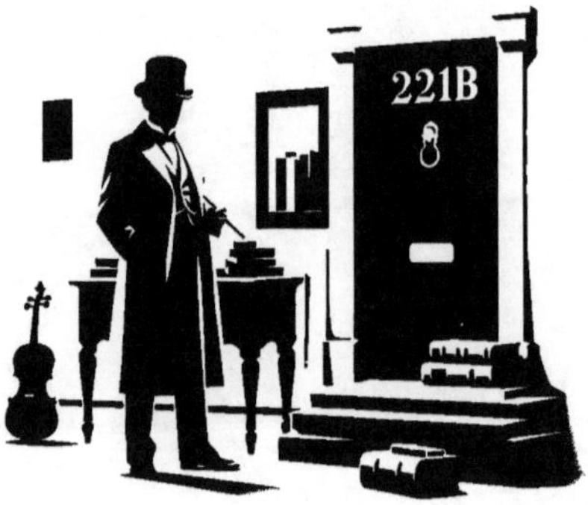
221B

221B: On Her Majesty's Secret Service

"MY NAME IS BARON ROBESPIERRE ROBUR DE MAUPERTUIS.

Some may know me as Robur the Conqueror. I now represent the Hephaestus Ring but that is not important. What is important is to accept we control a force that can destroy armies from afar. You witnessed a demonstration only a short time ago. That force cannot be wrested from us without incurring the most terrifying consequences. I should not have to add that what we accomplished once, we can accomplish again and again from any point on the continent.

"However, we have no intention of doing so...at least, not yet. That is entirely up to you. We have had enough of wasted time and opportunities, of self-indulgence and corruption and decadence. The great nations of Europe must reclaim their superiority on the global stage. We cannot do that whilst weak and pallid democracies persist in allowing so-called freedom to destroy us."

Sherlock Holmes snorted.

221B: On Her Majesty's Secret Service

First edition published in 2025
© Copyright 2025
Mark D. Ellis

The right of Mark D. Ellis to be identified as the author of this work has been asserted by him in accordance with the Copyright, Designs and Patents Act 1998.

All rights reserved. No reproduction, copy or transmission of this publication may be made without express prior written permission. No paragraph of this publication may be reproduced, copied or transmitted except with express prior written permission or in accordance with the provisions of the Copyright Act 1956 (as amended). Any person who commits any unauthorised act in relation to this publication may be liable to criminal prosecution and civil claims for damage.
All characters appearing in this work are fictitious. Any resemblance to real persons, living or dead, is purely coincidental. The opinions expressed herein are those of the author and not of MX Publishing.

Hardcover ISBN 978-1-80424-662-7
Paperback ISBN 978-1-80424-663-4
ePub ISBN 978-1-80424-664-1
PDF ISBN 978-1-80424-665-8

Published by MX Publishing
335 Princess Park Manor, Royal Drive,
London, N11 3GX
www.mxpublishing.co.uk

Cover and book design by Melissa Martin-Ellis

221B: On Her Majesty's Secret Service

221B

On Her Majesty's Secret Service

Mark D. Ellis

221B: On Her Majesty's Secret Service

✥

To and for Melissa—To me she is forever and always *The* Woman.

221B: On Her Majesty's Secret Service

FOREWORD

IN THE ARCHIVES of the Diogenes Club in Pall Mall, there rests a padlocked steel strong-box bearing the heraldic image of a lion and unicorn, the Imperial Seal of the United Kingdom. Printed beneath the seal are four characters: 221B. Below them is the warning: Official Secrets Act Protection.1889/1911.

One day before, as of the of this writing, I had placed the box within its specially designated receptacle with my own hands. There it will remain, untouched and unopened, for 100 years to the day. A qualified representative of the British government (assuming either one still exists) will, upon that date, make the final determination as to whether its contents should be revealed to other eyes.

The box is crammed with papers, nearly all of which are handwritten records of cases undertaken by myself and my friend, Mr Sherlock Holmes, in the service of the Lion and the Unicorn. In my published writings, I more than once alluded to missions we performed for the nation. I have refrained from revealing that, for many years, Holmes and I were active contract operatives for the counter-intelligence agencies of Her Majesty's Government. The umbrella designation at the time was Her Majesty's Secret Service, which encompassed diverse departments, such as the Foreign Office, the Home Office and the Defence Intelligence Branch.

On the official reports sent to Whitehall, our activities were attributed only to "221B," a designation which did not mislead anyone in the service after my first story about Sherlock Holmes appeared in *Beeton's Christmas Annual*.

It should come as little surprise to those reading these accounts a century or more hence, that Holmes's elder brother, Mycroft, was deeply involved in sending us forth to tilt at windmills. As I noted in the story published as "The Bruce-Partington Plans," Holmes described his older brother's position thusly: "You are right in thinking that he is under the British government. You would also be right in a sense if you said that occasionally, he *is* the British government."

At first resistant to my literary efforts chronicling the investigations of his gifted younger brother, Mycroft soon concluded my sensationalized and somewhat fictionalized accounts might provide a clever diversion. The more stories published about his brother's work as a consulting detective, the more obfuscation could be cast upon the actual reality of Sherlock and myself — not to mention, our increasingly famous street address.

As a former military man, I understood, if not always approved, of the actions taken by Mycroft and his colleagues to ensure the security of the Empire. Withal, I am compelled to admit that while I accepted the assignments offered me, I was less motivated by patriotism than by the lure of life-risk and the call of adventure. I also must confess how, at age 27, that same foolish allure brought me to the Battle of Maiwand, and painful introductions to a pair of Jezail bullets. Although I was invalided out, I recovered in due course, returning to my natural athleticism.

Holmes and I were young men, barely thirty, when we first took up this work. Both of us were at our physical and intellectual peaks. We found we worked well together and relished sharing the danger. As Holmes once said to me, "Watson, you were born to be a man of action. Your instinct is always to do something energetic."

Of course, our monetary compensation was more than adequate, which allowed me to purchase a medical practice in London. After we were joined by Miss Loveday Brooke, the nature of our assignments expanded — and not always in a positive direction, according to Holmes.

Unlike a similar cache of papers I deposited with the bank of Cox

221B: On Her Majesty's Secret Service

and Co., at Charing Cross, all of the cases contained in this strong-box are government property. They are simple case reports to Whitehall, dry overviews of our assignments and their outcomes. Inasmuch as I was prohibited from even talking about our missions, crafting these reports with the same flourish and attention to detail given to my published work seemed rather a wasted effort.

I will leave the task of fully fleshing-out these chronicles to future scribes if they are so inclined—that is, if and when a successor to Mycroft decides the Official Secrets Act is no longer pertinent. Upon reflection, I am not too sanguine about that eventuality.

As for myself and Sherlock Holmes, it is only a few days since we had a quiet talk — quite possibly the last we shall ever have — after our apprehension of a notorious agent of the Kaiser.

On the eve of war, I intend to rejoin my old regiment, if they will have me. Holmes will leave the comfort of his small farm on the South Downs, no doubt once more to tilt at windmills, in the service of the Lion and the Unicorn.

John H. Watson, MD
10 August, 1914.

221B: On Her Majesty's Secret Service

PART ONE

*T*HE YEAR '87 *furnished us with a long series of cases of greater or less interest, of which I retain the records. All these I may sketch out at some future date, but none of them present such singular features as these strange train of circumstances which I am constrained by the Official Secrets Act of 1889 from taking up my pen to describe.*

—John H. Watson, M D

221B: On Her Majesty's Secret Service

There are always some lunatics about. It would be a dull world without them.

— Sherlock Holmes

CHAPTER 1

North Cornwall, 20 April, 1887

THE GUARD CAME as a surprise.

The cliff overlooking the Penhallick Wharf was both barren and overgrown. Thickets of sea-buckthorn crowned the ridge, sprouting from cracks between naked granite outcroppings. The rocky ground sloped downward to the outer perimeter of the wharf.

Shielded by brush, Loveday Brooke gazed at a cluster of bright lights. They were arranged in an orderly row along a rectangular revetted stone pier below her position on the ridge.

A rusty-hulled merchant steamer of about 5,000 tonnes floated there, moored by heavy rope hawsers. At this height and distance, the vessel looked like a child's toy, floating on the gentle swells of the Celtic Sea. The odour of brine hung in the air. She heard the distant drumming of the surf. The sea reflected the moonlight with the colour of old silver.

The tripod-mounted arc lamps on the platform illuminated every detail with merciless clarity, including the ship's name and that of the company painted on the ship's bow in white letters: *S.S. Friesland* and below that, Netherlands-Sumatra.

Loveday counted at least a score of labourers moving back and forth, unloading freight from the emergency cargo hatch amidships. They manoeuvred hand-drawn carts down a gangplank stretching from the hold to the pier. From there, they rolled the carts toward a brick warehouse looming on a promontory at the far end of the quayside.

The stevedores moved deliberately and quickly. The fact they used the emergency hatch for egress to the hold implied two things: Time was a factor and the cargo was not large, either in bulk or volume. She could not identify the contents of the carts, so she reached for her binoculars.

Before she could raise them to her eyes, she heard the guard marching along the ridge-line behind her. Loveday froze and crouched down, turning her head in the direction of his footsteps, peering through the screen of brambles. The man walked in a leisurely manner, a long-barrelled , side-by-side Lancaster pistol dangling from a strap around his left shoulder. She noted the weapon sported a pistol grip made of chequered walnut.

The guard wore a beret canted at a rakish angle over dark hair, and a slate grey uniform jacket emblazoned with a badge she couldn't quite make out on the breast. He didn't look in her direction. He focused his attention on where he placed his booted feet.

Loveday didn't blame him, because the ground was quite treacherous. Still, she gritted her teeth in angry frustration. She hadn't expected to encounter anyone until she reached the dockyard itself, and that was why she had chosen the disguise of a worker — flat green cap, baggy faded blue overalls and scuffed, clumsy shoes.

To add to the illusion, she had tucked her shoulder-length chestnut hair firmly up under the cap and applied a combination of grease and soot to her features. There was nothing she could do about her height and build, but she gambled on being given only casual glances when she reached the wharf. She had brought along an old steel pipe-wrench found amongst her late father's few possessions. It served as a prop to add verisimilitude to the role she intended to play. However, she doubted she would be convincing if the guard found her in a place no labourer had any reason to be, prop notwithstanding.

Loveday tried not to move at all or even breathe. She slitted her green eyes in order to keep ambient moonlight from reflecting off them. The guard walked past her position without glancing in either direction. Some of the tension went out of her body. At the crest of the ridge, the man stopped and lit a cigarette with a sputtering match. The brief, sulphurous flare revealed a blunt-jawed, moustached face. Broadly built, he was at least a head and half head taller than she.

While he puffed on the cigarette, the guard made a slow visual survey of the area, from the distant ruins of Tintagel Castle to Trebarwith Strand. Loveday held her breath during the entire procedure, praying the tobacco smoke-induced tickle in her nostrils didn't build to a sneeze. Fortunately, the temperature was exceptionally mild for this time of year so close to the sea, and her teeth weren't inclined to chatter.

Finally, when her lungs ached and temples throbbed, the sentry began walking again. She inhaled short, shallow sips of air, timing them to coincide with the crunch of the man's footfalls on the pebble-strewn ground.

Turning her head slowly, Loveday followed the guard's progress. The ridge was obviously the man's assigned patrol route and his shift probably lasted from sunset to midnight or possibly all the way to sunrise. She hadn't taken into account a protracted game of cat-and-mouse with sentries. She doubted she could make her way down the ridge and join the work-crew on the wharf without being seen. The guard had to be dealt with.

Tightly gripping the handle of the wrench in her right hand, Loveday carefully arose and followed the man's path. Hefting the tool, she guessed it weighed over ten pounds, and was more than sufficient to lay the fellow out, provided she got close enough to land a blow to the back of his skull.

Due to her shoes, she could not walk on her toes, so she sacrificed speed for stealth, very aware of where and how she placed her feet, praying no stone turned underneath them.

As the guard's route took him toward a copse of brush on the seaward side of the ridge, he slowed his pace. He dropped the cigarette butt and crushed it underfoot. Loveday kept moving, holding the wrench in a double-fisted grip hands as if it were a cricket bat. A sound floated through the air, an almost apologetic cough, like a gentleman might make at a church service.

An icy hand clenched around the base of Loveday's spine as she watched the guard wheel around, leading with the Lancaster. His teeth bared in a startled snarl when he caught sight of her. Loveday froze in mid-step just as a dark mass rose from behind the man, as if a section of the thicket had detached itself. She glimpsed a blur of movement as she threw herself to the ground, beneath the barrels of the Lancaster. The wrench clattered against the rocks and her elbows impacted painfully against gravel.

Fabric rustled and the guard's gargling cry of surprise was quickly silenced when a man's hand came from behind his head, holding a thick cloth. It clamped itself over his nose and mouth. The guard groped desperately for the Lancaster but before he could secure a grip on the trigger, his struggles weakened. His body sagged as if his legs had turned to half-melted wax.

The man carefully lowered the guard to the ground, making sure he didn't hit his head on the stones. A film of moisture gleamed on the slack-jawed face and Loveday caught the whiff of a chemical tang. She recognized the odour as diethyl ether .

Loveday watched a blonde-haired man straighten up from beside the body of the guard, bringing the pistol with him. He stood slightly over medium height and was clean-shaven. Broad-shouldered with an athletic build, his black shirt and twill pants helped him blend into the shifting pattern of moonlight and shadows. His face held the bone-deep kind of tan that marked a man who spent a lot of time out-of-doors. He didn't appear to be much over thirty years of age.

He looked toward Loveday without smiling or speaking. Expertly, he broke open the Lancaster, checked the shells and snapped it shut again. Then he waved the square of cloth through the air, gave it a squeeze, shoved it into a pants pocket and announced, "The new mixture worked."

"Just as I thought it would," said a male voice, pitched low but not enough to dull its authoritative edge.

A tall man with crisp black hair in need of a trim stepped casually out of the shadows. He stood over six feet and was so lean he seemed considerably taller. He wore dark clothing much like the blonde man, except for a double-breasted Ulster topcoat of midnight-green. His hands were tucked into the pockets. His high-planed face suggested old storybook illustrations of sword-wielding highwaymen, a similarity not helped by the man's piercing blue-grey eyes and the alert, hawk-like set of his head. A faintly reckless smile creased his lips.

Withdrawing a black-gloved left hand from the pocket of his coat, he reached down to Loveday. "May I?"

She slapped at his hand. "You may not. You very nearly got me killed."

As she climbed to her feet, the blonde man pointed with the pistol barrel to the wrench lying amongst the rocks. "Saved you from it, rather. Even if you had gotten close enough to strike this poor fellow, the odds of you rendering him unconscious with one blow were astronomical."

Loveday uttered a scoffing sound of dismissal. She began brushing off her clothes. "Really."

"Really. You simply lack the reach or the muscle mass to manage it. Oh, you may have succeeded in stunning him, but you would have inflicted a degree of blunt force trauma that could have resulted in a cervical fracture, concussion or subdural blood-clots. I don't think you'd want that on your conscience. Regardless, the hammers were cocked, so he would have gotten off a reflex shot when he hit the ground, alerting everyone around the wharf."

"A matter of opinion," Loveday retorted, adjusting the bill of her cap.

"An informed opinion," said the taller man. "Doctor Watson has a little professional experience with this sort of thing, Miss Brooke."

Loveday inhaled deeply, put her hands on her hips and stared at the two men levelly. "I understand both you and Doctor Watson do...Mister Holmes."

"AH", SAID SHERLOCK HOLMES. "I wasn't sure if you remembered me. We passed each other on the way out and into the office of old Ebenezer Dyer, and we did not speak."

"I asked 'old Ebenezer' your name," replied Loveday. She took off her cap and shook out her hair impatiently. "I'd heard of you, of course."

"So you're a woman," observed Watson, his bland tone implying he was not surprised. "I thought you were too slightly built to pass as an a common stevedore, even a half-grown one. Your wardrobe is a good effort, however." He glanced over at Holmes with quizzical eyes. "You two have met?"

"Not officially," Holmes said. "But I can introduce you — John Watson, this is Miss Loveday Brooke of the Lynch Court Detective Agency."

221B: On Her Majesty's Secret Service

Stuffing her hair back under her cap, Loveday glared at Holmes suspiciously. "How do you know my name?"

"You are the only female operative employed by the Lynch Court agency, and since I saw you there, walking with ease into Ebenezer's private office, I deduced you weren't a client. The over-riding question is what you're doing on a remote part of the Cornish coast late at night, unsuccessfully disguised, as Watson put it, as a common stevedore."

"I could ask you two the exact same thing," she shot back. "Except for the stevedore bit."

"I presume your disguise is to help you penetrate the wharf?"

"Of course. How do you gentlemen intend to do it?"

Watson smiled for the first time. "Truth to tell, Miss Brooke, that isn't our intention...this is more of a reconnaissance, a scouting mission. A look-around."

"Spying, in other words."

"That is the precise word," said Holmes.

"Do you always bring bottles of potent anaesthetic on your look-arounds?"

Holmes angled an eyebrow at her. "We anticipate and adapt to new circumstances, Miss Brooke."

"Something of a policy," Watson said. "Anticipate and adapt. That's why we've been successful when we spy. So far."

The guard moaned softly and Watson dropped to one knee beside him, peeling back the man's right eyelid. "He'll be coming 'round soon, so it's best we gag and restrain him."

From the capacious left pocket of his coat, Holmes produced two lengths of cord and a long scarf. Loveday uneasily noted how he kept his right hand snugged in the other pocket. Holmes said, "Perhaps he should be dosed again."

Watson propped the man up in a sitting position, pushed his upper body forward and tugged off his jacket before pulling his arms behind his back. "At this concentration, the ether acted as a nearly instantaneous hypnotic. If I give it to him again without a proper recovery period, he could suffer nervous system damage or perhaps an oesophageal effect where he ends up choking to death on his own vomit."

He glanced toward Loveday. "Do you know anything about knots, Miss?"

She nodded. "A bit. My father was a sailor."

"A hand here, if you will, please."

Loveday kneeled beside Watson and the senseless guard. Swiftly, she looped the cord around the man's wrists, cross-wrapping and working out the slack. Holmes said approvingly, "The old reliable handcuff knot. You do know some useful things, then."

Loveday took the second length of cord and moved to the man's legs, sliding it under and over his knees. "Yes," she said. "And what I don't know, I can guess."

"A shocking habit."

"Nevertheless, I can speculate that you visiting the Lynch Court office for an audience with Mr Dyer wasn't for a job interview but to learn about an investigation that parallels one of your own."

"Or perhaps I just wanted to drop by for a visit with a former mentor and colleague. We are in the same line of work you know."

"Your reputation precedes you, Mr Holmes." Loveday's fingers swiftly crafted a bowline knot. "From what I hear, you act more as a consultant, working from an armchair in your Baker Street digs. There is also talk amongst colleagues like Mr Dyer that you and your doctor friend are most often engaged in work of a very confidential nature."

"All of our work is confidential in nature, Miss Brooke," said Holmes patronizingly. "Our clients expect that, do they not?"

The guard sighed. Loveday patted his bound knees and stood up. "Done and done."

Holding the scarf lengthwise, Watson inserted it between the man's jaws, tying the loose ends tightly at back of his neck, testing the gag with a finger to make sure he couldn't dislodge it with his tongue upon regaining consciousness.

Watson laid him back down and stood up, bringing the beret and jacket with him. He squinted at the insignia on the man's jacket. Worked in red thread, it appeared to be a circle surrounding a stylized mallet and anvil. He tapped it with a finger. "See this?"

Holmes nodded. "Straight-away. Hardly surprising under the circumstances."

"Our bully-boy may be uncomfortable when he wakes up," Watson said, fitting the beret over his hair, "but he's not going anywhere. We three most definitely should, however."

Loveday gazed at him sceptically. "And where should 'we three' go?"

Neither man answered. Watson thrust his arms into the sleeves of the jacket and busied himself buttoning it up. The fit was tight. Loveday asked, "What are you doing?"

"Adapting to changing circumstances."

Loveday sighed wearily. "Gentlemen, I suggest we stop playing coy with one another. Otherwise, we'll be tromping on each other's toes and heels."

Holmes inclined his head toward her. "Ladies first."

Reaching inside her overalls, Loveday produced a large envelope bearing the red wax seal of the Queen's Bench Division of the High Court. "I'm here to serve a bench warrant on a lunatic who is charged with a number of civil and criminal violations. My agency was hired to serve the warrant before he flees the country again. We were informed he could be found on this night in this place."

221B: *On Her Majesty's Secret Service*

Watson and Holmes exchanged glances, and after a thoughtful moment, Holmes shrugged. He said, "You are correct that I visited your firm to compare notes. The doctor and I have been engaged to locate the same man, but our investigation holds the priority position. I assumed I had made that clear to Ebenezer."

"You did," retorted Loveday. "But we had already been paid a substantial retainer by a desperate client...as the chief investigator on the case, I was not inclined to simply stand aside and allow freelance adventurers to have their way, regardless of what government department hired them."

Watson frowned. "You don't know of what you speak, young lady."

Loveday laughed scornfully. " 'Young lady'? Don't be absurd. You're not much older than I am."

Holmes demanded, "What is the name of the man you hope to find here?"

"Baron Robespierre Robur de Maupertuis."

Holmes smiled enigmatically. "Also known as Robur the Conqueror." His smile widened as he added, "And yes, he *is* a lunatic."

221B: On Her Majesty's Secret Service

I find, on looking over my notes, that this period includes the shocking affair of the Dutch steamship Friesland, *which so nearly cost us both our lives.*

— John H. Watson, MD

CHAPTER 2

THE *FRIESLAND* FLEW no flag, but Holmes, Watson and Loveday knew she was registered in Holland. The iron-hulled freighter, a Clydeside merchant steamer, looked old, low and clumsy. A smokestack rose from the high superstructure. Smoke wafted lazily from the wide funnel.

Peering through the eyepieces of a compact set of binoculars, Holmes watched the wooden crates being carted with haste down the gangplank and onto the pier. "So that's the boat which has been playing hide-and-seek with the maritime insurance companies of three nations these last few years."

"Ship," corrected Loveday, peering through her own binoculars.

"Pardon?" inquired Holmes absently.

"The *Friesland's* LOA looks like it measures out to over 100 meters, so that makes her a ship."

"LOA?" inquired Watson, squinting through a brass military field telescope with his right eye.

"Length Overall. I told you, my father was a navy man."

"I served in the army, in Southern Afghanistan," Watson replied. "About as far from sea-going vessels as it was possible to get."

"Judging by your tan, I thought it was either there or India."

Watson chuckled briefly. "This tan commemorates a recent visit to Málaga."

"That must have been pleasant."

"No," he replied. "It was not."

Holmes said, "More attention on our immediate objective, rather than the doctor's bronze glow, please,"

Lying on their bellies at the base of the cliff, hidden by scrub-brush and wedges of shadow, the three people studied Penhallick Wharf. An open area of at least twenty yards separated them from the perimeter. A narrow roadway paved with sand and crushed shells curved up and away from the cove to the coastal highlands. Loveday had hidden her bicycle there in the shrubbery along the verge.

The thumping beat of a generating engine throbbed in the air and Holmes noted a thick power cable snaking over the side of the *Friesland* to a big yellow-metal junction box resting on the pier. Connection cords stretched from the array of arc-lights to it.

Watson sniffed experimentally. "I smell burning coal."

"From the engine room of the *Friesland*," Holmes said. "They're feeding coal to an electricity-generator, which in turns powers the outdoor lights."

"Clever," said Loveday.

"Outdoor electrical lighting is becoming more commonplace," Watson stated. "Particularly in North American cities."

"And in France," Holmes said.

Watson lowered the telescope. "We managed to climb down here without being seen or breaking our necks. So what's the strategy for reaching the wharf itself?"

Loveday chuckled. "My plan is the same as it always was — to just walk right in with my trusty wrench, as if I have every right to be there. I didn't put on my fancy-dress clothes for nothing."

"Nor did I," said Watson, making sure the beret was still firmly seated on his head.

Loveday regarded him doubtfully. "You think you can pass yourself off as the sentry?"

"*A* sentry...I'm sure there is more than one. It's only temporary protective colouration so I can stroll in without being challenged."

My strategy is for all three of us to do that," stated Holmes. "We will just have to wait for the opportune moment."

"When will that be?" Watson asked.

Holmes raised his head from the eyepieces. "We'll know when it comes. Until then —" He turned towards Loveday who lay between he and Watson. "Who hired your agency to serve a warrant on the baron? That is normally the job of bailiffs after a legal judgment has been rendered, is it not?"

"Not even for-hire bailiff services wanted to touch the job...that is, not after two previous ones turned up dead — one in Belgium and the other in Greece."

"And the hiring party?"

Loveday hesitated a second before saying, "I'm not at liberty to divulge names, but they are a wealthy British family who years ago invested in the Netherlands-Sumatra shipping company, before its controlling shares were acquired by a conglomerate called the Hephaestus Ring. They're supposed to be an international trading consortium."

Holmes smiled enigmatically. "We've heard of them."

"Baron Maupertuis bought Netherlands-Sumatra from Hephaestus," Loveday continued, "and due to his malfeasance and misappropriation, the company went into receivership and eventually, bankruptcy. My clients were among the investors and creditors. The tangible assets — the small fleet of merchant vessels and freighters — were sold, and the profits shared. Except for the *Friesland*, which had been registered in Holland by the Hephaestus Ring. The representative who signed the Dutch registration on the part of Hephaestus was none other than Baron Maupertuis. Neither he nor the *Friesland* could be located for several years."

She flicked her gaze between Holmes and Watson. "I am sure both of you gentlemen are very aware of the background of this case."

Watson shifted the Lancaster slung over his shoulder. "We were briefed on the high court rulings. Unsubstantiated charges of bribery were made against various government officials. We were also told there have been numerous sightings of the *Friesland* along the Cornish coast for the past year."

"My investigations turned up the same reports," said Loveday. "I was finally able to narrow them down to this specific port...the seldom-used Penhallick."

"And you learned," Holmes interposed, "how every fortnight, the *Friesland* could be seen in these very waters. Last week, one of your sources let you know preparations for another port-of-call were underway, scheduled for this very night."

"How could you know that?" Loveday demanded. "Unless we share the same informant."

"That's the simplest and most likely explanation," Holmes said. "Double-dipping, I believe it's called. I'll have a word with him. Regardless, once we became aware of Lynch Court's involvement in the case, I paid a visit to Ebenezer to apprise him that the interested party Doctor Watson and I represent holds a prior claim on the baron."

Loveday sighed. "I can speculate upon the identity of your interested party —"

"Another shocking habit."

She ignored him. "— but I don't understand why they would be interested in a situation like this. Maritime insurance fraud is criminal but hardly a matter of national security."

Watson frowned at her. "You don't remember the hoopla over the Great Aeroship Mystery? The *Albatross?* Robur the self-proclaimed Conqueror and so-called Master of the Air?"

A line of concentration appeared on the bridge of Loveday's nose, barely visible due to the shadow cast by her cap's visor. "That was years ago, wasn't it? I was a child. I thought the whole matter was dismissed as a hoax dreamed up to sell newspapers."

"So did I," said Watson. "So did most of the world."

"What makes you so sure Baron Maupertuis and this legendary Robur are the same man?"

Watson side-stepped the question by asking one of his own. "Do you know what the baron looks like?"

Holmes shushed them, holding up a hand for silence. He tilted his head towards the moored ship. The rhythmic thud of the generator skipped a beat, then two, and stopped altogether. The arc-lamps flickered and went dark. He rose swiftly. "The opportune moment has come. Let's go."

They did not run across the open space, even though the diffuse moonlight was sufficient to illuminate their path. Running footfalls sounded distinctly different from those walking at a steady pace.

In a low voice, Loveday asked, "How did you know the lights would go out?"

"Coal-burning generators inevitably experience an interruption due to over-heating," Holmes answered. "I knew if we waited long enough, we'd be able to take advantage of that."

"In other words," Loveday said, shouldering her wrench, "you guessed."

Watson smiled. "More like speculated."

"I extrapolated from known data," Holmes said stiffly. "Not the same thing at all."

Although the lamps had gone out, the stevedores continued their work in the moonlight, exhorted by a loud, coarse male voice. Loveday murmured, "Gentlemen, on a scale of one to ten, what is the danger factor do you think we are walking into?"

Watson presented the image of seriously pondering the question. "A clandestine dockyard patrolled by armed guards, apparently overseen by a fugitive from justice? I'd say seven. Strong possibility of severe bodily harm, perhaps even being held prisoner if we're caught out."

"Ten," said Holmes curtly. "Our quarry is a seasoned professional criminal who is involved in activities he wants to keep secret. Not to mention he calls himself Robur the Conqueror. That speaks to advanced megalomania. Likelihood of torture, murder and being buried at sea — or in a shallow grave — if we're caught."

"Neither of you seem very worried at the prospect."

"It's only worrisome if we're caught," Watson said with a grim smile.

The generator began thumping again. The lenses of the arc-lamps flashed and a yellow glow slowly intensified. The light was not as bright as before. They saw deep shadows along the pier which had not been there before. They moved toward them, away from the light cast by the lamps. The odours of wet hemp, tar and oil floated in the air.

Loveday took the lead, walking confidently among the labourers, cap pulled low. Watson noted how none of them gave her a second glance. As he and Holmes passed a bench scattered with a collection of tools, he grabbed a crowbar, letting it hang from his left hand. He offered Holmes a long, industrial turn-screw, but he waved it away, selecting a wooden-handled longshoreman's hook instead.

As they strode down the dock in the direction of the warehouse, they caught snatches of slurred Geordie accents mixed with Cornish Gaelic. Watson understood very little of what was said, but the general tone of the voices sounded unhappy.

Holmes walked casually toward several crates of various sizes stacked in the bed of a two-wheeled cart. Watson and Loveday followed him. With the steel tip of the hook, he pried at the lid, lifting it an inch. Watson inserted the crow-bar into the opening. Loveday bent over the right wheel, pretending to tighten a nut with her wrench.

With a squeal of nails, the lid popped up. Pieces of black moulded metal lay neatly arranged within the crate. They resembled sections of wide gauge pipe cut in half length-wise, each one about a foot long. Setting aside the crowbar, Watson picked up a piece, rapping it with his knuckles and turning it in hands, surprised by its light weight.

"It looks like cast iron," Loveday said.

Watson passed the piece to Holmes who turned it in his hands, weighing it like a cut of meat at a butcher's shop. "It's a wrought alloy of some type, dense but thin-walled."

"A Ferroalloy," said Watson. "Perhaps Titanium? It was discovered here in Cornwall, after all."

"*Oi!*" bellowed a man's voice from behind them. They turned toward a heavy-set, bristle-jowled man dressed not dissimilarly to Loveday, standing on the gangway leading from the *Friesland* to the pier. He looked to be considerably wider than he was tall. "One o' you lot move that load over to the warehouse! You other two, get back to clearin' out the hold!"

Watson, Loveday and Holmes exchanged, quick, questioning glances. Loveday slammed down the lid of the crate and placed her wrench atop it. "I'll take the cart."

Watson eyed her doubtfully. "You won't be able to manage that weight."

Loveday spit in the palms of her hands, bent her knees, grasped the cart's handles, lifted and began rolling the cart forward. "I'm stronger than I look."

"You stand corrected, Watson," Holmes said dryly. "Again."

"After all of this time working with you, I really should be accustomed to it."

Over a shoulder, Loveday called, "If the man we seek is here, he's most likely at the warehouse. Meet me there when you can."

"You won't be hard to find in your fancy-dress clothes," Watson called back.

Axle squeaking, the cart and Loveday disappeared into the darkness. Holmes gazed after her thoughtfully. "She is swift in making up her mind and fearless in carrying out her resolutions. Rather a remarkable young lady."

Watson quirked an eyebrow. "Young lady? Don't be absurd. You're not that much older than she is."

"Oi!" shouted the man on the gangplank again. He gestured with a savage impatience. "Get over here!"

Holmes shrugged and started off. "Best we do as he says...I'd hate to be sacked on our first day."

As the two men drew closer to the light shed by the lamps, the heavy-set man's face compressed into a glower of suspicion. "Wait a bloody second...you're not part o' my crew!"

Watson stepped forward onto the gangplank, assuming a military posture. The Lancaster on his shoulder helped. "Cargo inspectors," he said briskly, indicating the insignia on the jacket with a thumb. "Stand aside."

The man's thickly bagged eyes darted from Watson to Holmes and then back again. "We're almost done unloadin' here!"

"Nevertheless," Watson continued marching along the ramp, face an expressionless mask.

Holmes, following closely behind, said sternly, "Permit us to do our jobs and we'll be out of your way, Mister—?"

221B: On Her Majesty's Secret Service

"Penhollow," the man replied resentfully. "Spargo Penhollow."

The two men pushed past him. Holmes said, "We shouldn't be more than three minutes, Mr Penhollow."

"I got orders to be done here by midnight so the ship can be back in her berth afore dawn, so don't dawdle."

Eyes straight ahead, Holmes and Watson strode to the end of the gangway and into the cavernous hold. The smell of brine, mildew and coal clogged their nostrils. The steady throbbing of the power generator vibrated through the steel bulkheads. A pair of arc lamps cast yellow halos at opposite ends of the hold.

"Not much left to look at," commented Watson. He nudged a box with a foot. "Or for."

Penhollow had spoken the truth. Only a score of crates remained, stacked ziggurat-fashion in the centre of the chamber. Watson tried to lift one of the crates by a corner, and when he couldn't, he snapped, "What the hell does Mycroft expect us to find in this God-forsaken spot? He never made that clear."

"That's because he doesn't have any expectations, only a pocketful of suspicions."

Holmes used the hook to pry open a lid. Both men stared at the contents for a silent second. Watson reached in and lifted out a metal cylinder bound with metal fittings. It was a bit over two feet in length. One end was brass-capped but perforated by four concentric rings of holes all of the same shape. The other end terminated in a square pistol grip. Grasping the brass cap, he twisted it to the right. It rotated with a series of clicks, like the cylinder of a wheel-gun.

"The pepper-box principle," he muttered.

Holmes said, "And one pocket's worth of brother Mycroft's suspicions."

Watson eyed the object carefully and handed it to Holmes. "It reminds me of a stripped down and miniaturized Nordenfelt rapid-firing gun."

"A Nordenfelt crossed with a Maxim automatic machine gun," Holmes commented, holding it in a double-handed grip and sighting down its length. "Rather awkward, and depending on its recoil, accuracy is probably not its strong suit."

"A machine gun pistol wouldn't need to be accurate," said Watson tensely. "The Nordenfelt rapid-firers were used in Afghanistan...they tore men to pieces but were difficult to manoeuvre into position. If such a weapon has been developed to be used like a handgun—"

"Oi!" The echo of Spargo Penhollow's roar bounced back and forth from the bulkheads. He stood at the opening the cargo hatch, his flesh-pouched eyes wide and bright with anger. "I just asked! You two ain't no inspectors!"

Watson turned to face him, shoulders squared. "Of course we are. Ask the baron."

"I don't work for no baron!" Penhollow shouted, stepping down into the hold. "Mr Zaharhoof pays me my wages and I just asked his man Rubadue and he tells me there ain't no inspectors dockside!"

Holmes returned the weapon to the crate. As a counterpoint to Penhollow's anger, he presented a calm, dignified demeanour. "Do you mean Basil Zaharoff, by any chance?"

"However you pronounces it, that's who I mean!" He hooked a thumb toward the hatch. "We'll all just go see Rubadue and get this straightened out one way or 'tother! Drop that hook and pistol and get movin', boyos!"

Watson and Holmes hesitated. Holmes tossed aside the hook. Penhollow's right hand dipped into his an inner pocket of his overalls and came out gripping a Bull-dog revolver with a two-inch snubbed barrel. "You there, Captain Bloody Cargo Inspector— drop that scatter-gun or I drops you."

"We're offering you no resistance, Mr Penhollow," said Watson reasonably.

"This is all a misunderstanding."

Penhollow snorted out a contemptuous laugh. "You're the one what's misunderstandin'! Leave go that pistol."

Watson exhaled a resigned breath. His shoulders slumped. The Lancaster strap slipped down and the weapon dropped toward the deck. His left hand snatched it by the grip, and squeezed the trigger. Both barrels exploded in flame and thunder.

221B: On Her Majesty's Secret Service

It is stupidity rather than courage to refuse to recognize danger when it is close upon you.

—Sherlock Holmes

CHAPTER 3

LOVEDAY HADN'T GONE far with the cart before she suspected she might have made a mistake. The cart was heavier and far more unwieldy than she had initially estimated. The handles were splintery. She wondered why she hadn't included a pair of sturdy work gloves as an integral part of her disguise. Such an omission flew in the face of Mr Dyer's praise of her as the most sensible and practical woman he had ever known.

Three years previously, by an errant spin of Fortune's wheel and the sudden death of her father, Loveday had found herself thrown upon the streets of London penniless and virtually friendless. While reflecting upon her marketable skills, she realized she had none except logic, intelligence, perseverance and a dollop of foolhardy courage.

Forthwith, she contacted her father's old navy friend, Ebenezer Dyer. She inveighed upon him to grant her a temporary position with his flourishing detective agency in Lynch Court. He quickly enough found out the stuff she was made of, and assigned her cases that brought an increase of pay and of reputation alike to the agency in general and to Loveday in particular.

The Netherlands-Sumatra case at first hadn't appeared to be much more complicated than delivering a document, but Mr Dyer hadn't even considered assigning it to another operative. He contended that in cases which involved following a suspect or serving a writ, women detectives were more satisfactory than men, for they were less likely to attract attention.

Within a few weeks of following leads and reviewing court transcripts and engaging with informants, she concluded the waters were far deeper and darker than Mr Dyer could have known. He obviously hadn't foreseen the involvement of Sherlock Holmes.

Although Loveday had heard tales and gossip about Holmes and Doctor Watson for the last few years — even from Mr Dyer — she did not realize the two men were so young. Before glimpsing Holmes in the Lynch Court office, she had imagined them as a pair of tweedy, middle-aged, moustached duffers with the senses of humour of average fence-posts. She certainly hadn't expected to enjoy being in their company as much as she had.

The path curved around the beach at an oblique angle. At the shoreline, she saw a steam packet of the pleasure boat kind that plied the waters of the Thames. A fashionable, aft enclosed cabin occupied almost half the vessel's length. A half-dozen dinghies were anchored around it.

When the quayside ended, Loveday had no choice but to follow a gravel path laid down through high weeds. It was made rough underfoot by loose flint and fist-sized granite chunks. The moonshine provided enough illumination so she could see where she was trundling her cart, but just barely. A string of lights glowed in the distance. A score of yards ahead of her she heard the crunch of cart-wheels on gravel, and a man's voice lifted in breathless song.

Stick him in a scupper with a hosepipe bottom
Stick him in a scupper with a hosepipe bottom
Way hay and up she rises
Early in the morning!

Loveday smiled. She remembered her father occasionally singing the shanty when she was a child and how her mother shushed and chastised him. She recollected the lyrics very well, but she repressed the the urge to join in with the chorus about a drunken sailor put into a bed with the captain's daughter.

A man came clumping along the path from the direction of the warehouse. He walked very fast and single-mindedly, breathing hard. He fetched the cart a sharp whack his his blackthorn walking stick while squeezing past it. Loveday caught only an impression of red hair, a scarred face and unkempt sideburns. He growled, "Move aside, boyo," before continuing on toward the pier. Loveday refrained from offering either an apology or a correction.

Despite the gnawing pain in her shoulders and back, Loveday wrestled the cart past heaps of rusted machinery. Most of the rusted husks of metal were so corroded as to be unidentifiable. Judging by the mounds of slag and the great litter of steel scrap, the area had served as a foundry at one time.

Three men marched past her in the general direction of quayside. They wore grey berets and jackets with the hammer and anvil insignia on the breast. Although they paid her no heed, Loveday's breath caught in her throat at the sight of them.

The guards held long leather leashes in their right hands and Lancaster pistols were slung over their shoulders. At the ends of the leashes strained and slavered three of the biggest mastiffs she had ever seen. The black-and-tan dogs panted, tongues lolling, drool dripping from their fang-filled jaws. Although she wanted to stop and rest, she feared she would draw the attention of the sentries, so she trudged on, the cart's axle squeaking. Anxiety and apprehension knotted in her chest.

The warehouse rose out of the darkness before her. The building looked much larger than it had from a distance. It resembled an ancient cathedral constructed of soot-stained brick. A round chimney, broken in half, punched upward from the roof. She guessed it had been built at the turn of the century when the Cornish copper and tin mining industry was at its zenith.

221B: On Her Majesty's Secret Service

Half a dozen oil lamps hanging from a rope strung across the wide entrance provided a wavering light. She saw the singing stevedore push his cart beneath them and through the doorway. She tried to quicken her pace. Once inside, she hoped she would be directed to the proper place to take the cart and someone would be there to unload. She caught whiffs of heated metal.

When she heard the steady throb of machinery, she realized she had entered more than a warehouse. A vista of great, clanking machines opened up. Mechanics wearing protective goggles, gloves and headgear operated the equipment. She saw drill presses, forges, smelters, crucibles. It was all lit by an array of arc-lamps.

The combined rattles, clangs and bangs were nearly deafening. Some of the machines shot sparks, emitting the sharp odour of ozone, while others spit jets of steam. Chain conveyors rattled in jerks and starts. A forest of girders supported a trussed network of overhead catwalks.

Because she could do nothing else, Loveday continued forward, her progress helped by interlocked concrete slabs that served as a floor. The hot air she breathed tasted stagnant, thick with the stink of grease and superheated metal.

She kept her eyes on the stevedore ahead of her, trying to imitate his steady, measured tread. Several times she dodged a flurry of sparks and once she barely avoided being scalded by a hissing spurt of steam. She tried to shut out the noise, the smell and the heat — it all felt like a physical assault. Perspiration filmed her forehead beneath her cap.

Passing a wire-screened enclosure, she glimpsed a line of humped power generators. Sweaty, bare-chested men walked to and fro with shovel-loads of coal to feed a flaming furnace. The wall behind them was studded with glass-encased needle meters, dials and levers. A uniformed guard stood outside the enclosure.

Up ahead, she saw the stevedore expertly manoeuvre his cart to the right and she duly followed him, squinting through the steam. She glimpsed four figures at the end of the main aisle, standing beside a long, streamlined object which reminded her of a rounded whale back. One of them appeared to be a woman wearing a broad-brimmed hat but a cloud of vapour blurred her view.

Perspiring and breathing heavily, Loveday saw the stevedore had stopped inside of a large room lit by oil lanterns. He stood mopping his brow with a bandana while a brawny man wearing a grey beret but no shirt heaved a crate from the cart. The wall was covered by stacked crates and boxes, row after row.

It felt blessedly cool in the room. Not even trying to repress a sigh of relief, Loveday released the cart's handles and they hit the floor with a double-thud. The palms of both of her hands were reddened and she was sure they had picked up a few splinters. She felt justified in leaning against the right cart wheel to pick them out.

Surreptitiously glancing out at the bustling work area and machinery, she suspected that all of the old ironmongery had been reused for a new purpose, powered by electricity generators. If the foundry had been resurrected for manufacturing, she could not imagine what it could possibly be producing.

A tall, very thin man appeared at the entrance, his dark eyes questing back and forth. He wore a tailored suit of dark blue serge and a rose-coloured tie. His thick, jet-black hair, parted in the middle, was as neatly trimmed as his moustache. He looked young, perhaps in his late twenties.

Loveday grabbed her wrench, squatted down and pretended to be adjusting the wheel of the cart, hoping he would ignore her. Instead, he purposefully strode to the cart, and reaching over her, he began examining the crates with pale, slim hands. He muttered something in a language that sounded like German.

"Pardon me," he said in accented English. "I am looking for a crate holding parts of my induction motor. My name should be on it."

221B: On Her Majesty's Secret Service

Loveday stood up and made a show of looking at the exteriors of the containers. Most bore the stencilled legend Care of Hephaestus but not much else. "I just roll the cargo, sir." She pitched her voice as deep as she could without sounding like a music-hall performer.

If the man noticed anything odd about her vocalization, he showed no sign. He tipped and rotated the crates, "Ja, I understand, but this crate has been shipped all the way from 89 Liberty Street, New York City, New York in the United States of America, and I am anxious to show my motor to the baron and—*ah!*"

His short exclamation was one of relief. He ran his fingers over a name printed on the surface of a crate at the very bottom of the cart. "This is me. My name, I mean."

Loveday saw *N. Tesla* stencilled just above Care of Hephaestus. "You are N. Tesla?"

"Nikola, *ja*. Nikola Tesla. I arrived in your country only the day before yesterday."

Loveday sensed he was eager for conversation. "From where, sir?"

As if by rote, Tesla stated, "From 89 Liberty Street, New York City, New York, United States of America. But I was born in Austria."

He gazed at Loveday steadily. A smile creased his lips. "I am a scientist and engineer, and I have been engaged by the baron to help him develop new technologies and to install an electrical lighting system on the grounds of the Paris World Fair — the Exposition Universelle — of 1889."

"Are some of the new technologies the power generators I saw on the way in, sir?"

"Not exactly...I modified them to my alternating-current operating system."

"You must be a very important man, Mr Tesla."

Tesla's smile widened. "Less than six months ago I was digging ditches for two dollars a day, so no, I am not. Your current station in life is not much different than mine only a short time ago. From a ditch to the Exposition Universelle. Life sometimes depends on a random spin of Fortune's wheel."

Loveday couldn't help but smile, too. "I'll remember that, sir."

"I do not know why a young lady like yourself is engaged in performing manual labour best suited to male stevedores, but hard times come to many of us, and so we must find ways to endure them as best we can...regardless of our sex."

Loveday's throat constricted in sudden panic. "Sir?"

Tesla blinked at her in confusion. "Do I overstep? Please pardon me — I assumed you were a young lady, not a young man."

His face flushed in embarrassment. "I beg your forgiveness." He reached for the crate. "I shall leave you to your work."

On impulse, her thoughts racing, Loveday laid a reassuring hand on his arm. In her normal contralto speaking voice, she said, "There is nothing to forgive, Mr Tesla. I was just taken aback that you saw through my..." she remembered Watson's words "...protective colouration. Yes, I needed immediate work and this was all that was available to me, so I disguised myself. Please don't tell anyone."

Tesla's smile returned. "Your secret is safe with me. I possess an advanced degree of perception...I often forget that what is viewed as total reality to most is only a transparent illusion to my eyes. I saw a young lady wearing the clothes of a labourer, while others would see only a labourer, and since all labourers in their universe are men, they gave you no more thought."

"You have a gift," Loveday said.

Tesla's smile faltered. "Most days it is a curse."

Grasping the corners of the crate, he heaved it up. He struggled to lift it clear of the cart. Loveday supported it by one edge until he secured his hold. It was surprisingly heavy. She said, "I'll help you carry your — what did you call it —inducement motor."

221B: On Her Majesty's Secret Service

"Induction motor. *Ja, danke.* I would hate to drop and break it before Mr Zaharoff and Madame Koluchy have a chance to look at it, as long as they are here."

"Who are they?"

"I believe they are investors in the Exposition."

"And in the baron's new technologies?"

"Ja. We share the same obsession. He calls himself a technocrat."

Loveday slid the handle of the wrench through a loop at the waist of her overalls. She and Tesla carried the crate out into the foundry. The man asked, "May I know your name, Miss?"

Loveday considered offering the man an alias, but decided it was unnecessary. If she successfully served the warrant, her name would be on the subsequent legal documents. Besides, she found the young scientist strangely endearing. This has been the night for meeting strangely endearing men, she thought.

"Miss Brooke will do for now, Mr Tesla."

Tesla nodded. "Call me Nikola."

As they walked toward the end of the aisle, she saw a man and woman standing near a long, matte black metal shape that resembled nothing so much as a bewinged throwing dart four meters in length. It rested atop a wheeled flat-car, the four wheels of which fitted into narrow-gauge metal tracks laid in the floor. The track led to a square opening in the seaward side wall, and slanted down at a 45 degree angle.

A well-dressed man standing at the rear of a giant dart glanced up as they approached. His impeccably tailored suit was rust-coloured, his tie dark red. Of medium height with a dusky complexion, his back-swept black hair held streaks of grey, as did the pointed goatee framing his mouth and chin. He held a gold-knobbed walking stick in his right hand. His obsidian eyes registered no reaction to the sight of Tesla and a slightly built workman. His face was studiedly expressionless and gave Loveday the feeling it would remain so while watching a newborn babe or a dying child.

Tesla whispered, "That is Mr Basil Zaharoff...he is very important, I am told. He says he is English, but I suspect otherwise."

Zaharoff turned away to speak to the woman. She was slender and elegantly dressed in an ankle-length lavender dress and short jacket. A light-blue mesh fell from the wide brim of her Duchess-of-Devonshire-style hat, and veiled her features.

"That is Madame Koluchy," said Tesla. "She, too, is very important and very interested in my earth-resonance concept. She is a nutritionist but I overheard her talking to Mr Zaharoff about something called Thunderstrike."

"And the baron?"

"You might say he is my sponsor. There he is."

A movement several feet above the metal dart caught Loveday's attention. Standing atop an elevated platform connected to a swinging boom arm, she saw a man wearing a steel-grey uniform. It looked much like those of the sentries but made of a superior material. It glinted with metallic highlights in the glow of the arc-lamps. Looking up at him, Loveday received the impression of a giant of a man, due to his height and enormous head set squarely on his broad shoulders.

Upon seeing Tesla carrying the crate, the metallic giant quickly climbed down the platform by means of a ladder. As he strode stiff-legged around the dart, Loveday was able to get a better look at him. Confirming her initial impression, the man possessed powerful shoulders and a strong head, with thick hair more white than grey. A short, crisp beard ran along his jawline. His bushy eyebrows were drawn sharply together above a prominent nose

His chest was broad and deep, his hips narrow, and he exuded an energy of vibrant health, obviously blessed with an iron constitution. Hot red blood obviously burned beneath his sun-browned skin.

221B: *On Her Majesty's Secret Service*

He was also not quite four feet tall, despite the thick soles on his high-topped boots.

Tesla set the crate on the floor and announced, "Here is my induction-motor, Herr Baron." He patted Loveday on the shoulder. "This fine lad gave me a hand."

The baron's eyes flicked from the crate to Loveday. They narrowed in suspicion. Loveday, enjoying drama of the moment, pulled off her cap, cast it to one side and shook out her hair. "Are you Baron Robespierre Robur de Maupertuis?"

Both Tesla and the baron stared at her in silent surprise. The baron nodded an affirmative. Loveday said, "So noted," reached inside her coveralls, produced the sealed envelope, and thrust it into the man's surprisingly large hands. "My name is Loveday Brooke, and I am duly authorized to act in the service of the High Court by hereby serving a warrant of control over real property in your possession, to wit, the *S.S. Friesland.* You are ordered to appear before the Queen's Division at the place, date and time you will find on the warrant."

Although she did not look directly at them, Loveday was aware of Madame Koluchy and Basil Zaharoff staring at her. Tesla stammered a few words in German, then regarded Loveday with an accusatory glare. "You misled me!"

"I did nothing of the kind, Nikola," she responded coolly. "I'm sorry if you feel a bit used, but the outcome of my job of work here was never in doubt. I would have found a way to serve the warrant, even had I not made your acquaintance."

"Just so, just so," murmured the baron, breaking the wax seal of the envelope and opening the flap.

"I've been led to understand you prefer to be known as Robur," she said, "As in the Conqueror."

"I have been known by that name," he replied, balancing a pair of pince-nez on the bridge of his nose. His deep voice held only a hint of a French accent. "I shall be again."

He unfolded the document and began reading, his lips moving. He examined the wording of the order itself, the date and time, and even fingered the official embossed seal. Twined around the middle finger of his left hand gleamed a golden ring. The ruby setting was cut to resemble a short-handled mallet.

Loveday waited without speaking and after a moment, the man carefully refolded the stiff square of paper along the crease and slid it back into the envelope.

She asked, "Do you understand the order?"

"What was your name again, Miss?"

"Loveday Brooke."

Robur chuckled. "I like that. You English are so clever when naming children. By what means did you get here?"

"Is that important?"

"I suppose not, since you obviously disguised yourself and blended in with the workers. I'm just wondering how you learned I would be here this night."

"There are many people in several countries curious about your whereabouts," she said non-committally.

"But very few who know of this place. Regardless, there isn't much point in discussing it, and I have neither the time nor the inclination to torture the information out of you."

Loveday felt her heartbeat speed up. With an edge to her voice, she asked again, "Do you understand the order?"

"Of course." Holding the envelope by opposite corners, Robur effortlessly ripped it and the document within in half. Both pieces fluttered to the floor. He peered past Tesla and Loveday and gestured with his right hand, as if he were attracting the attention of a waiter. He called out, "Oh, Vonn!"

"Destroying the order makes no difference to the Queen's

Division," Loveday said. "I will testify you confirmed your identity to me and that the warrant was legally served."

Robur sighed in weary exasperation. "I am well aware of that, Mademoiselle Brooke. And that makes no difference to me."

A grey-jacketed guard marched directly to Robur. The man stood at least six feet five inches tall with sloping shoulders and long, powerful arms. His blonde hair was cut short, close to his scalp. He was broken-nosed and beetle-browed. Loveday gauged him as a beast of a man. A big revolver rode in a leather holster at his right hip."Yes, sir?"

Robur pointed to Loveday and said, "Vonn, take this silly little *chine* to the cove and drown her. Don't choke her or otherwise abuse her, leave no bruises. Just hold her head beneath the water until she expires. Come see me when it's done."

221B: On Her Majesty's Secret Service

There is no man who is better worth having at your side when you are in a tight place than Sherlock Holmes.

—John H Watson, MD

CHAPTER 4

THE DOUBLE BARRAGE of buckshot smashed into the nearest arc-lamp, shattering the lens in a blinding miniature sunburst and a shower of glass shards. The report, magnified by the bulkheads and open space of the hold, was concussive.

Spargo Penhollow stumbled as if he had just received a blow, eyes dazzled and mind dazed. The bore of the pistol in his hand swept back and forth. He uttered a bestial roar as he struggled to recover his balance and his vision.

Neither Watson nor Holmes was inclined to give him the chance. They bounded across the hold and grabbed Penhollow's arms, trying to force them behind his back in hammerlocks.

As soon as they had secured their grips, they realized their mistake. The two men shared a swift eye exchange, acknowledging their error. Watson murmured, "Oh, bloody hell."

Although shorter than both Holmes and Watson, Penhollow was far stronger. They strained to push him against the bulkhead, their feet scraping the deck for purchase.

Penhollow brought both of his arms together as if he were clapping his hands. The backs of Watson's and Holmes skulls collided. Air left two sets of lungs in simultaneous, explosive whoofs.

221B: On Her Majesty's Secret Service

Holmes reeled away, but Watson maintained his grip on Penhollow's right arm. He cracked him hard across a clump of nerve ganglia on the wrist-joint with the barrels of the Lancaster. The man bawled out an obscenity and his revolver fell from numbed fingers.

Watson slid under and around Penhollow's arm, losing his beret in the process, and jumped onto his back. He applied a choke-hold with his left arm and dug into his pants pocket with his right hand. Penhollow lumbered across the hold, bellowing and swearing. He tried to dislodge Watson by furiously shaking himself like a big, wet dog.

Regaining his balance, Holmes put himself in Penhollow's path and delivered a bartitsu lateral kick-punch combination into his lower belly. The man grunted at each blow and slapped Holmes. His slab of an open hand connected with the side of his head, knocking him sideways against the stack of crates.

Watson increased the pressure of the arm around Penhollow's throat. The man drove an elbow into his solar plexus and propelled himself backward on wide-braced legs. He slammed Watson against a bulkhead, snarling a triumphant, "Ha!"

Holmes closed in again, bringing his left fist down on the bridge of Penhollow's nose. Blood squirted from his nostrils and he opened his mouth to gasp for air. Watson clapped the ether-saturated pad over it.

Penhollow uttered a gargling cry and tried to prise Watson's hand away. He careened across the hold, tossing his head in the manner of a mad bull. Then his eyes rolled up, he pawed feebly at Watson's arm around his neck, and toppled backward, pinning Watson to the deck beneath him.

Watson thrashed and elbowed his way out from under Penhollow's suffocating weight. Holmes helped him stand. "That went on a bit longer longer than I had wanted."

Watson rubbed the back of his head. "Think how I feel." He

checked the glass vial of diethyl ether. A rubber seal with a drip-nipple served as a stopper. It was slightly under half-full of the clear liquid. "We're getting much more use out this than I expected."

He returned the container and pad to his pocket while Holmes scooped up the pistol. He checked the cylinder. "We need to disembark immediately. If Zaharoff's man is who I think he is, we won't be able to brazen our way out the same way we brazened our way in."

"Rubadue was the name?"

Holmes nodded grimly. "Most likely Cuthbert Rubadue, a ruffian-for-hire originally from Edinburgh. We had a serious falling out during my Montague Street days when I was learning my trade. He earned a full stretch in Coldbath Jug and was released just last year. I've kept a weather eye on him since then. He's sure to recognize me."

Watson frowned. "Why would Basil Zaharoff hire a man like that? And what does he have to do with any of this?"

Holmes stepped cautiously toward the hatch opening. "Something else Mycroft will be exceedingly curious about."

He and Watson peered around the edge. The gangway was clear but they saw a burly man with red, bristle-cut hair and shaggy sideburns standing at its nether end. His face was marked with a vicious scar which ran from the bottom of his left eye straight down the cheek past the corner of the mouth to his chin He spoke animatedly with a half-a-dozen confused and irritated-looking stevedores. He wore a shabby herringbone coat and gripped a knotty shillelagh topped with a varnished, fist-sized knob.

"Rubadue?" inquired Watson quietly.

"The same."

The red-haired man glimpsed them at the hatch and pointed the knob of the blackthorn stick in their direction. In a raspy voice overlaid with a Scots brogue, he cried out, "Sherlock Holmes! Holmes the meddling, jumped-up jack! A drubbing ye've been owed these past eight years, and by God, this night the debt will be paid in full!"

"Hullo, Cuthbert," Holmes called. "Found gainful employment other than flimping, have we?"

A trio of gray-uniformed guards trotted along the pier from the direction of the warehouse. Three very large black-and-tan mastiffs pulled them forward by leather leashes. The workers quickly parted for them. Rubadue gestured to the gangplank and shouted to the guards, "Them two in the hold there! Don't let 'em get away! Set the dogs on 'em!"

Watson bent down, forcing his fingers between the edge of the ramp and the lip of the hatch. He heaved but the tripled-reinforced length of oak and metal did not budge. "Give me a hand, Holmes!"

"No time for that," Holmes said. "It's latched to the dock." He hefted the revolver. "The pistol is fully loaded. We could shoot the hounds if they come aboard."

Watson grimaced and straightened up. "I would prefer not to."

"Nor I." Holmes handed him the pistol. "You're a better shot than I am, anyway."

"Except when it comes to shooting Her Majesty's initials into the wall of our sitting room."

"I did that once and only once, and neither you nor Mrs Hudson have ever permitted me to forget it."

On the pier, Rubadue spoke intensely to the guards, apparently trying to impress upon them the urgency of the matter. The dogs milled around their legs, growling and snapping at stevedores who came too close.

"They have us have trapped here, you know," Watson said. "Suggestions?"

"We could always surrender."

"You'd receive your long-deferred drubbing."

"True, but I don't think Cuthbert would stop there."

"Neither do I," replied Watson. "Better part of valour, then?"

"Agreed." Holmes back-stepped from the hatch. "We need to get out into the open air and the only way is to go up." He unbuttoned his coat. "And with alacrity, too."

Watson shook his head in weary exasperation. "I hope Miss Brooke is faring better on her mission than we are on ours."

They found the access hatch of the hold and entered the dimly lit alleyway beyond. Taking one of the small oil lamps from a bracket, Holmes led them into a labyrinth of pipes and wheel-valves criss-crossing in all directions. They heard the steady drip of water and the rhythmic beat of the electrical generator, much louder now. The odour of mildew filled their nostrils. Dismantled pieces of machinery lay scattered on the deck. They carefully picked their way over it. Watson said disapprovingly, "This boat — ship — seems to be in poor shape...barely seaworthy."

"Apparently she's only used for short voyages," replied Holmes.

"Our obstreperous friend, Mr Penhollow, made reference to the *Friesland* needing to be safely back in her berth by dawn...that suggests her berth is relatively close by."

The two men strode quickly through the metal maze, Holmes bumping his head on low-hanging pipes more than once. Watson kept looking backward for signs and sounds of pursuit. He saw and heard none, but he didn't feel encouraged. Inhaling a deep breath and then exhaling it, he said, "I should tell you that I wrote up the notes of the Lauriston Gardens murder investigation in the form a novel."

"I am aware. I've seen you at your desk scribbling away for the past year or so."

"When I first broached the subject of chronicling the affair, you said, 'You may do what you like.' "

221B: On Her Majesty's Secret Service

"I remember. So you finally completed it."

"Not only completed it, but I submitted it and had it accepted by a publisher. I received word last week that it will appear in *Beeton's Christmas Annual* in December as *A Study in Scarlet*. I attribute the title to you within the body of the story."

Holmes' brow furrowed. "I believe I said the case was a tangled skein."

"You did. That was my original title but the editor didn't care for it and asked for a change."

"And the reason for telling me this now?"

Watson smiled without humour. "Just in case I don't make it through this night. I'd hate for you to be surprised while visiting a news agent come this Yuletide. Anticipate and adapt."

Holmes nodded. "Just so. Thank you for your consideration." He paused and added, "I'm not certain if Mycroft will be in a grateful mood, however. Your novel will make us public figures."

Watson scowled. "Well, Mycroft can just go and —"

Holmes came to a sudden stop, turning to look down the passageway. He put a forefinger to his lips. Watson tilted his head and listened. He heard a distant tap-tapping. Between one heartbeat and the next, the tapping rose in volume to a steady castanet clatter. Underlying the sound came grunting snarls of exertion.

Holmes put a hand between Watson's shoulder blades and pushed. "Run!"

They sprinted down the corridor as the rattle of sharp nails against metal grew louder. Their own thudding footfalls echoed and re-echoed. Watson ran as he had run few times in his life. His heart pounded against his ribs. The old bullet-wound in his leg began to burn as if a white-hot poker had been laid upon it.

The passage dead-ended against a heavy metal door with a wheel-lock centered in its rivet-studded mass. Holmes grabbed the wheel

221B: On Her Majesty's Secret Service

with his free hand as Watson staggered to a halt.

"The hatch!" Holmes snapped. "Help me open it."

Putting their hands on the wheel, they turned it violently. It didn't spin easily—it caught and squeaked during the rotation until they attained a steady hand-over-hand spin. They continued spinning until the lock completed its final turn and they heard the snapping of solenoids and latches. Putting his shoulder against it, Holmes pushed the door open, rusty hinges squealing.

The two men stumbled over the raised lip of the hatchway. Watson pointed the revolver down the passageway and squeezed the trigger three times. The gunshots sounded like handclaps, magnified a dozen times.

The muzzle flash briefly smeared the darkness with strobing tongues of flame. Little flares sparked in the murk as the rounds struck and ricocheted from metal. They heard a series of staccato clangs, as if a blacksmith pounded on an anvil at an inhumanly fast tempo, as bullets bounced from bulkhead to bulkhead.

Watson aimed high, not wanting to shoot the hounds, only to drive them back long enough so they could shut and seal the hatch. After the third shot, he threw himself backward and Holmes pulled the hatch closed with a reverberating boom.

Watson gulped air, leaning against the hatch. Heavy weights slammed against it from the outside and they heard growls of frustration. He and Holmes hastily backed away from the door.

"What in God's name has Mycroft gotten us into?" demanded Watson breathlessly.

"Our orders were only to observe," said Holmes. "We've gotten ourselves into this specific situation."

"Mycroft can bloody well get us out of this specific situation...we're owed that much!"

"Only if we can get a signal to him," Holmes replied, turning away to examine their surroundings, holding the lamp high. They stood in a chamber that at one time served as a tool room, judging by the table chain-vise and various hammers, sledges and wrenches scattered atop it.

Holmes saw rusty, staple-shaped ladder rungs bolted to the bulkhead. They stretched up a shaft to an round iron hatch. Putting one foot on the lowest rung, Holmes tested his weight on it, then stepped upward, holding the lamp in his right hand. "An inner-hull maintenance accessway, I wager."

"It probably hasn't been opened in years," Watson said in a low voice. He added, "Men with guns and ill intent will join the dogs shortly, Holmes."

"I am very aware, Watson," Holmes responded impatiently, putting his feet on another rung and then another. He examined the rim of the hatch with the lamp and placed his left hand against it. He pushed. It didn't move.

Watson carefully put his ear close to the door. He heard the scratching scramble of clawed feet on the deck and the murmur of male voices. Feigning calm, he said, "The hound-masters are on their way."

Holmes stepped onto a higher rung and put his right shoulder against the metal disk, bracing his legs on the ladder. He pushed. Rust sifted down from the rim, stinging his eyes and dribbling into his mouth. He spit out the grit and pushed harder. The disk shifted and he shouldered it up and to one side without making too much noise, other than a low metal-on-metal grind.

Holding the lamp ahead of him, Holmes struggled up through the round opening. He received only an impression of a low-ceilinged chamber leading into a crawlway. He opened his mouth to call to Watson, but the man thrust his head and shoulders through. He whispered tensely, "They're trying to get the door open."

Holmes helped him up and out and they pushed the hatch-cover back over the iron-rimmed hole. They heard the clank of the wheel-lock and men raising their voices in angry, confused shouts. They had expected to find two cowering interlopers.

Watson and Holmes soft-footed their way into the cramped crawlway. They could walk along it only sideways, shuffling like crabs. Holmes lit their way by the dying flame of the lamp. After a few yards, the passage curved slightly to the left, following the contours of the hull. They navigated around a mass of pipes as the lamp-light flickered and went out.

They found and climbed up a short flight of stairs by feel alone and exited the crawlway into a properly wide and lighted corridor. Both men gusted out sighs of relief, although Watson pointed out, "We're still trapped. We need a better means of defence than what we have."

As they passed through double swinging doors and continued down the passage, they glimpsed a closet to the right. Holmes peered in and saw it held cleaning and custodial supplies. He paused for a thoughtful second, then entered.

Grabbing a push broom and a heavy, long-handled mop, Holmes returned to the corridor. Watson demanded, "Are you providing the means of cleaning up our blood and viscera after the hounds of hell are done with us? Very considerate."

Holmes smiled wryly. "You said we need a better means of defence. You still have the ether, do you not?"

Face registering puzzlement, Watson produced the vial from his pocket. Realization shone in his eyes when he looked at the mop. "Hounds of hell deterrent. Very clever."

"Anticipate and adapt."

Ahead of them they saw another set of double doors bisecting the corridor. The left-hand door bore a red-painted legend accompanied by an upward pointing arrow: WAY OUT. At the same time, from the opposite end of the corridor came the rapid pattering of padded feet and the clicking of claws.

221B: On Her Majesty's Secret Service

"The beasts found another way up here!" blurted Watson, finger tightening on the trigger of the revolver.

The two doors sprang apart, and the three mastiffs rushed in between them, lithe and frighteningly swift. Black-rimmed lips drew back from their fangs in a contortion of blood-lust. They uttered wet, snarling grunts as they ran.

Without speaking, Holmes thrust the mop-head toward Watson who applied a liberal splash of anaesthetic over the thick cotton strands. The two men back-pedalled down the corridor as the mastiffs raced three abreast toward them. The centre dog pulled out ahead of his companions and for a split second, Watson was reminded of a savage, triple-headed Cerberus.

The hound left the deck in an arching leap straight for Holmes' throat. The beast's great forepaws struck his chest and bowled him over. He fell back with his feet braced against the dog's belly, at the same time shoving the mop head into its open maw.

He used the animal's momentum to carry it over his body. It tumbled snout over rump to land gracelessly on its back. The mastiff scrambled clumsily back to all fours, shook its big head, uttered a prolonged retching sound, then fell over onto its left side, paws twitching fitfully.

The other two dogs slowed their charge to stiff-legged walks as their sensitive noses encountered the painfully sharp aroma of the ether. When they saw their comrade lying senseless, they hesitated, growling deep in their massive chests.

Keeping the pistol trained on the hounds, Watson helped Holmes to his feet and they both carefully backed to the door. Holding out the mop full-length, Holmes swung it in short flat arcs. One dog made a forward lunge and received a wet slap across the muzzle. It staggered and slammed into its companion, eyes rolling, sneezing explosively. The third hound snapped at the mop-head, stopped itself from sinking its fangs into it, and wheeled away from the fumes in revulsion, snorting and coughing.

Holmes and Watson pushed open the doors and lunged through them. The doors had no locks or drop-bars, only a pair of metal handles in elongated U shapes. Watson slid the blunt-end of the broom-handle through them. He braced it tightly just as the doors shook under the repeated impacts of the two mastiffs hurling themselves against it. The hounds growled and snarled on the other side, and faintly, they heard the shouts of men.

"I fear I'm losing my abiding affection for canines," Watson muttered.

"A righteous man regardeth the life of his beast, but the tender mercies of the wicked are always cruel," intoned Holmes. "Blame the dogs' owner, not the dogs."

Watson held up the vial of ether. It was three-quarters empty. "We can't keep this up indefinitely."

"Nor do we intend to," Holmes said, whirling around toward the flight of stairs leading upward. "Let's get out of here before our improvised barricade gives up the ghost."

The stairs took them through an open hatch. They emerged on the quarterdeck, in the shadow of the superstructure that supported the *S.S. Friesland's* bridge. No one could be seen behind the dirty panes of glass. The sea air smelled thankfully fresh and clean after the dank atmosphere and ether fumes of the lower levels of the ship. They could still hear the steady throb of the generator and the sounds of activity from the wharf. The deck of the ship looked deserted.

Pulling the door of the hatchway closed, Watson secured it with the simple hook and eye-bolts screwed into the frame. He knew it wouldn't prevent the men and mastiffs from reaching the deck, only slow them down.

Warily, they stepped out from the shadows and into the moonlight, moving toward the seaward-facing port side. They circled the base of

221B: On Her Majesty's Secret Service

the mast towering amidships and the loose heap of cargo netting that lay around it. Holmes held the mop out before him like a medieval knight's lance. Watson reflected that his friend should have looked ridiculous, but under the circumstances, did not.

A voice rasped from behind them, "Ye look like a right bleedin' idjit standin' there with yer mop, Holmes. Ye plan to swab the deck after yer drubbin'?"

Holmes and Watson turned in a slow circle, surveying the six men stepping out from behind the mast. Rubadue marched across the deck from aft. The men were all stevedores and carried a variety of hooks, cudgels and pry bars amongst them. One held a Webley revolver.

Rubadue patted the palm of one hand with the knob of his shillelagh. His lips peeled back from tobacco-stained teeth in a victorious grin. "We got the drops on ye, so now it's yer turn to be accomodatin'. Drop the shooter and the mop."

Holmes smiled. "Not that it is an unusual state for you, Cuthbert, but you are more than a bit over your head here."

Rubadue laughed contemptuously. It was not a pleasant sound. "Look who's talkin'."

"Aren't you the least bit curious as to why I'm here?"

"Nay. 'Tis not my — whatdoyecallit — baileywick. If the boss wants to know somethin' from someone, he has experts to call." He gestured with the blackthorn stick, pointing first to Holmes and then to Watson. "Do as I says. Drop 'em. Yer schoolboy tricks won't work this time, Holmes."

Holmes glanced toward Watson, nodded and they placed mop and pistol on the deck at their feet. Rubadue laughed again. "Sherlock Holmes, the meddling, jumped-up jack."

"Cuthbert Rubadue, the prostitute's pick-pocket."

The Scotsman's grin disappeared and he took a threatening step

55

forward, lifting his shillelagh. Holmes' right hand dipped into his coat pocket and came with out with a brass pistol. He raised it smoothly. It was long barrelled and exceptionally wide-bored, like a wheel-lock from the 16th century. Cuthbert rocked to a halt, eyes widening first in fear and then incredulity.

Holmes continued to raise the pistol until he pointed it directly overhead. He squeezed the trigger. With an eardrum compressing pop, a flare streaked from the bore, seemingly propelled by by a ribbon of spark-shot smoke. When it was but an ember glowing among the stars, the projectile burst apart, burning with brilliant white fire against the dark sky.

"What the bloody hell —" Rubadue began. He broke off and gestured to the stevedores, yelling, "Grab 'em, lads!"

At the edge of the cove, where the calm waters joined with the open sea, a flare rocketed skyward and exploded into a ball of coruscating orange flame. The stevedores stared at it, not moving.

Holmes announced, "Gentlemen, out there is a boatload of officers from the Defence Intelligence Branch. They are on their way here right now. If they find you aboard the *S.S. Friesland,* you will be arrested and prosecuted as enemies of the Crown."

He glanced toward Rubadue. "That includes you, Cuthbert. We'll have to reschedule that drubbing."

The labourers fled across the deck in all directions, dropping their makeshift weapons and tools along the way.

"Boatload?" inquired Watson. "Five at most."

Holmes glanced out to sea. "Seven, if you count Mycroft twice." His gaze returned to Rubadue. "Are you still here, Cuthbert?"

Rubadue didn't answer. His hands tightened around his shillelagh. Wood creaked. His lips worked as if he had difficulty speaking. He snarled hoarsely, "A bloody trick!"

Watson bent down and retrieved the pistol from the deck. "Not bloody," he said. "You said it yourself...a schoolboy trick." He cast a sour look toward Holmes. "And of course it worked, didn't it?"

Sherlock Holmes shrugged negligently. "Don't they always?"

221B: On Her Majesty's Secret Service

A complex mind. All great criminals have that.
—Sherlock Holmes

CHAPTER 5

LOVEDAY STRAINED BRIEFLY against the arms pinning her, but Vonn tightened his grip on the collar of her shirt, expertly twisting it against her throat like a choke leash. She gagged, gasped briefly for air and then stopped struggling. Although dread knotted in her belly like an icy fist, she met Robur's thoughtful stare with a challenging one of her own.

"That is a foolish decision" she husked out. "I'm not here alone."

The man cocked his head at her. "No?"

"There are others working with me to locate you."

Eyebrows raised, Robur made a mocking show of looking around, even peering under one of the conveyor frames. "And where may they be located, Mademoiselle Brooke?"

"I'm sure you understand my reluctance to reveal anything to you,"

Robur made an impatient shooing gesture toward Vonn. "Take her."

"Wait!" Tesla placed himself beside Loveday, laying a protective hand on her right forearm.

Robur's eyebrows drew down. "Do not interfere, Nikola. Keep your place."

"With all due respect, Baron," Tesla said earnestly, his eyes glistening like damp pieces of obsidian, "surely you realize that any violence against this young woman will only compound your legal liabilities. She obviously did not come here on her own accord. She was dispatched, therefore, she can be traced."

Robur glanced at Loveday expectantly "Well? What have you to say to that?"

Loveday's composed expression did not alter. She had spent years developing and perfecting a poker face, hiding her feelings and innermost thoughts behind a pose of clinical, almost serene detachment. She stated unemotionally, "I took lodgings in the village. I rented a bicycle. I sent a wire to my employer in London. Yes, I can be traced. Easily."

Robur appeared to lose all interest in the conversation. "You can be traced and your drowned body can also be found washed up on one of the beaches in the area. Easily. A rented room and bicycle will only expedite identifying your corpse. Poor, foolish *petite fille*, she must have fallen from the cliffs whilst taking a midnight stroll, no doubt a doomed lover's tryst. How tragically romantic." He snapped his fingers. "Nikola, step aside. Vonn, take her."

Vonn jerked Loveday backward. She cried out, "Sherlock Holmes!"

Robur held up a peremptory hand, halting Vonn. "Explain."

"Sherlock Holmes and Dr Watson are operatives of the British Secret Service. They are here for you."

Robur shook his head in weary exasperation. "I've never heard of them. A ridiculous name...'Sherlock Holmes.' Typically British."

A man, panting and gasping, raced forward. Loveday recognized the red-haired man with the blackthorn cane as the same rude fellow she had met on the path. His face glistened with perspiration. Judging by his expression, he teetered on the verge of panic.

He ran past Robur without speaking and only halted when he reached Zaharoff and Madame Koluchy. He spoke to them in a frantic whisper, gesticulating with the shillelagh. Zaharoff's eyes went wide and he blared out, "Sherlock Holmes?"

He swung toward Robur, reaching out with his walking stick. "Stop! Let her go!"

Robur said, "Hold on that, Vonn."

The guard didn't release Loveday but he didn't move.

Zaharoff looked around anxiously. "We must flee...or rather you and Madame Koluchy must not be found in my company. I own this property, so therefore I have the legal right to be here, but both of you are sought by the authorities."

Robur's face twisted into a ferocious mask of anger. "Why are you suddenly so fearful, Basil?"

Zaharoff took a steadying breath. "I have certain mutually beneficial connections within the British government. But two agents of her Majesty's Secret Service named Holmes have been prying into my affairs. So far, my solicitors have kept their enquires at bay, but if I am found consorting with the alleged mastermind of the Brotherhood of Seven Kings and Robur the Conqueror, my connections will be severed. None of us can afford to be compromised."

In a velvet-soft voice, touched with an exotic foreign accent Loveday could not place, Madame Koluchy said, "You are right, Basil...we can't risk the Ring's exposure. Robur and I will retire to the launch."

"No!" barked Robur, hands clenching in fists. He thrust his head forward. "I will not abandon my prototype!"

Zaharoff opened his mouth to argue. Nikola Tesla chose that moment to snatch the wrench hanging from the loop on Loveday's overalls. He used it to strike Vonn directly on his right elbow joint.

The man cried out in angry, agonized surprise. He staggered back, clutching at his arm with his left hand. To Loveday, Tesla shouted,

221B: On Her Majesty's Secret Service

"Fly, Miss Brooke!"

She grabbed his hand and yanked him forward. "You too, Nikola!"

They ran at an angle toward the nearest machines. The route took them away from the exit but it provided cover, particularly near the smelting furnace. Loveday wasn't sure if the guards would be given the order to shoot, but she did not care to chance it. Because of the noise, they couldn't hear gunfire, but a spark flared from a dark iron framework ahead of them, leaving a white smear.

Loveday and Tesla changed direction, bending almost double. Loveday assumed the uniformed guards hadn't been ordered to apprehend them alive. She guessed they would fan out all over the foundry to outflank them and cut off possible avenues of escape. Her heart pounded against her ribcage like a trapped bird, but her thoughts remained clear.

A certain cold professionalism swept over Loveday. She took the wrench from Tesla and gripped it tightly. These were far more ruthless people than she had ever imagined and she had no intention of falling under their power again. She couldn't help but wonder what had become of Holmes and Watson, and who the second secret service agent named Holmes might be.

Avoiding areas where workers congregated, Loveday and Tesla crept quickly through the centre of the foundry, feeling the thunder of machinery in their bones. They breathed shallowly against the cloying stench of molten metal near the smelter. They changed direction several times. Tesla did his best to move swiftly but when he recoiled from a jet of steam he slipped on the damp floor and nearly fell. He whispered breathlessly, *"Es tut mir leid."*

She patted his arm reassuringly and then tensed, squatting down. She pulled Tesla with her. On the other side of a clattering conveyor belt, Vonn loomed up, a misshapen apparition striding through a billow of steam. He moved uncertainly, wiping at the beads of

221B: On Her Majesty's Secret Service

perspiration on his brow. He carried his Adams .540 revolver awkwardly in his left hand. Loveday realized that Tesla had rendered his right arm temporarily useless, so attempting to fire accurately with his left hand put valuable machinery, as well their operators, at risk. She doubted he had been given orders to do so.

On impulse, Loveday flattened herself on the floor, peering beneath the conveyor belt. A bit over two metres away, she saw Vonn's booted feet and legs. A plan sprang full-blown into her mind. It was desperate, and even a trifle ridiculous, because it was such a long shot. She decided to trust her instinct and go ahead.

With her hands, she pantomimed to Tesla what she intended to do. He stared at her in disbelief and shook his head vigorously. She glared at him and mouthed, "Stay here!"

Using her elbows and the sides of her feet, Loveday wormed her way forward. The wrench in her hand made progress difficult, especially when she had to manoeuvre over and around support struts and upright posts.

Vonn shifted position only a few inches in the short time it took Loveday to reach him. She gambled that the man would choose to keep visually surveying the area, hoping either she or Tesla would show themselves long enough to fire another, more accurate shot. He was oblivious to his immediate surroundings.

Hiking herself up on her knees as far as she could without having her hair tangled up in the underside of the conveyor, Loveday raised the wrench and brought it down hard on the toe of Vonn's right boot. Even over the mechanical racket, she heard him scream.

Loveday scrambled out from under the conveyor, wrench held high. Face contorted in pain, Vonn danced backward, a half-hobble, half-limp. He levelled the revolver at her but she swung the wrench and struck the barrel, ripping it from his hand with a semi-musical clang of metal against metal.

The impact stung her fingers, loosening her grip. Vonn's left hand lashed out and encircled her wrist, painfully crushing flesh against bone. He shook her savagely. The wrench fell and slid out of reach. Teeth bared in a silent snarl of rage, Vonn closed his right hand around the slim column of Loveday's throat.

She felt as if an iron collar constricted her windpipe. Dark amoeba-like spots swam across her vision. Effortlessly, Vonn lifted her from the floor by wrist and throat walked her toward the conveyor belt. She struggled, losing all scruples. Her knee slammed into his groin and she raked at his eyes with the fingers of her free hand. Vonn grunted and lowered his head so she only clawed away his beret. The snarl on his face became a grin of vicious satisfaction.

The light of consciousness suddenly went out of his eyes with the suddenness of a candle being extinguished. Loveday felt his body shudder, then his grasp relaxed, his hands dropping away. He fell forward. Gasping for air, she pushed Vonn aside. He fell half-across the conveyor belt. It whisked him away toward the open, glowing maw of the smelting furnace.

Massaging her throat, Loveday blinked away the floating spots. She saw Sherlock Holmes reaching out his left hand to steady her. The other gripped the wrench. It glistened with a spattering of scarlet. Right behind him, she saw John Watson. Both men looked dishevelled and out-of-breath, as if they had either been running or fighting or both. Her surge of relief made her light-headed for a moment.

Loveday coughed and said hoarsely, "Thank you, Mr Holmes."

He extended the wrench, handle-first, toward her, regarding her with a grave gaze. "Now you see how it's done."

The entire foundry became a pandemonium of running people, bellowed orders, counter-orders, curses in different languages and the occasional gunshot. Cutting through it all piped the piercingly distinct shriek of police whistles used by the Metropolitan Police.

The cacophony of machines eased as they fell silent in one section after another. "The generators are being shut down," Holmes

221B: On Her Majesty's Secret Service

commented. "Mycroft and company must have made landfall."

"Who is Mycroft?" asked Loveday.

"If he wishes to tell you," said Watson dourly. "He'll do so himself."

Tesla hesitantly stood up. Watson reached for the pistol in his waistband, but Loveday checked his motion with a gesture. "No, he's a friend. He helped me escape from Robur and the others."

Another gunshot echoed throughout the building and Tesla flinched. Holmes said, "He should stay where he is for the time being. I have a sense matters will become quite complicated soon enough."

Holmes, Loveday and Watson sprinted toward the far end of the facility. To avoid armed sentries, they zigzagged through the maze of machinery. Most of it had been abandoned by its operators. They heard voices raised in angry protest and saw men milling about. One of them caught and held Loveday's attention.

A tall, large-framed man stood frowning down at Basil Zaharoff and Robur. His corpulent body was draped in a dark tan gabardine greatcoat with a yellow scarf at his throat. His hair was black, his head massive. His face held a sharpness of expression she recognized as a mirror image of that held by Holmes. His eyes were a peculiar pewter-grey colour.

Five men dressed in nondescript brown suits the colour of Windsor soup brandished pistols, disarmed guards and patted down machinists. They moved very efficiently. Police whistles hung from cords around their necks. No bodies or injured people were in evidence, so the brown-suited men had apparently fired their weapons into the air for effect. Robur and Zaharoff stood with their hands raised. Of Madame Koluchy, there was no sign, nor did Loveday see the red-haired man.

The big man looked up at the approach of the three people. His lips pursed in disapproval. In an aggrieved baritone, he stated "I assumed you would have the consideration to be waiting for me, Sherlock. We had to find our own way in here."

Holmes grinned in genuine amusement at the man's irritation. "We tried, Mycroft, but Watson and I were unavoidably delayed by a triumvirate of hell-hounds, and their equally dogged handlers. We talked our way off their menu, but they're still afoot, so be watchful if you care to take a tour of Penhallick Wharf."

"Not likely. You know how much I hate fieldwork." His eyes shifted to Loveday. "Who is this, then?"

"Ask her yourself, Mycroft," snapped Watson. "I believe she can speak."

"We've heard her," offered Holmes. "Several times, in fact."

The big man's eyes narrowed in annoyance. He said, "My name is Mycroft Holmes, Miss. I represent a certain branch of the British government. That is all you need to know for the moment. And you are?"

"My name is Loveday Brooke, a private investigator. You must be the other Secret Service agent named Holmes Mr Zaharoff mentioned. I take it you and Sherlock are related."

"Brothers," grunted Mycroft.

"I'm the younger," said Sherlock. "In case you wondered."

"Why is an operative of the Lynch Court Detective Agency here?" Mycroft demanded. He glanced toward Sherlock. "You said you had impressed upon Ebenezer Dyer the need to stand aside."

Loveday's nerves were stretched wire-taut but some of her confidence was returning. She stepped forward, staring levelly at Mycroft. "As I explained to your brother, my agency has important clients to answer to."

Her gaze shifted to Robur, who did not look at her. "I served the warrant of control on Baron Maupertuis as I was duly authorized by the court to do, after which he ordered my execution. Mr Zaharoff there is a witness as is a Mr Tesla, who I'm certain will support my allegation. A third person, a woman identified to me as Madame Koluchy, was also present. I do not see her here."

While she spoke, Zaharoff and Robur maintained neutral expressions. Mycroft turned toward Zaharoff, "Kathryn Koluchy was here tonight?"

When Zaharoff did not answer, Loveday said, "She was indeed, up until a few minutes ago, as well as a disreputable looking man with red hair. He is missing, too. Perhaps you should check to see if a steam launch is still tied up in the cove."

Mycroft blew out a sigh. It sounded like the working of a fireplace bellows. "We saw the launch departing as we arrived. As time was of the essence, we allowed it to be on its way. Had we known Madame Koluchy might be aboard, at best we could only have questioned the woman, not arrested her."

He turned to face Zaharoff. "You, however may face such an eventuality before the night is done. Explain yourself, sir."

Zaharoff drew himself up in an attitude of outraged dignity. He lowered his hands "I shall not. You have no legal standing here, Mr Holmes. This facility is my private property and the wharf itself is under exclusive lease to me, so I may engage in my own private business, unmolested. Whatever issues you have with any of my guests, I suggest you attend to them directly and not use me as either your go-between or surrogate. As it is, unless you have a writ or a warrant specific to me, I demand you depart immediately, else my solicitors shall make this egregious trespass a matter of public record. I have friends at the *London News.*"

Mycroft did not move, nor did his expression alter while Basil Zaharoff spoke. Then he inquired quietly, "A warrant is what you request, sir?"

Zaharoff nodded. "I do."

"Very well." With a speed astonishing for a man of such size,

221B: On Her Majesty's Secret Service

Mycroft struck Zaharoff across the face with a broad, fat hand like the flipper of a seal. Zaharoff reeled backward, falling against the end of the black metal dart. He put a hand to his face and stared at Mycroft in silent incredulity.

"You are a bounder, sir," Mycroft declared matter-of-factly. "Worse than. You are a convicted arsonist, a convicted bigamist, a convicted swindler, an imposter, an arms dealer and a war profiteer. Nor are you even remotely English by birth. You have connived, bribed and blackmailed your way into British society, industry and the halls of power. Currently, through means far more foul than fair, you are scheming to merge a pair of armament companies, Maxim and Nordenfelt. That is your first step in establishing a weapons manufacturing monopoly. We also know you have financial dealings with the Hephaestus Ring...which is a hollow dummy business, formed to disguise and disperse the assets of an international criminal enterprise."

Robur finally spoke, regarding Mycroft with contempt. "You are mistaken, *gros homm.*"

Mycroft permitted himself a sardonic smile at being addressed as "big man." He stepped forward, towering like an oak over the much smaller man. "How so, *nain?*"

At being called "dwarf," Robur swept the assembled people with black, rage-filled eyes. "You stand in the way of a mighty organization, the full extent of which you have yet to comprehend."

"I wouldn't make that assumption." Sherlock Holmes strode directly past Robur to the dart resting on its wheeled flat-car. After a swift visual examination, he struck the hull with his knuckles. It rang like a gong. "This is your contrivance, isn't it?"

"It is not a contrivance."

"I submit it is an updated version of your legendary flying machine, the *Albatross,* with which you terrorized and even extorted several nations, nearly twenty years ago."

"This is a prototype," Robur retorted, as if begrudging each word. "but much improved over the original. The completed version will be much larger, of course."

"Of course. What is its motive power?"

"You would not understand."

"Probably an electrical induction motor," ventured Loveday. "Invented by Nikola Tesla. An Austrian genius brought here under false pretences."

"A genius," repeated Holmes as if the word tasted sour. "One of many recruited to serve the 'mighty organization' you alluded to, Robur."

"What do you mean, Sherlock?" demanded Mycroft.

"Watson and I have done our own research over the last year or so. The Hephaestus Ring is more than a merchant consortium or even a criminal enterprise. Its true origins date back centuries. It is older than many countries and functions almost as a nation unto itself. It even has a national purpose...to dominate the Earth through the institution of a global technocracy."

Mycroft's eyebrows rose then lowered. "A global what?"

"A society controlled by an elite class of technical geniuses. Hephaestus is overseen by a renegade group of brilliant intellects, who see themselves as superior beings and whose mission is to control the lesser minds of the world — all the rest of us. Some of these 'technocrats' have brought themselves to our attention over the years...among them the man calling himself Captain Nemo, a rogue French astronomer named Professor Mirzarbeau...and most recently, a man known as Moriarty."

Holmes's gaze returned to Robur, who met it unblinkingly. "Judging by what Watson and I found aboard the *Friesland*, it's not difficult to extrapolate that the Ring and Basil Zaharoff are engaged in an interdependent but mutually compensatory undertaking to develop, use and profit from new mechanicities...specifically those of a military nature." He took a step closer to Robur, sudden anger glittering in his eyes. "The future the Hephaestus Ring foresees is one of unending warfare."

Robur chuckled and glanced down at the hammer ring on his left hand. "Not unending, Mr Holmes...just until we have established a technocratic state...then there will be war no more. Our plans are complex but our goals are for the greater good."

"Complex plans conceived by criminal minds. Complex and criminal are two words that adequately sum up your character."

"My body may be small —"

"But you have schemes colossal enough to challenge God," Holmes broke in, not bothering to blunt the edge of sarcasm in his voice. "You've made quite clear the ultimate aim of the Ring's superior intellects."

"Perhaps so. But you've overlooked that scattered beneath our superior intellects is a vast system of support. Minions, in other words." He cut his eyes to the right. "The lesser minds who live only to execute the Ring's commands."

The gunshot sounded like the slamming of a giant door. Mycroft cried out and stumbled, clapping a hand to his upper left arm. He fell to one knee. Zaharoff squawked in fear and threw himself to the floor. Instinctively, Holmes dropped into a crouch, aware of the brown-suited agents doing the same all around him. He glimpsed Loveday and Watson jumping to cover behind one of the machines. She cried out, "It's Vonn, the man Robur ordered to drown me!"

Vonn lurched toward them like an automaton, gripping a revolver in both hands. Holmes stared at him in horrified fascination. The left side of his face was a red mass of blisters, his hair a layer of smouldering peach-fuzz. The sleeve of his jacket was scorched black. Apparently, his brush with the smelter had been brief but severe. He limped as he walked, squeezing off two more shots. The bullets struck the exterior of the dart, ricocheting away. A mechanic standing nearby howled in pain and clutched his midsection.

"Watson —!" Holmes shouted. At that instant, Robur head-butted him in the groin. Pain flared through his pelvis. Fighting the impulse to double over, he grabbed the smaller man by the collar of his tunic. Robur fought free and ran toward the dart in a hobbling hop as if his knees could bend only so far.

Vonn fired again. Watson drew the Bull-dog pistol from his waistband, took aim and squeezed the trigger. The round punched a small hole through Vonn's right shoulder. Two brown-suited agents returned fire at the same time. The triple-impacts lifted the man off his feet and slammed him down on the concrete floor. He made no movement afterward.

Straightening up, Holmes attended to Mycroft, helping him to stand. It wasn't easy. The big man inspected the entrance and exit holes in his gabardine coat-sleeve with rueful eyes. "Missed my flesh, surprisingly enough."

"It is, considering how much of it there is to miss," Holmes said with a relieved grin.

The foundry building filled with a humming drone. The sound climbed higher in pitch. The black dart on the flat-car vibrated violently. A tongue of blue flame jetted from the exhaust aperture. Sherlock Holmes pulled his brother away from the sudden blast of heat. The car's four wheels turned within the tracks in the floor. It rolled toward a square opening in the wall, picking up speed.

"Robur," snapped Holmes, kicking himself forward, ignoring the needles of pain in his groin. He was aware of Watson running up behind him, revolver in hand.

The agents aimed their pistols at the black craft, but Mycroft bellowed, "No shooting! The bloody thing is bullet-proof! You'll put us all at risk!"

"For the love of God, Holmes!" Watson shouted."What are you doing?"

221B: On Her Majesty's Secret Service

Holmes had no answer to that. He wasn't sure himself. He sprinted after the flat-car, running to the right of the flame hissing from the dart's exhaust. The car reached the edge of the opening, tipped forward and plunged out of sight.

Holmes didn't slow his pace. Instead, he shucked out of his coat. Without hesitation, he launched himself into space, arms extended. He heard Watson cry out angrily, "Dammit — *Sherlock!*"

Holmes absently noted that Watson had called him by his first name, something he only did in states of exceptional agitation. The flat-car rolled to the bottom of the ramp and jarred to a halt amid a great splash of sea-water. Then the dart shot forward, the prow cutting a foam-edged V as its momentum carried it out into the cove. In the split-second before he hit the dark water in a dive, Holmes glimpsed a length of heavy rope trailing from a cleat at the dart's portside.

Holmes knew the waters of the Atlantic would be cold but the icy temperature nearly made him blurt a profanity. He stroked furiously through the boiling wake, hearing the whine of turbines throttling up. His flailing left hand secured a grip on the end of the rope. He managed to close his right hand around it just as the craft gave a leaping forward surge.

Dragged along in the frothing backwash, Holmes kept his mouth tightly shut to prevent seawater from filling it. Rolled and tumbled about by the turbulence, he climbed hand over hand along the rope, his shoulder sockets burning. He felt a distant wonder at the true nature of the dart. He hadn't expected an ocean-going craft. He hoped it was not a submersible, like Nemo's much-debated *Nautilus*.

With a muscle-wrenching effort, he twisted his body atop the humped hull. Panting, he looped the rope around his left hand and tied it off. Raking his wet hair from his eyes, he inched toward the open canopy. He glimpsed the back of Robur's head in the recessed cockpit, both of his hands gripping a steering yoke. A transparent windscreen protected him from the spray and backsplash as the dart churned through the cove toward the open sea.

Straddling the hull, Holmes inched forward until he was within reach of the cockpit. He grabbed a handful of Robur's hair. He slammed his face hard — but not as hard as he could have — against the steering yoke. "That's for your low blow! Reverse course! Now!"

Robur uttered a cry of pain mingled with anger. He half-turned in the pilot's chair, saw Holmes and roared, *"Jeune imbécile méprisables!"*

Robur pulled back on the yoke. and pushed a control stick forward. With a muffled boom, the dart's speed doubled and the prow rose above the waves. Lateral thrust pushed Holmes backward. He slid down the hull as the machine lifted from the ocean with frightening swiftness. He frantically grabbed for hand and footholds but the surface was too smooth. The rope snapped taut around his left arm, biting into his wrist, but it prevented him from falling.

The dart continued to rise. Wings unfolded on both sides of the craft. They were ribbed and scallop-edged, much like those of a bat. They appeared to be made of a very thin, durable black-alloy. With a pop of displaced air, the wings spread to their full extension. Holmes estimated each one was equal in length to his height. He heard a faint, strained whine.

The craft's nose dropped as the ship levelled out. The hull vibrated and shuddered, airspeed slowing. A hundred feet below, the surface of the Atlantic flashed by, the reflection of the moon and stars little more than a pattern of fleeting specks. The slipstream tore at him as Holmes laboriously pulled himself forward, his left hand tight around the rope. From the cockpit, Robur shouted, "Too much weight! My prototype is not fully flightworthy! We will go down!"

Eyes narrowed against the slap of the wind, Holmes said loudly, "You can always go back!"

221B: On Her Majesty's Secret Service

"No — *you* can!" Robur whirled and snatched Holmes by his collar and sleeves, dragging him across the hull toward the cockpit.

Grunting with the exertion, Robur delivered a flurry of blows. His eyes shone wild with panic. Holmes realized the man was mad with fury and terror. His only thought was to batter Holmes from the aircraft, so as to lighten the load and remain airborne. Holmes defended himself instinctively. Robur's fists hit only his arms, elbows and shoulders, but the punches were powerful and expertly delivered.

Robur's left fist, reinforced by the heavy hammer ring, penetrated Holmes' guard and crashed against his cheek, splitting the skin. The blow stunned him, and for a second his senses blinked out. Galvanized by the sudden blaze of pain and the taste of blood, Holmes went on the offensive. He caught Robur's left hand in a vise-like grip. With every iota of his strength, he lunged forward and slammed it against the edge of wind-screen. Even over the rushing wind, he heard bones snap.

Throwing back his head, Robur howled in agony. He fell against the steering yoke. The dart yawed and went into a stomach-turning spin. Holmes nearly went over the side. He glimpsed a span of dark water wheeling crazily below.

Pushing Robur aside, Holmes grabbed the yoke and pulled it back. The aeroship's spiralling descent slowed and finally ceased, barely fifty feet above the sea. Robur lay crumpled against the inner wall of the cockpit, his eyes closed, face ashen, apparently unconscious.

Quickly, Holmes unwrapped the rope from his forearm so he could work out the intricacies of the aeroship's pilot mechanism unencumbered. As soon as he touched the yoke, Robur erupted into furious life. His left foot came up in a straight-leg kick into Holmes' right side. The tremendous force slammed all the wind from his lungs. He felt a rib break.

221B: On Her Majesty's Secret Service

Robur swarmed all over him, clawing, kicking and man-handling him out of the craft with his uninjured hand. Teetering on the edge of the cockpit, trying to refill his lungs, Holmes fought to maintain his balance by keeping one hand on the rope.

Robur rammed a shoulder into Holmes' belly and knocked him completely out of the cockpit and onto the starboard wing. The alloy sagged beneath his weight. The aerocraft tipped to one side. Leaning over the edge of the cockpit, Robur stretched out his right arm to push Holmes into space. He screamed, *"Meurs, bâtard!"*

As Holmes slipped off the wing, he looped the rope around Robur's wrist and tightened it with a jerk. He plummeted toward the black water below. He didn't have time to assume a vertical position to enter the sea in a dive, so he curled himself into a tight ball.

The cold water smashed into him, sending fireballs of agony through his ribcage, but the fall did not daze him. He stroked to the surface, spitting the salt-water from his mouth. The brine stung his lacerated cheek like carbolic acid.

Clearing his water-occluded vision with a shake of his head, he saw the bat-winged aerocraft briefly outlined against the moon. He glimpsed a small body dangling by one arm from a rope under its streamlined fuselage. Faintly, at the edge of his hearing, Holmes heard a prolonged scream. Then both shapes were lost in the darkness.

Treading water, Holmes looked for and found the distant arc-lamps still glowing on the pier of Penhallick Wharf. He began a dog-paddle toward it, gritting his teeth against the pain of his injuries. He did not swim far or for long when he heard the steady *chug-chug* of steam-pistons. He saw a packet cutting a white wake in his direction, coming from the wharf.

After a minute, he was able to see Watson, Mycroft and Loveday standing on the deck in front of the wheelhouse. Only Loveday seemed pleased to see him, her soot-stained face creased in a relieved smile. Mycroft and Watson scowled down at him.

The boat slowed and came alongside. Holmes hauled himself aboard by dint of a short ladder Watson lowered to him. Dripping wet and shivering, he found a keg on which to sit near the boilers. Breathlessly, he said, "I would not refuse an offer of brandy, if there's any to be had."

Mycroft uncorked and extended a silver flask. Holmes accepted it and took a long pull, appreciating the liquid fire scorching his throat and warming his belly. Loveday draped his Ulster coat over his shoulders, gingerly touched the laceration on his cheek and said, "I suppose it's only polite to enquire after your health."

Holmes probed his ribcage with one hand and winced. "Yes, the forms must still be observed, and yes, I do appear to be intact, but I feel a bit tenderized."

Mycroft snorted. "We can see that. Accept it as the cost of behaving like a headstrong schoolboy."

Holmes met Watson's stare, seeing the anger in his eyes. He said mildly, "Anticipate and adapt, remember?"

"You didn't do either one," Watson snapped. "You reacted on impulse. You simply couldn't bear to see Robur escape — not because he is a criminal, but because of your own vanity. He still got away and you're a beat-to-hell, half-drowned dog. All for nothing."

"Robur escaped with his aeroship," Mycroft interposed. "A mechanism we could have studied and emulated for the benefit of England."

Holmes smiled, despite the pain. "I believe you'll find the prototype, if not Robur himself, by alerting the Royal Navy to initiate a search in these waters. Although man may indeed actually be meant to fly, the aerocraft was not...at least, not for any great distance. Robur told me that himself, not to mention when last I saw him, he was no longer in control of it."

Mycroft nodded, his glower easing. "That's a step in the proper direction. I shall contact Admiral Hood first thing in the morning and see what he can do."

"What will be done about Zaharoff and the Hephaestus Ring?" asked Loveday. "And the *Friesland*?"

"Unless we apprehend Robur," Mycroft replied unhappily, "our legal recourse is limited. The *Friesland* can and will be turned over to the Netherlands-Sumatra creditors, and we've let Zaharoff and the Ring know we're aware of their activities. They won't dare act with such impunity henceforth. Whether that will be a good thing is for the future to determine."

Holmes handed Mycroft the flask. "If I upset any of you by my actions, please understand that it was an inadvertent by-product of the circumstances."

Watson said sarcastically, "The circumstances being that you always believe you can succeed where all others might fail, Sherlock. What you never fail at is finding opportunities to test yourself...regardless of how unnecessary those tests might be."

Holmes nodded contritely. "Perhaps you're right, Watson. But as Miss Brooke will attest, the best way of successfully acting a part is to be it."

Loveday cocked her head at him quizzically. "And just what part are you being?"

Sherlock Holmes shivered, drew his coat tighter about himself and leaned his head back against the warm wall of the wheel-house. "Apparently, the headstrong schoolboy who enjoys playing tricks." He paused and added, "The problem is, I no longer know if I'm acting a part or being it."

He closed his eyes.

221B: On Her Majesty's Secret Service

PART TWO

IT WAS SOME time before the health of my friend, Mr Sherlock Holmes, recovered from the strain caused by his exertions and injuries suffered in the spring of '87. The whole question of the Netherlands-Sumatra Company and of the colossal schemes of Baron Maupertuis is too recent in the minds of the public, and too intimately concerned with politics and finance, to be a fitting subject for this series of sketches, even if the details were not restricted under the Official Secrets Act.

— John H. Watson, MD

221B: On Her Majesty's Secret Service

The most winning woman I ever knew was hanged for poisoning three little children for their insurance money.

—Sherlock Holmes

CHAPTER 6

1 March, 1889, Paris

MADAME KATHRYN KOLUCHY raised her crystal snifter of Leyrat Partage brandy to the four men gathered around the table. "Gentlemen, I salute you."

The oak-panelled conference room in the Aliments en Plein Essor Inc. offices overlooked the Avenue de la Bourdonnais. The Avenue, lined with many massive brick and stucco buildings constructed in the 1850s following the edicts of Napoleon III, served as the seats of businesses such as Foods On The Rise, Inc.

The conference room's baroque early 18th century furnishings provided an anachronistic Olde World contrast to the building's modern facade. A very tall, upright cabinet of walnut inlaid with intricate scrollwork and figures of pagan deities dominated the room. It was topped by heavy mountings of gold-chased ormolu. Four legs supported it, resting on ball-and-claw casters.

The men seated at the mahogany table responded to the toast with varying degrees of enthusiasm, sipping from their glasses. Madame Koluchy turned and raised her goblet to the life-size marble bust of Archimedes above the door. *"Trinquer!"* she said loudly.

She took a sip of brandy, then turned to survey the faces of the

221B: On Her Majesty's Secret Service

men. They stared at her, impatient for the meeting to begin. She was in no particular hurry. Kathryn Koluchy wore a casual afternoon frock of teal blue, the tailored lines emphasizing the lean, feline beauty of her body. Tall for a woman, her wine-red hair wound in a coppery braid tightly around her well-shaped head. Her features were classic and haughty with a high-bridged nose and eyes of a blue so deep as to approach violet. Her complexion was very white, with the faint bluish under-tint of a true redhead.

Tiny diamond earrings glittered at her delicate lobes. On her right hand gleamed a ring made of a coppery metal with the setting in the form of a smithy's hammer hovering vertically over an anvil. The hammer of Hephaestus, the Greek god of fire, craftsmen and metal-forging, was set with a bright ruby.

Madame Koluchy looked like a regal holdover from a previous century of European aristocracy, with just enough modern exoticism to make her appearance doubly striking.

"To the Ring," she said. "And to the memories of our inspirations."

On shelves bracketing the likeness of Archimedes rested sculpted marble busts of Emperor Kublai Khan, Hypatia and Hero of Alexandria, as well as Leonardo Da Vinci, Archytas of Tarentum and Cornelis Drebel.

The effigies of the men — and one woman — represented on the shelves had been hailed as scientists, geniuses and visionaries, possessing the most extraordinary intellects of their time. Some opined their attributes were more than extraordinary—they bordered on superhuman. Madame Koluchy held that opinion about herself, as well.

In another time, another place, Kathryn Koluchy might have been a Cleopatra or at the very least, a Barbara Villiers. But in this time and place, she was the empress of a phantom empire composed of an interconnected group of secret societies.

221B: On Her Majesty's Secret Service

At a very young age, Kathryn inherited the contradictory title of Queen of the Brotherhood of the Seven Kings. Her much older husband, Count Carlos Luchino Vincenzo Koluchy, chieftain of the Brotherhood, claimed the organization originated after the consolidation of seven major criminal secret societies in the Middle Ages — an achievement credited to Catherine de Medici.

By the time Madame Koluchy assumed control of the society at age 23, after the assassination of the Count, the Brotherhood had grown into an organization spanning most of Europe with tendrils reaching into the Near East. It cut for itself a sizeable slice of every illegal pie within its sphere of influence.

After a few years, Kathryn found the focus solely on crime too limiting. Even as a child she knew the key to true riches lay in amassing power, by taking control over the socio-political environment. She learned early she was not unique in that drive. She dealt daily with men — and the occasional woman — who shared the same obsession, whether they were industrialists, government officials, princes, kings or self-proclaimed religious leaders.

Among those people were representatives of the Hephaestus Ring, a loose affiliation of inventors, engineers and technologists who found the mainstream of their trades stultifying to ambition. Allegedly, the roots of the Ring extended back to the time of Archimedes and his analytic mechanisms. Members could be found on every continent, in every country, in every era. Some names were famous, such as Swift and Focault, other names were infamous, such as Mabuse and Moreau.

The Ring had crafted the means to finance their projects through exploiting investors or outright thievery. Despite their occasional outlawry, they did not consider themselves professional criminals. They shared far loftier common goals, regardless of their individual motivations.

The Hephaestus Ring, unlike other secret societies, was not an organization devoted to finding new members, but it was not opposed to expanding the ranks of its material resources. The Brotherhood of Seven Kings had those resources, and was willing to supply them.

In 1879, upon mutual agreement, the Brotherhood absorbed the Hephaestus Ring. In doing so, the primary policy of both organizations shifted. The first decision turned Kathryn Koluchy's widespread criminal network into a force that could make or destroy nations. She set for the Ring the goal of unifying the entire world under its control, by expunging all non-productive elements — including nations.

The most efficient way to attain such a goal lay in science. Madame Koluchy oversaw a permanent research staff devoted to the development, creation and exclusive possession of technological breakthroughs which were as much as twenty years ahead of mainstream industries.

Certain inventions were auctioned to the highest bidder or created for specific third parties upon demand. The Hephaestus Ring became a magnet for wealthy international business concerns. Due to investment from industry, the Ring grew exceptionally powerful. By 1885, the Ring had developed a clandestine network of political puppeteers who pulled the strings of the world's institutions and leaders.

Although the blend of organized crime and organized science proved very profitable, particularly through military applications, a tipping point was fast approaching. The Exposition Universelle was only two months away, and thereafter the Hephaestus Ring intended to call the tune for the global dance amongst all countries.

Kathryn Koluchy and every member of the Ring knew the tune. Most of them fashioned their lives according to the melody. The current Echelon were brilliant, eccentric and even ruthless men, but Madame Koluchy was their undisputed leader. They all wore Hephaestus rings identical to the one on her left hand.

221B: On Her Majesty's Secret Service

She sat down in her chair at the head of the table. Carved from antique oak and lined with old tapestries, the back and arms were set with enamelled medallions. She raised her glass one more time. "To Thunderstrike and to the future it will usher in."

She and the four men drained their glasses. The portly and bald-headed Professor Mirzarbeau did so in one gulp and wiped his mouth with a none-too-clean handkerchief. He looked the part of a quaint little Anglo-French scientist. His clothes were old and shabby. His blue eyes appeared monstrous, magnified by thick lenses in round gold-rimmed spectacles.

Mirzarbeau was one of Europe's leading astronomical physicists — or he had been until his pet theory that Earth and all the other worlds in the solar system were living organisms forced him to retire from his position at the Academy of Sciences. Embittered, the man withdrew from academia, but his theories intrigued Madame Koluchy.

She arranged the financing to construct a massive telescope of Mirzarbeau's own design, which he called, unsurprisingly enough, the Mirzaroscope. Endless tinkering with it occupied most of the man's time and attention. He was positive that with its use, he would be able to not only prove his theories, but harness a new celestial energy force he referred to as the Violet Flame. His experiments into the Flame's effect on light refraction had already borne fruit.

Mirzarbeau's hatred of academia was shared by the elderly man who sat next to him. Rail-thin and hook-nosed, his complexion was swarthy except for the paler hue of his upper lip and jawline, where he had recently shaved off a moustache and beard. A red turban enclosed the top and sides of his head. He wore a beautifully tailored lounge coat of navy-blue serge.

His colleagues addressed him only as Prince Dakkar, even though that was not the name by which he was known. As one of the most feared, and even hated men since Bonaparte, he was consumed with paranoia every time he set sail from his isolated island fortress of self-exile. Dakkar's fears were not without merit. A number of nations had, in absentia, sentenced Captain Nemo to death for crimes ranging from piracy to mass murder, so when in Europe, he took pains not to draw attention to himself.

Dakkar was one of the oldest members of the Ring. He saw no reason to share his creations, such as the notorious *Nautilus,* with corrupt countries. He saw the Thunderstrike project as the most practical way to end the rule of the greedy and feeble-minded. If the undertaking were successful, his status as an international fugitive could be reversed.

The man seated across the table from Dakkar was a slightly built blonde man in his early thirties. Julius Wendigee, with his wire-framed spectacles, mild blue eyes, and neat, although unremarkable wardrobe, resembled a librarian or law clerk. Born in Holland, he and his family had immigrated to South Africa in the 1840s. He returned to Europe in his teens to earn a degree in electrical engineering. His advanced theories and inventions attracted the attention of the Hephaestus Ring. After they arranged an important position for him at Société Electrique Edison in Paris, Wendigee didn't require much persuasion to join them.

Wendigee didn't think of himself as a true genius in the class of an Edison or even a Tesla — he was merely a well-bred Afrikaner who was horrified by the growing unrest in South Africa's black townships and British mistreatment of the Boers. He viewed Thunderstrike as the most straightforward way of wresting control of South Africa away from the English and modelling it on Belgium's Congo Free State.

To Wendigee's right sat a short, round-bodied, thin-legged little man who went by the name of Silvanus Cavor. Middle-aged with a chubby, red face and wide-set brown eyes, he wore an overcoat with leather patches on the elbows. He called himself a physicist, but as far as anyone knew, he held no degree. His invention of — or discovery, no one was sure which — of a remarkable substance he called Cavorite had earned his place at the table.

In a chair at the table's far end lounged Colonel Sebastian Moran. A tall, rangy man, Moran's bronzed, weather-beaten face was stamped with a perpetual scowl. His eyes, faded to the pale colour of old steel, were partially concealed by the black lenses of half-glasses. A heavy, leonine moustache swept down from his upper lip and curved along his jawline. His tawny hair was so sun-bleached it appeared almost white.

His velvet-trimmed Newmarket coat of deep burgundy made Moran appear to be a well-to-do country squire, which he was. He owned both a manor house and estate, and a lavishly palatial home in Mayfair. He also ran an opium smuggling syndicate, but that was only a sideline. His primary vocation was acting as chief-of-staff to Professor James Moriarty, one of the Ring's most important affiliates.

Without preamble, Madame Koluchy announced in English, "I have just learned from my sources that the main structural work on the Iron Lady is projected to be completed in two weeks time. At the end of this month on the 31st, Gustave Eiffel himself is scheduled to conduct an inauguration tour restricted to journalists, dignitaries and government officials, including our new prime minister, Monsieur Tirard. From today forward, we will use the date of the tour as our working deadline."

Julius Wendigee shifted uncomfortably in his chair and cleared his throat. Kathryn cast him a questioning look. "Julius?"

In his guttural Afrikaner accent he said, "Our technicians have manufactured Tesla's coils and resonant transformer circuits. Test models are complete and if all goes well, they will ready to be installed during the final phase of construction."

"But?"

"But Nikola's diagrams deal in theoretical energy magnification. He never tested the apparatus on this scale." Wendigee sighed, paused and added, "In order to minimize the chances of failure, we need him back with us."

"The search for our wayward friend continues," Madame Koluchy replied. "It continues even as we speak. At last report, his whereabouts have been narrowed down to a specific region, and his exact location may be revealed before the day is out. Regardless, he cannot elude us forever."

"It's been nearly two years," said Dakkar. "If he is under the protection of the British Secret Service —"

"He is not." The woman's eyes flashed with angry impatience. "He is running from them as well as from us. We can proceed under the assumption that Nikola Tesla will be found."

"Let us assume *nothing*," Moran said stiffly. "We have planned our campaign carefully but every military commander must allow for the unforeseen...like the incompetence of Basil Zaharoff at Penhallick, for instance."

Kathryn Koluchy shrugged. "We must use men, and men fail. Part and parcel of any undertaking, particularly one as complex as this one. Besides, Zaharoff's access to other manufacturing facilities remains a boon to our operations."

"Unless," said Dakkar, "he decides we jeopardize his own position."

"Frankly, I prefer Basil's past involvement with the Ring remain a matter for the courts and not the security services of England."

Mirzarbeau said uneasily, "If we've drawn even a slight suspicion from British intelligence, they will inform Deuxieme Bureau. We may have to reconsider our timetable."

"The Ring has its own connections within the Bureau." Kathryn favoured the rotund scientist with a patronizing smile. "The good doctor is premature in his apprehension."

"Is he?" enquired Colonel Moran, his voice a lion-like rumble.

221B: On Her Majesty's Secret Service

"Random factors must always be considered, Madame."

She turned toward him. "We have a means to provide for all contingencies."

Moran's scowl deepened. "What about this man Holmes?"

Kathryn held her condescending smile in place. "Which one?"

"Both...but the younger Holmes is on the scent of my employer."

"He is under observation by our people."

"When will 'our' people take action?" Moran did not even try to hide the disdain in his tone and bearing.

"Soon."

"No, not soon. Immediately. I speak for the Professor on this. I represent his interests here."

"Colonel, you enjoy a deserved reputation as a soldier and big-game hunter, but murdering a man with such influential contacts within the Secret Service would only draw the kind of attention we wish to avoid. It is not a sound tactical strategy at this juncture."

"What do you know of tactics, Madame?" Moran's shaggy eyebrows drew together at the bridge of his nose. "What are you but a career criminal posing behind a curtain of respectability? You are a purveyor of patent medicines, miracle cures and so-called health foods. Sheer quackery."

"Despite what you may think, I am a nutritional scientist, a healer."

Wendigee leaned forward, elbows on the table. "There is no quackery about her, Colonel. There are authentic accounts of her wonderful cures which cannot be contradicted."

Moran laughed derisively. "The Professor has studied her for the last few years and it seems that under her treatment in health resorts such as Saltburn-On-Sea, weak, sickly and more importantly, wealthy people became strong and vital again by consuming a substance called Herakleophorbia IV. Or so they claim." His eyes

221B: On Her Majesty's Secret Service

bored into those of the woman. "How is this magic food possible, Madame?"

She met Moran's stare unblinkingly. "What I do and how I do it remains more than ever my secret."

"Although I am the Professor's right-hand man," replied Moran, "I opposed an alliance with you because of your secrets. Your personal history suggests you are primarily a schemer and counter-plotter, not a general."

"And you, sir, are primarily a card cheat. An exceptionally successful and notorious one, but a cheat nonetheless."

The other three men at the table stirred uncomfortably. Dakkar ventured, "Colonel Moran makes a solid point...from a mechanic's point of view, the more moving parts, the more chances for a malfunction. How can you be so sure of yourself?"

Kathryn Koluchy fixed her dark eyes on Dakkar. "Captain—if I may call you that— it is fortunate I have such high respect for you and your accomplishments, otherwise I would say something quite rude and ill-befitting a lady."

Planting the flats of her hands on the table-top, she pushed herself to her feet. "It is best we have this out. I have known for some little time one of you sees Thunderstrike, whether it is a success or failure, as way for a quick infusion of capital to fund your own plans."

Mirzarbeau blinked at her owlishly from behind the lenses of his spectacles. "That is an outrageous accusation, Madame. How have you come to learn this?"

A cold smile played over Madame Koluchy's lips. She strode over to the upstanding cabinet and flung open the doors. Within it stood a switchboard bristling with thousands of tiny relays and complexities of naked circuitry. Pinpoints of light glowed here and there among the clicking relays as they opened and closed with blinding rapidity.

"My Analytical Engine," she announced, still staring at

221B: On Her Majesty's Secret Service

Moran. "One of only two fully operating models in the world, although I know Professor Moriarty attempted to hire Leonardo Quevedo to tinker together his own version — after copies of the original schematics by Charles Babbage and Ada Lovelace came into his possession. One of his secrets."

Moran's scowl twisted into an expression of astonishment, then resentment.

"All of my decisions regarding Thunderstrike are made by this machine," Madame Koluchy continued. "The Engine is a virtually infallible mechanical organism, developed by the brightest minds I could find, including Augustus Van Dusen, a man who is known as 'the Thinking Machine.' I collected all information, all data, all potential rewards and risks regarding Thunderstrike and followed the plan of action it developed."

Putting her hands on her hips, she swept her gaze over the faces of the men at the table. "If the plan fails, it will not be through any flaw in the Engine. It will be through human error, because we deviated from the course of logic it outlined, or we did not act on its recommendations."

Kathryn focused her hypnotic eyes on Wendigee. He swallowed painfully. "Julius, you paid me a compliment earlier about my wonderful cures. One of my wonderful cures is specific to the treatment of betrayal."

Wendigee coughed. His eyes watered. His lips stirred as he began to speak. He doubled over, leaning against the table as a sudden dry-heave racked him. He put a hand over his mouth and brought it away with pink sputum glistening in the palm. He gasped, "What have you done to me?"

"That particular cure was added to your brandy," she answered matter-of-factly. "A poison which remained inert in your metabolic system until it reacted to the sudden surge of fear-fuelled adrenalin, triggered by my words."

Sweat sheened Wendigee's face. His eyes bulged in terror.

221B: On Her Majesty's Secret Service

"Kathryn, I didn't betray you or the Ring, I only intended —"

"—To delay the installation of the transmitters in the tower until I agreed to pay you more." Madame Koluchy's voice came as sharp as a whip-crack. "That is the type of betrayal the Analytical Engine warned me about. Nothing more complicated than naked greed."

Wendigee's mouth opened and closed like a landed fish. He coughed violently again, his spectacles flying from his face. Sebastian Moran leaned away from him. The man's body sagged toward the floor, sliding down from the chair to the carpet. He lay there, body twitching, bubbles of pink foaming on his lips. He continued to breathe, but his respiration was harsh and laboured.

Silvanus Cavor, his complexion paper-white, pushed his wine glass away from him. In a querulous voice, he said, "I think I want to go home."

Moran stared at him angrily. "Shut your hole." He returned his glare to Madame Koluchy. "You served all of us the same poison, didn't you?"

"I considered it," she replied coolly. "But the Engine made Julius' perfidy quite transparent. Even if I had, I would not create a poison without developing an antidote." She showed the edges of her teeth in a sardonic, mocking grin. "I'd hate to be accused of sheer quackery."

Moran averted his eyes, his face reddening in embarrassment. Mirzarbeau self-consciously cleared his throat and said, "Madame, Julius may have earned the action you took against him, but without his electrical engineering genius to replace that of Tesla we are —"

Madame Koluchy turned her head called, "Cuthbert!"

A red-haired man in butler's livery opened the door and hurried her toward her. "M' lady?"

"The Engine's decryption, please."

"Just completed." He handed her a small card. She glanced at it and nodded toward Julius Wendigee on the floor. "Please deal with that in the customary way."

Cuthbert Rubadue bent over Wendigee, sliding his hands under the man's armpits. He grunted softly as he swung the limp body of the Dutchman across the yoke of his shoulders. He quickly left the room the same way he had entered it.

"Julius has a fiancee, you know," said Mirzarbeau quietly.

"Yes," replied Madame Koluchy. "Sara. She is one of our agents"

Tapping the corner of the card against her lower lip, she closed the doors of the cabinet and the Analytical Engine fell silent."Don't fear that this sudden vacancy creates a vacuum."

The three men regarded her doubtfully. "What else could it be?" Dakkar demanded. "Julius was not as visionary as Nikola Tesla, but he was a brilliant engineer in his own right. We have no one to replace him."

Kathryn Koluchy picked up her brandy snifter from the table and strolled over to the window, pushing aside a curtain to gaze over the Champs de Mars. She said, "We have Nikola Tesla...or at least we will by the end of the week... if not sooner."

"We've located him?" snapped Moran, sitting up straight in his chair. "At last?"

"The Analytical Engine has." She brandished the card. "I will be dispatching an officer of the Echelon to retrieve him forthwith."

"What if Tesla doesn't want to be retrieved?" Mirzarbeau asked.

"Tesla has an unfulfilled employment contract with the Hephaestus Ring and the Iron Lady...his wants are irrelevant."

Madame Kathryn Koluchy's gaze travelled up the thousand foot length of the wrought-iron lattice-work tower, from the massively broad base to the elegant spire on top. The Eiffel Tower was several kilometres away but it dominated the Paris skyline. She raised her goblet and said softly, *"Trinquer!"*

221B: On Her Majesty's Secret Service

Criminal cases are like fevers... they should be taken in hand within twenty-four hours.

—Loveday Brooke

CHAPTER 7

London, Lynch Court, 2 March

EBENEZER DYER SAID, "I admit that the dagger business is something of a puzzle to me, but as for the lost necklace — well, I should have thought a child would have understood that when a young lady loses a valuable article of jewellery and wishes to hush the matter up, the explanation is obvious."

"Sometimes," replied Loveday Brooke calmly, "the explanation that is obvious is the one to be rejected, not accepted."

Dyer and Loveday had been jangling at one another a good deal that morning. Her short temper was in part attributed to the grit-laden east wind which had set her eyes watering on her way to an early appointment at Lynch Court.

Dyer stood behind his writing table, hands clasped behind his back in a "parade rest" posture. A powerfully built man in his mid-50s with weather-beaten features and carefully trimmed brown hair and moustache, he still retained military habits from his years in the Royal Navy. He faced Loveday with the weary exasperation of a school-teacher lecturing a gifted but argumentative student.

"I don't see how you can approach a problem with that foremost in mind," he said. "It's a cognitively inconsistent position."

"To be aware of all possibilities? Hardly."

"If," Dyer said, bringing his hand down with emphasis on his table, "you lay it down as a principle that the obvious is to be rejected in favour of the abstruse, you'll soon find yourself having to prove that two apples added to two other apples do not make four."

Loveday snorted, but delicately. "You remind me of another smug logician I know."

Dyer frowned at her. "Perhaps we should run this matter past your Baker Street Boys before we go further. Mr Holmes might have some input —"

Lawson, the young clerk, stuck his head into the office. "Mr Hawke is here, sir."

It was a fortunate diversion. "Bring him in, Lawson." Dyer turned to Loveday. "This is the Reverend Anthony Hawke, the gentleman at whose house Miss Monroe is staying temporarily. He was an Anglican clergyman, but gave up his vocation some twenty years ago when he married a wealthy lady. Miss Millicent Monroe has been sent over to his guardianship from Pekin by her father, Sir George Monroe, in order to get her out of the way of a troublesome and undesirable suitor by the name of William Wentworth Danvers."

The last sentence was added in a low and hurried tone as Mr Hawke entered the room. He was a man close upon seventy years of age, white-haired, clean shaven, with a full, round face to which a small nose imparted a somewhat guileless expression. His manner of greeting was urbane but slightly flurried and nervous. He gave Loveday the impression of being an easy-going, good-tempered man who, for the moment, seemed unusually perplexed.

He glanced uneasily at her before sitting down. Dyer hastened with introductions, explaining Loveday was the enquiry agent he

221B: On Her Majesty's Secret Service

had assigned to get to the bottom of the matter now under consideration.

"In that case, there can be no objection to my showing you this," said Mr Hawke. "It came by post this morning. You see my enemy still pursues me."

As he spoke he took from his pocket a big, square envelope, from which he drew a large sheet of paper. On the paper, there was, roughly drawn in black ink, two daggers about six inches in length, with remarkably pointed blades.

Dyer looked at the sketch with interest. "We'll compare this drawing and its envelope with that which you previously received." He opened a drawer of his writing-table and removed a similar envelope. From it he drew a square of paper. On it there was drawn one dagger only.

He placed both envelopes and their enclosures side by side, and in silence compared them. Then, without a word, he handed them to Loveday, who, taking a glass from her reticule, subjected them to a similarly careful and minute scrutiny.

Both envelopes were of precisely the same make and were each addressed to Mr Hawke's London address in a round, school-boyish sort of hand — the hand so easy to write due to its lack of individuality. Each envelope likewise bore a Cork, Ireland and a London postmark. The sheet of paper, however, that the first envelope enclosed bore the sketch of one dagger only.

Loveday laid down her glass. "The envelopes have been addressed by the same person, but the last two daggers have not been drawn by the same hand. Dagger number one was drawn by a timid, uncertain and inartistic hand — see how the lines waver, and how they have been patched here and there? The person who rendered the other daggers, I should say, could do better work."

Mr Hawke's eyes widened. "You don't mean to say I have two enemies pursuing me in this fashion! What does it mean? Can it be — is it possible that these things have been sent to me by some secret society in Ireland mistaking me for someone else?"

Dyer shook his head. "Members of secret societies generally make sure of their targets. I don't think we should build any theories on the Cork postmark...the letters may have been posted from there for the sole purpose of drawing off attention from some other quarter."

"Is there some reason to suspect an Irish organization is involved?" Loveday enquired. "Do the Fenians carry a grudge against you?"

Mr Hawke shuffled his feet and cleared his throat."Before I left the church, I served as a clergyman in County Cork and denounced the violence of the Irish Republican Brotherhood during the Rising of '67. As did many of the Catholic and Anglican clergy. But that was more than twenty years ago."

Dyer declared sharply, "The probability of an Irish political society having a hand in this affair is so remote it is not worth entertaining."

"Agreed," said Loveday."Mr Hawke, would you mind telling us a little about the loss of the necklace? There must be some connection between the missing diamonds and the daggers."

Dyer turned toward her. "I think that the episode of the drawn daggers — drawn in the double sense — should be considered as a thing apart from the loss of the necklace. After all, it is possible that these daggers may have been sent by way of a joke — a rather foolish one — by some harum-scarum fellow, bent on causing a sensation."

Mr Hawke's face brightened. "Ah! Do you think so? It would lift such a load from my mind if you could bring the thing home to some practical joker. Now I come to think of it, my nephew, Jack, is not quite so steady a fellow as I should like him to be...he must have a good many such scamps among his acquaintances."

"A good many such scamps," echoed Loveday somewhat sarcastically. "Nevertheless, I think we are bound to look at the other side of the case, and admit the possibility of these daggers having been sent in sober earnest by persons concerned in the robbery, with the intention of intimidating you and preventing full investigation of the matter."

Mr Hawke's face fell once more. "It's an uncomfortable position to be in. It did not occur to me before, but I remember now that I did not receive the first dagger until after I had spoken very strongly to Mrs Hawke, before the servants, about my wish to set the police to work. I told her I felt honour-bound to Sir George to do so, as the necklace had been lost under my roof."

"Yes...she entirely supported Miss Monroe in her wish to take no steps in the matter. Indeed, I should not have come round as I did last night to Dyer, if my wife had not been suddenly summoned from home by the serious illness of her sister."

Dyer asked, "Did Mrs Hawke or Miss Monroe give any reason for not wishing you to move in the matter?"

"All told, I should think they gave about a hundred reasons—I can't remember them all. For one thing, Miss Monroe said it might necessitate her appearing in the police courts, a thing she would not consent to do, and she certainly did not consider the necklace was worth the fuss I was making over it. And that necklace, sir, has been valued at over nine hundred pounds, and has come down to the young lady from her mother."

"And Mrs Hawke?"

"Mrs Hawke supported Miss Monroe in her views in her presence. But privately to me afterwards, she gave other reasons for not wishing the police called in. Girls, she said, were always careless with their jewellery, she might have lost the necklace in China, and never have brought it to England at all."

"Quite so," said Dyer. "I think I understood you to say that no one had seen the necklace since Miss Monroe's arrival in England. Also, I believe it was she who first discovered it to be missing?"

"Yes. Sir George, when he wrote apprising me of his daughter's visit, added a postscript to his letter, saying that his daughter was bringing her necklace with her and that he would feel greatly obliged if I would have it deposited at my bankers', where it could be easily got at if required. I spoke to Miss Monroe about doing this two or three times, but she did not seem at all inclined to comply with her father's wishes.

"Then my wife took the matter in hand — Mrs Hawke, I must tell you, has a very firm, resolute manner — she told Miss Monroe plainly that she would not have the responsibility of those diamonds in the house, and insisted they should be sent off to the bankers. Upon this, Miss Monroe went up to her room, and presently returned, saying that her necklace had disappeared. She herself, she said, had placed it in her jewel-case and the jewel-case in her wardrobe, when her boxes were unpacked.

"The jewel-case was in the wardrobe right enough, and no other article of jewellery appeared to have been disturbed, but the little padded niche in which the necklace had been deposited was empty. My wife and her maid went upstairs immediately, and searched every corner of the room, but, I'm sorry to say, without any result."

Loveday nodded thoughtfully. "Miss Monroe has her own maid?"

"No, she has not. The maid — an elderly native woman — who left Pekin with her, suffered so terribly from sea-sickness that when they reached Malta, Miss Monroe allowed her to land and remain there in charge of an agent of the P. and O. Company, till an outward bound packet could take her back to China. It seems the poor woman thought she was going to die, and was in a terrible state of mind because she hadn't brought her coffin with her. I dare say you know the terror these Chinese have of being buried in foreign soil. After her departure, Miss Monroe engaged one of the steerage passengers to act as her maid for the remainder of the voyage."

"Did Miss Monroe make the long journey from Pekin accompanied only by this native woman?" asked Dyer.

"Friends escorted her to Hong Kong — by far the roughest part of the journey. From Hong Kong she came on in the *Colombo*, accompanied only by her maid. I wrote and told her father I would meet her at the docks in London...the young lady, however, preferred landing at Plymouth, and telegraphed to me from there that she was coming on by rail to Waterloo, where I might meet her."

Dyer cast a meaningful glance in Loveday's direction. "She seems to be a young lady of independent habits, doesn't she?" He turned back to Mr Hawke. "I suppose you and Sir George Monroe are old friends?"

Mr Hawke smiled fondly. "He and I were great chums before he went out to China — now about twenty years ago — and it was only natural, when he wished to get his daughter out of the way of young Danvers's impertinent attentions, that he should ask me to take charge of her till he could claim his retiring pension and set up his tent in England."

"What was the chief objection to Mr Danvers's attentions?"

"Well, he is a boy of only one-and-twenty, and has no money into the bargain. He has been sent out to Pekin by his father to study the language, in order to qualify for a billet in the Customs, and it may be a dozen years before he is in a position to keep a wife. Now, Miss Monroe is an heiress — will come into her mother's large fortune when she is of age — and Sir George, naturally, would like her to make a good match."

"I suppose Miss Monroe came to England very reluctantly?" Loveday enquired.

"I imagine so. No doubt it was a great wrench for her to leave her home and friends in that sudden fashion and come to us, who are all strangers to her. She is very quiet, very shy and reserved. She goes nowhere, sees no one. When some old China friends of her father's called to see her the other day, she immediately found she had a headache, and went to bed. On the whole, she gets on better with my nephew, Jack, than with anyone else."

Dyer absently smoothed his moustache. "How many persons does your household consist of at the present moment?"

"We are one more than usual, for Jack is home with his regiment from India. As a rule, my household consists of my wife and myself, butler, cook, housemaid and my wife's maid, who just now is doing double duty as Miss Monroe's maid, also."

Dyer dug out his watch from his waistcoat and opened the cover. "I have an important engagement in ten minutes' time, so I must leave you and Miss Brooke to arrange details as to how and when she is to begin her work inside your house, for, of course, in a case of this sort we must, in the first instance at any rate, concentrate attention within your four walls."

"The less delay the better," said Loveday. "I should like to attack the matter at once and have it resolved by evening."

Mr Hawke thought for a moment. "According to present arrangements, Mrs Hawke will return the day after tomorrow, so I can only ask you to remain in the house till the morning of that day. I'm sure you will understand that there might be some little awkwardness in —"

"Oh, quite so," interrupted Loveday with a laugh. "How would it be if I assume the part of an interior decorator in the employ of a West End firm, sent by them to survey your house and advise upon its redecoration? All I should have to do is walk about your rooms with my head on one side, and a pencil and notebook in my hand."

Mr Hawke nodded a trifle nervously. "I have no objection. But if by any chance there should come a telegram from Mrs Hawke, saying she will return by an earlier train, I hope you will make some excuse, and not get me into hot water, with her, I mean."

Loveday stood up, reaching for her reticule. "You may rely upon my discretion, Mr Hawke."

221B: On Her Majesty's Secret Service

TWELVE O'CLOCK struck from a neighbouring church clock as Loveday lifted the brass knocker of Mr Hawke's front door in Tavistock Square. She had stopped by her Gower Street flat to change into a costume she felt more befitting her masquerade — a deep purple dress with tight sleeves and full skirt, and a matching top hat with a red silk band and veil. It sat at enough of an angle on her head to imply self-confidence. With her reading glasses, reticule, umbrella and notebook, Loveday Brooke looked the very model of modern female professionalism.

Be the part, she murmured to herself as the door began to open. An elderly man in butler's livery admitted her and showed her into the drawing-room on the first floor, requesting she take a seat.

A single glance around showed Loveday that if her role as interior decorator had been real instead of assumed, she would have found plenty of scope for her talents. Although the red brick house was comfortably furnished, it bore the unmistakable impint of early Victorian days.

Loveday took stock of the faded white and gold wall paper, the chairs covered with lilies and roses in cross-stitch, and the knick-knacks of a past generation that were scattered about on tables and the mantelpiece. A yellow damask curtain divided the back drawing-room from the front one in which she was seated. From the other side of this curtain there came to her the sound of voices — those of a man and a girl.

"Cut the cards again, please," said the man's voice. "Thank you. There you are again — the queen of hearts, surrounded with diamonds, and turning her back on a knave. Miss Monroe, you can't do better than make that fortune come true. Turn your back on the man who let you go without a word and — "

"Whisht!" interrupted the girl with a playful laugh: "I heard

the next room door open — I'm sure someone came in."

The girl's laugh seemed to Loveday utterly devoid of the echo of worry that the circumstances warranted. She repressed a sigh of ennui. Not for the first time did she feel the cosy matters Dyer assigned to her were both trivial and beneath her talents. She doubted the "Baker Street Boys" would have wasted their time on such a domestic mystery. Still, there was a quality to the girl's voice that struck a faint chord of familiarity.

Mr Hawke entered the room, and almost simultaneously the two young people came from the other side of the yellow curtain and crossed towards the door. The young man was a good-looking, smiling young fellow, with dark, twinkling eyes, neatly clipped hair and regulation regimental moustache. Since he fitted the general description of "scamp," Loveday assumed he was Hawke's nephew Jack.

The girl was flaxen-haired, blue-eyed, slightly built and beautiful in a child-like way. She wore a very stylish peach-coloured afternoon frock. She appeared perceptibly less comfortable with Jack's uncle than she was with Jack, for her manner changed and grew formal and even apprehensive as she came face to face with the old gentleman. She gave Loveday a brief, appraising glance, which held a hint of both suspicion and challenge.

"We're going downstairs to have a game of billiards," said Jack, addressing Mr Hawke, and throwing a look of curiosity at Loveday.

"Jack," said Mr Hawke, "what would you say if I told you I was going to have the house re-decorated from top to bottom, and that this young lady had come to advise on the matter?"

Loveday repressed a smile at the very couched bit of mendacity that passed his lips.

"Well," answered Jack promptly, "I should say, 'not before its time.' That would cover a good deal."

Then the two young people departed together and Loveday went straight to her work.

"I'll begin my survey at the top of the house," she said. "Will you kindly ask one of your maids to show me through the bedrooms? Preferably the one who waits on Miss Monroe and Mr Hawke."

The maid who responded to Mr Hawke's summons was in perfect harmony with the general appearance of the house. In addition to being somewhat elderly and faded, she was also remarkably sour-visaged. She carried herself as if she thought that Mr Hawke had taken a great liberty in thus requesting her attendance.

In dignified silence she showed Loveday over the topmost floor, where the servants' bedrooms were situated, and with a somewhat supercilious expression, watched her making various entries in her notebook. She led the way down to the second floor, where the principal bedrooms of the house were.

"This is Miss Monroe's room," she said, as she threw back a door. The room that Loveday entered was, like the rest of the house, furnished in the style that had prevailed a generation before. The bedstead was elaborately curtained with pink lined upholstery; the toilet-table was befrilled with muslin and tarlatan out of all likeness to a table.

The one point that chiefly attracted Loveday's attention was the extreme neatness throughout the room — a neatness that was carried out with so strict an eye to comfort and convenience that it seemed to proclaim the hand of a first-class maid. Everything in the room was, as her father used to say, squared to the quarter of an inch.

"This room will want some money spent upon it," said Loveday, letting her eyes roam critically in all directions. "Nothing but Moorish woodwork will take off the squareness of those corners. But what a maid Miss Monroe must have. I never before saw a room so orderly and, at the same time, so comfortable."

The maid nodded. "I wait on Miss Monroe, for the present, but, she scarcely requires a maid. I never before in my life had dealings with such a young lady"

"She does so much for herself, you mean?"

"She's like no one else I ever had to deal with. She not only won't be helped in dressing, but she arranges her room every day before leaving it, even to placing the chair in front of the looking glass."

"And to opening the lid of the hair-pin box, so that she may have the pins ready to her hand," observed Loveday, bending over the Japanese table, with its toilet accessories.

Another five minutes were all that Loveday accorded to the inspection of this room. "Please tell Mr Hawke that I wish to see him."

The maid and Loveday found the man in the drawing room, looking much disturbed, with a telegram in his hand. He said, "From my wife to say she'll be back today. She'll be at Waterloo in about half an hour. If she finds you here —"

"Set your mind at rest," interrupted Loveday. "I've done all I wished to do within your walls."

"Done all you wished to do!" echoed Mr Hawke in amazement. "Do you mean to tell me you've found something — the necklace or the daggers?"

"Don't ask me any questions just yet... I want you to answer one or two instead. Can you tell me anything about any letters Miss Monroe may have sent or received since she has been in your house?"

"Sir George wrote to me about her correspondence, and begged me to keep a sharp eye on it, so as to nip in the bud any attempt to communicate with Danvers. So far, however, she does not appear to have made any such attempt. With regard to letter-writing, she has a marked and most peculiar objection to it. Every one of the letters she has received, my wife tells, me, remain unanswered still. And if she wrote on the sly, I don't know how she would get her letters posted — she never goes outside the door by herself, and she would have no opportunity of giving them to any of the servants to post, except Mrs Hawke's maid, and she is beyond suspicion in such a matters."

"I suppose Miss Monroe has been present at the meal table each time that you have received your daggers through the post — you told me, I think, that they had come by the first post in the morning?"

Mr Hawke nodded. "Yes, Miss Monroe is very punctual and has been there each time. Naturally, when I received such unpleasant missives, I made some sort of exclamation and then handed the thing round the table for inspection, and Miss Monroe was very much concerned to know who my secret enemy could be."

"No doubt," said Loveday. "Now, Mr Hawke, if by chance you should receive by the evening post one of those big envelopes and find that it contains a sketch of three drawn daggers —"

"Good gracious!" exclaimed Mr Hawke. "Am I to take it for granted that I am doomed?"

"I don't think I would if I were you," answered Loveday dryly. "I want you to open the big envelope that may come to you by post this evening, just as you have opened the others — in full view of your family at the table — and to hand 'round the sketch it may contain for inspection to your wife, nephew and Miss Monroe. Now, will you promise me to do this?"

"Oh, certainly...but I shall feel so very much obliged to you if you'll enter a little more fully into an explanation. You place me in a miserable position. Are you returning to Lynch Court now?"

"I have a few stops to make first." Loveday looked at her lapel watch. "Please come to the office by eventide. I shall then be able to enter into fuller explanations, I hope."

221B: On Her Majesty's Secret Service
Sherlock has all the energy of the family.
— Mycroft Holmes

CHAPTER 8

London, Pall Mall

THE TELEGRAPH KEY clattered. The rapid-fire staccato clicks resolved themselves into letters of the alphabet, shifted about and formed words, floating in the thought-ether.

PARIS, 2 MARCH, 11:34 AM

DEATH OF JULIUS WENDIGEE

STOP

FOUND FLOATING IN SEINE APPROX. 1900 HRS LAST NIGHT

STOP

CAUSE OF DEATH BELIEVED TO BE HEART FAILURE STOP

BODY IDENTIFIED BY FIANCEE

STOP

POST-MORTEM REPORT WHEN AVAILABLE

ENDIT.

The click-clack of the key ceased but Mycroft Holmes continued to sit in his chair, his eyes closed, fingers interlocked over his stomach. He re-read the mental image of the telegram, murmured, "Confound it!" and opened his eyes. He reached over to the telegraph unit on his sideboard and keyed in the Message Received signal.

221B: On Her Majesty's Secret Service

Mycroft Holmes was not pleased, but then, he rarely was — at least not for more than ten seconds a day. He usually experienced those ten seconds when his afternoon tea arrived at precisely at five past three, delivered by his secretary, Austin Westbury.

Many things displeased him—first and foremost, the realization that as he passed forty years of age, he owned far fewer comfortable shoes and far more trousers with very wide waistlines. Although never slender as a youth, he was a much wider man now than when he had first began working for the Diogenes Club.

He had been recruited during his first year at Oxford. Initially, his job was to audit the club's books, due to his extraordinary faculty for figures. His work was so exemplary, his superiors decided an accountant's position squandered a remarkable resource. They saw Mycroft's gift lay in his omniscience. The intelligence services began by using him as a convenience, but in very short order, he had made himself indispensable.

Of course, that had been almost twenty years before, yet his office space in the archives still did not have a window to look through while he sipped his afternoon cup of Darjeeling. However, it had been his decision not to have the electric laid on, choosing instead to illuminate the space with several stained glass dragonfly oil lamps, both desk and floor models. They cast a rich, golden light over the entire room.

Mycroft Holmes had served as a professional intelligence officer for most of his adult life. As such, he was used to working underground, both figuratively and quite literally. As a younger man, he had visited his share of spy nests and anarchist rabbit warrens hidden amongst the cellars of various locations in Limehouse and Whitechapel. It was during that period he realized he had no taste at all for field work.

His personal warren was not a cellar. but a windowless office suite beneath the west wing of the Diogenes Club in Pall Mall. The club had a pair of three-story wings and a baronial main hall upon which had been built an octagonal tower with the brass Diogenes seal facing Waterloo Place.

The club's motto — *Ex Tenebris Lux, Amore Patrlae Vinett,Quaerite Veritatem, Vivant Leo et Unicornis* — was embossed around the outer rim of the seal: Out of Darkness, Light, The Love of Country Conquers, Search for the Truth and Long Live the Lion and Unicorn.

There was also a portico with Greek columns, a glass-domed conservatory, and behind the building, a tennis court adjacent to formal garden.

Mycroft saw very little of the Diogenes Club grounds other than the dining and reading rooms. His suite could only be reached by an elevator concealed in a corner of the carriage house at the very rear of the west wing. His private office was shaped like the inside of a drum, with high bookshelves rising nearly to the ceiling.

He sat at a large, very old desk, with many pigeonholes. The desk had come with the office and although no one said as much, every director of the Diogenes was expected to sit at it.

Mycroft had no staff other than his middle-aged secretary Austin, but he was linked to the Department of Operations at the Home Office by a direct telephone line, as well as an old but reliable telegraph unit. He kept the gadgetry out of sight, hidden within a sideboard behind his thickly upholstered desk chair. A voice-pipe apparatus, connecting him with Austin's small reception area, sat at his right elbow.

At the moment, the news of Julius Wendigee's death pre-empted Mycroft's displeasure with shoes and waistlines. He was much more concerned with the fact that Wendigee and Nikola Tesla were once colleagues, and now the Dutchman from South Africa was dead. Years before, both men ad been hired at the same time by Société Electrique Edison in Paris. When that piece of common biography was uncovered, Wendigee was put on the watchlist of possible associates of the power brokers known as

221B: On Her Majesty's Secret Service

The Hephaestus Ring.

Over the past year and a half, Wendigee had done very little worth watching. He continued to work at the Société Electrique as a high-ranking engineer, and become engaged to a French woman named Sara, with whom he often strolled along the Seine.

The man had supervised the installation of the lighting system for the upcoming Paris Exposition, and was frequently seen on the grounds by operatives of the Deuxieme Bureau. Julius Wendigee seemed the opposite of extraordinary, and therefore of no interest to the Hephaestus Ring. But he didn't seem the type to suddenly drop dead and fall into the Seine, either.

Repressing a sigh of ennui, Mycroft decided it was time to stop grousing and get back to work. He lifted the stack of papers from the "in" basket on his desk and began to read. From long practice and concentration, he could read upward of two thousand words per minute. As he possessed almost total recall, he retained everything his eyes scanned, and indelibly imprinted it on the photo-sensitive plate of his mind.

Most of the sheets of yellow foolscap were daily reports from diverse government departments, from the Admiralty to the Office of Rail and Road. A select group of operatives — Mycroft called them conduits — monitored all data circulating through all branches of the British government, had it printed and passed it on to the Diogenes Club.

No bit, gram or germ of intelligence that came into Mycroft's hands was ever discarded. Something that today seemed inconsequential could be of enormous import a year down the road. He read the text quickly, turning each absorbed page face-down on the desk.

There were reports about the hybridization of grain, of engagements and weddings, pages upon pages about various public figures, both at home and abroad, One sheet held a little article snipped from an Irish newspaper called *The Southern Star.*

221B: *On Her Majesty's Secret Service*

The headline read: Electrical Miracle Or Clever Trick?

"26 Feb.—

The fishing village of Glandore, just off the Cork Road between Skibbereen and Clonakilty, had recently played host to a man who demonstrated a strange and unique ability to control electricity, locals say.

Professor Hasellmeyer, late of Serbia, was engaged in experiments at an archaeological site in Glandore, known locally as the 'Druid's Altar' this Saturday last. The weather had been uncommonly mild and a body of holiday-makers visiting Glandore village were drawn to the professor's activities. He claimed with what he called a resonant transformer circuit of his own design, he could transmit electrical energy to any point on Earth. The circuit was described as little more than four vertical metal rods, joined at the top and supporting a centre transmission apparatus. With it, the professor brought forth miraculous and colourful coronal discharges into the air, tapped he said from the energies of the Earth at the centre the stone circle.

When asked the nature of his trickery, Professor Hasellmeyer grew offended and denied the involvement of sleight-of-hand. He explained in the strongest possible terms that his experiments in the wireless transmission of electricity were not meant for the edification of the public and were far from complete. He furthermore stated he had come to the secluded site in order to continue his work unmolested. According to one witness, he appeared so discomfited by their attention that the holiday-makers acceded to his wishes and left him to his labours. No one is certain if the Professor has taken lodgings in the area, or is merely passing through."

Mycroft studied the article for several silent seconds and picked up the speaking tube of the voice-pipe. He blew into it and faintly he heard the signal-whistle at the other end. Austin's voice responded, "Yes, Mr Holmes?"

"I need to know if there is a newspaper in County Cork,

Ireland, called *The Southern Star.*"

"Yes, sir."

"I need to know immediately. Contact Stead at the *Gazette.*"

"Of course, sir."

"Also enquire of him about a Serbian scientist named Hasellmeyer."

"Understood."

Mycroft did not appear to be excited but he felt his pulse and heart-rate speeding up.

Earlier that day, when the telegraph had stuttered out the message regarding Julius Wendigee's body being fished out of the Seine, he had not foreseen a relationship to much of anything else, certainly not to a minor event last week in West Cork.

At first glance, neither news item shared the slightest connection, but the compilers of the disparate scraps of data knew Mycroft could cross-index, collate and consolidate it all far faster than any calculating machine. Like his younger, more energetic brother, he possessed a tidy and exceptionally orderly brain, with a great capacity for storing facts and reaching conclusions.

Therefore, he instantly saw the link between the death of electrical engineer Julius Wendigee of South Africa and the electrical demonstration of Professor Hasellmeyer of Serbia. Mycroft was always suspicious of coincidence, so he had become a subscriber to the principle of synchronicity.

After the Penhallick Wharf affair, Mycroft inveighed upon the Home Office and the Defence Intelligence Branch to prioritize a watch on the Ring's known membership. So far, it had come to very little. Recently, an underworld informant by the name of "Porlock" who operated on the fringes of Moriarty's network had offered his own suspicions that the Professor was deeply involved in an undertaking with the Ring, but no direct proof was forthcoming.

221B: *On Her Majesty's Secret Service*

Even so, the Hephaestus Ring did not fall under the umbrella of an illegal organization. No formal criminal charges had ever been filed against it. Nor was it a paramilitary political group like the Radicals. Although it espoused the social philosophy called "technocracy," the Ring was more akin to an exclusive lodge, like the Golden Dawn.

Even that comparison was inadequate and misleading. Mycroft privately preferred "supra-nation," inasmuch as technocratic doctrine could be freely practised within any industry or on any street corner. As such, the Hephaestus Ring could extol the virtues of overthrowing world governments in favour of a totalitarian technocracy without fitting the legal definition of subversive.

In the nearly two years since the Penhallick Wharf fracas, Mycroft had learned several criminal syndicates were reorganized to operate interdependently, overseen by the Hephaestus Ring. He theorized the connections linking the networks could be swiftly severed when the danger of exposure or charges loomed. Few European courts were inclined to engage in lengthy and expensive prosecutions based only on suspicions that a legitimate business concealed illicit activities, such as Kathryn Koluchy's Foods On The Rise firm in Paris.

Mycroft had hoped Nikola Tesla would serve as the linchpin of such litigation. As the main witness against the Ring, due to being directly sponsored by Baron Robespierre Robur de Maupertuis, his testimony would be more than damning — indeed, it could prove fatal to the group's continued existence.

But both Robur and Tesla had vanished on the same night, within minutes of each other. Although earnestly sought by police departments all over the United Kingdom, no trace of either man was found. Fragments of Robur's prototypical aeroship were dredged from the sea, but not a body.

In the aftermath, Mycroft learned all he could about Nikola Tesla's background and character, assuming the Austrian inventor feared both the Ring and the British authorities. He extrapolated that a man of his intelligence would go to ground rather than flee across borders. Most likely, he would take an alias but as a dedicated scientist, he would not totally abandon his work

As for Robur, over the last month, phantom aeroship sightings had been reported in the southwestern United States. Although the American authorities officially dismissed the reports as hoaxes or misidentifications, officer John Strock of the American Federal Police privately suspected that Robur the Conqueror, or at least his creations, were still extant.

Repressing the urge to resort to his snuff-box, Mycroft returned to his reading, forcing himself to focus on the eclectic collection of data. Much of it appeared nonsensical but he knew none of it was meaningless.

After ten minutes, Austin walked in, carrying a tea-tray and a saucer with three shortbread biscuits. Mycroft looked at the clock on his desk and with a distant sense of surprise saw the time was precisely 3:05.

Austin, a thin man with a thin moustache and thinning gray hair, placed the tray on the desk He said, "I telephoned Mr Stead. He said there is a new broadsheet called *The Southern Star* published weekly in Skibbereen. Unfortunately, he could offer no information about a Professor Hasellmeyer."

William T. Stead served as the editor of the *Pall Mall Gazette* and although he was a reformer and held liberal views, he was a patriot and completely trustworthy—at least as far as Mycroft was concerned.

Austin filled the cup from the pot and then returned to his desk. He would retrieve the tray, pot, cup and saucer in thirty minutes' time.

Mycroft sipped his tea, wondering if a switch to coffee might help to sharpen his thought processes. The Tesla-Wendigee-Hasellmeyer conundrum nibbled at his nerves the same way he nibbled at the short-bread. He prided himself on always starting with unvarnished facts before he even considered a conjecture. Based on a balancing and an analysis of vectors, he reached conclusions. This situation required a leap of faith and swift action.

After a few moments of contemplation and tea consumption, he reached a provisional conclusion. He did not care for it at all.

Very little actually upset Mycroft Holmes, but he could be disturbed. and the newspaper clipping from Ireland disturbed him a great deal — he felt certain if the Defence Intelligence Branch conduits thought the item worth bringing to his attention, others would take notice of it as well.

He shook his head and whispered, "Merde." It was the single profanity he permitted himself, and then only whilst alone in his office. He never employed swear words anywhere else, not even within earshot of Austin.

Officially, the Diogenes Club brain trust did not directly oversee any field operatives of Her Majesty's Secret Service. Unofficially, his brother, Sherlock, John Watson and most recently, Loveday Brooke, could be called upon in an as-needed basis. Mycroft had recruited the female private enquiry agent, teaming her with Sherlock and Watson, working under the code-name 221B.

He had great faith in 221B, although the three had very contrasting personalities. Withal, they worked well together, despite the initial reluctance of Sherlock to include Miss Brooke. The successful resolution of the Vatican cameos assignment and the case of Isadora Persano's remarkable worm had proved her resourcefulness to the point that Mycroft harboured no hesitation whatsoever about dispatching her on lone assignments, if circumstances warranted it.

One personality trait all three people shared was a lack of enthusiasm for report writing. Watson and Miss Brooke apparently took turns at producing them. The reports which held a dearth of finer details but were packed with journalistic whos, whats and wheres, were written by Loveday, and the ones which read like Penny Dreadfuls were penned by Watson, who entertained literary aspirations. Mycroft found the work of both authors rather engaging, and so refrained from offering criticisms.

He understood that the majority of commanders fell into the sin of not delegating authority and insisting upon supervising every course of action personally. He sometimes wondered if he tended to go a bit far in the opposite direction, assuming his operatives would succeed at anything they were instructed to do.

He had not called upon 221B in nearly three months, since they had investigated the disappearance of Whitehall clerk, Mr James Phillimore. He knew he would have to summon them again before the day was done, and they wouldn't like it a bit. Miss Brooke was a career woman and would accept the assignment regardless, but Sherlock and Watson worked for the Diogenes Club solely at their own discretion.

As a former military man, Watson was bound by duty to Queen and Country, but he was not reticent about expressing his displeasure. Sherlock would no doubt insist that his detective work took precedence, as well as his current obsession with exposing James Moriarty. Nevertheless, Mycroft knew his brother would ultimately do what he was asked, whether he liked doing it, or not.

Mycroft Holmes was certain no one else—definitely not the man calling himself Professor Hasellmeyer—would like it, either.

221B: On Her Majesty's Secret Service

While all people are agreed as to the variety of motives that instigate crime, very few allow sufficient margin for variety of character in the criminal.

—Loveday Brooke

CHAPTER 9

London, Lynch Court

"IT IS A miserable position!" Mr Hawke exclaimed, as he took the chair that Loveday indicated.

"You're repeating yourself, sir," Loveday said.

Mr Hawke rolled the latest edition of the *Evening Standard* into a cylinder with nervous fingers and tapped it against his knee. "I not only received the three daggers for which you prepared me, but I got an additional worry for which I was totally unprepared. Immediately after dinner, Miss Monroe walked out of the house all by herself, and no one knows where she has gone. It seems the servants saw her go out, but did not think it necessary to tell either me or Mrs Hawke, feeling surely we must have been aware of the fact."

"So, Mr Hawke has returned," said Loveday. "I suppose you will be greatly surprised if I informed you that the young lady who so unceremoniously left your house, is at the present moment, to be found at the Charing Cross Hotel, where she has engaged a private room in her real name of Miss Deirdre Dalton."

Mr Hawke's eyebrows crawled up his seamed forehead. "Eh! What? Private room? Real name Dalton! I'm bewildered!"

"I'm not surprised. The young lady whom you welcomed into your home as the daughter of your old friend, was in reality a person engaged by Miss Monroe to fulfill the duties of her maid onboard the ship. Her real name is Deirdre Dalton, and she has proved herself a valuable co-conspirator in carrying out Miss Monroe's scheme which she devised with her lover, Mr Danvers, before she left Pekin."

"How do you know all this?"

Loveday replied, "It seems that Miss Monroe must have arranged with Mr Danvers that he was to leave China within ten days of her doing so, travelling the same route by which she came, and to land at Plymouth. There, he was to receive a note from her, apprising him of her whereabouts. As she was onboard ship, Miss Monroe appears to have set her wits to work with great energy; every obstacle to the execution of her plan appears to have been met and overcome."

Loveday lifted the index finger of her right hand. "Step number one was to get rid of her native maid, who might have proved troublesome. I have no doubt the poor woman suffered from sea-sickness, as it was her first voyage, just as I equally have no doubt that Miss Monroe worked on her fears, and persuaded her to land at Malta, and return to China by the next packet."

Raising another finger, she said, "Step two was to find a suitable person, who for a consideration, would be willing to play the part of the Pekin heiress among the heiress's friends in England, while the young lady herself arranged her private affairs to her own liking.

"That person was quickly found amongst the steerage passengers of the *Colombo* in Miss Deirdre Dalton, who had come onboard with her mother in Ceylon. You know how cleverly this young lady has played her part in your house — how, without attracting attention to the matter, she successfully shunned the society of her father's old friends, who might have been likely to involve her in embarrassing conversations, and how she carefully avoided the use of pen and ink lest —"

"Yes, yes," interrupted Mr Hawke; "but shouldn't we go at once to the Charing Cross Hotel, and get all the information we can out of her — she may bolt, you know."

"I do not think she will. She is waiting there patiently for an answer to a telegram she dispatched more than an hour ago to her mother, Mrs Maureen Dalton, at 14 Woburn Place, Cork City, Ireland."

"How is it possible for you to know all this?"

"Oh, that last little fact was simply a matter of astuteness on the part of the man whom I have deputed to watch the young lady's movements today. You met him this morning...a Mr Lawson. I have to thank those 'drawn daggers,' that caused you so much consternation, for having put me on the right track."

"Ah," said Mr Hawke, drawing a long breath; "I hope you are going to set my mind at rest on that score."

"Would it surprise you to be told that it was I who sent those three daggers to you this evening?"

"You! Why?"

Loveday replied, "Those roughly drawn sketches that to you suggested terrifying ideas of violence, appeared to me to suggest the herald's office rather than the armoury...the cross fitchy of the knight's shield, rather than the poniard. If you will look at these sketches again, you will see what I mean"

Loveday produced the drawings from the office writing-table. "To begin with, the blade of the dagger of common life is, as a rule, at least two-thirds of the weapon in length...in this sketch, what you would call the blade, does not exceed the hilt in length. Secondly, note the absence of guard for the hand. Thirdly, let me draw your attention to the squareness of what you considered the hilt of the weapon, and what, to my mind, suggested the upper portion of a crusader's cross. No hand could grip such a hilt as the one outlined here."

Mr Hawke gazed at her with wondering eyes. "How could you possibly know all of this?"

"After I left your home today, I went straight away to the British Museum, and there consulted a certain work on heraldry, which has more than once done me good service. There I found my surmise substantiated. Amongst the illustrations of the various crosses borne on armorial shields, I found one that had been taken by Henri d'Anvers from his own armorial bearings, for his crest when he joined the Crusaders under Edward I. Since then, it has been handed down as the crest of the Danvers family."

"Danvers?" repeated Mr Hawke.

Loveday nodded. "Someone in Cork sent to your house, on two occasions, the crest of the Danvers family. With my mind full of this idea, I left the museum and next visited the office of the P. and O. Company, and requested the list of passengers who arrived by the *Colombo*. The only passengers who landed at Plymouth besides Miss Monroe, were a certain Mr. and Miss Dalton, steerage passengers who had gone on board at Ceylon on their way home from Australia. Their name, together with their landing at Plymouth, suggested the possibility that Cork might be their final destination.

"After this, I asked to see the list of the passengers who arrived by the packet following the *Colombo*, telling the clerk who attended to me that I was on the look-out for the arrival of a friend. In that second list of arrivals I quickly found my friend—William Wentworth Danvers by name."

"The effrontery! In his own name, too!"

"Well, you see, a plausible pretext for leaving China could easily be invented by him — the death of a relative, the illness of a father or mother. And Sir George, though he might dislike the idea of the young man going to England so soon after his daughter's departure, was utterly powerless to prevent his doing so.

221B: *On Her Majesty's Secret Service*

"When I came to your house today, another important item of information was acquired. As I waited a few minutes in your drawing-room, I overheard a fragment of conversation between your nephew and the supposed Miss Monroe. One word spoken by the young lady convinced me of her nationality and even place of origin. That one word was the monosyllable 'Whisht.'"

Mr Hawke blinked in surprise. "What does that have to do with anything?"

"Have you ever noted the difference between the 'hush' of a Londoner and that of an Irish native? The former begins his 'hush' with a distinct aspirate, the latter with as distinct a W. That W is a mark of nationality which is never lost. Now Miss Dalton's was as pronounced a 'whisht' as it was possible for the lips of a Corkwoman to utter."

"And from that you concluded Deirdre Dalton was playing the part of Miss Monroe in my house?"

"Not immediately. When I went up to her room, in the company of Mrs Hawke's maid, I found the orderliness of that room was something remarkable. The orderliness of a lady in the arrangement of her room, and the orderliness of a maid, are two widely different things, believe me."

Hawke's eyes reflected his inner perplexity. "How so?"

"As I stood there, looking at that room," Loveday answered, "possibilities quickly grew into probabilities. Now, supposing that Miss Monroe and Deirdre Dalton had agreed to change places... the Pekin heiress, for the time being, occupying Deirdre Dalton's place in her humble home in Cork and vice-versa...what means of communicating with each other had they arranged? How was Deirdre Dalton to know when she might lay aside her assumed role and go back to her mother's house? There was no denying the necessity for such communication.

"We must credit these young women with having hit upon a very clever way of meeting those difficulties. An anonymous and startling missive sent to you would be bound to be mentioned in

221B: On Her Majesty's Secret Service

the house, and in this way a code of signals might be set up between them that would not direct suspicion to them. In this connection, the Danvers' crest, which it is possible that they mistook for a dagger, suggested itself naturally, for no doubt Miss Monroe had many impressions of it on her lover's letters.

"As I thought over these things, it occurred to me that possibly dagger number one was sent to notify the safe arrival of Miss Monroe and Mrs Dalton at Cork. The two daggers or crosses you subsequently received were sent on the day of Mr Danvers's arrival at Plymouth, and were, I should say, sketched by his hand. Now, was it not within the bounds of likelihood that Miss Monroe's marriage to this young man, and the consequent release of Deirdre Dalton from the onerous part she was playing, might be notified to her by the sending of three daggers to you?

"Accordingly, after I left your house, I made a sketch of three daggers exactly similar to those you had already received, and had it posted to you so that you would get it by the late post. Your agitation was such you didn't notice the lack of a Cork postmark on the envelope.

"Furthermore, I had Mr Lawson watch your house, and gave him special directions to report on Miss Dalton's movements throughout the day. The results I anticipated quickly came to pass. For the last couple of hours, a remarkable cross-firing of telegrams between the hotel at Charing Cross and Cork has been going to and fro along the wires."

"A cross-firing of telegrams! I do not understand."

Loveday said, "As soon as the telegraph office imparted to me Mrs Dalton's address in Cork, I telegraphed her, in her daughter's name, desiring her to address her reply to Lynch Court, not to Charing Cross Hotel. About three-quarters of an hour afterwards I received in reply this telegram, which I am sure you will read with interest."

Loveday handed a telegram — one of several that lay on the writing-table — to Mr Hawke. He opened it and read aloud: "Am

221B: *On Her Majesty's Secret Service*

puzzled. Why such hurry? Wedding took place this morning. You will receive signal as agreed tomorrow. Better return to Tavistock Square for the night."

Mr Hawke blinked in confusion. "The wedding took place this morning? My poor old friend! It will break his heart."

"Now that the thing is past recall, we must hope he will make the best of it," said Loveday. "In reply to this telegram, I sent another, asking as to the movements of the bride and bridegroom, and got this reply: 'They will be at Plymouth tomorrow night; at Charing Cross Hotel next day, as agreed."

"So, Mr Hawke," she concluded, "if you wish to see your old friend's daughter and tell her what you think of the part she has played, all you need do is watch the arrival of the Plymouth trains."

A quick rapping came from the office door. Loveday said, "Miss Dalton, right on time."

"Miss Dalton!" repeated Mr Hawke in astonishment.

Loveday rose and went to the door. "I telegraphed her, just before you arrived, to come here to meet a lady and gentlemen involved in this matter, even though it is after office hours....no doubt she thinks she would find here the newly married pair."

Opening the door, Loveday allowed the entrance of the bewildered young woman she had seen earlier in the day. She was dressed far less stylishly now. The girl stopped short and stood silent in the middle of the room, the picture of astonishment and distress. Mr Hawke also seemed at a loss for words, so Loveday took the initiative.

"You may sit if you wish, Miss Dalton," she said, placing a chair for the girl. "Before doing so, you should know the whole of your conspiracy with Miss Monroe has been brought to light...the best thing you can do will be to answer our questions as truthfully as possible."

With a suddenness that surprised even Loveday, the girl burst into tears. "It was all Miss Monroe's fault from beginning to end! Mother didn't want to do it — I didn't want to — to go into a gentleman's house and pretend to be what I was not. And we didn't want her hundred pounds —"

"Oh," said Loveday contemptuously,"A hundred pounds was your share?"

"We didn't want to take it," said the girl, between sniffles and dabbing at her eyes with a handkerchief monogrammed with a pair of overlapping cursive M's; "but Millicent said if we didn't help her, someone else would, and so I agreed to —"

"What we want," interrupted Loveday impatiently, "is for you to tell us what has been done with Miss Monroe's diamond necklace — who has possession of it now?"

Deirdre Dalton's tearful eyes widened. "I've had nothing to do with the necklace—it has never been in my possession...Millicent gave it to Mr Danvers two or three months before she left Pekin, and he sent it on to some people he knew in Hong Kong, diamond merchants, who lent him money on it."

Loveday nodded. "I suppose Mr Danvers retained part of that money for his own use and travelling expenses, and handed the remainder to Miss Monroe to enable her to bribe such a foolish creature as yourself and practice a fraud that ought to land you in jail."

The girl's face turned deadly white. "Oh, don't do that — I haven't touched a penny of Millicent's money!"

Loveday looked at Mr Hawke. "Your decision."

He rose from his chair. "I think the best thing you can do, Miss Dalton, is to get back home to your mother in Cork as quickly as possible, and advise her never to play such a risky game again. Have you any money in your purse? No — well then here's fifty pounds for you, and lose no time in getting home. It will be best for Miss Monroe — Mrs Danvers, I mean — to come to my house and claim her own property there. At any rate, there it will remain until she does so."

The girl left the office with incoherent expressions of gratitude. Before she went through the door, she cast Loveday an over-the-shoulder glance. Her smile seemed more triumphant than relieved. *Be the part,* thought Loveday.

Mr Hawke sighed. "I appreciate you sorting out this business in such a swift manner, Miss Brooke. I doubt that consulting detective who is the rage of the cheap periodicals could have done nearly as well."

"Oh, right," said Loveday. "Hemlock Jones or some such?"

"I believe so,"Mr Hawke replied distractedly. "I only hope Mrs Hawke will approve of what we have done when she hears all of the circumstances of the situation."

"I feel sure she will," Loveday said. "Mr Dyer will be in touch with you about our fee. Good evening, Mr Hawke."

Loveday escorted the old man to the door and let him out. She noted it wasn't quite dark and was a little surprised there had been so much activity throughout the day. The door to Dyer's private office swung open and he stepped out. He smiled at her. "Very well done...and in record time."

Loveday glanced at her watch. "I won't be late for my bartitsu lesson, if nothing else."

"You probably could've dragged the case out for another full day, however."

"That occurred to me but I could not have tolerated one more day of the tedium." She shook her head. "This was all a rather ridiculous matter, full of ridiculously entitled people engaged in ridiculous things."

The smile disappeared from Dyer's face. "The ridiculous cases are how we earn our livelihoods, our bread and butter, Loveday. I'm sure you're more engaged by the cases you share with Sherlock and that burly friend of his, but none of those have been forthcoming as of late."

221B: On Her Majesty's Secret Service

"Those cases are decided by a higher authority than Mr Holmes and John Watson."

"Still —"

The outer door opened and a man's husky voice called out, "Miss Brooke?"

Both she and Dyer recognized the voice. Not allowing the surge of excitement she felt to show on her face or be heard in her voice, she responded, "In here, Mr Tangey."

A lean, middle-aged man wearing the dark blue pseudo-military uniform of the Corps of Commissionaires strode in. He handed an envelope to Loveday. "I was told to inform you a cab will arrive to take you to Baker Street within a few minutes."

Nodding curtly to Dyer and Loveday, he very quickly left the office. Dyer said, "He didn't seem inclined to linger, did he?"

"It's late in the day and most likely he wants to finish his deliveries." She opened the envelope and took out the telegram. The message imprinted on the paper was short but exactly what she had hoped it would be.

ATTN 221B

COME IF CONVENIENT.

IF INCONVENIENT COME ALL THE SAME.

M.

Loveday folded the message and put it in her reticule. "The hunting horn has sounded," she murmured with a sardonic smile.

Dyer stared at her reproachfully. "May I presume that is a summons from your government liaison?"

"You may certainly presume but I am bound not to validate. I hope you understand."

"I hope you understand that your occasional involvement with Her Majesty's Secret Service does not keep you safe from being sacked if your duties here begin to suffer?"

Loveday presented the picture of pondering the query.

"Actually, I think it does keep me safe. Through my involvement with the Secret Service over the last two years, I've brought several very richly remunerative cases of a sensitive nature to the Lynch Court Agency...certainly more rewarding than exposing a music hall romantic melodrama dreamed up by two silly twits of girls."

Dyer stiffened. "You're not threatening to resign, I hope?"

Loveday sighed and turned her attention to unrolling the copy of the *Evening Standard* Mr Hawke had left behind. "I prefer to think we were just reminding each other of several pivotal points in our relationship. Now I shall wait for my cab and peruse the newspaper. At my earliest convenience, I will add up and present to you all chargeable hours I spent engaged in earning today's..."

She trailed off, paused and intoned, "Bread and butter."

221B: On Her Majesty's Secret Service

You have an extraordinary genius for minutia.

—John H Watson, M D

CHAPTER 10

London, Baker Street West

"WHICH IS IT today?" Sherlock Holmes asked. "Complete fabrication or a mere exaggeration?"

John Watson did not deign to glance up from his writing pad and swiftly moving fountain pen. "Neither, but you *have* just given me an idea for an opening line of dialogue."

"You're welcome."

Holmes stood at Watson's desk for another few seconds, balancing several slim reference books in the crook of his left arm. Watson ignored him long enough for Holmes to lose his patience and return to his place at the bow window. More noisily than strictly necessary, he dropped the volumes atop a bookcase. Taking his long-stemmed briar pipe from the breast pocket of his morning coat, he peered at the bowl and asked, "Pass me my tobacco pouch, would you?"

"It's in the coal scuttle."

"No, it's on your desk there, just underneath the *Evening Standard.*"

Lifting the newspaper, Watson retrieved the Persian slipper, eyeing the worn leather and threadbare silk inlays with distaste. The upcurving toe bulged with tobacco. He tossed it to Holmes. "You *do* remember this is my slipper?"

Holmes expertly snatched it from the air. "I also remember you

221B: On Her Majesty's Secret Service

never wore it."

"Why on Earth would I wear only one slipper?"

"It's one of a pair. You still have the other."

"Again — why would I wear only one slipper?"

"What good did the two of them do you?"

"They're mementoes of my service in Afghanistan. I never intended to use them as footwear."

Holmes took a generous pinch of brown shag from the slipper and thumbed it into the bowl of his pipe. "You make my point for me."

Watson gusted out a sigh, and turned his attention back to his writing pad. Holmes lit his pipe with a match, puffed on the stem, exhaled a plume of smoke and asked, "Seriously, Watson — what are you working on?"

"If you must know, it's a chronicle of the Agra treasure case. The provisional title is *The Sign of Four."*

"Melodramatically purple. I suppose the events are still fresh in your memory?"

Watson put down his pen. He said wearily, "Yes, Holmes, they are...believe it or not, I can even remember how the woman I'm going marry brought the case to us."

"Is your upcoming marriage the reason you're growing a moustache?"

Watson reflexively touched his upper lip with a forefinger, running the tip over the bristles. "Not precisely. But I'm actually re-growing it...I had one when you and I first met."

"Queens regs required you to have a full moustache whilst in the army. All commissioned officers had to — but you shaved it off shortly after we moved into Baker Street. That was almost eight years ago."

Watson shrugged. "I grew weary of maintaining it, keeping it trimmed and free of debris. It required more labour than shaving every few days. Besides, as you proved, it is easier to disguise oneself when clean-shaven."

Turning to face him, Holmes exhaled another cloud of smoke. "Muttonchops would have been quite the impediment to your imposture of a Morisco antiquarian in Málaga during that Paradol Chamber business."

Watson winced. "I still think a skin-stain would have been just as effective as a sun-tan. Less painful, at any rate."

"Regardless, why are you growing — regrowing — a moustache?"

Watson shifted in his armchair uncomfortably. "Mary saw a photograph of me in my Army uniform and remarked how dignified I appeared. She also mentioned that when I return to private practice, facial hair would bolster my professional persona...add a touch of gravitas."

Holmes turned to the window. "May I assume that with a wife and a full-time medical practice, your time working with me, much less for the Diogenes, will be somewhat truncated?"

Watson did not reply immediately. When he did, his voice was flat. "I suppose you should."

"Furthermore, with a fully regrown moustache, you won't be inclined to accept missions where you're expected to infiltrate the National Union of Women's Suffrage."

Watson laughed, "That would be a safe enough assumption, yes. I'm surprised Mycroft hasn't proposed something like that already."

Holmes did not respond. He stared out the window, apparently distracted by the faint clatter of horse-hooves on cobblestones and the jingle of harnesses. Although barely four o' clock, the afternoon sun sank beneath the irregular skyline of London, bathing the room in faded copper hues as it did so. Holmes continued to puff single-mindedly on his pipe. A gray-white cloud wreathed his head. The finger of his left hand tapped a nervous ditty on the window pane.

Watson realized that not only was Holmes in a state of nervous agitation, their sitting room was a shambles. Books were stacked in corners and chairs, a stench of sulphur dioxide tinged the air from a glass fractionating column on the table, a thick sheaf of letters was precariously pinned to the top of the mantel piece by the blade of a jackknife. The open violin case lay carelessly across the lounge chair, and various unidentifiable objects could be seen just about everywhere.

Sniffing the air, he realized how severely their sitting room reeked of old smoke and the lingering fumes of chemical experiments. He said, " Holmes, if you're going to further pollute our atmosphere, please open the window."

"It's rather too cold outside for that."

"And it's rather too intolerable inside. I've already gotten complaints from Mrs Hudson."

"So have I."

"Now you're getting them from me."

With an exasperated sigh, Holmes opened the window wide, allowing the chill March breeze to push its way in. Watson snatched at the papers ruffling on the desk, glaring at his friend's back.

The loose pages of the *Evening Standard* flapped. Watson quickly slapped his hand down on them. A pen-and-ink illustration on a back page caught his eye. It depicted a bat-winged aircraft in the night sky, casting two beams of light at a frightened-looking man on a hilltop. The headline emblazoned on the newsprint read: "Phantom Air-Ship — Aerial Navigation A Reality?"

Watson glanced up at Holmes, who pretended not to have noticed. Tapping the page, he demanded, "Is this why you placed the newspaper on my desk, Holmes? So I'd be sure to read this article?"

Holmes continued gazing out the window. "Which article?"

221B: On Her Majesty's Secret Service

"This one, of course." Clearing his throat, Watson turned up the flame of his desk lamp, and began reading in a portentous tone: " 'From our correspondent at the *Dallas Statesman* – About 1 o'clock last Monday morning, the inhabitants of Denton, who were still astir at that hour, claim to have seen an air-ship passing rapidly over their city. Some merely said they saw a bright light, whilst others went so far as to say they saw a cigar-shaped flying machine and heard human voices coming from it.

" 'A credible witness, whose reputation for truthfulness cannot be assailed, stated, 'When I first ascertained the character of the object, it floated about three hundred feet above the earth and seemed to be about fifty feet long, of a cigar shape with two great wings thrust out from each side; a broad tail or steering sail behind, and a long beak or blade resembling Heriot-Watt on a ship, in front.

" 'A search light threw its rays far into the night ahead of the craft, beside which even the luminosity of the moon paled. A row of windows along the side gave out smaller lights, the source of which must have been stored electricity, as there was no smoke, as far as I could see, and I could see very plainly, nor was there the slightest sign of a smoke-stack.' "

Lowering the paper, Watson stared at Holmes expectantly. "So...what do you make of it?"

Holmes turned to face him. "Most likely the same thing you do. Our former acquaintance Baron Robespierre Robur de Maupertuis has upgraded his prototype aeroship into an advanced model."

"Why are you so sure Robur still lives?"

Holmes arched an ironic eyebrow. "Other than the fact his body wasn't found with the wreckage of his flying machine, and in nearly two years time, it has yet to wash up on any beach?"

"Or," ventured Watson, "you're still so angry about the battering he gave you, you refuse to admit he died at sea and cheated you out of a tit-for-tat."

221B: *On Her Majesty's Secret Service*

"I'm not that childish. Being battered on occasion is part and parcel of our business."

"But assailants have never escaped from you before." Watson took a deep breath and added sympathetically, "He hurt you, Holmes — broken rib, fractured cheek-bone, massive contusions. As well as your physical injuries, your pride was so severely injured you had to take a rest cure at Colonel Hayter's estate."

Holmes nodded impatiently "Where the Colonel introduced me to the pain-easing benefits of morphine mixed with cocaine. But that's neither here nor there. If this news item has a basis in reality, then the two most likely possibilities are patently obvious: Either an enterprising technologist has built his own aeroship based on Robur's design or Robur himself is gadding about the lone prairies of Texas on test flights of his latest aircraft."

"There are more than just those two possibilities," Watson said.

"But not likely ones." Holmes paced across the floor from the bow window to the mantelpiece and back again, leaving a trail of smoke in his wake, like an errant locomotive. "Mycroft has kept the known and even potential members of the Hephaestus Ring under observation since the Cornwall incident. Basil Zaharoff closed down his secret foundry shortly after the raid, without ever revealing what it was manufacturing in the first place."

"True," Watson admitted. "And we never did learn what became of the *Friesland's* cargo, since Zaharoff's solicitors and his connections in the government blocked Mycroft's efforts to confiscate it. By the time the case made its way through the courts, all of it had been dispersed to parts unknown."

Holmes paused at the mantelpiece long enough to flip through the latest correspondence affixed to the wood. "Exactly. You and I found firearms aboard the *Friesland*, but they were being off-loaded at Penhallick Wharf, which suggests they had been manufactured elsewhere. Texas, perhaps."

"That would be appropriate but when last heard of, Zaharoff

was living in Spain."

"With considerable holdings...including a mistress and a munitions factory."

"None of that proves Robur survived."

Holmes continued to pace. "Nor does it disprove it...but we have plenty of circumstantial evidence that if the Ring has the means to conceal manufacturing facilities, they certainly have the means to hide someone from the prying eyes of Her Majesty's Secret Service, particularly if both are laying low in a foreign country."

"Even so, I thought your current fixation on tracking down and bringing James Moriarty to the dock superseded everything else."

"I would not call it a fixation, Watson."

Watson forced a chuckle. "Oh, no? Don't you suspect there are two Moriartys?"

"I've dropped that theory."

"That's a relief."

Holmes extended three fingers. "I'm now exploring the possibility of three Moriartys."

Watson stared at him in silence for a second, closed his eyes and pinched the bridge of his nose. "Holmes —"

"Whether one Moriarty or three, his name has been associated with that of the Hephaestus Ring for several years. If the Ring has plans, Moriarty most likely knows about them, and the reverse is also true."

Nodding in reluctant concession, Watson said, "Perhaps we should consult Mycroft...he might have some insights or recent intelligence to share. But the airship article was printed in this afternoon's edition of the *Standard*. Mycroft won't see it until tomorrow."

"I believe Mycroft has something he wants to discuss with us before then."

concede you may have a point and I will take it under serious consideration. But I don't think this moment is the proper time to remove yourself from our triad."

Watson and Holmes exchanged a long, silent look. Sighing in exasperation, Watson stood up from his desk, and turned down the lamp. "You're right. I shouldn't toss both you and Loveday into the deep end without a bit of prior notice...certainly not until I hear what Mycroft has to say."

"My thoughts exactly," said Holmes, unsuccessfully repressing the relief in his voice.

After collecting hats, coats and the page from the *Evening Standard*, Watson and Holmes left their flat, calling to Mrs Hudson not to wait dinner for them. They stepped out onto Baker Street, glancing up and down the avenue for cabs. Although all of the street lamps had yet to be lit, they saw dray and delivery wagons clop-clopping along, and even a few bicyclists in the dimming light. Pedestrian traffic was not heavy, consisting mainly of people walking home from work.

From their left, an anonymous black four-wheeler rolled up directly in front of them, drawn by a pair of equally black horses. The coach was completely enclosed. The glass in the windows was tinted, so they knew it was a private conveyance. The door bore an unobtrusive lion and unicorn sigil worked in gold leaf, identifying the coach as property of the Crown.

That accounted for the brace of horses. Broughams built for officials of Whitehall and the palace were sturdier and often reinforced with sheet metal for protection of the passengers and important cargo. Cobb, the driver was a white-haired man wearing a top hat at least five seasons out of style.

Holmes walked briskly to the coach and opened the door. Loveday Brooke glanced quizzically at him from within. "You're surprisingly prompt, Mr Holmes. I just passed Tangey on his way back to the Foreign Office. He was climbing into a cab himself."

Holmes touched the brim of his Homburg. "The unofficial

motto of 221B is 'We Can But Try,' Miss — ah — Loveday." He surprised himself by feeling suddenly glad to see her, even though his stomach jerked in a nervous spasm.

She smiled wanly. "Miss Brooke will do just fine, Mr Holmes. No need to make both of us uncomfortable."

Holmes covered his sudden surge of embarrassment by gesturing to Watson to precede him into the passenger compartment. Watson slid in beside her, giving Loveday a quick appraisal. She wore a stylish purple dress, top hat and violet gloves. She rested her right hand on the curved handle of an umbrella, the stainless steel ferrule planted firmly on the cab's floor. In the other she held a modest reticule.

"Fancy meeting you here, John," she said. "Again."

He grinned. "We always seem to be going to the same place."

"Fair to say. I received my summons at Lynch Court mere minutes before the cab arrived."

Holmes pushed in beside Watson and thumped on the ceiling with a fist. It started off with a lurch. "At least it's a nice evening for a drive."

"It might rain later," she replied. She tapped the ferrule of her umbrella on the floor. "But I'm always prepared. Anticipate and adapt, correct?"

Holmes nodded. "Correct."

The cab rolled in the direction of Pall Mall. The congestion of late afternoon London traffic thinned somewhat. Loveday peered at Watson by the feeble light from the exterior lamp "Are you growing a moustache, John?"

Self-consciously, he fingered his upper lip. "Thinking about regrowing one. Mary says I should."

"She thinks it will add dignity to his medical professional persona," Holmes stated. "Gravitas."

Watson cast him a warning sidewise glare.

Loveday nodded. "I can see that. How is Mary?"

"Fine...busy planning the wedding. The actual date has yet to be decided, but we're hoping for the month of May."

"A large affair?"

"Small to the point of intimate, I wager. Neither Mary nor myself have many friends, or much in the way of family members to invite."

Loveday made a vague, waving gesture. "The three of us have that in common." She leaned forward, looking past Watson to Holmes. "Speaking of family, do you know what Mycroft wants to see us about?"

"Not specifically," Holmes answered, "but I'm fairly confident it has to do with Robur."

She nodded. "Due to that piece in the *Standard* about the airship seen in Texas. Hardly seems an emergency, though."

Holmes grunted contemplatively. "It must be urgent if Mycroft couldn't wait until tomorrow."

"I didn't have any plans for this evening," declared Loveday, "except for my bartitsu club."

Holmes raised his eyebrows meaningfully. "Go on."

Watson asked, "Bartitsu is a men's-only sport, isn't it?"

"It's not a sport," Holmes and Loveday said simultaneously and they both chuckled.

"It's a self-defence system that combines elements of boxing, jujitsu, French savate and la lance...single-stick fighting," Loveday said, "but I prefer the umbrella to the cane. Mr Holmes put me on to bartitsu, and I've pursued my own training over the last year."

"Who did you find to instruct you?" Holmes asked.

"Pierre Vigna. He was reluctant at first but I changed his mind."

"How?" Watson asked.

221B: On Her Majesty's Secret Service

"I offered him double his rate."

Watson nodded, "Of course."

She gazed at Holmes. "May I ask who instructed you?"

"Not Vigna."

Loveday's full lips quirked in a smile. "You're rather a hard man to get to know."

"So I've been told, Miss Brooke."

"We've worked as occasional partners for the better part of two years."

"Colleagues," Holmes corrected her. "We don't need to know any more about each than our professional credentials. I presume that's why you prefer me to address you as 'Miss Brooke.'"

Loveday nodded curtly. "Very true. But I presume you know all about me, anyway."

"Not really." Holmes folded his arms over his chest and looked straight ahead. "Only that you were born in Chiswick twenty-nine years ago. You were named after your maternal great-grandmother. You have no siblings. Your father Terrence was a second lieutenant aboard the *HMS Undaunted*. Your mother, Alice, passed away of scarlet fever while he was at sea. You were 15 years of age. After resigning his commission and leaving the Navy, your father took a supervisory position at the Thornycraft Shipbuilding Company. He lost his life in an industrial accident in 1882, for which he was held responsible."

"That's enough, Holmes," Watson cautioned quietly.

Holmes paid no heed. "Your father was deeply in debt, and after his passing, the debtors swarmed all over you and what was left of his estate. Learning that much of the debt was due to fraud, you set yourself the task of exposing the swindler. You were successful, but in the process, you cut yourself off from your place in society. You therefore sought a permanent position with the Lynch Court detective agency as an operative of Ebenezer Dyer, where you've been ever since."

221B: *On Her Majesty's Secret Service*

Loveday's lips tightened. "Perhaps for not much longer."

Holmes did not acknowledge her remark. "You are gifted with what Alfred Binet calls an 'eidetic memory' and therefore are an outstanding investigator. After three years of exemplary service with the Lynch Court agency, Ebenezer promoted you to chief detective which is quite an accomplishment. How and why you ended up working for the Diogenes Club and Mycroft, is, of course, obvious." Holmes turned his head, looking past Watson into her eyes. "Talent recognizes genius...as do I."

Loveday started to speak, stopped herself and smiled crookedly. "I'm not sure, but I think that's the closest to a compliment from Mr Holmes as I'm ever likely to get."

Watson said flatly, *"I'm* sure."

221B: On Her Majesty's Secret Service

Nothing clears up a case so much as stating it to another person.

—Sherlock Holmes

CHAPTER 11

IT WAS DARK by the time the coach wheeled into the wall-enclosed courtyard at the rear of the Diogenes Club. They disembarked and Holmes said to the driver, "I doubt we will be long... please wait for us."

Cobb nodded, respectfully tipping his top hat. "Those are my orders, sir."

Holmes looked down St. James Street at a hansom cab four blocks away, stopped at the kerbside, parked between two streetlamps. It was barely visible in the gathering gloom and fog.

"Did you say you saw Commissionaire Tangey climbing into a cab on Baker Street, Miss Brooke?"

Loveday glanced at him with a puzzled eye and then in the direction he was gazing. "I did. Is that significant?"

"Not necessarily, although most commissionaires get around town on foot or by bicycle."

"Unless time was of the essence."

"How many minutes between Tangey delivering Mycroft's summons to you in Lynch Court and the arrival of Mr Cobb?"

Loveday pursed her lips thoughtfully. "No more than ten minutes."

221B: *On Her Majesty's Secret Service*

"Certainly not sufficient time for Tangey to reach Baker Street with our summons without taking a cab."

"Is there something we need to know about Tangey?" Watson asked.

Holmes turned away. "Not yet."

Loveday, Watson and Holmes entered the club grounds through a delivery gate. They walked across the compound to the side entrance of the carriage house. With a key taken from her reticule, Loveday unlocked the door.

Their path lit by four paraffin lamps hanging from the ceiling rafters, the three people wended their way past and around the four carriages and a coach kept there for safekeeping and protective coloration.

The Diogenes Club security protocols weren't elaborate or complex — there was little reason for them to be. Mycroft controlled everything from various pigeonholes in his antique desk, including a self-destruct system for the file room.

When the panels of the lift hidden behind a stack of harness and tack slid aside, they knew Mycroft had pressed the release button. Through an elaborate mirror and periscope system, he had watched them arrive.

The lift cage was so small it barely accommodated the three of them, but Holmes once opined it was probably just large enough to contain Mycroft. The lift deposited them in a narrow, stone-walled corridor. Wire-encased ceiling bulbs shed a cold illumination.

They strode past an open door. The dimly lit room beyond contained a litter of ancient weaponry, from swords to maces to battered suits of armour. Bookshelves lined the walls and stretched to the ceiling.

The chamber held the archives of the Diogenes Club — trophies of past missions stretching back to the mid-seventeenth century. The pronounced odour of must and even mildew irritated

221B: On Her Majesty's Secret Service

their sinus passages as they walked past.

Loveday wrinkled her nose. "Smells like my gran's basement."

The door to Mycroft's suite of offices was unlocked. Watson, Holmes and Loveday walked through the reception foyer, past Austin's tidy desk. He was gone for the day. Holmes picked up the voice-pipe and blew through the funnel. They heard the distant shrill whistle and then Mycroft's annoyed voice: "Confound it, Sherlock...I know you're here. No need to announce yourself."

The three people exchanged grins as they entered Mycroft's office and seated themselves in hard wooden library chairs before his battleship of a desk. Watson remarked, "I always feel like I've been called to the headmaster's office when I come in here."

"I suppose we could meet at the Red Lion," Mycroft said darkly. "I enjoy beer. But that would hardly be regulation. I hope you realize I would never send for 221B if I didn't consider the matter of the utmost import."

"Our time is your time," Watson said in a dry tone that implied he didn't mean it. He made an exaggerated show of opening and consulting his pocket-watch.

Loveday said, "John is just being a twit, you know."

Mycroft eyed Holmes impassively. "You are in need of a haircut, little brother. I'm surprised Mrs Hudson let you go out in such a state."

"At least I *do* go out now and then, big brother."

Mycroft didn't respond. "I have news that may concern our wayward Austrian genius, Nikola Tesla." He held out a square of newsprint. "I can read this to you, if you wish. That would save the three of you passing it around or looking over each other's shoulders."

"Aloud, then," said Holmes. He handed Mycroft the folded page from the *Evening Standard.* "When you're done, you can read this. To yourself."

221B: *On Her Majesty's Secret Service*

Mycroft frowned but began reading aloud the dispatch from Ireland's *Southern Star.* When he finished, he unfolded the newspaper page of the *Standard,* his eyes flitting back and forth over the text and the illustration. After he was done, he raised his face to the three people sitting opposite him. "A surprising confluence of events...and I haven't been completely surprised by anything in this line of endeavour for a very long time."

"Both stories share several intriguing commonalties," Holmes said.

"Assuming either story can be accepted at face-value," pointed out Loveday.

"Under the current circumstances," said Mycroft, "we should. We have Mr Tesla, a native of Austria, who was sponsored by Robur to develop electrical technology for the Hephaestus Ring. He disappeared nearly two years ago. Barely a week past, an electrical engineer named Hasellmeyer made his presence known in Ireland, claiming he hailed from Serbia — part of the Austro-Hungarian Empire and Austria's neighbour. It is not much of a suppositional stretch to imagine Hasellmeyer and Tesla are one and the same."

"Why didn't Nikola return to Austria after all this time?" asked Loveday. "Why go on the stamp in the United Kingdom?"

Mycroft shrugged. "Most likely he feared all points of exit to the Continent would be under surveillance, either by British authorities or the Hephaestus Ring or both."

Holmes said, "And there is the matter of Julius Wendigee, a former colleague of Tesla's, found dead in Paris just last night."

"He was engaged to install the electrical light system of the Paris Exposition grounds," replied Mycroft.

"A task that was also intended for Nikola," said Loveday. "According to our brief conversation at Penhallick two years ago."

"Three common factors," said Watson holding up three fingers.

221B: On Her Majesty's Secret Service

"Where does a flying machine in Texas fit into this?"

Mycroft regarded him gravely. "In the wake of the Penhallick Wharf affair, I contacted the intelligence and police agencies in Europe and America — every country where Robur and his first airship, the *Albatross,* had been reported back in 1868. John Strock, an officer of the Federal Police in Washington DC, contacted me a month ago about sightings of both a winged aeroship and a mystery submersible in the U.S. state of Ohio."

"Robur's prototype was designed to operate in both water and the air," Holmes said thoughtfully. "We have evidence of that."

"The identity of the brain behind these sightings in Texas and Ohio remains an open question," said Mycroft. "For all we know, it could be the man known as Captain Nemo who accessed Robur's blueprints and combined both functions into a single craft."

"A flying machine in Texas," Watson intoned, ticking off the items on the fingers of his right hand. "A fugitive Austrian performing electrical experiments in Ireland, a Dutch electrical engineer and former workmate of Tesla found dead in Paris. Both the dead Dutchman and the fugitive Tesla possessed expertise useful to the International Exposition."

"And according to the fugitive in question," said Loveday, "Kathryn Koluchy is an investor in the Exposition and her firm, Foods on The Rise, is based in Paris."

She added, "I should like to mention this is the second time County Cork has figured in a case I'm involved in today. Most likely it is an unrelated coincidence."

"What was the nature of the case?" asked Watson.

"Bread and butter. Easily solved. A little thing."

Holmes said, "It has long been an axiom of mine that the little things are infinitely the most important."

"Be that as it may." Mycroft swivelled his chair around to reach into a pigeon-hole in his desk. "Mathis, my Deuxième

221B: *On Her Majesty's Secret Service*

Bureau opposite number, sent me a detailed overview of the exposition grounds on a set of glass slides. I have never found the time to view them."

"Do you have a magic lantern?" asked Holmes.

Mycroft removed a flat, paper-wrapped package and carefully placed it on the desk. "Yes...supposedly the newest model...called a Choreutoscope."

He opened another compartment and removed a large brass and wooden-walled box with a thick telescoping glass lens projecting from one side of it. He placed it on his desk, aligning the lens with the nearest wall. "Hopefully, I can remember how it operates."

From a drawer, Mycroft removed a short candle, lit the wick with a match, and placed it within a hollow cylinder atop the lantern. A disk of white light appeared on the wall. He unwrapped the paper from the package, revealing a rectangular cartridge with a small crank attached to one end. He inserted the opposite end into a narrow slot between the lens casing and the lantern surface. He carefully turned the crank on the rectangle.

Within the circle of light appeared a collection of blurred images, overlaid by a faint grid pattern. Adjusting the lens, the images came into focus. A jumble of buildings, roads and even waterways popped into sharp relief, as if looking down from a high angle.

Mycroft cleared his throat and stated, "The grounds of the Exposition Universelle, as rendered by one of the architectural staff."

"Didn't France just have one of those exposition things?" Watson asked.

"You're behind the times, doctor. That was back in 1878...it was not a success, either financially nor culturally. Five years ago, the French government decided that the birth of their Republic should be celebrated — and vindicated — during the centennial year of the 1789 Revolution. So, it was decreed by President Jules Grévy, that there should be held, from May sixth until November sixth, 1889, the Paris World's Fair, also called an international exposition."

"How is this fair different from the one before it?" Loveday enquired.

"From what I understand, the basis of this exposition was devised so that the affair will show a profit...a substantial one, unlike the three previous Paris expositions. The government, which had borne the entire cost of the other fairs, have paid for less than a third of the costs for mounting this one. Investors from industries all over the world are supplying the capital."

Holmes uttered a wordless murmur of surprise. "I had no idea it covered so much ground."

"Over ninety-six square kilometres," said Mycroft, slowly turning the cartridge's crank. Different images appeared, mainly of buildings with ornate facades. "Including the Champ de Mars, the Trocadéro, the Quai d'Orsay, a part of the Seine, and the Invalides esplanade."

Holmes repressed a smile. Mycroft's pronunciation was flawless. His facility with languages had been a source of pride since his teen years.

"Transport around the Exposition grounds will be partly provided by a three-kilometre, narrow gauge railway," continued Mycroft. "The fair has two main sites—the Trocadéro and the Champ-de-Mars house the Fine Arts and industrial exhibits. The Esplanade des Invalides is housing the colonial exhibit and several state-sponsored pavilions, as well as the International Theatre."

On the wall appeared a bizarre male figure dressed in a bright red velvet doublet with winged collar and puffed sleeves. His face was hard and bony, his smirking lips framed by an upturned moustache and goatee. A two-feathered cap sat at a rakish angle on his head. Seated before a chess-board, the figure's right leg

221B: On Her Majesty's Secret Service

was crossed over the left. It terminated in a cloven hoof.

"Good Lord," Watson said with a barely repressed laugh. "What is that — or should I say, who?"

"You would be right on both counts," replied Mycroft. "That is Mephisto, the chess-playing automaton...also known as an automatic android. It caused something of a stir in professional chess-playing circles here in London ten or so years ago. Designed and constructed by an artificial limb manufacturer named Gumpel, this Mephisto is a more refined version of the original, prepared to make his debut at the Exposition."

"Oh," said Watson. "I've heard of similar novelties...just a man inside of a costume, pretending to be an automaton."

"Not in the case of Mephisto," Holmes said. "Allegedly, it has been thoroughly examined and found to be a true machine. It has won many games and even a tournament. Quite the remarkable advance in automation, from what I have read and heard. I'd be interested to make its acquaintance."

Mycroft turned the crank backward to restore the previous image of the fairgrounds.

"What about that eyesore of a skeleton tower there on the Champ-de-Mars?" asked Loveday.

Mycroft chuckled and adjusted the lens, increasing the magnification "The president and numerous commissioners of Paris all agreed that the 1889 exposition should feature something special and memorable. A *clou* — a highlight that would give the entire undertaking a visual signature, a structural symbol of French culture. After rejecting a proposal for a 300 metre tall guillotine, the Committee decided that a nine hundred and eighty-four foot all iron tower would be a more appropriate symbol — a structure surpassing in height any construction ever built."

Loveday pursed her lips in disapproval. "Who came up with that idea?"

221B: On Her Majesty's Secret Service

Mycroft replied, "There were several predecessors, at least conceptually. In 1833, a British engineer proposed a 1,000-foot cast iron column to commemorate Parliamentary Reform. American engineers had a similar idea for the 1876 Philadelphia Exposition but neither of those went beyond the rough blueprint stage."

Mycroft turned the crank and the black and white photograph of an ordinary looking grey-haired and bearded man appeared. "An architect and civil engineer named Gustave Eiffel first suggested the idea to the Exposition committee. His company built the framework for the Statue of Liberty. Eiffel was at work on the plans for this tower even before the announcement of a competition for a design. Since his company has built it, the tower belongs to Eiffel. Only he has the financial resources, the professional reputation and the political leverage to carry the project to a successful completion."

"And is it completed?" Holmes asked.

"According to Mathis, it will be by the end of this month," answered Mycroft. "There have been unforeseen delays regarding the electrical and lift systems. Quite the monumental project, all things considered."

"Rather phallic, isn't it?" Loveday asked dryly.

Mycroft shifted uncomfortably in his chair. "I suppose that's a subjective interpretation...however, some Parisians, particularly the tower construction crews, have nicknamed the tower *la dame de fer...* 'the Iron Lady.'"

"Why is that?"

"Due to the way the four support pylons are covered with a lacy 'skirt' and how they are enhanced with fine decorative arches. Too fanciful for my taste." Mycroft permitted himself a smile "You might say it's a bit too French, Miss Brooke."

"I'm reminded of a giant lightning rod myself," Watson said meditatively. He glanced toward Mycroft. "How did the article from the Irish newspaper describe Professor Hasellmeyer's transmitter? Four vertical metal rods, joined at the top?"

Mycroft, Loveday and Holmes stared intently at the image of the tower on the wall. Loveday made a "hm" sound. She asked, "Is it possible Nikola was assigned the task of making the tower the opposite of a giant lightning rod? A device to transmit electricity?"

"The tower is made of puddled iron," said Mycroft, "which has undergone a special kind of processing to make it purer and even more durable than steel. I suppose using it as an energy transmitter is within the realm of extreme possibility."

"For what practical purpose?" enquired Holmes. "To make Paris a literal city of lights, instead a metaphorical one? If the Hephaestus Ring is involved with the Exposition, a Promethean gift of bringing light to darkness does not fit their character."

Watson commented, "Perhaps they intend to force Parisians to pay good francs for that gift."

Mycroft grunted. "Our only possible direct source of information is the so-called Professor Hasellmeyer. Therefore, you three will leave tonight for County Cork to find him. Take the train from Euston station to the Port of Holyhead and then the ferry to Dublin. At the Pearse railway station, you will board a private train which will convey you non-stop to Skibbereen. I'll arrange for you to be met there by Inspector Keegan of the Royal Irish Constabulary. He will conduct you to this Glandore village or see that you get there."

Loveday and Watson stared at Mycroft incredulously. "You expect us to leave tonight?" she demanded.

Mycroft inclined his head in a curt nod. "If my own conduits saw that news item from *The Southern Star*, it is very likely so did those who supply data to the Hephaestus Ring. They've probably already dispatched a team of retrieval agents."

"What was that about a private train?" Holmes wanted to know.

221B: On Her Majesty's Secret Service

"A locomotive and two cars. It waits on a siding in the Dublin railyard for just such a use. To quickly transport our own agents anywhere within the borders of the kingdom. It is occasionally used by the aristocracy. The crew are on standby. They will be alerted to have the train ready when you arrive." He paused and added, "The locomotive was christened *The Wraith.*"

"That's all well and good," Loveday said. "But I obviously did not bring a change of clothes or much of anything else with me." She raised her umbrella and reticule. "I'm not accustomed to traveling this light."

"Our coachman will drop you by your lodgings and wait while you put together some luggage." Mycroft looked toward his brother and Watson. "The same for you two. Take all the time you need...as long as you are aboard the 11 o'clock ferry to Dublin."

Loveday eyed Mycroft suspiciously. "Assuming Professor Hasellmeyer is indeed an alias of Nikola Tesla's — of which I am not convinced — and also assuming we find him in Ireland, what do you expect us to do with him? He's not a criminal. In fact, I owe him my life."

Mycroft sighed. "It's a matter of character. Your prior interaction with the man indicates he felt protective toward you. I won't go so far as to claim Mr Tesla trusts you, but he does know you and that will give us an advantage over anyone sent from the Ring. I doubt he'd run from you. He will be more inclined to heed your words."

"My words regarding what, specifically?"

"That he should return to London with you and place himself under our protection."

"Based on what little I observed of Nikola's character, it's a fifty/fifty proposition whether he will agree. He's managed to escape detection for two years...what if he decides to continue gambling on his own resources?"

Mycroft shrugged. "Then you must do what you think best. Do not force him."

Loveday nodded and stood up. "Very well, then."

Watson came to his feet, automatically looking at his watch. "Mary is off with the Forresters in the Cotswolds for the week, but I suppose I have time to dash off a wire to let her know I'll be away from Baker Street."

Mycroft frowned. "That may not be wise, doctor."

Watson scowled at the big man. "I'm not going to Ireland without telling her. Cork is a dangerous place...a hotbed of rebel activity."

"You misunderstand. I meant only to suggest that all three of you could presently be under observation and any telegram you send from a commercial venue might be intercepted."

Mycroft pushed a blank message pad across the desk to him. "Write what you wish, and I'll send it from here."

Only a little mollified, Watson used a pencil to quickly jot four lines, assuming he wouldn't be charged by the character. Holmes walked closer to the image of the exposition grounds displayed on the wall. He studied it for a few silent seconds, eyes narrowed.

Mycroft asked, "Something, Sherlock?"

Holmes glanced over his shoulder at his brother, smiling ruefully. "Nothing specific. I just have the distinct feeling that sooner rather than later, I will need to know my way around the grounds of the Exposition Universelle."

221B: On Her Majesty's Secret Service

Violence is sometimes a duty.
— John H. Watson, MD

CHAPTER 12

WHEN THEY STEPPED out of the carriage house, they were greeted by a freezing drizzle. Watson hunched his shoulders and tugged up his coat collar. "You were right to bring your umbrella, Loveday."

"I usually am." She popped opened the canopy. "It should accommodate the three of us."

Holmes remained under the overhang, surveying their surroundings. He saw the brougham waiting for them in the courtyard with Cobb the coachman in his perch, the brim of his hat pulled low and his chin tucked into the folds of a scarf. Watson ducked under the umbrella and cast Holmes a questioning glance. "Are you waiting for something?"

"As a point of fact, I am. You two go ahead, but look over to your left. If you see a cab up the way, stop and pretend you've forgotten something. Return to me. Pat your pockets. Don't overact." He added wryly, "Be the part."

Loveday smiled but Watson only rolled his eyes. They walked towards the coach. When they were within a few yards of it, they came to halt. Watson patted his coat pockets and he and Loveday came back to the carriage house.

"The cab is still there," reported Loveday. "It hasn't moved since you pointed it out."

"How is that important?" Watson demanded peevishly.

"In and of itself, it isn't," replied Holmes. "But combined with the fact that Cobb the driver of our coach apparently had the opportunity to trade in his old hat for a current model while we were occupied with Mycroft makes the situation a little sinister."

Watson frowned. "He has a new hat?" He started to turn.

"Don't look at him," Holmes warned.

"I wasn't," Watson retorted defensively. "So if Cobb has a newer hat than earlier, it stands to reason that's also a newer Cobb."

"Or an entirely different one." Loveday angled the umbrella so the canopy hid their faces from the street. "Or most likely, not a Cobb at all."

"My feeling is that it's Commissionaire Tangey," remarked Holmes.

Both Watson and Loveday blinked at him in surprise. After a few seconds, Watson ventured, "I presume you will be explaining that."

"I will, but not at the moment. We need to agree on a course of action."

"Personally," said Loveday, "I don't feel like walking or running through Pall Mall in the rain, I can tell you that much."

"Then let's ride in relative comfort," said Holmes, starting off for the brougham. "If there's danger, we'll meet it head-on but halfway."

Watson fell into step beside him. "So your course of action is to stick our heads into the trap, and then improvise."

"Adapt," Holmes corrected.

Loveday crowded forward, trying to cover Watson and Holmes with the umbrella. She said quietly, "You could argue that it's not really a trap if you know it's a trap."

"I knew the ambush at Maiwand was a trap before I rode into

it," Watson replied. "I was still shot."

"Only twice, wasn't it?" enquired Loveday.

"Once was quite enough. I don't suppose there are any weapons amongst us?"

Loveday smiled cryptically. "That all depends on what you mean by weapons."

They reached the side of the coach. The door hung open. Instead of allowing Loveday to enter, Holmes gazed up at the man seated in the driver's box and said conversationally, "Good evening, Tangey. What have you done with Mr Cobb?"

The man stared down at him, struck speechless for a long a moment. He uttered a sound between a cough and croak. Holmes lifted a warning right hand. "No need to deny it. Just nod and answer my questions as quietly as you can. You're acting under duress?"

Tangey pulled down the scarf wrapped around the lower portion of his face. "Bless you, Mr Holmes, I am indeed being forced. Mr Cobb is all right but being held in the hansom back there with a knife at his throat. Two men inside, one in the box. I never saw them before but they are a rough lot. They claim they are following orders."

Holmes raised sceptical eyebrows. "Mr Cobb is being threatened to ensure your cooperation?"

Tangey cleared his throat. "They hold my wife, sir. I had a feeling you smelled something awry when you asked about her health at Baker Street."

"What are your orders?"

"Simple, sir. I will drive you and your friends to a street in Soho. We will be followed by the other cab to make sure I obey. Once we reach our destination, you will disembark. Mr Cobb will be released, I will return home, and my wife will be safe."

"And what happens to us?" Watson asked.

"I don't know, doctor," Tangey said sorrowfully. "But I was

told there will be no harm done if we all do what is expected of us. But they did not expect you to pierce my masquerade so quickly." The man paused and said in a voice choked with emotion, "I can't tell you how sorry I am about this...somehow they knew about my wife's condition and they—"

"Just so," Holmes said curtly. He gestured toward Loveday. "We should get underway before our watchers become suspicious."

Tangey shoulder's slumped in relief. "Thank you, sir...God bless you."

They climbed aboard the brougham, Loveday first followed by Watson, then Holmes. They had hardly gotten settled when Tangey whipped up the horses, and the coach plunged away at a furious pace through the misting streets.

"Now that we're safely caught in the bloody trap," Watson said acidly, "you can spare your fellow captives a few moments to explain why."

Holmes raised an eyebrow. "I don't know the why of the trap as of yet, but the moving parts are obvious. The puppet-master is well acquainted with our procedures and even some of our cases. Most probably, our lodgings as well the Diogenes are under near constant surveillance and that includes personnel such as Commissionaire Tangey and Mr Cobb's antique chapeau."

"Who would have the resources to do that?" Loveday asked. "The Hephaestus Ring?"

Holmes shook his head. "Not necessarily."

The coach lurched to the left, then back again. With a wordless utterance of annoyance, Loveday clapped a hand to her hat to keep it in place.

Holmes went on, "Watson, you may recall how in the case of the stolen naval treaty, Mrs Tangey was an early suspect in the crime, due to her fondness for drink. Even after her exoneration, her fondness continued and Commissionaire Tangey has sought help for her alcoholism ever since, employing the catch-all euphemism of a 'health condition.'"

"I remember," Watson said. "The wretched woman was little more than a drunkard. You intervened with Mycroft on poor Tangey's behalf so he could maintain his position at the Home Office and still be eligible for his Coldstream Guards pension."

"That was kind of you," said Loveday.

Holmes shrugged. "Easier than training someone new. At any rate, when Tangey delivered Mycroft's summons to Baker Street he appeared uncharacteristically distressed, and I sensed his state was not due to over-exertion."

"Ah." Watson nodded in satisfaction. "You asked him about his wife...something you have never done before this evening. He seemed very startled, even frightened."

"He acted a bit strangely at Lynch Court as well," said Loveday. "But I found it even stranger to see him climbing into a cab after he made his delivery to Baker Street."

"Whereupon that cab followed our coach to Pall Mall," Watson stated, "and while we were occupied at the Diogenes, Mr Cobb was replaced by Commissionaire Tangey." His eyes narrowed as a thought occurred to him. "Why go to the trouble of buying a new hat for the imposture instead of just taking the one worn by Cobb?"

Holmes chuckled. "The success of the switch depended on the hat. Our puppet-master knew no amount of coercion or threats could force Cobb to break his discipline or violate his oath of service. Therefore if something dire happened to the hat during the inevitable struggle to replace Cobb with Tangey, the plan would be undone. Therefore, it was far simpler to have a new hat on hand than concerning oneself with the safety of the old one. Besides, who notices the age of a coach driver's headgear?"

"I presume that's a rhetorical question," said Loveday with unmistakable sarcasm. "As for a question that isn't rhetorical —

what do we intend to do when we reach our destination?"

"I would say that all depends on the destination," Holmes retorted.

Loveday lifted her umbrella and put the thumb and forefinger of her left hand on the metal end tip. She began working it back and forth. "You asked about weapons, John."

He and Holmes stared as she pried the tip away to reveal a sharp, gleaming spike four inches in length. She said, "After I began bartitsu training with the single-stick, I had this umbrella specially modified for self-defence. The handle and shaft are reinforced with steel, making it a useful cudgel or makeshift rapier. Several of the ribs have very sharp points covered by rubber, and they can be swiftly removed from the canopy, if need be."

Holmes said grudgingly, "Ingenious."

"Elementary." Loveday reached into her reticule and produced a set of heavy brass knuckles. "I also have this."

"That is rather less so," commented Holmes. "But probably more effective in the long run than a trick umbrella. Give them to the doctor, please."

Watson took the knuckles and slipped the rings over the fingers of his left hand. He experimentally punched the palm of his right. He winced. "Ow. These will do." He glanced at Holmes. "What about you?"

"I'll see if I can't eke by on my own wits and training," Holmes answered, peering through the window. "We appear to have reached a rather questionable neighbourhood."

Loveday looked through the tinted glass and her lips compressed. "I'd call it forbidding."

With a clopping of hooves and the squeak of leather harness, the brougham traversed long lines of dull brick houses that were relieved only by the lamp glares of public houses at the corners of intersections. Tangey guided the horses down a narrow lane and then hauled back on the reins, calling out to the horses, "Hononny. Ho."

After setting the brake, Tangey clambered down and opened the coach door. Holmes, Watson and Loveday disembarked cautiously. They looked around at the rain-damp brickwork of the buildings rising on all sides of them. The drizzle had stopped. Gazing in the direction whence they had come, they saw the hansom clatter to a stop at Bateman Street.

Tangey pointed toward Firth Street. "I am to tell you to walk that way and keep walking until someone tells you to stop."

"That's it?" demanded Watson, fingers clenching around the brass knuckles. "What of Cobb?"

"He is supposed to be waiting for you here by the time you return and will drive you anywhere you to need to go." Tangey trudged toward the parked hansom. "I'm sorry again about all this. Please don't think ill of me."

Watson sighed. "All right, then. I suppose we'd better start walking and get this over with, one way or another."

Holmes and Loveday nodded in agreement. They began marching toward Firth Street, with Loveday between the two men. They had not gone far when she whispered, "Mr Holmes — I imagine you're already aware of this, but we are being followed."

Holmes nodded. "Since we left Tangey."

Watson asked lowly, "You don't think it's as commonplace as a pair of footpads, do you?"

"I fear not. Most probably an escort to make sure we're headed in the right direction."

Loveday's lips tightened, "If they meant us harm, surely it would have been easier to do so while we were inside the coach?"

"Too attention-getting," said Holmes. "Three agents of Her Majesty's Secret Service assassinated in one of the Crown's own conveyances? That would make headlines for weeks."

Watson nodded grimly. "But three people murdered by a gang of street thugs in Soho in furtherance of a robbery is a story easily controlled, and quickly forgotten."

"Except," Loveday said, "this thuggery is far too much work for street ruffians to undertake."

None of them had raised their voices much above a murmur, nor had they looked behind them as they continued to walk. Keenly aware of the dangers that could await them in the dark doorways of the buildings they passed, they kept their attention divided between the stealthy footfalls behind them and the silent shadows that lurked ahead.

A lone street-lamp a dozen yards away showed an alley mouth gaping open on their right. They ducked in and quickly went around the corner, flattening against the wet wall. They froze there, listening. The soft crunch of multiple shoe soles on pavement paused. After a moment, the sound began again, but slower and more cautiously.

Holmes, Loveday and Watson walked deeper into the labyrinth of Soho's back alleys and courtyards. Holmes said, "The next corner is Regent Street. We go left there, and hurry."

As they moved forward, four large men stepped out from the murk between two buildings and stood with their arms folded, blocking the way. Loveday stopped and glanced back. Three broadly built figures approached from the rear. All of them were dressed similarly in threadbare coats, battered bowlers and a couple with flat-caps

Watson looked over at his partners. "They don't appear to be armed, at least."

As soon as the word "armed" left his lips, a man loomed in their path. He brandished a flexible riding crop about three feet in length, covered by a layer of cross-stitched rawhide.

"Yer goin' in the wrong direction, chums." He slapped the flat tongue of the weapon against the palm of his hand. "Turn about."

"What if we prefer this route?" Holmes asked.

The man chuckled, a phlegmy sound of genuine amusement. He smacked the tongue of the crop against his hand again. "This is loaded with lead...it won't kill ye, but 'twon't tickle ye neither, if I decide to get unfriendly."

They looked behind them. The man standing at the centre of the other three had drawn a long-handled knobbed nautical cosh known as a Solomon's Bar. Holmes said softly, "Classic caught between a rock and a hard place."

Loveday hefted her umbrella. "I vote we chance it."

At that moment all seven of the men shuffled forward, half-circling them warily. The first man who had spoken said, "If ye don't turn yourselves about, we'll do it for ye...and we won't be gentle."

He reached for Loveday. She lashed out with the handle of the umbrella. The shock of the solid connection thrilled up her arm, and a grunt of surprised agony rewarded her. The man went down, clutching his fractured right wrist with his left hand. He almost immediately rolled back to his feet, grimacing in pain and shame.

In the same moment, Watson feinted for the face of one man and shifted his attack to the man beside him. In a flurry of jabs and uppercuts, he forced the man back, clasping his scarlet-streaming nose with both hands. He swore sulphurously in a Brummie accent.

Holmes knocked the wind out of the man carrying the loaded riding crop with a front-thrust kick to his solar plexus. As he doubled over he dropped the crop and Holmes snatched it up. Whirling, he squared with another man just as Loveday came up. As the man raised the Solomon's Bar cosh above his head, Loveday lunged forward in a fencer's pose, leading with the umbrella.

221B: On Her Majesty's Secret Service

Four inches of razor-pointed steel stabbed through the back of the man's hand. He bellowed in pain, dropping the cudgel. Sliding his punctured hand into his left armpit, he staggered to one side and cleared a path.

The three of them ran, Watson punching a man out of his way with his brass-weighted left fist. They sprinted into the nearest adjacent alley. After two turns, it opened directly onto the rear court of an old brick building bearing the legend in peeling white paint: DOMBEY AND SON STORAGE. A stack of crates lay on a platform at the base of a loading dock.

Holding the hem of her skirt high, Loveday raced toward it. She blurted breathlessly, "Let's take cover and regroup."

Not bothering to argue, Holmes and Watson joined her behind the crates, hunkering down and panting. Holmes still gripped the appropriated crop. He gave it an experimental snap and grunted in approval. They heard coarse male voices raised in shouts. Watson said, "They'll find us in a minute or two, you know."

Holmes raised his head above the edge of a box. He had only half-grasped the details of their surroundings when the platform suddenly began to drop beneath them. They heard the squeak and creak of cables and cogwheels. The freight elevator descended down a shaft with walls made of stone blocks. It dropped about three metres, then stopped with a clang.

Holmes and his friends carefully stood up, and squinted away as an arc-lamp blinked on, pinning them inside a white circle of blinding brilliance. In the darkness beyond, two men spoke in hurried whispers. One them said loudly and angrily, "Bleedin' eejits ended up where you wanted 'em in the first place, sir."

"So noted, Mr Carker."

The light's painful brightness dimmed. Holmes blinked, trying to clear his vision. By degrees his sight returned and he caught a glimpse of a figure moving away, walking quickly toward the left. A cultured voice said, "You may step off the platform. The freight lift brought you to the basement of my warehouse...if you had simply done as you were told, you could've taken the stairs."

Holmes, Loveday and Watson stepped forward tentatively. The room was not as their imagination had pictured the basement of a warehouse — the walls were pine-panelled and the ceiling was surprisingly high. Comfortable armchairs were set about, with a round mahogany table as their focal point. Teapot, cups and even saucers with biscuits sat atop it, as well as a bronze dinner bell.

At the table sat a man. Not a particularly impressive man at first glance, despite his expensive fawn-coloured suit with a red silk foulard at the throat. His eyes had the colour and quality of onyx. Slightly behind the chair rose an arc-lamp, its lens still glowing. His black gaze fixed on Holmes, and when their eyes met, Basil Zaharoff said, "You're later than I wished."

Holmes responded with a slight nod of acknowledgment. "Perhaps if your invitation hadn't been so subtle, we would have arrived on time."

Zaharoff smiled. "Possibly I was too melodramatic, but it was a practical method."

"Is terrorizing Commissionaire Tangey and Mr Cobb while holding Mrs Tangey hostage your idea of practicality?" demanded Watson.

Loveday glared at Zaharoff. "Not to mention having your men pursue us through the back alleys of Soho."

Zaharoff chuckled, but it sounded forced. "Mrs Tangey was never in any danger. I sent one of my female operatives posing as a hat saleswoman to pass the time with her and share a bottle of sherry."

Loveday smiled, "As my employer Mr Dyer says, women operatives are more satisfactory than men because they are less likely to attract attention."

"Your employer sounds like a perceptive man. At any rate, as soon as Mr Tangey agreed to cooperate, my operative quit the premises, but left behind the sherry."

Zaharoff's genial smile disappeared. "As for you lot, there was no need for violence. You were never in danger."

"Our violence was the result of erring on the side of caution," said Holmes coldly. "If your men are complaining, perhaps they should find another line of work. There was no need for the level of subterfuge which brought it about."

"Like you, I prefer to err on the side of caution, and that is why I rely upon my own private intelligence network, rather than knock at the door of 221B Baker Street, begging for an audience. I do not wish my presence in London known."

"Known to whom, Mr Zaharoff?" Loveday asked.

"In point of fact, that is one of the matters I wished to speak to the three of you about." He waved to the chair. "Please, Miss Brooke, take a seat. You too, Doctor Watson, Mr Holmes. Help yourself to refreshments."

They hesitated. After exchanging glances, Holmes shrugged and stepped forward, sitting down in the chair directly opposite Zaharoff. Loveday and Watson followed his example, but none of them sampled the tea or biscuits. He noticed but said nothing.

Leaning back in his chair, Zaharoff reached for a cut-glass humidor on a side table. He removed a cigar, then extended the container towards Holmes and Watson, who shook their heads politely. With a miniature scissors, Zaharoff neatly clipped one end of the cigar, inserted it beneath his moustache, and ignited the other end with a match. When a blue haze of smoke formed around his head, he spoke again.

"Our first meeting was not auspicious, and for that I apologize."

Loveday chuckled. "This second one is not much of an improvement, sir...however, I do owe you some thanks for interfering when Robur ordered his man to kill me. I presume you were motivated by practicality and pragmatism, not sentiment."

Zaharoff gingerly puffed at the end of his cigar. "A correct presumption. And it is that same practicality which draws me to speak with you tonight. I have found myself in an interesting quandary, and wish to discuss it with you."

"Get on with it, then," Watson said impatiently. "We have a train and a ferry to catch."

"Understood. I have an offer to make for your services, and you cannot consider it adequately until you have a complete grasp of the background."

Holmes settled back in his chair, stretching out his legs and crossing them at the ankles. He folded his arms over his chest. "You understand that we cannot speak on the behalf of any of our national security offices."

"Of course. Your legal powers are restricted by the very nature of your work. You cannot officially arrest anyone, but can take them into custody and have them bound over for arraignment by governmentally constituted tribunals. I am also aware that you seldom deal with matters of state."

"You seem to know a lot about us," Watson observed.

"I've made your business my business ever since that unfortunate night at Penhallick Wharf. I am still dealing with the repercussions of that incident. Now, I ask that you hear me out."

"Speak then," said Holmes.

Zaharoff exhaled a stream of smoke. "Nearly three years ago I was first contacted by a representative of the Hephaestus Ring. She is known to certain departments of the English government and police agencies in Europe as Madame Koluchy. She openly admired my work, my organizational ability and my modest talent for timing. She told me something of the Ring's goals, and I will admit to being most intrigued. I was promised that if I accepted her offer, I would be directly in line for a position with what she called their Echelon."

Loveday cocked her head at a quizzical angle. "Echelon?"

"That is the term for the Ring's ruling council...the heads of different divisions, so to speak."

"You know who they are?"

Zaharoff held up a hand. "Allow me to finish."

Loveday inclined her head in a gracious nod with only a slight, but unmistakable overtone of mockery. "Please do."

"The Ring's offer was moderately attractive," continued Zaharoff. "I gave it serious thought but after the affair at my private iron-works in Cornwall, I decided to reject it. My current position is, I feel, an enviable one. I am effectively at the top of my profession, popular, sought-after, and despite the opinion of Mycroft Holmes, respected. I also wield a fair amount of power, and am completely autonomous in my operations. If I were to agree to throw full-in with the Hephaestus Ring, I would lose a good deal of my independence of action, which is very precious to me."

"How did the Ring react to your decision?" Holmes asked.

"I haven't informed them of it, as yet. We are still doing business with each other but at a rather longer arm's-length than previously."

"What about the Ring's goals?" asked Watson. "Don't you share them?"

Zaharoff shook his head. "There are many things about the Ring of which I do not approve. The main one being their ultimate aim is to unify all industries and sciences under their sole control."

"Such an arrangement would encroach upon your own aspirations?" enquired Holmes.

Basil Zaharoff's eyes sparked with a brief flash of anger, quickly veiled. "Yes...and one of my aspirations is a knighthood. But the Ring has not proven easy to refuse. In the last couple of years, they have presented me with samples of their technology for use in my own vocation."

"Such as those hand-held repeating guns we found in the hold of the *Friesland?*" Watson asked.

"Those were prototypes, but yes. The weapons had been fabricated according to the Ring's design and they proposed I could use my resources to have them mass-produced for use in a future war...one in which I would share the profits."

"Generous of them," commented Loveday. "Where are the weapons now?"

Zaharoff shrugged. "I have no idea, and that was done deliberately. I ordered them removed from Penhallick but I did not say to where. I left that up to the Ring to decide."

Holmes said sardonically, "You are wise."

"I do not wish to become obligated to this group whom I distrust."

Watson asked dubiously, "If you distrust them so much, shouldn't you be monitoring their activities?"

"I allowed one of my men to be my eyes and ears within the Ring," Zaharoff continued, "but I fear he has been seduced, either by their philosophy or by Madame Koluchy or a combination thereof. I have not received a report from him in months, and that was a garbled communique sent through a back-channel, regarding the Paris Exposition, Thunderstrike and something called an Analytical Engine."

"A computing machine," said Loveday. "As a child I was acquainted with the daughter of Ada Lovelace, who collaborated on the engine's design with Charles Babbage. She was a brilliant mathematician."

Zaharoff waved away her words. "Be that as it may, if my man Rubadue has indeed turned his coat, then I may find myself the target of a scheme to eliminate my influence in global affairs altogether."

"From what I remember of Cuthbert Rubadue," replied Holmes, "if he were seduced, it was most likely not due to a woman or a social philosophy but by a matter of basic economics. Perhaps you could simply raise his rate."

Zaharoff sighed wearily, smoke curling from his nostrils. "My preoccupation with this entanglement has become a waste of resources. I want to be done with the Hephaestus Ring, Madame Koluchy, Robur, the Echelon — all of it. Precious time and attention are being diverted from operations of great complexity and their commensurate rewards."

"What services do you wish from us?" demanded Watson.

"All I wish from you, Doctor Watson, as well as from Miss Brooke and Mr Holmes, is your understanding and appreciation of my position. I am being wooed by this distasteful but stubborn group which you suspect me to be a part of. I want to assure you, that is not the case. At the present time, the Hephaestus Ring is only able to contact me by indirect, devious channels, which is the way it will remain. I have one last contractual obligation to fulfil. After that, I would like to suggest we consolidate our resources to stand against them."

"In other words," said Holmes with unmistakable sarcasm, "we go after the bigger game, and leave you alone."

Zaharoff chuckled. "Exactly. In exchange, I will provide more material assistance, such as names, locations, descriptions and plans of the Echelon."

Loveday, Holmes and Watson exchanged uneasy glances. Loveday ventured, "We'll have to consult a higher authority—"

"Why?" asked Holmes bluntly. He fixed a challenging stare on Zaharoff's face. "We have a tacit agreement, under the condition that you supply what information you have about Professor James Moriarty."

Zaharoff met the stare with a suspicious one of his own. "I know the name. It is a peculiar request. I expected you would be more interested in the man we know as Robur the Conqueror."

Loveday leaned forward. "Does he live?"

Zaharoff hesitated before saying, "I believe he does, but I have not laid eyes on him since that night in Cornwall, so he very well may not." He directed a slit-eyed stare at Holmes. "What is your interest in this man, Moriarty?"

"Have you met him?"

"Never."

"Nor have I, but you may consider compiling a dossier on the man as a show of trust."

"Trust needs to be mutual, Mr Holmes. At this moment, I suspect you don't believe me to be an honourable man, therefore you see no reason to treat me honourably."

Holmes sat up straight in his chair. He snapped, "Do you think you can trust the Ring not to destroy you, if you continue to refuse them?"

A hint of a smile touched Zaharoff's lips. "Allow me to say, rather immodestly, that I may take a great deal of destroying." He tapped off a half-inch of ash from this cigar. "Very well. I will alert my network to accrue all that can be accrued about this man Moriarty."

Holmes nodded and stood up. "I hope our next meeting will be under more amicable conditions."

"As do I." Zaharoff picked up the bell from the table and gave it a single shake.

Before the echoes of the chime faded, Holmes, Loveday and Watson felt rather than heard a door open behind them. Heavy-soled boots clumped on the floor. Zaharoff said, "Mr Carker, safely escort our guests up the stairs and back to their coach, please."

Loveday, Watson and Holmes arose, seeing a saturnine, dark-haired man in a frock coat and work shoes standing expectantly at the foot of the staircase. Holmes paused and turned back toward Zaharoff. Dispassionately, he stated, "You do realize that at some point in the near future, *you* will become the bigger game."

Zaharoff showed the edge of his teeth in a half-grin, half-snarl. "I do indeed, Mr Holmes. But I intend to be such big game no hunter in the world will dare put me in their sights." He made a shooing motion with his hands. "Au revoir. Until we meet again."

221B: On Her Majesty's Secret Service

PART THREE

DURING MY LONG *and intimate acquaintance with Mr Sherlock Holmes, I had never heard him refer to his relations other than his brother, and hardly ever to his own early life. This reticence upon his part had increased the somewhat inhuman effect which he produced upon me, until sometimes I found myself regarding him as an isolated phenomenon, a brain without a heart, as deficient in human sympathy as he was pre-eminent in intelligence. His aversion to women and his disinclination to form new friendships were both typical of his unemotional character.*

Or so I had erroneously and somewhat foolishly believed.

— John H. Watson, MD

I have seen too much not to know that the impression of a woman may be more valuable than the conclusion of an analytical reasoner.

— Sherlock Holmes

CHAPTER 13

The Irish Sea, 3 March

HOLMES LEANED ON the railing of the *PS Banshee's* foredeck and drew in deep lungfuls of air. The odour of brine and kelp and the wet, wild wind sent a shiver of excitement through him, although he wasn't quite sure why. Other than a to-and-from voyage to America in his youth, his experience as a sailor was limited.

The hull vibrated as the *Banshee's* steam turbines pushed it through the Irish Sea, the prow parting the waters in foaming waves. The muted roar of the paddle-wheel threatened to drown out the steady thump of the ferry's oscillating engine. The double smoke-stacks belched cinders and fumes, but fortunately the breeze blew them aft.

Although very close to dawn, Holmes could see only a gray emptiness of waters stretching to a deeper gray on the horizon, which he assumed was Ireland. The rising sun smudged the eastern sky with a faint orange hue. Fog drifted over the sea's surface as a light, gossamer mist.

Holmes took a cigarette from a case in an inner pocket of his long coat. Cupping his hands around the strike lighter he managed to set fire to the tip after only two attempts. He relished the bittersweet smoke mixed with the tang of salt. He stood and meditatively puffed on it, letting the restless panorama of rolling waves, the deep rumble of the ship, and the thundering power of the ocean fill him.

Holmes glanced behind him at the elevated bridge housing. Through the glass he made out the outlines of several crewmen. He assumed Watson and Loveday were still resting in their compartments below, trying to overcome mild cases of seasickness. For some reason, he had been spared, but then he had eschewed the left-over mutton stew that passed as a late supper in the dining car of the Holyhead train.

The *Banshee* was a big ship, over three hundred feet in length and the last of the paddle-steamers plying the sea between Holyhead and Dublin. She was loaded to the scuppers with crates of dry goods, pig iron, beans, bolts of cloth, and the passengers who sat amongst the deck cargo, if they couldn't afford a cramped, humid cabin. The voyage comprised only four hours, so most people didn't feel the expenditure worth it. Holmes felt too keyed up to sleep, so he prowled the deck, anxious, eager and excited.

After leaving Soho, they had been safely picked up by a disgruntled but unharmed Cobb with his old hat intact. They stopped by Baker and Gower streets for changes of clothing and a few odds and ends, including his magnifying glass and Watson's medical bag. They managed to reach the last train out of Euston Station with only minutes to spare.

The train was late arriving at the Port of Holyhead but the Dublin ferry's departure had been delayed long enough for them to board her. Holmes suspected a telegram or telephone call from the Diogenes Club had held up the *Banshee* at the dock until he, Loveday and Watson arrived.

Exhaling a wreath of smoke, Holmes wondered darkly whether he had done the right thing by striking a bargain with Zaharoff, insofar as receiving information regarding James Moriarty. He knew Loveday disapproved of him making such an arrangement without informing Mycroft, but he was accustomed to following his own instincts. He had never asked Mycroft for permission to do anything while growing up, and he was not about to start now. He respected his brother's intellectual and analytical gifts, but Mycroft's own confidence in them quickly became intolerable without a brake being applied.

Regardless of Watson's scepticism about Moriarty, Holmes possessed the ability to recognize and classify repeating patterns in both nature and events. Over the last five years he had sensed a conscious power behind a multitude of unsolved crimes of varying sorts — forgeries, robberies, and murders. They all shared certain commonalities, like the invisible signature of an artist. It wasn't until the affair of John Openshaw and the five orange pips that the signature had become visible. The problem lay not in deciphering the signature but in determining whether it belonged to Professor James Moriarty, late of Stonyhurst College; Colonel James Moriarty of the Royal Engineers; or Stationmaster James Moriarty of Worting Junction. Three Moriarty brothers, triplets, he suspected.

The sky lightened as a pale, weak sun climbed into the sky. The dark gray line on the horizon acquired more definition. Holmes squinted toward it, trying to discern details. A footfall sounded on the deck behind him. Before he could turn, a petite young woman padded up beside him, walking with an easy grace. She wore a deep red coat with a satin-lined hood that cast the upper half of her face into shadow.

"Good morning to ye, sir," she said politely in an unmistakable Irish lilt.

Quickly covering his surprise, Holmes nodded amiably. "Good morning, Miss. We're in sight of Ireland. I think we should dock in Dublin shortly after full daybreak."

Her lips curved in a smile. " 'Twill be good to see the hills of home again after so long away from them."

"You've been away?"

"Aye, in Australia these last three years. Mam and I went there to take care of her brother, Liam, who'd been hurt in the gold-diggings in Queensland."

She paused and tugged back her hood, revealing a roses and cream fair complexion with cornflower blue eyes framed by masses of honey blonde hair. Her face had a classical beauty except for an upturned nose and impudently smiling mouth. "I don't suppose ye'd have one of those to spare?"

Holmes narrowed his eyes in momentary confusion, then realized she had gestured to the cigarette in his right hand. "Of course, Miss."

He took out his case and allowed her to make the selection. As she placed it between her full lips, he extended the lighter toward her. Ignoring it, she plucked the cigarette from the index and middle finger of his hand, expertly applied the glowing tip to the one in her mouth, puffed, got it going and handed it back to him.

She inhaled deeply. "That is good quality."

"My tobacconist in London has a fine reputation."

Exhaling a stream of smoke from her delicate nostrils, she replied, "Well deserved. Thank ye, Mister—?"

Holmes returned the case and lighter to his coat pocket. "Holmes. Sherlock Holmes."

She showed no sign of recognition. "My name is Deirdre D'Alton."

Noting how her French pronunciation was on a par with Mycroft's, Holmes assumed she had practised for some time. "Pretty name."

" 'Tis a fine name for an actress, do ye think?" Her blue eyes seemed to sparkle even in the dim pre-dawn light.

Holmes felt a smile tugging at the corners of his mouth. "I would hesitate to offer an opinion, Miss."

She laughed, a gay trilling. "Ye look like an actor yourself, certainly with that classic profile. Another Henry Irving ye are."

Holmes chuckled dryly, resisting the impulse to mention his own experience at treading the boards as well as his many impostures. He vividly remembered what Baron Dowson said to him the night he before he was hanged: "What the law has gained the stage had lost." However, sitting in his little cell adjacent to the gallows, Dowson was drunk and understandably dejected by his failure to penetrate Holmes' disguise of a Russian saboteur-for-hire.

"So, you aspire to be an actress?"

"Nay, I *am* an actress — the theatrical world just hasn't discovered it yet."

"Perhaps you may make your mark at the Gaiety Theatre in Dublin," replied Holmes. "I understand it is much like the one in London...with an audience capacity of more than one thousand. In such a venue, the world at large will certainly discover your gifts."

Deirdre D'Alton flicked the cigarette over the rail. She turned a glorious smile on him. "Ye are very kind, sir."

Holmes' heart suddenly stumbled, then began to race. *She's lovely,* he thought.

"Unfortunately, I will only be passing through Dublin, on my way to Cork City to join my mam."

"She is not still in Australia?"

Deirdre shook her head. "Nay. Her brother — my uncle Liam — died and so we have returned home. I spent a few weeks in London, a guest of friends while my mam came on to Cork." She paused and asked, "Have ye ever been there?"

"I plan to make a visit very soon. West Cork."

Her smile faltered, replaced by a wary expression. "D'ye now? That is interestin'."

"Why is that?"

The deck rocked underfoot as a swell lifted the ferry. Deirdre stumbled, snatching at the rail to restore her balance. She fell against Holmes as he reached out to steady her. He felt her body heat, even through the fabric of his coat. He did not draw back. The rail prevented him.

She gazed up at him. "Ah, ye *are* a gentleman, aren't ye?"

Holmes groped for a response. He made a motion to gently disengage and saw Loveday Brooke and Watson approaching from aft. Although Loveday's face held no particular expression, she quickly averted her eyes when their gazes met. Watson appeared puzzled at first, then his mouth quirked in an amused grin.

Feeling foolish and angry because he did, Holmes quickly shifted position and stepped away from the girl. Watson said, "Message from the captain — we'll dock within the hour."

Holmes straightened his coat, noting how Deirdre did not turn to face Watson and Loveday. He said, "I'm sure that news came as a relief to your stomachs. By this way, this is Miss Deirdre D'Alton." He added a trifle hastily, "We've just met."

Loveday circled her, smiling a hard, humourless smile. "Shouldn't that name be pronounced Dalton? I said it that way earlier today and you did not correct me... Deirdre."

Holmes and Watson stared at the two women, eyes going wide. Hands on hips, Deirdre pivoted to gaze directly into Loveday's face. She laughed. "I didn't correct ye because ye were so bloody proud of yerself, Miss Brooke. I didn't want to spoil yer half-minute of triumph."

"So, you two ladies are acquainted?" Watson ventured mildly.

"We met briefly yesterday afternoon," replied Loveday. "You recall me mentioning a case where County Cork figured tangentially?"

"The bread and butter one?"

Loveday nodded. "The very same. This young woman was

involved in a case of identity transfer."

Curiosity overcame Holmes' puzzlement. "Explain."

Loveday gestured toward Deirdre. "Deirdre Dalton impersonated a certain Miss Millicent Monroe, passing herself off as the daughter of a family friend whose host family had not seen the girl in many years."

Holmes regarded her with a slit-eyed glare. "Why?"

Loveday took a breath and quickly outlined the broad details of how and why the two young ladies switched names and places for a period of time in furtherance of an elopement. At the conclusion, Holmes uttered a little grunt of approval. "Excellent work, Miss Brooke."

Loveday smiled in appreciation but said only, "Rather basic, actually. Once I realized it was a childish matter of role-playing not stolen diamonds, the resolution was swift."

"Apparently everyone performed splendidly in their chosen roles," said Watson. "Miss Monroe, Miss Dalton and even you, Loveday."

Loveday directed a stern stare toward Deirdre. "I feel that Miss Dalton did the more professional job. Despite what she told me earlier, I suspect the entire plan was hers. She was obviously confident enough in her talent as an actress to defraud an entire household."

Deirdre performed a pirouette and a little half-curtsy. "I'd call it disarming them." Lifting her chin and affecting an aristocratic pose by placing her right hand on her waist, she enunciated in a drawling English upper-class accent, "It was not quite as difficult a role as you might imagine, donchaknow, since Millicent and I had a long time to rehearse on the voyage over. I turned in a credible performance as Miss Monroe, while she was spared the reverse."

Holmes said, "Very well done...I admit your innocent act was effective on me."

"It wasn't an act, Mr Holmes, at least not entirely." She reverted to her normal speaking voice. "I saw Miss Brooke in the company of two handsome gentlemen when she boarded the ferry last night ...I was understandably curious if her being here had anything to do with me. She'd threatened to turn me over to the police, after all."

"I still might," Loveday said coolly.

"Mr Hawke would have to file charges and he's not likely to do so. He paid for my fare back to Ireland, remember?"

"There is still the matter of the one hundred pounds you received from Miss Monroe, although you claimed you hadn't touched a penny of it."

"I haven't...the money is with my mam in Cork City."

"And what of Millicent?"

"Off on her honeymoon, I hope. Fair-play to her and her man."

"Why do you say that?" Loveday asked.

Deirdre shrugged. "Her father planned to marry her off to one of his business partners, probably only a hundred years older than she. She claimed the old *bodach* was stupid and cruel. Since I bear the name of Deirdre of the Sorrows, who preferred death to a forced marriage, I determined to help Millicent flee hers. She offered me the hundred pounds for my part in the plan, insisting it was a small enough price for her freedom."

She turned back to Holmes. "When I saw ye standing out here alone, I decided to make yer acquaintance and learn what I could about why ye were here in the company of Miss Brooke."

"Did you find out anything useful?"

She shook her head. "Not much, but I did enjoy our conversation, nevertheless. I can't help but wonder that being as how Miss Brooke is a detective, the three of ye aren't involved in some sort of investigation in the wilds of West Cork."

"And if we are?" interjected Watson. "I'm Doctor John Watson, by the way."

"Charmed. Well, Doctor, if yer destination is indeed West Cork, I hope ye know yer way around. Ye three are just the type of Sassenach mollycoddles that skangers and Fenians are on the watch for."

"We have a contact there," Watson replied. "A policeman in Skibbereen named Keegan."

Deirdre snorted out a scornful laugh. "An RIC officer? Ye'd be better off paradin' around with bull's-eyes painted on yer backs."

Holmes asked, "What actions would you suggest mollycoddles like us take to minimize the risk to themselves?"

Deirdre grinned. "Find someone who knows West Cork and is known in West Cork, like someone whose family has roots in the heart of the rebel county."

"I wonder, could that someone be you?" demanded Loveday.

"Could and is. My late uncle Liam was born in Skibbereen. I speak Irish, my family's name is known along every borreen, every hill, dale and village up and down the coast, from Inchydoney to Dingle."

"A ridiculously inappropriate proposal, Miss Dalton. We are engaged on a confidential assignment for the Crown."

Holmes said thoughtfully, "That may be all the more reason to take Miss Dalton's offer under serious advisement."

Loveday stared at him, surprised into speechlessness for a long moment. "Please tell me you're joking."

Holmes said, "Watson and I operate a bit differently in Baker Street than you do from Lynch Court. We have our own network of local operatives to call upon when necessary."

"The Irregulars," Watson commented with a smile.

"Exactly. They know neighbourhoods, streets and alleys. Engaging Miss Dalton to render a similar service could simplify matters, especially since time is of the essence."

Loveday stepped close to Holmes and said quietly, "We need

to discuss this privately before it goes any further."

Holmes and she locked eyes for a long second. He glanced toward Deirdre Dalton. "Will you excuse us a moment, please?"

The young woman nodded and stepped several paces away, gazing out at the distant lights of the Dublin waterfront just emerging from the darkness. Loveday, Watson and Holmes huddled together. Loveday spoke first in a sharp whisper: "Are you mad, Mr Holmes? She's a civilian."

"So are we, Miss Brooke. But even you cannot deny the scheme she and her confederate concocted was clever and very effective."

Loveday nodded grudgingly. "I said as much to our client." She sighed and shook her head. "We must maintain a strict need-to-know policy with her."

Watson said, "Regardless, we may be putting her at risk. She has the right to know about that possibility."

"Agreed."

Loveday shook her head again. "She's barely one step above a criminal."

"We deal with criminals on a daily basis. I don't get that sense about her."

"After the flagrant way she flirted with you, I wouldn't expect you to. I don't trust her."

"There is no reason why you should," Watson said. "But under the circumstances, trust is not a priority. Amongst the three of us, we already have agreements with informants, double-agents, and freelance assassins."

"Let's not forget Basil Zaharoff," said Loveday. She sighed and glanced over at Deirdre standing at the rail. "Very well...but she's too young and in my opinion a bit too full of herself."

Holmes and Watson exchanged poorly repressed smiles. Loveday noticed. "What?" she challenged.

Holmes straightened up. "Nothing." He called, "Miss Dalton, would you join us, please?"

Deirdre walked over to the three people. Without preamble, Holmes said, "There is an element of danger in our mission to West Cork."

"Where in West Cork?", asked Deirdre warily.

"A village called Glandore."

"I know it. What kind of danger are ye expecting in such a wee place as that?"

"Unfortunately, I can offer no details. Does that dissuade you?"

"Not really," Deirdre replied frankly. "There was an element of danger anytime I took a walk in Australia, from sunstroke to snakebite."

"Would five shillings a day to act as our guide and liaison be acceptable?"

Without hesitation, Deirdre extended her right hand. "Accepted."

Holmes took her hand in his own and she formally pumped it. She said, "Done and done. And I may yet find an opportunity to practice my thespian arts."

"We intend to depart Dublin by direct rail for Skibbereen as soon as we reach Pearse station. If you like, we can stop in Cork City, so you may get word to your mother."

"I'll send a wire to her from Pearse station as to my changed plans."

A bell tolled from the bridge. Over the clangour, a crewman bawled, "We make port in half-an-hour, mark! One half-hour! Collect your luggage and prepare to disembark!"

Deirdre turned toward the starboard side of the *Banshee*, saying over her shoulder, "I have a portmanteau to retrieve. If we are separated, we'll meet on the dock."

221B: On Her Majesty's Secret Service

Holmes, Watson and Loveday hung back as the passengers assembled. Watching Deirdre disappear into the mill of people, Loveday said, "I'll say this for her — she's very game, even in the face of unknown danger."

Watson forced a chuckle. "It's unknown to us, too. But yes...Miss Dalton is very charming, don't you agree, Holmes?"

"The fair sex is your department, Watson," Holmes replied dismissively, very aware of Watson's juvenile attempt to trap him into saying something indiscreet. He eyed the sky, noting how the colour shifted from a charcoal grey to the colour of pewter. A motion in the low clouds caught his attention. For a fraction of a second, he caught an impression of movement, like a black distortion streaking just beneath the overcast.

He stiffened. "Did either of you see that?"

"See what?" demanded Loveday, looking up. She shaded her eyes with her hands

A piece of sky directly overhead shifted, scraps of a violet-hued cloud dropping away to reveal a winged craft soaring towards Dublin at a height of a thousand feet. Lights on the matte-black hull flashed red and white.

"What the bloody hell?" murmured Watson in wonder.

The craft flipped over on its port side wing, ascending at the same time. It changed course, and with a sound like the distant ripping of coarse cloth, surged off to the northwest, where it was quickly lost in the distance. The three people stood and continued to gaze skyward. A few curious passengers looked up as well, but seeing nothing, they went on about their affairs.

After a long moment, Holmes said grimly, "I think we know what the danger is now, Watson...as well as the man who poses it."

The less experienced a doctor is, the higher are his notions of professional dignity.

— John H. Watson, MD

CHAPTER 14

County Cork, Ireland

THE HEADWATERS OF the Arghistan swirled with blood. The screams of drowning people blended with the rushing of the current to make a babbling cacophony of terror.

Watson placed his feet carefully on the backs the thrashing flood victims, using them as stepping stones to cross the waterway. He did not look at their faces but he knew who they were, all the same — his comrades from the Fifth Northumberland Fusiliers, his colleagues from St. Bartholomew's and even the entire faculty of the University of London Medical School.

But since he had to get to the other side of Arghistan River to visit his brother Henry, he was left with no choice but to use the drowning and dying people as stepping stones. He felt bad about using them so, but they didn't seem to mind.

As he put his weight on the back of a man who looked like Thaddeus Sholto, he lost his footing. The man floundered beneath him, pitching Watson into the river. The current swept him away with all the other dying people, carrying him further away from his brother. A pink silk scarf was tossed from the opposite bank. He caught it by instinct. Lifting his head clear of the surface, he saw Mary resolutely tugging on the scarf. She called to him but he could not hear her.

Watson's surge of relief was replaced by cold horror when the grinning black dwarf he knew as Tonga rose from the river midway to the bank and began spitting poisoned darts at him through a long blowgun. The scarf parted and the bloody surface of the Arghistan closed over his head.

He felt a strong hand grip his shoulder and his body made a blind lunge for the surface. Only when he saw Holmes leaning over him, hand on his shoulder, did he realize he was not in Afghanistan and not drowning.

"Are you all right?" Holmes asked, straightening up.

Watson blinked at Holmes and then squinted away from the sunshine streaming in through the train carriage's windows. He heard the steady clatter of wheels and the creak of springs. Pushing himself into a full sitting position on the cushioned seat, he cleared his throat. "Why wouldn't I be?"

Holmes put his hands into the pockets of his black-and-white checked Norfolk jacket, regarding him with a hesitant smile. "I heard you say something."

Watson knuckled his eyes. "I was only dreaming."

"I thought as much. You called out for Mary. Would you care for a bite of breakfast or a spot of tea?"

Looking to the front of the coach, Watson saw Tennyson, the valet, attending to Loveday and Deirdre. They sat a low table made of dark, highly polished wood. The clean-shaven black man in trim butler's livery lifted the silver cover away from a serving tray. Arrayed upon it were a porcelain teapot and cups as well as saucers filled with fried eggs and wedges of toast. He caught a whiff of freshly smoked kippers and his stomach somersaulted. He had almost recovered from his bout of sea-sickness, but the jolt and jounce of the railway that carried him and his companions into rural West Cork set his belly to roiling again.

"No breakfast, thank you," he said to Holmes. "Perhaps some tea when I'm more awake."

Holmes nodded in understanding and turned away. "It's been a very tiring last twelve hours."

"Only twelve?" Watson asked, feigning surprise.

"Closer to thirteen, if that makes any difference."

Swallowing a yawn, Watson ruminated how the hours since arriving at the Diogenes Club seemed to be far more than twelve or thirteen — they felt endless. A weariness had settled into his bones, borne of the long train ride from London to Holyhead followed by the ferry trip to Dublin. He had tried to sleep in the little compartment aboard the *Banshee* but his nausea prevented him from fully relaxing.

After disembarking from the ferry, the four of them took a coach to Pearse station, arriving a little after six o' clock in the morning. After asking about the location of the *Wraith*, they were quickly conducted by the stationmaster himself to the rail line, upon which waited a massive steam locomotive, awesome in its size.

From the tip of the pilot obstacle-remover to the rear wall of the engineer's cab housing, the machine measured twenty-five feet. The leading drive wheels were even taller than Holmes.

Decorated with yellow lightning stripes, the words *HMSRW Wraith* were emblazoned in scarlet paint on the side of the cab. All the brass parts from drivers to rods to the rivet heads shone with a bright polish. A lion and unicorn sigil was inscribed on a proud silver plate bolted onto the coachwork. The locomotive reminded Watson of a slumbering prehistoric beast, a behemoth of black cast iron skin and heavy brass bones.

There was a Pullman passenger coach-car coupled to the fuel tender behind the locomotive, a long streamlined affair with the exterior painted a deep red with yellow trim. The interior held four comfortable, cushioned bench-style seats, upholstered in deep green plush that matched the carpet. The walls were decorated with artful wainscoted panels and the windows were draped by green-and-yellow tasselled curtains. The rear of the car was equipped with a small but functional kitchen and washroom, both partitioned off from the rest of the carriage.

They were greeted by Tennyson, who welcomed them aboard and explained that the train's permanent service staff consisted of an accomplished engineer, a fireman, a mechanic, and himself. He expressed a bit of surprise at the presence of Deirdre, since he had been told to expect only three passengers, but he accepted the addition without challenge.

Tennyson described the locomotive as part of the "Teutonic" class, a recent upgrade from the earlier "Dreadnought" class, equipped with a duplex-drive. A much improved boiler system increased the train's overall efficiency and speed. For the security of important passengers, the coach's exterior walls were composed of bullet-impervious metal panels. The glass in the windows was double-paned and augmented by a mixture of Prince Rupert's Drops. The undercarriage springs ensured a smooth ride.

At the time, Watson had been too long without sleep, decent food and peace of mind to pay much attention to praises sung about a mere train. Deirdre seemed impressed but she was so excited by the prospect of an adventure with agents of Her Majesty's Secret Service, the details of their means of transport did not overwhelm her. Once everyone had chosen their places in the carriage, the trip to County Cork began. Watson realized he had been too hasty in his dismissal of the locomotive's qualities.

A prolonged groaning came from deep within the machine, followed by a nerve-stinging squeal of steel grinding against steel. The great wheels spun, sparks spewing from the point where the rims met the rails. A clattering jolt shook the train from the prow to the passenger car.

The *Wraith* shuddered and the locomotive surged forward,

wheezing and panting. Smoke boiled from the stack. The iron wheels turned slowly on the rails, finding traction as the locomotive strained to pull the fuel tender and the swaying passenger car. The train rolled along the stretch of tracks built on an elevated causeway, building momentum as it moved out of the rail-yard and the city proper. Within minutes, the locomotive increased its speed and the side-to-side sway of the carriage all but disappeared.

Not long after that, Watson had fallen asleep, his head against a window, eased into slumber by the train's iron gallop. For the sake of his dignity as a physician, he hoped he hadn't snored or slumbered with his mouth open. He assumed he hadn't cried out during his nightmare. Generally, he did not remember his dreams unless they were particularly vivid, and then he rarely dissected their imagery. Even the appearance of Tonga, whom Holmes had shot during the chase on the Thames a year before, faded from his memory.

He shifted position, massaging a kink in the back of his neck. He felt sticky and uncomfortable, as he always did after sleeping in his clothes. He had fetched a set of tweeds designed for country wear from Baker Street but hadn't yet changed into them. It appeared Holmes, Loveday and Deirdre had already traded in their travelling clothes for garb more suited to rusticity. He stretched, wincing at the flare of pain in his shoulder. The wounds inflicted by Jezail bullets never let themselves be totally forgotten, only endured or ignored.

Running a hand over his jawline to determine whether he needed a shave, he suddenly realized the growth of bristles on his upper lip irritated him. He decided to razor away his fledgling moustache. He could always regrow it when the process would be less of a distraction.

Watson had accepted hardship while in the field in Afghanistan — sleeping on the ground with a rock as a pillow, attending to bodily functions behind bushes or while sitting on logs, even using using dry sand to wash his feet. Still, not a single hour had passed since being invalided out of the Army that he had ever missed even a minute of those rough-and-tumble days. He knew he was capable of repeating them if necessary — he just hoped it would never be required.

Now with the hands of the clock on the carriage wall pointing toward ten in the morning, the shadows of dawn had long receded from the vast green fields and burned away the last of the fog. The sun climbed high enough in the sky to at least tease the possibility of a bright day, and his spirits rose.

The railway passed into a tunnel punched through a huge granite outcrop. After less than a minute, the train emerged into the light on the other side, and Watson gave himself to the scrutiny of the passing countryside rippling by like easy green waves.

The train chugged through a shallow valley, with escarpment ridges to the north and south. Farmlands rolled past the windows on either side of the train, a vast blanket of green and early spring growth. Herds of sheep and red cows grazed on the flanks of hills. He saw more trees between the open fields, climbing up the slopes.

The train rumbled over a trestle spanning a blue, fast-rushing river and he idly wondered if there were any differences between salmon-fishing in Scotland and Ireland. He didn't feel particularly enthused to find out.

He had visited the city of Belfast whilst in the Army, but had seen little of the legendary Irish countryside. Although it struck him as a bucolic, placid landscape, mind-clouds of worry prevented him from enjoying what he now saw of it through the windows.

Tennyson walked past him on his way to the kitchenette and said, "We should arrive in Cork City for a brief stopover within the hour, sir."

Watson thanked him and his attention was captured by a gay

laugh from Deirdre. She chatted animatedly with Loveday and Holmes at the breakfast table. The journey was all just a lark to her. Holmes and Loveday appeared cheerful as well, as if they were enjoying a holiday excursion.

Suppressing a profanity-seasoned sigh, he took his valise from beneath his seat and went quickly to the wash-room to shave, comb his hair and change into his brown tweed jacket, trousers and hiking shoes.

Watson joined his companions at the table. If anyone noticed the lack of whiskers between his nose and upper lip, they made no mention of it. Deirdre greeted him with a friendly, "Did ye sleep well, John?"

She looked so damnably fresh and fetching in her green cardigan and knitted red tam, he felt obliged to growl, "Actually, young lady, I prefer Doctor."

Deirdre swiftly dropped her gaze. Loveday regarded Watson disapprovingly as he sat down beside her. She handed him a cup of tea. "It's still hot, but you could use some sweetening — Doctor."

"I apologize. I feel a bit rusty and mean this morning. Miss Dalton...you and I haven't been properly introduced, other than an exchange of names and I fear I'm being a bit short with you."

"We've had little time or opportunity for much more than that," pointed out Holmes, sipping at his own tea. "It's been rather a full last few hours."

"We should remedy that post-haste," Watson said, dropping a sugar cube into his tea. "We haven't discussed with each other or Miss Dalton what we saw from the deck of the ferry this morning."

Holmes paused, the rim of the cup at his lips. His eyes flicked first to Loveday, then to Deirdre. She gazed at Watson in puzzled surprise. "What did ye see?"

Holmes lowered his cup. He said quietly, "Need to know, old fellow."

"Which she does, in my opinion," Watson replied, turning in his chair toward the kitchenette. "Tennyson, how long until we reach Skibbereen?"

The man peered around the edge of the partition. "Our stop in Cork City shouldn't take longer than fifteen minutes. I estimate we'll arrive at Skibbereen station no later than noon."

"From there, I'll be yer guide to Glandore," Deirdre said. "We'll have to engage a coach or go by horseback."

"I'm sure Inspector Keegan has arranged transportation," Loveday said.

Watson nodded. "Presumably, the inspector will require a need to know why we're there, yes?"

Yes," replied Loveday reluctantly.

"Under the circumstances, so should our young guide. If she doesn't like what she hears, she can disembark at Cork City and join her mother."

Holmes placed his cup in the saucer. "Very well. Miss Dalton, my friends and I are searching for an Austrian scientist who may be staying in Glandore, most likely under an alias. His name is Nikola Tesla. He is not a criminal, but he is in hiding. Unfortunately, Tesla is also sought by a man who most certainly is a criminal. He is known as Robur. His infamy stretches back some twenty years — probably before you were born — when he terrorized several nations of the world with a flying machine of his own invention."

"Flyin' machine?" Deirdre echoed, her eyes widening. "Not like a hot-air balloon?"

"Not like a balloon at all. Robur was born of French aristocracy, with the hereditary title of baron, which means very little since the peerage system was abolished forty years ago. Still, he was a child of privilege and a prodigy. By all accounts he was an engineering genius by the time of adolescence. While testing an ornithopter he had built, he went over a cliff and broke both his legs. He was very short as an adult, as a result of his atrophied legs, although he created special braces to allow him to walk."

Deirdre's eyes narrowed. "Ye mean he's one of them wee men?"

Loveday chuckled. "If you mean he's a short fellow, yes. But his ego is anything but wee."

Watson said, "Robur is most decidedly a megalomaniac, which may well be related to his short stature...but that didn't prevent him from becoming a respected military engineer in the French army during the Crimean War. But like most men of genius, he was a misfit in the military and had no patience for the chain-of-command. During the demonstration of a new type of bomb-carrying glider he had developed, he disobeyed orders and was seriously injured in an explosion which killed several soldiers. He was court-martialled and dishonourably discharged. Yet another insult to his ego."

"Regardless of his ego or his height," Holmes broke in a trifle impatiently, "Robur is a technological genius...he has produced inventions far ahead of their time. The only mind that could rival his is the man known as Captain Nemo."

"What made Robur a criminal?" Deirdre asked.

"Incensed by his treatment at the hands of the army, he created a flying machine he called the *Albatross*. In order to intimidate nations to disarm, he threatened to drop bombs on their militaries if they did not accede to his demands. Fortunately, the machine was damaged and sank into the ocean."

"Robur was believed dead," Loveday interposed, "but he survived by hiding in plain sight. He reclaimed his family name of Maupertuis and title of baron."

"With the help of a criminal organization," said Holmes, "Robur has apparently perfected a new flying machine, an aeroship more advanced than his first one. Miss Brooke, Dr

Watson and I saw this craft flying above us at dawn this morning as the ferry approached the port of Dublin."

Watson said grimly, "It is obvious Robur is either following us or his destination is the same as ours. Or both."

Deirdre pursed her lips thoughtfully. "Is this wee mad feller floatin' around in the sky really such a villain as you make him out to be?"

"He's a killer," stated Loveday flatly. "He ordered one of his men to drown me. I was an inconvenience, and his reflex action was to get rid of me. Like swatting a fly."

Deirdre swallowed hard. She looked toward Holmes. "He means harm to the Austrian scientist fella, then."

"He means to bend Nikola Tesla to the will of his criminal organization...and that certainly means harm to both his person and the rest of the world."

Deirdre shrugged. "That settles it then. Ireland is part of rest of the world, last I looked."

Holmes laughed appreciatively. "Very perceptive, young lady."

Watson and Loveday joined in with the laughter, and the tension around the table dissipated. Watson said, "We still don't know exactly what or who we may be facing...I feel distinctly underdressed, even though I packed my reliable old Adams."

"All I have is my trick bumbershoot and brass knuckles," Loveday said.

Tennyson leaned in. "Beg pardon, ladies and gentlemen, but I believe I can help to supply your armament deficiencies. If you will follow me."

Tennyson walked purposefully toward the rear of the car. Mystified, Watson, Holmes and Loveday followed him. Deirdre elected to stay seated and finish her kippers on toast. Before they reached the kitchenette partition, Tennyson paused and faced the wall, pressing his fingers against a protruding knob within an ornate design element.

With a faint series of clicks, a long rectangle of the coach wall fell open, not unlike a drawbridge. Small chains connected it to a retracting pulley within the recess. They stared at the array of weapons clipped neatly to the panel. Loveday uttered a wordless exclamation of surprise and reached for a Bull-dog double-action revolver with hard rubber grips. She hefted it, popping open the five-round cylinder to make sure the weapon was unloaded, then sighted along the front and rear targetting notches, testing the trigger action.

"This will do," she said. "Manageable weight, accurate and easy to conceal. Thank you, Tennyson. I presume you will supply me with ammunition?"

He nodded. "All you may need, Miss Brooke."

Holmes extracted a matched pair of flat, ivory-handled throwing knives with five inch black blades. Both were sheathed within thin leather forearm scabbards.

Watson angled an eyebrow. "Really, Holmes? Didn't you bring the Webley?"

"I did, but it spoils the line of my jacket." Holmes carefully thumbed the edge of a blade and cast a questioning glance at Tennyson. "Sheffield?"

Tennyson inclined his head. "Of course, sir. Nothing but the finest steel for our passengers."

Watson grunted, picking up a nickel-plated Remington derringer. "You must have some interesting passengers, Tennyson."

"If I may be so bold, sir...you have no idea."

Smiling, Watson weighed the gun in his palm and gave it a swift visual examination. "A Model Type II, over-and-under barrels. Yes, this could be quite useful as an adjunct to my tried-and-true service revolver."

The shriek of the locomotive's whistle announcing their imminent arrival at the Cork City station came to them. They felt the train lurch and begin to slow. After thanking Tennyson, they retook their seats at the table.

With the weight of the derringer in his jacket pocket, Watson felt a bit more equipped to face whatever awaited them. He noticed that Loveday and Holmes seemed a bit more relaxed as well. Sipping his tea before it went completely cold, he said, "A firearm isn't an instrument associated with the dignity of the medical profession, but in this instance, I prefer it to a stethoscope."

With a napkin, Loveday rubbed the Bull-dog pistol's front sight. "I prefer not to use one at all, but as my father was wont to say, it's better to have a tool and never need it than need a tool and not have it." She looked over at Holmes, who had rolled up his coat sleeve to strap a sheathed knife to his forearm. "But throwing knives up your sleeves, Mr Holmes? Isn't that a rather an..." She paused, groping for the right word: "*Ungentlemanly* choice of self-defence accoutrements?"

"I don't imagine I will be using them against gentlemen, Miss Brooke. I suppose I should have brought along the loaded riding crop I took from Zaharoff's man?"

"Whether you are skilled in the use of the knives is the point I'm making."

Holmes regarded her with feigned confusion. "What is today's date, pray tell?"

"Now you've done it," Watson said to Loveday reproachfully.

"The same as it was when we boarded the train," said Loveday. "The third."

Holmes snapped his right hand up and forward. The knife sped across the width of the coach and struck a paper calendar hanging on the opposite the wall. The tip of the blade embedded itself in the centre of the small square enclosing the numeral 3.

"Is it still the third, pray tell?," Holmes asked innocently.

Loveday rolled her eyes. "Point taken."

Deirdre Dalton laughed and clapped her hands delightedly. "Knives and guns and flying machines! Oh, this is going to be so much fun!"

221B: On Her Majesty's Secret Service

Horses: dangerous on both ends and crafty in the middle.

— Sherlock Holmes

CHAPTER 15

THE BRAKES CAUGHT and held as the *Wraith* ground to a hissing stop in front of the depot in Skibbereen. Men and women standing on the platform stared in surprise at the massive locomotive as it pulled up, disgorging Tennyson, who placed a set of portable steps at the coach door. Loveday and Deirdre exited first, followed by Watson and Holmes, who carried the luggage. The noonday sun hung bright in a surprisingly cloudless sky. The temperature felt much milder than in England. The air held the scent of hot grease and peat smoke.

Tennyson gestured to the railyard behind the station and said, "We will find an appropriate siding upon which to wait."

Holmes said, "We'll keep you apprised when we can. I presume you will wire Mycroft that we've safely arrived?"

"Wire who, sir?" Tennyson asked flatly, his expression studiedly blank.

Holmes smiled. "I misspoke. Thank you, Tennyson."

They moved into the waiting room of the station which was occupied only by the ticket seller and a handful of men, women and babies. Watson was on the verge of asking the old man behind the ticket window if anyone had asked for them, when a voice behind them called, "Mr Sherlock Holmes?"

They turned and saw a middle-aged, middle-sized man

wearing a rumpled herringbone suit coat and baggy beige trousers. His tousled brown hair needed a comb and his pale, puffy jowls needed a shave. He looked as if he had awakened moments before from a not-too-restful slumber and stumbled over to the depot.

"I am he," said Holmes, stepping forward and extending a hand. "These are my associates, Misses Brooke and Dalton, and Dr Watson."

The man pumped his hand and released it quickly. "I'm Inspector Keegan of the RIC." His accent sounded more British than Irish. He eyed Deirdre distrustfully. "I was told to expect only three of you."

"Miss Dalton was engaged as our local guide on the trip over," said Holmes.

Keegan did not shift his gaze from Deirdre. "I recall a Liam Dalton living hereabouts twenty or so years ago."

"My late uncle," said Deirdre quietly, with a touch of sorrow in her voice. "He went out to make his fortune in Australia and passed away there."

Keegan grunted softly. "He was wanted for questioning in regards to his part in the Fenian Rising. He was suspected of murdering a constable."

"As I just told you," Deirdre said, a sudden edge to her voice, "my uncle has passed. The Rising happened before I was born."

Holmes said coldly, "I'm sure you'll agree that neither Miss Dalton nor her uncle could have any relevant information for the Constabulary."

Keegan looked at him with a glint of anger in his eyes. "Skibbereen is called the 'cradle of Fenianism' due to the rising of 1867. We have long memories here."

"On all sides," Watson said. "which has no bearing whatsoever on why we've been despatched from England."

"So let's get to it, shall we?" asked Loveday.

Keegan's lips worked as if he intended to say something else — or spit — then he jerked his head toward the door. "Let's take a walk. Too many ears about."

Deirdre slipped her arm through Holmes'. "Let's," she said, a defiant note in her voice.

Keegan led them through the frosted glass-fronted door and off the platform toward a gravel-covered footpath. As they walked along it, under the still-leafless branches of a great oak, the inspector said, "I received two wires from London — one last night and one early this morning. Both were from the Defence Intelligence Branch and both signed 'M.' Is this someone known to you?"

"Very well," said Loveday lightly.

"A little too well, on occasion," Watson said.

"He's like a brother to me," Holmes commented casually.

"The first wire was in regards to a story printed in the Southern Star news-sheet about a German professor conducting electrical experiments at the Druid's Altar site in Glandore. This 'M' of yours was anxious to know if my office knew his current whereabouts."

"And?" prodded Watson.

"I replied no," said Keegan. "The incident in question happened a week ago and the scientist in question — Hasellmeyer? — was not engaged in an unlawful activity, so there was no reason for us to look into it."

A startled rabbit leaped from the cover of a clump of grass and bolted across the path. Keegan jumped slightly in surprise, his right hand instinctively going for the pocket which held his pistol. Deirdre chuckled and said, "One of the Other Crowd, keeping an eye on us."

"Other crowd?" Loveday repeated.

Keegan uttered a scoffing sound. "The lass means fairies."

"The Fae," Deirdre corrected. "They take the form of animals, so as to spy on us mortals and make sure we behave."

Holmes nodded. "Understandable in today's world. Inspector, what was the nature of the second wire from London?"

"Informing me of the arrival of three agents of the Crown and requesting I give you full cooperation. So, in that spirit, I despatched my only day-duty constable over to Glandore and Leap village early this morning, to ask questions about this Hasellmeyer fellow while I questioned the editor of the *Southern Star*... he could offer no intelligence other than what was published."

"Did the constable you sent to Glandore learn anything?" Loveday wanted to know.

"Only that a foreigner arrived in the village over a fortnight ago, staying at Clancahill Castle hotel. It was said he visits the ancient sites in the area, like Knockdrum, the Three Fingers Standing Stones and most frequently, the Druid's Altar."

"A Serb?" inquired Watson.

Keegan shrugged. "No idea...couldn't even get his name. Glandore is a busy fishing and boating port, so it isn't difficult to move about unnoticed. The foreigner most likely is the Hasellmeyer you're looking for."

"Is the hotel a real castle?" Loveday asked.

Keegan smiled but it looked forced. "At one time, I suppose. The place has changed hands many times since the 12th century, so it's fairly typical of all castles in the region. An Irish-American hotelier named McShinnock acquired it about five years ago and modernized the place. He lives there with a small staff."

"Is he popular in the village?"

"He lost a leg fighting in the American Civil War and made his fortune in the following years...I believe the Yanks call it 'carpetbagging.' Now he fancies himself a descendant of Irish chieftains...he commissioned a set of portraits supposedly of his ancestors that he has hung in the receiving room. He's quite the crippled old eccentric."

Keegan's smile widened. "The locals have taken to calling him King Kevin."

"Your constable must have spoken to his Irish half," commented Deirdre. "Otherwise you wouldn't have gotten a name of the foreign visitor."

Keegan said sourly, "After all these years here, I'm accustomed to the clam-mouth treatment from the locals, but not from a Yank. I suspect he's a supporter of the IRB...the Irish Republican Brotherhood. Much of their financing comes from America, you know."

"How long have you been in Skibbereen?" asked Watson.

"I was assigned here from the Wicklow RIC barracks in '66...I was just twenty-one years of age. The next year was the Rising and a fellow officer was shot dead whilst standing next to me, lighting a cigarette." He paused a few seconds and added in a faraway tone, "Theo was my age."

"That must have been horrific," Loveday said sympathetically.

"I stayed on through the whole thing, trying to find the man who put the bullet through Theo's head. Years went by and I worked my way out of uniform and became an inspector. Never did find the killer."

The path wound around the foot of a low gentle hill, and dipped into a green declivity. They stopped at the top of the grade and looked ahead of them. The river Ilen sparkled amid rush-crowded banks. In the distance, on the opposite shore, they saw a churchyard surrounded by an ancient stone wall, as well as row upon row of small grey headstones.

Deirdre murmured, "The famine burial ground at Abbeystrewery cemetery...the 'pits,' Me mam said there must be ten thousand people buried there, thrown into mass graves without any coffins or even words said over them."

If Keegan heard her, he paid no attention. He continued to

march along. Beyond the riverbank stretched Skibbereen proper, with narrow, twisting streets lined on either side by blocky brick buildings and shopfronts. Freight wagons and donkey-led carts rumbled along the cobblestone street. As a market town, the air carried the lingering under-scent of livestock and cabbages.

When the inspector led them past the doorways of pubs and eatries, Holmes noticed people quickly withdrawing into the darkness of the interiors or pretending to be engrossed in other activities, like rolling cigarettes or tying boot-laces. No one spoke to them, even though the inspector addressed a few men by their first names in desultory greetings.

They walked past a pub where the skirl of pipes, the music of a fiddle and the drumming rhythm of a bodhran spilled out the open door and into the street. Impulsively, Deirdre danced a few graceful steps of a slip jig, drawing appreciative laughter and a smattering of applause from passers-by. She performed an exaggerated curtsy and flashed a mischievous grin at her admirers. " 'Tis good to be back home."

Renewing her tight hold on Holmes's arm, Deirdre whispered tensely, "Keegan's paradin' us around, ye know...showin' us off to tell the Fenians we're under the protection of the RIC."

"Isn't that to our advantage?" Holmes whispered back.

She shook her head. "It depends on the Fenian mood today. They may look at us as a challenge."

Most of Skibbereen's businesses were strung along High Street with livery stables out on the edge of the town, on the Baltimore Road. Keegan pointed to a livery yard that boasted a big barn with the name CRONIN'S painted across the front. They saw several carriages and buggies for rent in an adjacent lot. "We can get our transportation here."

Watson raised an eyebrow. "You're going with us?"

"I intended to, aye. The route can be tricky. The legendary Irish country roads, you know."

Loveday gestured toward Deirdre. "We engaged this young lady to guide us."

Keegan sighed. To Loveday's ears, it sounded like one of relief. "Very well," he said. "I have the town's own affairs to attend to. Some folk out near Toe Head reported seeing a sort of flying machine this morning so I have to look into it."

Holmes, Watson and Loveday exchanged swift glances. Holmes asked, "Where is Toe Head in relation to Skibbereen?"

"East of here. Out on the coast on the edge of the sea, near Tragumna. They claimed they saw it dive right into the water."

"Did they report it as winged?"

"Not that I'm aware." Keegan snorted. "They were the ones who did the flying, belike — from over-drinking of the poitin." He turned away. "You could take rooms at the Clancahill if the hour is too late to return."

The man said his goodbyes without shaking hands and marched back in the direction from which they had come. Watson gazed after him thoughtfully. "I don't think that man enjoys his job much."

Loveday replied, "We can't blame him." She looked toward the fenced-in enclosure holding a dozen horses. "Do we want to travel by buggy or saddle?"

Watson squinted toward a roan gelding. "I haven't been on horseback since Afghanistan, almost eight years ago."

Holmes asked, "What mode of transport do you recommend, Miss Dalton?"

"Please call me Deirdre. I would suggest horseback, because the roads are not the best and even the best are still bad. West Corkers call carriages 'suicide gigs' because they tend to turn over with a change in the weather. With horses, we are not bound by the roads and can go cross-country by taking to the open fields."

Holmes nodded reluctantly. "Seems logical, but horses and I

have an uncertain relationship."

Loveday asked, "How long has it been since you've been a-saddle, Mr Holmes?"

"I don't remember." He began walking toward the animals. "But I was born in North Riding, Yorkshire, after all."

Loveday grinned. "Ah, Yorkshire...and another piece of the puzzle falls into place."

"Do you ride, Miss Brooke?"

"Every other Sunday through Hyde Park."

Cronin the liveryman was a spindly gentleman with salt-and-pepper whiskers who chewed snuff. He greeted them cordially, if a trifle uneasily. "Aye, we have horses and tack for daily rental...I require a twenty pound deposit beforehand — unless you're on RIC business, then it's fifty pounds."

Deirdre laughed. "Nay, not police business...the inspector was kind enough to show meself and me friends the way here so we could give ye our money."

At the sound of her voice, Cronin's attitude became less wary. He said, *"Dia dhaoibh."*

"Dia is Muire dhuit," responded Deirdre."We're riding to Glandore."

Cronin eyed the position of the sun in the sky. "I would recommend making haste or staying the night there. Some wild country 'twixt here and there...not safe for travellers after dark."

"I'm looking forward to seeing some wild country," Holmes said. He took his grey fore-and-aft billed travelling cap from a pocket and settled it firmly on his head.

"Do ye need ladies saddles?"

"Not I," replied Loveday. "I'm have riding trousers under my skirt."

"As do I," Deirdre said. "Besides, I've never ridden a side-saddle."

They walked around the animals, studying their legs, withers and eyes. They selected four horses. Loveday chose the roan gelding, Watson a sorrel, and Holmes a mature white mare, mainly because she nuzzled him by way of a greeting.

Expertly, Loveday and Holmes bridled and saddled their own mounts and helped out with Deirdre's and Watson's. All of the horses were calm enough to allow their luggage to be tied onto the backs of the saddles without protest.

Deirdre hesitated before climbing aboard her horse, a chestnut mare of medium size. Holmes lifted her into the saddle and made sure her feet were secured within the stirrups. She thanked him sweetly. Loveday murmured, "I should have foreseen that part of her act. So should've Sherlock."

Watson chuckled. "What makes you think he didn't?"

Loveday scowled at him. "Because he's a man?"

They mounted up, took reins in hand and started their horses at a walk out of Skibbereen. The horses clopped past a small group of men dressed as labourers who stood on the roadside carrying shovels and pick-axes. They stared at them with open suspicion as they passed. Holmes commented, "We seem to have attracted an unusual amount of attention."

"It's a small town and we're strangers," said Loveday.

"And seen in the company of an RIC officer, who, I submit, isn't very popular with the citizenry."

Deirdre looked behind her at the men, intoning softly, " 'I was hunted through the mountains like a traitor to the Queen and that's another reason why I left old Skibbereen.' "

Watson said, "Present company excluded, I hope."

The four of them followed an old, overgrown road that traced its way across hilly acres of good pasture. In the distance, they saw grazing cattle and the roofless, burned-out ruins of houses, the homes of dispossessed tenant farmers.

"We never discussed whether our destination is the Druid's

Altar or the hotel in Glandore," Loveday said, riding abreast of Deirdre.

"Both are in the same direction at this point," she replied. "We should reach a crossroads and make up our minds then." She added, "The Druid's Altar's real name is Drombeg...it means 'small ridge' in the old tongue."

Watson said, "I throw my vote in for the Druid's Altar or Drombeg or whatever it is called... I'm very curious about it."

Loveday asked, "What about you, Mr Holmes?"

He shrugged. "The Druid's Altar seems the most likely place we'd find our quarry on a fine day like this one...assuming we get there before sunset."

Deirdre said, "Then we must ride cross-country for a few miles and meet up with the Cork Road."

She turned her mount to the left, crossed a shallow ditch choked with wet weeds and crossed into a field. She trotted ahead, displaying complete control over her mount. On impulse, Holmes urged his horse into a gallop, riding abreast of Deirdre for a moment before racing ahead. She grinned and urged her mare into a long-legged lope. After exchanging exasperated glances, Loveday and Watson followed suit.

Formations of granite and limestone thrust up through the soil, making the rich grasslands an obstacle course. Holmes did not mind. He was in a good mood, the best he had been in for longer than he cared to remember. He took keen pleasure in racing through West Cork on horseback, as he expertly wended the white mare between the outcroppings. It awakened rare, nostalgic memories of his childhood in Yorkshire, recollecting how he recklessly rode his pony over hill and dale.

The four people rode down a slope through a deep, thickly wooded gully between two rocky ramparts. The tall trees were fir and oak and poplar, the ground carpeted with yellow and blue wildflowers and high grass.

Deirdre said, "This way should bring us out on the Cork Road between Union Hall and Leap Village. Drombeg is but a few minutes away from there."

The path terminated abruptly at the edge of a tumbled rockfall of boulders clogging the gully. They reined their horses to a halt and studied the stone jumble. Watson said, "That looks deliberate...perhaps dynamited."

"But not recently," Loveday said. "Look how overgrown it is. Perhaps it was done during the Rising, to slow down police pursuit of Fenians who were cutting across the fields to reach the Cork Road."

Holmes swung off the saddle. "Or to lay an ambush. I'll see if I can find a way to lead the horses across or around it."

Handing the reins of his horse to Watson, he walked forward, working his way slowly through broken branches and brush. He threaded a path between and over the mossy stones. The air felt cool and fresh beneath the trees, although he noticed the absence of birdsong.

Deirdre said, "Be careful, Mr Holmes. There are also bogs about."

Before Holmes could reply, a whip-*crack* split the air. A bullet struck a rock close to his left foot, leaving a white scar on the dark surface as it ricocheted away.

He lunged behind a granite outcropping, heart trip-hammering in his chest. He heard Loveday cry out, "Sherlock—!"

"I'm all right," he called. "Stay there!"

A male voice shouted, "The rest of ye, keep to yer saddles! Don't make us shoot ye out of 'em!"

Holmes peered over the rock. He heard the scuttle and scuff of movement at the crest of the ridge. "What do you want from us?"

"Are ye armed?"

"Not at the moment." He twisted around, looking toward his companions. They sat astride their horses, crouching low, eyes

221B: *On Her Majesty's Secret Service*

watchful. He hoped neither Loveday nor Watson would try to reach for their firearms.

"What are ye doin' out here, other than trespassin'?"

"We don't mean any harm. We're only passing through to the Cork Road."

There came a long period of silence. Holmes heard whispers and then the man shouted again, "Stand up — hands in the air. Do it slow!"

Holmes stood up carefully, raising his arms. Two men broke out of the shrubbery at the lip of the ridge. They wore shapeless dark clothes and broad-brimmed hats, casting their features into shadow. Scarves covered their lower faces. The taller of the pair carried an old bolt-action Enfield rifle. The other man cradled a shotgun in his arms. The pants and shoes of both men were wet and splashed with green algae and mud.

They dropped to the gully floor and approached Holmes, expertly navigating their way through the litter of granite and shale. The man with the rifle said, "Ye are English." It was not a question but more of an accusation.

Holmes nodded. "Obviously."

The man drove the stock of the Enfield into his stomach. Holmes grunted, bending nearly double, pain flaring through his torso. He gasped in a lungful of air. The man with the shotgun kept his gun trained on Watson, Loveday and Deirdre. He demanded, "Are ye spies for the Crown, then?"

Grimacing, Holmes straightened up. "As I said, we're passing through. We have no interest in the Irish Republican Brotherhood —"

The butt of the rifle struck him in the belly again, slamming almost all oxygen from his lungs. Holmes fell to one knee.

"Who said anything about the IRB?" the man snarled. "What do ye know?"

Holmes struggled to breath. Surreptitiously, he slid his right hand into his left sleeve. His fingers touched the handle of the

206

knife scabbarded to his forearm. He did not want to draw the weapon because he knew if he did, he would have no choice but to use it.

He heard a drumming of hoofbeats and Deirdre crying out, *"Cuir uait!"*

Lifting his head, Holmes saw her spring from the saddle and rush forward over the scattering of stone. "Leave him be!"

The man with the shotgun snapped at her in angry Irish. Deirdre responded in kind with a confusing torrent of words. Holmes continued to kneel on the ground as the three people engaged in a rapid-fire exchange of Gaelic, complete with foot-stamping and arm-waving.

Deirdre moved to stand over him, placing her hands on his shoulders. She shouted, *"Duine ata gealita! Gealita!"*

The two men stepped back, lowering their weapons. The man with the Enfield said sourly, "Ye can do better than a gobshite in a silly hat, lass."

They clambered up the rockfall and disappeared over the crest of the ridge. Holmes arose, gusting out a sigh of relief. "Thank you."

He sat down on a boulder, kneading his midsection. Deirdre called over her shoulder, "It's fine now. Ye can come up."

Watson and Loveday quickly dismounted, tying the reins to nearby shrubbery. Their horses were content to graze. Rushing forward with his medical bag, Watson demanded, "What in God's name was all that about, Holmes?"

"I'm not certain, but I recognized one of the men from that group we saw as we left Skibbereen. By his shoes. I wager they questioned Mr Cronin who was only too happy to supply what he knew of our destination."

"That's exactly what happened," stated Deirdre. "The fellow who carried the rifle met up with one his mates and they managed to get ahead of us by going through the bog. They didn't admit so, but they're Fenians. He said they'd keep their eyes on us. Not sure if that is good or bad."

Watson opened his bag, removing his stethoscope. Holmes waved it away impatiently. "I've only been a bit battered. Hardly a new experience."

"Right," retorted Watson sarcastically, stowing the instrument back into his bag. "Part and parcel of our business."

Loveday looked toward Deirdre. "What did you say to persuade them to withdraw?"

"First, that Mr Holmes spoke the truth about us only passing through on the way to Glandore. Second, I told 'em I was the niece of Liam Dalton, whose name they recognized as a patriot who fled Old Skibb after the Rising."

Holmes asked, "What did the fellow mean when he said you could do better than a 'gobshite'?"

"Oh, that." Deirdre laughed. "I also told them you and I were betrothed and if they took the life of my husband-to-be simply because he was English, I would curse their own unions to the end of their days. I don't know if they believed me, but they didn't care to chance it."

Loveday stared at her in nonplussed silence, then laughed. "Very convincing. Congratulations on finding the perfect opportunity to employ your Thespian skills."

She glanced from Deirdre to Holmes. "Assuming that's all it was."

Holmes adjusted his cap and stood up. "Let's find another way through."

221B: On Her Majesty's Secret Service
The unexpected has happened so continually in my life that is has ceased to deserve the name.

—John H. Watson, MD

CHAPTER 16

THE MIDDAY sky was as blue as a Danube dream, full of wispy white clouds with the air stirred by a fresh ocean breeze. Tesla thought about all of his unrealized dreams while growing up in Smiljan and blinked back tears of self-pity.

Then the oily spanner slipped on the bolt and he skinned a knuckle against the sharp-cornered flange of the conductor. Turning his face toward the sky, he shouted angrily and earnestly, *"Dösbaddel!"*

Rather than hurling the tool aside in frustration, Tesla continued to arrange the two metal insulating rods on either side of the conducting cylinder, joining them to the top frame. The sunlight struck highlights on the circle of damp standing stones rising from the shallow depression at the head of the broad valley. The fourteen megalithic stones loomed all around like weathered, forbidding sentinels, standing guard over the aeons and keeping their own silent counsel. Ages of erosion had carved deep fissures and furrows across the surfaces of the stones.

A bramble-crested ridge overlooked the site. Below the perimeter of the megaliths, the valley rolled to cliffs that dropped away to a mirror-calm sea, the surface shimmering a teal green in the afternoon sunlight. Far in the distance on the horizon, dark storm clouds gathered.

Despite the wild beauty of the place, the so-called Druid's Altar felt like an evil place to Tesla. He sensed many lives had been lost here over the centuries, most of them by violence.

Making sure the transmission circuit was positioned precisely at the centre of the circle, he tightened down all the nuts and double-checked with a sextant and tape measure. His initial experiment with the energy-magnifying apparatus had not been fully completed due to the arrival of curiosity-seekers. He hoped his efforts would not be interrupted today.

From the time he was in his teens, Tesla's primary scientific goal had been to develop a power transmission system. He theorized that one day humanity could harness and amplify the planet's own electrical charge, transmitting it anywhere in the world to provide free energy for all.

He envisioned his transmitter as interacting with naturally occurring geomagnetic vortices, places that generated both positive and projective frequencies. He foresaw the Earth itself as the medium for conducting the telluric currents, with no need for wires or other artificial conductors.

By the flipping of two levers, Tesla activated the circuit. His hearing registered a hum, like a distant swarm of bees. As the circuit built to a charge, he felt a faint needles-and-pins prickling sensation on his exposed hands and face. He backed away a few paces. Settling wire-rimmed spectacles on the bridge of his nose, he focused his attention on the process. He was so engrossed, he did not even turn around when a female voice inquired from behind him, "Professor Hasellmeyer, I presume?"

Although the voice sounded familiar he didn't remove his gaze from the cylinder. "Go away, please."

"I'm afraid I can't do that right now, Nikola."

Tesla wheeled around, snatching off his eyeglasses and letting them dangle by a ribbon attached to the lapel of his jacket. It took him a moment to overcome his astonishment and recognize the two men standing there as the pair he had encountered nearly two years before in Cornwall. He instantly knew Loveday Brooke. The pretty blonde girl standing slightly behind her was a stranger.

"Loveday!" he blurted, self-consciously adjusting his tie. "How nice to see you! What in heaven's name are you doing here?"

"I assure you it's not by happenstance," she replied, her eyes flicking over the circle of stones and then to the transmitter frame. "As I'm certain you are aware, since you went to the trouble of disguising your appearance by cutting your hair short and doing away with your moustache."

She waved toward her companions. "You may remember Mr Holmes and Dr Watson."

Tesla nodded toward them. "Gentlemen."

Watson said, "Good to see you again, even though you look nothing like the man I remember."

Holmes gestured to the young woman. "This is Miss Deirdre Dalton, our guide."

Tesla inclined his head in a short bow. "Charmed."

She nodded in return. "I'm sure." She added, "If I may be so bold, you could use some instruction in the art of theatrical make-up. The white streaks of talcum at your temples are a trifle obvious."

Tesla laughed. "I shall take that under advisement, Miss Dalton."

"You've been running for a long time," said Holmes. "But I'm afraid your pursuers have finally run you to ground."

Tesla frowned. "Other than you, who might those pursuers be?"

Loveday said, "You know very well. Otherwise you would not have assumed an alias."

He nodded in abashed acceptance of her words. "How did you find me?"

She stepped forward. "The prelude to locating you was a bit problematic, but we saw your horse and gig at the foot of the path. We left our own mounts there, hobbled and waiting. We should get back to them."

Lifting a hand, Tesla said, "Stop — you mustn't come too close. There is an electric charge building in the immediate vicinity."

Loveday came to a halt. "Dangerous?"

"Not yet."

Watson eyed the framework closely. "What exactly is that device?"

Tesla shrugged. "In plain language, it functions like a pump to draw telluric current from the Earth's electromagnetic energy field, and then drive it back, disseminating it through the ground."

"For what reason?"

"If my theory proves out, then electricity could be sent to carefully attuned receiving circuits. By achieving energy resonance, I can conceivably transmit power to anywhere on the planet."

"But why are you experimenting in this place?"

"I've long suspected some ancient civilizations were aware of telluric currents and constructed monuments over the vortex points in order to manipulate them—such as the Great Pyramid of Giza, Stonehenge and here at Drombeg stone circle, called the Druid's Altar. What little archaeological study done here estimates its construction to be a minimum of five thousand years ago."

"The time of the pyramids," Loveday said.

Tesla nodded. "Just so. It is my conviction that the prehistoric megalithic sites are the geodetic markers for naturally occurring power points which comprise the electromagnetic grid of Earth energies. The stone circles and dolmens of Ireland, Britain and

Brittany may serve as batteries and transmitters of geomagnetic energy. I call it the science of telegeodynamics."

Sceptically, Holmes said, "I've encountered those theories before but they've been dismissed as pseudoscience. Sheer eyewash."

Tesla chuckled but there was little real humour in it. "Perhaps it is just the hobby of a madman, hiding out from the world. I'm guessing you found me because of that article in the Skibbereen newspaper."

"Yes," Loveday answered. "But we wouldn't have, if certain agencies were not actively searching for you in the first place. The British Secret Service, for one."

"The Hephaestus Ring for another," said Watson.

"And Robur specifically," declared Holmes.

Tesla swallowed convulsively. "He is dead!"

"If he is, then someone else has carried forward with the development of his flying machine. We saw it this morning over the waters off Dublin. And we've heard a report that it was seen here, very close by, in fact."

"Why would Robur or the Hephaestus Ring want me?" demanded Tesla. "They already have my induction motor and—"

Holmes cut him off with a sharp gesture. "They have your invention?"

"A modified prototype of a new model, shipped to the foundry in Cornwall with the intention of mass-production."

"You didn't think to recover it?"

"It was very chaotic that night, you might remember," Tesla retorted resentfully. "So no, I did not. Besides, about a year later, I sold the license for an earlier model of my motor, and have been living on the proceeds, even though I am running low on funds. Fortunately, the proprietor of Clancahill Castle has extended me credit, although I fear he is growing impatient."

Holmes, Loveday and Watson exchanged inquisitive glances. Watson ventured, "Is it possible your modified motor could have been adapted to power Robur's aeroship?"

Tesla shifted his feet uneasily. "I see no reason why not, with the application of the appropriate electro-engineering aptitude."

Loveday said, "I think we had best move on." She reached for Tesla's arm. "We'll go with you to the hotel for your things and settle your bill. We have a train waiting in Skibbereen."

He evaded her hand. "Nein, not yet."

"Nikola, you are in grave danger."

Tesla's jaw muscles clenched in a show of stubbornness. "I need to complete my experiment. I was unable to the last time I was here. It will not take long."

A shivery, tingling vibration passed through the ground beneath everyone's feet. Deirdre backed away, uttering a wordless cry of alarm. The beehive hum rose in pitch. Threads of electrical energy crackled up and down the length of the cylinder, forming a luminous aura around the centre.

"It's working!" Tesla exclaimed. "Do you feel the current?"

"We'll be electrocuted!" shouted Deirdre, eyes alight with panic.

Tesla spared her a patronizing, over-the-shoulder smile. "We're perfectly safe while it's building the charge."

The halo around the shaft exuded flaring strings. The tendrils spit outward in all directions, one of them passing by Tesla's cheek, fanning it with a hot, tingling shock. He clapped his hand to his face, crying out. Loveday secured a grip on the collar of his coat and hauled him backward, away from the stone circle's perimeter.

Deirdre asked fearfully,"What is happening?"

Stumbling on a loose stone, Tesla said, "My oscillating apparatus is drawing telluric energy from the Earth...when it has built a sufficiently strong charge, it should—will—transmit it into the conductive layer in the upper atmosphere."

Holmes touched his right ear and frowned. "Is that odd sound part of the experiment?"

Loveday looked his way, puzzled. "I don't hear anything."

Tesla's eyes narrowed. "I think I do...like a rustle of waxed paper."

Watson glanced up. For a fraction of a second, he caught an impression of movement, like a dark distortion against the blue of the sky, skimming toward them from the direction of the sea. "Anybody see that?"

Holmes heard a swishing whisper which almost instantly became a booming pressure against his eardrums. A piece of sky fifty feet overhead shifted. The air shimmered, like water sluicing over a pane of dusty glass. Ambient violet waves rippled and dropped away to reveal a dark-hulled, winged craft constructed to resemble a bat-winged creature of prey. The long prow put them in mind of a pterodon's pointed beak.

The five people stood rooted to the spot, paralysed by astonishment for what felt like a chain of interlocking eternities. No one spoke. Then, in an eerily calm voice, Holmes said, "Invisible...the aerocraft can be made invisible."

In a tone hushed by awe and wonder, Tesla replied, "Most likely by a selective manipulation of light waves, the bending of the visible spectrum. There is a French scientist named Mirzarbeau who claimed he has created a method of reducing the refractive index of physical objects through a force he calls the Violet Flame...there is also a man called Griffin involved in the same field of research—"

Holmes interrupted, "Mirzarbeau is a member of the Hephaestus Ring."

The craft was coloured a flat, non-reflective black with a projecting bow sharper than the stern. The spindle-shaped fuselage looked to be about thirty feet long with a glass-enclosed superstructure above the prow. For the briefest of instants he glimpsed the outline of a broad-shouldered, bearded man behind the glass, his face forbidding and impassive.

"Robur?" he murmured to Tesla. "Very much not dead?"

The hull was of an alloy Holmes remembered from the prototype in Cornwall. The ribbed and scallop-edged wings were composed of a thin substance he was still unable to identify. He estimated their span to be a minimum of fifty feet.

He saw two fan-turbines placed on either side of the keel and he adduced that their spin, driven with extreme speed by the engine, propelled the craft through the air. From the undercarriage protruded a long metal-walled tube, brass-capped and perforated by concentric holes all of the same diameter — like the bores of multiple guns.

"Sherlock Holmes!" The raspy, metallic voice blasted forth from the aeroship. "Loveday Brooke! Nikola Tesla! Stand where you are!" The words were spoken in a monotone with faint, fuzzy crackles following each syllable.

"Jesus, Mary and Joseph," breathed Deirdre. "Is that the wee villain you spoke of?"

"Not sure," Loveday side-mouthed to her.

Holmes said calmly, "Watson, you and Miss Dalton were not included in the command to stay put. Whoever spoke doesn't know who you are or doesn't care."

"I don't feel particularly neglected," Watson said.

"Good, because the aeroship crew seem primarily interested in Miss Brooke, Tesla and myself. I suggest we split up, with you taking charge of Miss Dalton and Tesla. Miss Brooke and I will go in another direction."

Loveday stared at him incredulously. "We will?"

Watson clenched his fists. "This tactic sounds suspiciously like another of your headstrong schoolboy tricks, Holmes."

"A trick it may be, but it is neither headstrong nor schoolboy.

If we don't take action, then we will all be captured or worse."

With an edge in his voice, Watson said, "Holmes, if you haven't noticed, there's a rapid-firing gun aimed at us. We're the proverbial fish in the barrel...if we move, it may fire."

"It may, but the fire will be directed at Miss Brooke and myself. They won't risk Tesla. Get him and Miss Dalton away to safety. Miss Brooke and I will join up with you later." He cast his eyes toward Loveday. "That is, if you are amenable to my strategy."

Loveday inhaled sharply and nodded. "Even so, a distraction would be helpful."

Leaning forward, Tesla whispered, "I believe one is in the offing. My transmitter should have built up quite a charge by now."

Tension felt like a length of heavy wet rope coiling in Holmes' belly. Static electricity suddenly stung the flesh of them all, like the simultaneous bites of a thousand ants.

A blinding column of blue-white light erupted from the centre of the stone circle. Threads of blue witch fire streaked along the hull of the aeroship. For an instant, the entire surface of the fuselage blazed with a webwork of electrical energy. The machine lurched violently.

"Now!" shouted Holmes throwing himself to the right, aware that Loveday followed close on his heels. They raced toward the thicket bordering the Druid's Altar.

At the periphery of his vision, Holmes glimpsed spear-points of yellow flame flickering beneath the craft's undercarriage. There came a rattling roar, and a fusillade of bullets gouged up great gouts of turf and struck Tesla's framework, knocking it over with a loud clatter.

He and Loveday dove headlong into the thicket, rolling together through the briar-tangle of foliage. They crawled to the edge of a small clearing. A storm of bullets ripped along the brush-line, sending up a flurry of leaves and twigs. Holmes crouched over Loveday, using his body as a shield. When the barrage ceased, she elbowed him away. "You're no more invulnerable than I am, Mr Holmes. Besides, they're shooting blind."

"Force of habit." He straightened up, peering through the screen of shrubbery. "I think we distracted Robur long enough for Watson to get our two young wards away from the Druid's Altar. Robur will focus his attention on us if the electrical discharge did not damage his ship."

Breathing hard, Loveday raked her hair away from her face. "Why are you so sure Robur is aboard? That wasn't his voice we heard."

"I saw him, for a few seconds. Also, you and I were singled out. Tesla was almost an afterthought, although presumably his retrieval is Robur's primary mission. We both earned his wrath at Penhallick Wharf — me more than you, however."

"That is supposition."

"Drawn from experience with the type. I injured Robur, and he has waited nearly two years to injure me in return. I'm counting on his fixation to even the score — it will allow you the time to get away."

She hunkered down as a bat-winged shadow momentarily blotted out the sunlight. "Why just me? Why not both of us?"

Holmes touched her skirt. "First of all, you're not dressed for it. Secondarily, it was I who broke Robur's arm and caused his prototype to crash. As far as he's concerned, I'm the entrée'. You're just a mildly appetizing side dish."

"Somehow," she said, with a note of ironic humour in her voice, "that sounds vaguely insulting."

"I didn't mean it to be. Do you understand my reasoning?"

She silently considered the logic of his words for a moment. She nodded brusquely. "Understood."

221B: *On Her Majesty's Secret Service*

"Stay here until you see the aerocraft alter its course and come after me. Then move out in the opposite direction. Try to work your way back to where we left the horses and then to Clancahill Castle."

Again, quietly, she said, "Understood. Good luck, Sherlock."

They looked into each other's faces for a long, tense moment. Without another word, Holmes rose and loped quickly across the glade and into the overgrowth on the other side. He fought his way through a blackthorn barrier, ignoring the scratches on his face and hands and damage done to his clothes. He looked over his shoulder in a quick, single glance.

The aerocraft dropped suddenly from where it had hung poised in the sky. It swooped down, head-on. The snout of the rapid-firer protruding from the undercarriage flickered with flame. Bullets punched a cross-stitch pattern in the dirt in front of, and to the left of him.

Holmes dove to the right, then spun and ran in the opposite direction, staying beneath a canopy of trees and ferns. His heart raced and his throat constricted. He could not help but draw a parallel between himself and a rabbit pursued by a hawk. He did not like the feeling.

He put all of his energy and concentration into running, changing direction several times and tearing his way through tangles of vegetation. Penetrating the under-brush became like burrowing his way through to the bottom of a wet, green haystack.

Holmes raced through a copse of bracken, slapping the fronds aside. Then, he nearly pitched into empty space. Digging in his heels, he rocked to an unsteady stop. Directly in front of him the lip of a gully sloped downward for ten feet. At the bottom of it spread a very smooth and invitingly open space of dark green. He leaped down. The instant he did, he realized there was something ominous about the flat emerald expanse below.

With a painful contortion of his body, Holmes twisted and

turned in mid-air, spread-eagling himself. He fell full-length, with a moist slap and a splash of ooze.

He realized that if his snap judgment had been wrong, the shock of impact would have knocked all the air out of him. Instead, he was wet and covered in slime, but unhurt. He lay perfectly still, gazing up at the sky, doing his best to look like a lump of sludge. After five minutes, he saw the aeroship glide past in the direction of the sea. It wobbled in flight, trailing smoke, so possibly the transmitter's energy discharge had inflicted some damage.

The cold mixture of soil, water and slime crept up to his ear lobes. His soaked Norfolk jacket dragged at him. He moved toward the opposite side of the gully, then realized he could move easily only in one direction — down.

The words "Grimpen Mire" flared in his mind, but he he knew quagmires did not actually suck anything down. Victims of bogs died by drowning, by thrashing around in mindless terror until they sank beneath the fluidized surface.

Carefully, he extended both of his arms, dispersing his weight over the largest possible area. He glanced around at his surroundings, cursing the fact that his leap had dropped him virtually into the middle of the morass. The fingertips of both hands were a long way from anything that fit the loosest definition of solid footing.

Although he knew it was possible to swim in mud, he also knew the progress was excruciatingly slow and swiftly burned up an enormous amount of energy. The odds of becoming too exhausted to do anything but flounder around and drown were very high.

He squirmed about, clawing aside the semi-solid layer of muck lying atop the surface. The opposite side of the gully was closer, by perhaps a foot. It rose from the bog as a sheer wall of ivy-covered granite, six feet high. The slime crept up to the corners of his mouth as he studied the rock face. He doubted that he

221B: On Her Majesty's Secret Service

could struggle across the mire and reach it before he sank.

Even if he did, the stone was too smooth to afford handholds until a narrow ledge halfway up. Still, he inched his way toward it by spreading his arms and pushing aside the mire while kicking. He managed to move forward but with maddening slowness. Each movement resulted in a loss in buoyancy.

Loveday's voice said softly, "So much for the main course."

Twisting his head up and around, Holmes saw Loveday kneeling on top of the rock. He winced at the sight of the woman's thorn-torn blouse and generally dishevelled appearance. "Miss Brooke, what are you doing here?"

"I'm afraid I became bewildered about which direction to go so I followed you. Obviously a mistake."

"Easy to become mistaken, under the circumstances."

"It appears you're sinking in a bog, or am I mistaken about that?"

"Fair to say," Holmes retorted dourly. "I don't suppose you have a rope handy?"

Loveday shook her head. "Sorry, no…and the vines around here aren't very sturdy, either. I could try to find my way to the horses and elicit John's help…if I'm not shot in the process."

"I think Robur has moved on."

Loveday nodded. "The time is better spent finding a way to get you out of there, anyway."

"How?"

She grinned. "Anticipate and adapt. Or simply improvise. Permit me."

Standing up, Loveday swiftly began unbuttoning her skirt, fingers working at the waist-band. She tugged it down, revealing brown corduroy riding pants beneath. She stepped out of the skirt. By twirling and tightly twisting the fabric lengthwise, she fashioned a thick rope nearly four feet in length.

"I'll toss this to you and haul you out," she said, lying down flat on the rock and wriggling forward until her upper body hung over the rock edge. The tight-twisted skirt dangled at the end of her right arm.

"You make it sound so simple, Miss Brooke."

"I do not mean to, because I doubt it will be. Are you ready?"

He freed his right arm from the slime with a wet pop. "As I will ever be."

Loveday leaned far over and snapped the skirt toward him. Holmes flailed for it and managed to secure a grip on corner. With both hands Loveday grasped the nether end, drawing it toward her. She hooked the toes of her boots into a crack to anchor herself. "Try to climb."

Holmes put all of his weight onto the skirt by cautious degrees. He gripped it with his other hand and heaved himself upward. The bog clung to his body, but he pulled himself up along the length of the skirt, hand over hand, shoulder muscles protesting under the strain. With trembling arms, he laboriously climbed, placing one hand over the other until his waist and then his hips came loose from the morass with a protracted sucking sound.

Gritting his teeth, he fought his way upward until he could rest most of his weight on the narrow ledge. Loveday released the skirt. It dropped into the bog, joining his cap. Her fingers closed over his right wrist, then his left.

Holmes kicked himself up. With a surprising display of strength, Loveday hauled him the last few inches over the top of the rock and fell backward. The man came with her. For a moment, the two people lay there, gasping and panting.

"Well done," he husked out. "You are stronger than you look, just as you said years ago."

"Please get off me," Loveday grunted, squirming beneath him.

"Sorry." He tried to push himself up by fatigue-weakened arms. "Force of habit."

221B: *On Her Majesty's Secret Service*

"That's all very well, but I don't want John or someone to come along and find us like this."

"Too late," said Watson. They turned their heads to the left and saw him standing at the very edge of the mire. Although breathing hard, his bramble-scratched face was creased by a half-smile. "I've been looking for you two but I didn't expect to find you both here...but then I didn't expect any of what happened today."

Wearily, Loveday and Holmes manoeuvred themselves into sitting positions. She said, "I'd say that's a reaction we all share."

Holmes reached out with a finger and flicked away a speck of algae clinging to the tip of Loveday's nose. "Permit me."

221B: On Her Majesty's Secret Service

Criminals no longer stalk about as they did fifty years ago with blunderbuss and bludgeon...they plot, plan, contrive and bring imagination and artistic resource to their aid.

— Loveday Brooke

CHAPTER 17

A GENTLE RAIN began to fall during the ride to Glandore village. Holmes did not object, since it washed away a considerable coating of bog slime and mud from his sodden clothes. He rode his horse on the right side of the canvas-covered gig driven by Tesla. Reins in hand, the Austrian sat squeezed between Deirdre and Loveday. Watson rode to the left. The other two horses were tied to the rear.

Loveday offered him the use of her umbrella, saying it would be of little use to a man wearing bog-soaked clothes like Holmes, but Watson declined. "Thank you, but no...I don't wish to be further encumbered."

Holmes said, "Risking pneumonia as a show of solidarity with me is appreciated but totally unnecessary, Watson. I need a good rinsing off."

"One generally doesn't contract pneumonia from being out in inclement weather, Holmes."

Tesla asked petulantly, "In that case, why can't we go back for my apparatus?"

"It's been shot to blazes for one thing," Watson replied. "For another, we now know to an absolute certainty that the Hephaestus

Ring wants you very badly."

"Am I under arrest?"

"No," said Loveday curtly. "Nor are you free to go at the moment. Not until we've all had a chance to discuss a few things, such as how you were recruited into the Hephaestus Ring by Robur."

"I was not recruited," Tesla shot back angrily. "The first time I ever heard of the Hephaestus group referred to as a 'ring' was on that night at Penhallick Wharf. Until then, I presumed Hephaestus was a privately owned company devoted to scientific research and development."

"If you were not recruited, you must have been hired," Holmes said.

"That is exactly what I was. Over three years ago I resigned my position with Thomas Edison, due to his stubbornness and vanity. I found myself unemployed and even unemployable. I had no choice but to accept any menial job that came my way. Baron Maupertuis — whom you call Robur — contacted me about my induction motor. I went to work for him, not this Hephaestus Ring organization of yours."

Loveday's eyebrows knitted at the bridge of her nose. "So, from whom have you been hiding these past two years, Nikola? You said Robur is dead."

The man sighed. "Like any industry, any field of endeavour, there is a network of gossip mongers. I learned from several sources that Robur drowned when his prototype flying machine crashed."

He learned forward to peer past Loveday. "Due to you, I was told, Mr Holmes."

"Pieces of his aerocraft were found," Holmes said. "But not his body."

Tesla frowned. "I am not certain of the baron's fate now. I thought I glimpsed him on the air-ship, so it's possible my information network was incorrect."

"Has that gossip network informed you of the news about Julius Wendigee?" asked Loveday.

Tesla stiffened in surprise. "Julius? We briefly worked together at the Société Electrique Edison in Paris."

"His body was found floating in the Seine two nights ago. The cause of death is thought to have been heart failure."

"That is tragic."

"And highly suspicious," stated Holmes. "According to our sources, Wendigee was working to install the lighting system on the Paris Exposition grounds."

"That was the job I was initially offered," Tesla said uneasily.

"Wendigee replaced you but he apparently was not considered irreplaceable, because when the Ring learned where you could be found and retrieved, his employment was terminated. You must have had some inkling."

Tesla's face registered fear. "I do not know who I was hiding from, really. I just had the sense I was being hunted. I took an alias and did what I could to go to ground."

"You just had a sense?" Watson enquired doubtfully.

He nodded. "My instinct for survival is strong. It can fail me sometimes but when I am right, I am very right indeed...as today has proven."

Watson smiled at him coldly. "I have the instinct you're dissembling, Nikola."

"If not outright prevaricating," said Loveday.

Nikola's spine stiffened. "You are questioning my honour."

"Not at all," replied Holmes. "Just the degree of your transparency."

Tesla blinked at him. "I don't understand."

"You will."

Deirdre shook her head and smiled ruefully. "This has been a

221B: On Her Majesty's Secret Service

very unique way to earn five shillings, I must say."

"Even more interesting than posing as an heiress to earn a hundred pounds?" Loveday challenged.

Deirdre's smile widened and she glanced over at the bedraggled Holmes swaying in the saddle. "Playing Millicent was actually a very pedestrian role...no, this is far more interesting with a much more talented cast. Mr Hawke was a ham-fatter."

Loveday couldn't help but laugh.

The harbour of Glandore stretched out before them, a lighter grey contrasting with the deeper grey of the late afternoon sky. Anchored fishing boats bobbed on the waters of the bay, but the quays were empty, except for heaps of dredge netting and haphazard piles of burlap sacking.

Deirdre pointed out a pair of small rocky islands at the mouth of the harbour. "They're called Adam and Eve...the advice given to sailors navigating the waters for the first time is to avoid Adam at all costs and hug Eve."

After a few minutes of traversing a muddy lane stretching along the side of a hill, Tesla drew the gig to a halt within the forecourt of Clancahill Castle. A low ornamental wall partially enclosed it. Holmes wasn't very interested in the structure's authenticity or architecture. Since the rainfall had increased he was more concerned with its potential as a shelter. Still, he noted the stone walls were massive, towering up at least three floors and spreading out laterally in a pair of large wings to the right and left. The backside of the castle perched on the edge of the hillside. The front was built on a less steep slope.

At first glance the walls looked featureless but he noticed small projections and even cracks here and there. He saw deep-set windows on either side of the great arched doorway and a man standing upon the upper crenelations, watching their every move.

221B: *On Her Majesty's Secret Service*

A stableman draped in an oil-cloth cloak came forward to take charge of the gig and the horses. Tesla led them through the doorway and into a vast stone-floored hall. The walls were bare granite, except where covered by huge tapestries displaying medieval battle scenes and a banner displaying a family coat-of-arms. The crest featured a stylized animal standing on its hind legs. It could have been a wolf, a dog, or a fox rampant.

An elaborate gasolier hanging from the ceiling cast a warm, wavering pool of illumination from scores of flickering gas jets within lotus shades. They saw a grand staircase at the far end of the hall. A broadly built, square-jawed man wearing black and white butler's livery stood alertly on the first landing, a shotgun tucked casually under his arm. He stared at them impassively.

Tesla lifted a hand in greeting. "It's all right, Éowyn...these are my friends, visiting from England."

Éowyn jerked his head toward an adjacent room. "Yer expected."

As they walked in the direction he indicated, Watson murmured, "Not the most welcoming concierge I've ever seen."

"How could we be expected?" Loveday asked, mystified.

The receiving room lay off the hall directly across from the entrance. Framed life-size oil portraits of men in different period fashions hung on the four walls. Although the palette and technique were unremarkable, all the paintings were noteworthy for sharing a striking resemblance to the sharp-featured, ginger-haired man with shaggy, silver-tipped sideburns who stood before the hearth. He used a poker to shift a square of paper to the top of several flaming logs.

He wore a deep red blazer and matching tie. He turned toward them as they entered. His movements were stiff and awkward, due to missing his left leg from the knee down. He leaned on a heavy oak cane with the grip artfully carved in the likeness of a grinning fox head..

"Hello," he said jovially with an accent that Holmes marked as Bostonian but with a bit of an exaggerated Cork lilt. "You're a bit late."

He surveyed their faces with a swift glance, smiling at Holmes who stood in an ever expanding puddle of dirty water. "Appears you've fallen into a bit of a bog hole, young man."

"One reason for our delay," replied Holmes. "The other being that we did not know we were expected. You are —?"

"Kevin McShinnock," he said, half-stepping, half-lurching forward to take Holmes by the hand. He squeezed it hard. "You're very fortunate to be alive. I apologize for the unpleasant welcome to dear old Skibbereen and West Cork."

"Not at all...I look forward to returning under more congenial circumstances one day."

McShinnock nodded. "You'll be wanting a shower-bath to get off the mud, and if you let me have those things of yours, I'll see whether my housekeeper can get them cleaned up a bit for you."

"Thank you," Holmes said sincerely. He gestured to his companions, introducing them one by one. When he spoke Deirdre's name McShinnock barked out a laugh.

"Ha! So you're our little wren twittering the news about our visitors. Good thing you did, else our lads could've shown your friends a hard time."

Holmes cocked his head toward her quizzically. "Twittering the news?"

Deirdre cast him a coy smile. "When we were set upon, I told the men who you were and where we were going."

"And word reached you, Mr McShinnock?" Loveday enquired.

"Not just from the lass...first thing this morning a constable from old Skibb came knocking, wanting to know all about our professor here. Not long after, I received a message about the four of you being squired about the town by Inspector Keegan."

"The Fenians keep you informed of Royal Constabulary

business?" Watson asked, surprised.

"Not always, but when a monster of a locomotive stamped with a lion and a unicorn seal roars into the train station, and the passengers are greeted by Keegan himself, that's newsworthy enough to be shared with me. Your presence has made quite the stir in various quarters."

Loveday cocked her head at him quizzically. "Such as?"

"Let's get you settled in your rooms." McShinnock gestured toward the door. "The hotel is empty at this season, so you may have your pick. I'll have your luggage brought around. Over supper, we'll talk all about your day. Oh, not you, Professor—stay a bit...we have business to discuss, as well as the matter of your bill."

He took Tesla by the elbow and guided him toward a chair. The younger man looked to be on the verge of protesting but his shoulders slumped in resignation. "Very well."

"This is all moving a bit too fast for me," said Watson. "Who said anything about staying the night?"

McShinnock smiled condescendingly. "You're free to return to Skibbereen but it's nearly nightfall, it's raining and the way back is more treacherous in the wet and the dark." He looked Loveday and Holmes over with a critical eye. "Besides, some of you could use a rest."

Watson chuckled. "Only some of us?"

They went back into the great hall. The shotgun wielding man named Éowyn waved them up the stairs to the first floor. He indicated doors on either side of the corridor. "The water closet is at the end there...we recently had the latest model of shower-bath installed, Mr Holmes. You can leave your soiled things on the chair there and the housekeeper will take them away for cleaning. When your luggage gets here, I'll put yours in the shower-room."

"We can all use a bit of scrub," said Loveday. "So leave some hot water for the rest of us, please."

"Little chance of running out, Miss," Éowyn said pridefully. "Everything in the castle is strictly up-to-date, modernized by King Kevin. We're almost completely self-sufficient and even have our own gas-works to heat and light the place. We're the pride of West Cork, as far as hotels are concerned."

"Is that why you carry a shotgun?" asked Watson.

Éowyn stiffened. "Just following security procedures, sir. I shall leave you to it."

He turned on his heel and marched back down the stairs to the landing. Led by Loveday, the party moved along the corridor, opening doors and adjusting the gas wall brackets. They all shared a similarity in layout and furnishings. Loveday, Watson and Deirdre chose their rooms by the numbers on the doors.

Holmes went straightway to the shower-room. There, he found a selection of robes and towels laid out on a shelf. He removed all items from his pockets, and took off the forearm sheaths. He stripped out of his clothes, placing them outside the door on a chair. The shower was an unusual-looking contraption made of an intricate network of gleaming aluminium tubes, nozzles and control valves. He stepped into the stall and after some experimentation, he adjusted the water so as to be as hot as he could stand it. The entire bathroom quickly filled with billowing clouds of steam as he watched muddy water swirl down the drain.

Holmes soaped himself up, working a lather all over his body. His midsection showed rifle-stock inflicted bruising but the hot water reduced the soreness. He found a single-edged, ivory-handled safety razor on a recessed shelf and he methodically shaved by feel, scraping off two day's growth of bristles without seriously nicking himself. He stayed beneath the shower longer than necessary, wanting to scrub every microscopic grain of the bog from his pores. When his fingertips wrinkled and turned pink, he decided he was as clean as he was likely to be. He rinsed himself with jets of cold, clear water.

221B: *On Her Majesty's Secret Service*

He felt much better when he stepped out of the shower. Putting on a robe and towelling his hair dry, he walked through the steam and stubbed the toe of his right foot on his valise, right inside the door. He picked it up and left the bathroom, padding barefoot down the carpeted hallway to the room he had earlier chosen for himself. As he passed Watson's and Loveday's rooms he rapped on the door, announcing, "The WC is free."

Once inside his room, he turned up the lamps and looked through his luggage for a change of clothes. Fortunately, he had packed a shirt, waistcoat, trousers, tie and a pair of socks. He was relieved to find his Webley still in an inner side-pocket of the valise. After a moment's contemplation, he decided to strap the throwing knives to his arms. As he stood before the full-length mirror, knotting his tie, he heard a rapping the door. He called, "Come in."

Deirdre entered, carrying his trousers and Norfolk jacket. "King Kevin's house-keeper said this was the best she could manage."

The young woman had changed out of her travel outfit to a powder blue shirt waist blouse and black skirt. "She dried the jacket over the stove, but to get all of the bog-smell out of it, you might want to have it dry-scoured when you're back in London. Your trousers are a loss, I fear."

"Thank you. How are you settling in?"

"Fine...the room is comfortable, although the bed is a bit too soft for my taste."

"We'll return to Skibbereen the first thing in the morning and the train will have you in Cork City in no time."

"With my five shillings?" She put the coat and trousers on the bed and stood behind him.

Addressing her reflection, Holmes answered, "I think we should manage a bit more than that sum. After all, you saved me from a beating...or worse. That alone was worth the five shillings."

"By passing you off as my fiancee'?" She smiled demurely. "I hope I did not embarrass you. 'Twas all I could think of at the moment."

"Faced with a problem of that sort, the grand thing is to be able to reason backward. I have no criticisms of your choice of tactic."

Deirdre did not respond for a tick of time and then she chuckled. "I've never met anyone like ye, Mr Holmes."

Holmes smiled. "As my friend Doctor Watson has had reason to observe, it is fortunate for English society that I am unique."

"Nay...ye're more than that, I say. Fascinating is the word."

Holmes forced a laugh. "I've been called many things — foolhardy, vainglorious and even intolerable — but never that."

"Yer own Miss Brooke — Loveday — thinks ye are, y'know."

Holmes paused in the final tug of his tie. "She has never implied so."

"Nor would she, but I can tell. She's a little of jealous of me, too."

His eyebrows rose toward his hairline. "Jealous? I can scarcely countenance that."

"Why would she not? I'm younger than she is for one thing and she thinks I may distract ye."

"Distract me from the mission?"

"Aye. And from her."

"Perhaps she is just acting a part, like you often do. Miss Brooke's brain governs her heart. She also sees than I'm a century or two older than you, as well."

Deirdre shook her head dismissively. "I'm twenty-one, yer thirty?"

He turned toward her. "Thirty-five this past January, if you please."

233

She stepped close to him, reaching up to adjust his tie. "Even better. Me mam and da were those same ages we are when they were married."

Holmes stared at her, transfixed by and made uncomfortable by her loveliness. He experienced a momentary difficultly in both breathing and speaking. "Miss Dalton—"

"Deirdre."

"—Miss Dalton," he repeated, letting a stern edge slip into his voice. "This is rather inappropriate. You were hired as a guide."

"You can keep the five shillings if that is what's bothering you."

Holmes was startled into laughing. He gently placed his hands on her shoulders and pushed her back half-a-pace. "I cannot imagine worse husband material than myself, but I am flattered that you are misconcepted enough to think otherwise. As Andrew Marvell wrote, 'Had we but world enough and time.' "

Quietly, she quoted in return, " 'The grave's a fine and private place, but none I think there do embrace.' "

Dismayed by her tone and words, Holmes tentatively cupped her cheek with his right hand for barely a second. "You are a very long way from that fine and private place. Do your best to maintain the distance."

They heard the distant brass tolling of a bell. Holmes reached for his jacket and gave it quick sniff. The lapels were only a little damp and the smell of the bog was faint enough so he quickly slipped it on, returning his magnifying glass, briar pipe, cigarette case, strike-lighter and compass to the pockets. "That is our summons to supper, I wager. After the generosity shown to us by our host, the least we can do is be prompt to the table."

Deirdre nodded. "Aye. Of course. And Mr Holmes...?"

"Yes, Miss Dalton?"

"I wasn't acting with you just now. What's acting is Loveday pretending her brain governs her heart. Just like you."

He locked eyes with her and nodded curtly. "So noted." He offered her his arm. "Shall we?"

She linked arms with him. "We shall."

As the pair stepped out into the hallway, Watson and Loveday emerged from their rooms more or less simultaneously. They both looked considerably fresher and drier than they had only a short time before. Loveday had changed to a burgundy walking dress and rearranged her hair so it fell loose about her shoulders.

She said quietly, "My luggage appears to have been left unsearched but I've transferred the Bull-dog." She indicated her reticule.

Watson patted his coat pocket. "I'm bringing along the derringer in an abundance of caution." He sniffed the air and said cheerfully, "I catch a whiff of roast mutton. I didn't realize I was so hungry until this moment."

Descending the staircase, they saw Éowyn no longer stood at his post on the landing. They reached the great hall and the rich aroma of stew lay in the air like an enticing perfume. They followed the savoury smell across the great hall into the receiving room.

McShinnock and Tesla sat at the far end of a dark teak table that occupied most of the centre of the floor. There were seven place settings, cut crystal decanters and a very large ceramic tureen cast in the shape of a slumbering sheep.

Tesla jerked upright in his chair and started to speak, but McShinnock laid a hand on his arm. "Ah, you're just in time." He indicated the table with a sweep of his arm. "Come and be seated. I should add we have an unexpected guest."

They heard a faint rustle of movement and a scuff of feet from behind them. The four people turned as a very tall, slope-shouldered man stepped from behind the right-side double door. He wore a steel-grey uniform. It held a dull sheen, as if made of a very fine metallic mesh. A round badge bearing the silhouette of a hammer and anvil against a crimson background was emblazoned on the left breast of his tunic. He held a big round-barrelled, multi-bored pistol in his right hand, supporting it with the other.

The left half of the man's face was normal of flesh and contour, the other half was no face at all. A raw red mass knitted into a network of glassy scar tissue reached down beneath his chin and around to the right ear. His eye was still there, and although it glared with a milky blue hatred, it did not see. Deirdre bleated in wordless fear.

In a voice barely above a horrified, revolted whisper, Loveday husked out, *"Vonn."*

"You still remember, Fröken Brooke," he intoned flatly. "It is fitting that my face, the face you made, is the last one you will ever see."

He raised the barrel of his weapon. Loveday did not shrink back. She stared at him, unspeaking and unblinking. Holmes tensed, giving his right wrist a little shake and a knife slid into his palm. Casually, he stepped in front of the firearm. "I was the one who struck you, Vonn."

"And I was the one who shot you," announced Watson. "Or one of three."

Vonn said, "I will attend to all of you after I conclude matters here with Fröken Brooke."

McShinnock rapped on the floor with his cane and shouted, "Not here at my table, sir! It is simply not done! We agreed to talk with all parties involved first, did we not?"

Vonn's lips peeled back from his teeth in a sneer. "I am not here to talk. I am here to reclaim lost property. If you truly believed I wanted to discuss the issue first, then you are a far greater fool than my first impression."

McShinnock levered himself out of the chair, supporting himself with one hand on the table and the other on his cane.

221B: On Her Majesty's Secret Service

"These people are my guests and are under my protection."

Vonn's sneer became a contemptuous grin. "And whose protection are you under, old man?"

Kevin McShinnock returned the grin with a wide, gap-toothed one of his own.. "You have to ask? *Éowyn!*"

Three life-size oil paintings on the walls slid aside, revealing dark cavities beneath. Within each niche stood a large man, each with a shotgun levelled at Vonn. The man in the centre was Éowyn.

McShinnock said, "The spirits of my ancestors watch over me."

221B: On Her Majesty's Secret Service

We live in a utilitarian age. Honour is a medieval conception.
—Sherlock Holmes

CHAPTER 18

"**A** SCATTER-GUN makes a right awful mess of things," McShinnock said, sitting back down. He lifted his truncated left leg. "Especially at this range, as I can attest."

Vonn's gaze went from one pair of shotgun barrels to another. He shrugged, lowering his pistol. "Very well. Let us talk."

"After supper." McShinnock pointed to far end of the table with the ferrule of his cane. "Put the fancy shooter there. The rest of you take seats and help yourselves. We'll pass on the saying of grace just this once."

Holmes, Loveday and Watson hesitated. Watson's fingers edged across his waist-coat toward the pocket where he had stowed the derringer. He caught Holmes' eye and raised questioning eyebrows. Holmes subtly shook his head. Deirdre did her best to hide her fright. She started to speak, but Loveday put a warning finger to her lips. Holmes pulled out a chair for her close to Tesla. Watson did the same for Loveday.

Holmes gave the weapon on the table a swift visual examination. The end of the barrel held six bores arranged in a circle. A black torus-shaped magazine was positioned just before the trigger guard. "I assume it's the same model repeating pistol that was shipped to Cornwall on the night we all met each other?"

Vonn grunted, pulled out a chair, spun it around, thrust it between his legs and dropped into it. The gun was within arm's reach. He said, "With some refinements since. Six rotating bores instead of four, and the drum carries 50 rounds of 45-70 calibre ammunition." His lips lifted away from discoloured teeth in vulpine grin. "We call them 'Rattlers.'"

"Speaking of the night we met," said Watson conversationally, "why aren't you dead?"

Vonn chuckled with a sound like two pieces of chipped pottery grinding away at one another. "I was three-quarters of the way in that condition but a combination of providence and an experimental medical procedure pulled me through."

Watson's eyes narrowed to suspicious slits. "I find that exceptionally dubious."

"That is because you don't know Madame Koluchy and her miracle cures, like Herakleophorbia."

"No, it's because I'm a former army doctor and I know the kind of damage bullets inflict on the human body as well the tissue and neurological trauma resulting from third-degree burns."

Vonn turned his maimed face toward him. "You have weightier matters to worry yourself over, Englishman."

McShinnock lifted away the lid of the steaming tureen. "Help yourselves. No need to stand on ceremony."

"No wine or beer?" Vonn asked.

"Never discuss business on an empty belly or a drink-addled brain."

"I'm not hungry," Vonn said sullenly, crossing his arms over his chest. "Besides, I am a vegetarian."

"You'll eat," growled Éowyn from his niche in the wall. He shifted the barrel of the shotgun toward him. "When King Kevin says eat, you eat, a poncey vegetarian or no."

Watson took the initiative and began ladling stew into Blue Willow bowls. He passed them around, while Holmes filled water glasses and Loveday made sure everyone had spoons and forks. Holmes sat down and put his throwing knife on his lap, covering it with a linen napkin. For the next few minutes, everyone occupied themselves with the stew. It tasted as delicious as it smelled. Even Vonn partook, although he preferred to spear vegetables with his fork. Still, eating while literally under the gun did not make for a pleasant repast or aid in digestion.

Without preamble, McShinnock said, "My local branch of the family is from Carberry, just down the road from here, even though the ancient family seat is in Limerick...the name is derived from O'Sionnaigh which means 'fox'. " He lifted the head of his cane above the level of the table.

"The McShinnocks fought with the other clans in Munster against Baron Fitzgerald in 1261," he continued. "All the Norman castles along this coast fell into Irish hands. My family was promised this one but the clans returned to feuding and very few of the agreements were ever honoured."

Vonn glared at him. "I thought we were going eat first and talk later."

"This isn't business talk, laddy-buck. More of a biography, so everyone will have an idea whose hospitality they're enjoying."

Vonn glowered at him but did not respond. He went back to fishing for vegetables.

"I left Ireland in Black '47 on one of the famine ships bound for Boston," McShinnock went on. "I wasn't but fifteen or so years of age. My father was dead, killed by English soldiers in a food riot, so it was just me, my baby sister and my mother. Both of them died from the cholera during our first Massachusetts winter. I did what I could to survive in the East Boston slums...taking factory work, joining the gangs, thieving, apprenticing myself out, and I even did a turn as a rail-layer on the Mississippi and Missouri railroad. It was a very hard life, and I learned many hard lessons...but I also learned how to spot and act on opportunities."

He paused to dip a chunk of bread into the stew and take a bite. Tesla watched him in nervous silence, as if he feared McShinnock would suddenly strike him with his cane.

"Then came the war against the Confederacy," McShinnock continued. "I joined the Ninth Massachusetts Infantry, an Irish regiment fighting on the side of the Union. We were in many engagements, saw many battles, including Little Round Top and Fredericksburg. I was resourceful, so I got through them all with little more than scratches. I rose through the ranks to Captain Major.

"During a skirmish in Cold Harbour, a rebel guerilla took off my right leg at the knee with an old shotgun, firing point-blank from ambush. I could have died, but fortunately the regimental surgeon happened to be nearby and saved my life. The entire regiment was mustered out in June of '64."

Deirdre looked at him sympathetically. " 'Tis a very awful thing to have happened...war between peoples is a terrible thing."

McShinnock reached over and patted her hand. "But opportunities can be found, child. After the Confederate surrender, I decided hobbling around an old soldier's home pissing into a pot was no life for me. So I took what money I had—including my army pension — and a brand-new crutch and went down south to buy up distressed hotels in Georgia, Alabama and the Carolinas."

McShinnock sighed sadly. "I'm not proud of myself...I took advantage of the Southerners but since I had lost a leg fighting them because they wouldn't give up their slaves, I took Johnny Reb's property for pennies on the dollar to compensate myself. Yes, I was what they called a carpetbagger...I tricked and connived and cheated to gain what I wanted."

"O'Sionnaigh the Fox, indeed," observed Loveday disapprovingly.

McShinnock acknowledged her words with a curt nod. "I wanted more than mere land and money. My dream was to come back home, to Eire, to Ireland and live in a grand style until the end of my days."

Holmes looked around and nodded. "It appears you managed that."

"You'd be surprised how many here and elsewhere wanted to take it all away. You see, Mr Holmes, I also dreamed of freedom for my country. Right after the war, I became involved with the Fenian Brotherhood and the struggle to free Ireland from British rule. I raised and even stole money to finance many of their activities, including the Skibbereen rising."

"You weren't suspected?" Loveday asked.

"I operated under a code-name...'Altamont'."

"Are you still involved with the brotherhood?" Watson asked.

McShinnock shrugged. "Only in the role of a kindly grand-da who always has a word of advice or a place to hide my IRB lads if they've run afoul of the constabulary."

Loveday said, "You're also King Kevin in these parts."

He chuckled. "Aye, I'm well-indulged on that score. But I'm a reasonable monarch...I don't ask for much but respect. So, that's my story...make of it what you will."

Somewhere in the room, a clock chimed faintly. Holmes counted five times. Surreptitiously he checked his watch and saw it was not quite half-past seven.

At the sound, McShinnock's demeanour changed. He fixed his eyes on Vonn. "I'm ready to talk a bit of business with you now, if you keep your toy out of reach and are reasonable yourself."

"What business can you have with that bastard?" Loveday demanded angrily.

Vonn pointed his fork at her, sighting along its length as if he were aiming a pistol. "Part of my business involves you."

Loveday met his gaze steadily. "He's a hired killer. The reason he looks the way he does is because he tried to kill me."

"Yes, Mr Vonn mentioned that in passing."

Vonn smirked. "Shall I explain a few things to the arrogant British bitch, your highness?"

McShinnock nodded. "If you are so moved."

"Two years ago, my employer, Baron Robespierre Robur Maupertuis, contracted with that man —" He pointed his fork at Tesla "—for an important job of work. He paid for his transportation from America to France as well as a substantial advance against his wages. Mr Tesla never delivered. He is in serious breach and I have been assigned to make him stand and deliver by any means necessary."

Tesla asked a voice barely above a whisper, "How did you find me?"

An imitation of a smug smile creased Vonn's lips "The Hephaestus Ring has resources beyond your abilities to understand."

"Oh, please," Loveday said disdainfully. "You learned of his likely whereabouts the same way we did...by one of your agents coming across that little article in the *Southern Star* broadsheet. By a childishly simple process of elimination, you deduced Nikola was staying here — at the only hotel in Glandore."

Vonn's smile faltered. "The how is immaterial."

Holmes regarded him expressionlessly. "What is your understanding of the important job of work that can only be performed by Mr Tesla?"

"I didn't say only he could perform it, only that he did not."

McShinnock playfully ruffled Tesla's hair, while he flinched away. "Our young fugitive here told me his job was to electrify the Paris World Fair grounds but he had suspicions about the situation."

"Like what?" Watson asked.

Tesla cleared his throat. "I heard the baron refer to something called 'Thunderstrike' in a conversation with Madame Koluchy and Mr Zaharoff."

Holmes raised expectant eyebrows. "Well, Mr Vonn?"

The man shrugged. "Meaningless."

"You don't know what Thunderstrike is, do you?"

"That, too, is irrelevant."

"Who assigned you the task of finding Nikola? Robur personally or Madame Koluchy?"

"That has no relevance, either," Vonn said impatiently.

"I beg to differ. Where is Robur? Is he still aboard the airship?"

"As I said to your doctor friend, you have weightier matters to face. Nikola Tesla will fulfil his contract. It is that simple."

Watson cast a challenging glance toward McShinnock. "How did you get involved in this?"

Laughter lurked at the back of McShinnock's throat. "By simple dint of answering a knock at my door early this morning, when one of Inspector Keegan's constables came by. He sought information about the young professor here — who, thanks to Mr Vonn, I now know is Nikola Tesla — because the inspector received an enquiry from the Defence Intelligence Branch in London.

"Of course, I told the constable nothing and sent him on his way. Shortly after, Nikola left the hotel to visit the stone circle at Drombeg and shortly after that, messages came flying in about the arrival of a train and you four being escorted around town by Keegan. There was some back-and-forth with my lads, so I was busy for a while there. Then late this afternoon, came another knock at my door and another visitor."

Holmes tilted his head toward Vonn. "Him?"

"Him. Mr Vonn came right to the point, I'll give him that. He presented a photograph of a man known to me as Professor Hasellmeyer, claiming it was actually of a man named Nikola Tesla who owed his employer a great debt. He knew from his own enquiries that Mr Tesla was a guest here at Clancahill Castle...I was burning that photo right as you arrived."

"Why?" asked Loveday.

"Track covering...a habit of a lifetime. In any event, Mr Vonn also knew that as we spoke, Mr Tesla was returning from Drombeg in the company of criminal confederates who he claimed had caused him a great injury a couple of years ago."

"All-in-all, a perfectly ordinary set of circumstances," Holmes said dryly. "Did Mr Vonn here explain how he happened to be part of this?"

"Yes," answered McShinnock. "As I said, he was forthright about it, including the fracas in Cornwall. He told me he had travelled here in an air-ship invented by a genius named Robur...a name I recognized from the newspapers many years before. He called the flying machine the *Terror.*"

"The *Terror,*" echoed Holmes, enunciating slowly as if tasting the syllables. He directed a stare toward Vonn. "Melodramatic to the point of parody, but I'm sure Robur felt the name was fitting."

Vonn's mocking grin turned his ruined face into a macabre leer. "The *Terror* is vastly superior to the *Albatross,* with greater abilities, such as operating under the sea and even overland."

"And the ability to render itself invisible," Watson put in. "Quite the improvement."

"No doubt due to contributions by other members of the Ring," said Loveday. "Like Captain Nemo."

"And Professor Mirzarbeau," Holmes said. "I'd like to learn more...is Robur aboard the *Terror,* waiting for your return?"

"I'm done answering questions," Vonn said bluntly.

Watson turned to McShinnock. "Did Vonn tell you how he tried to apprehend Nikola and kill the rest of us at the Druid's Altar?"

McShinnock lifted his right shoulder in a shrug. "Not in so many words, but it was not difficult to draw that inference, particularly since the only choice he gave me was cooperating with him or being killed myself."

The gaze Loveday turned toward Vonn glinted with barely repressed fury. "Why should any of us cooperate with you?"

Vonn stared at McShinnock. "Perhaps you should field that question, Your Highness."

McShinnock nodded. "Vonn informed me if I did not turn all of you over to him upon your return here, he would use the airship to destroy my castle, bringing it down brick-by-brick, and kill me and mine very dead indeed in the process."

Watson uttered an incredulous laugh. "And then you invited him to stay for dinner?"

"Only after he showed me his fancy shooter and counted the number of holes it could put in me with one pull of the trigger."

Vonn said, "His Highness here implied he was willing to give up Tesla for additional considerations."

"Such as?" enquired Loveday.

"That is what we're discussing right now." McShinnock completely shed his pose of jocular host. He leaned forward, his face an unsmiling mask. There was a dangerous edge to his voice when he spoke. "Mr Vonn, I provided you with a bit of my background in order to give you the idea that I am not easily defeated by circumstance, nor am I intimidated by threats. I also do not tolerate disrespect. Apparently, that message was not successfully conveyed. Whether Mr Tesla here owes Robur the completion of a contract is a matter for the courts to determine. He is not a runaway slave to be chased down and hauled back to a plantation in chains."

Vonn snorted. "This is an extra-legal affair...the entity I represent has its own courts."

"In that case, why should I not hold you to ransom and cut a deal with that entity myself? Or have Éowyn take you out back and kill you right now?" His lips stretched in a savage grin. "When a man has no sense of honour himself, he cannot comprehend it in others."

Vonn gaped at him, his mouth opening and closing as he struggled to find words. "I have men posted around the castle. If this is some kind of clumsy trick—"

"Or," McShinnock continued, "I can have you arrested by the Royal Irish Constabulary and simply let the judicial system deal with you, your master and the entity you represent." He paused, inhaled deeply and shouted sharply, *"Inspector Keegan!"*

The fourth portrait of a McShinnock ancestor on the wall slid aside and Keegan stepped out of the niche. He wore a damp raincoat and held a long-barrelled revolver. He eyes were fixed on Vonn. He announced dispassionately, "You are detained in the name of the Crown."

The scar-faced man uttered a squawk of dismay and reached out frantically for the machine pistol. McShinnock leaned forward and with a looping over-arm, smashed the snout of the fox-head atop his cane against the knuckles of Vonn's right hand.

Shouting a curse, he withdrew his hand and lunged for the weapon with his left. Without otherwise moving, Holmes threw the knife with a blurring snap of wrist and forearm. The blade pierced the back of Vonn's hand, the razor point slicing through the palm and pinning it to the tabletop. His splayed fingers contorted, like the fluttering wings of a butterfly transfixed by a pin.

Holmes said flatly, "That's for the 'British bitch' remark."

Vonn's lips writhed back from his discoloured teeth in a snarl. Rising from his chair, Holmes snatched up the machine pistol, aware of shotgun barrels swinging to cover him. He was careful to keep its multiple bores pointed at the floor.

Keegan stepped around Holmes, reaching out to work the knife loose from Vonn's hand. "Quick thinking, Mr Holmes."

"Thank you, Inspector." He turned toward McShinnock. "This was all a ruse to stall for time, wasn't it?"

"Not all of it," McShinnock said defensively. "It was my supper-time. I like to eat early, even though the staff has been on alert all afternoon. Vonn arrived while the rest of you were cleaning up. I'm guessing his machine is out there nearby."

Watson's frowning face reflected his inner confusion. Then, his eyes brightened and he laughed. "You're were waiting for the inspector to get here!"

"One of my messengers informed me Inspector Keegan and two of his constables were in Toe Head, making enquiries about a flying machine. I was able send a messenger, informing him of Mr Vonn's visit and the precautions I had taken."

Keegan handed the throwing knife back to Holmes. "I was instructed to arrive by the back way so I could enter the castle unobserved. One of the hotel staff escorted me to a hiding place in this room."

McShinnock rose to his feet. "I may have refurbished and updated my castle but I've kept much of the original layout...like the network of secret inner wall passages and tunnels, and observation points."

Deirdre's eyes widened. "Which you disguised with those portraits."

"Just so, lass."

"And the clock striking five," Loveday said. "was the signal the inspector had arrived." She smiled. "Very crafty."

McShinnock tapped the carved fox-head. "I prefer resourceful, but crafty will do. As you said, 'O'Sionnaigh the fox, indeed.' "

Vonn clumsily wrapped a napkin around the knife wound in his left hand. "Why didn't your men just shoot me instead of playing this ridiculous game?"

"A messy shotgun murder in my hotel?" McShinnock managed

to sound scandalized. "Other than the fact I prefer to stay out of court, it's not much of an inducement for the tourist trade. This isn't the Wild West, sir. Besides, I didn't care for your manner...acting as if you had the moral right to drag this young man out by the ear, as well as avenging yourself on a young lady whose only real affront was objecting to being murdered. I think you need to stand in the dock for that alone." He paused and added, "There is still the issue of Mr Tesla's unpaid bill for room and board."

He glanced over at Keegan who stood behind Vonn, a proprietary hand on his shoulder. "I'm sure you can find even more criminal charges, Inspector."

"I can indeed," Keegan said. "Although I imagine London will take charge of him."

He tapped Vonn on the shoulder hard. "Up you go. Turn around. Put these on."

Keegan handed the man a pair of handcuffs. Vonn placed them around his wrists and clicked them shut.

"You've had experience." Keegan turned the lock in both shackles. "These darbies fit tight but unless you struggle, they shouldn't cause you any discomfort."

Vonn growled, "Where are you taking me?"

"To the jail in Skibbereen. I have a coach and constables waiting near the harbour for us. The good news is, the rain has stopped...bad news is, it's March in Ireland, so not for long." He turned back toward McShinnock. "You'll need to come to town and swear out a complaint."

McShinnock replied, "I'll be there tomorrow morning...by the way, what you may have overheard about my past was just an old crippled eccentric blowing smoke."

Keegan permitted himself a thin smile. "I never thought otherwise...Your Highness."

As Keegan marched Vonn out into the great hall, Watson

221B: On Her Majesty's Secret Service

hurried after him. "Vonn said he had men around the castle."

"My own men are only a minute's walk away," Keegan said over his shoulder. "They're still looking for a sign of this fabled flying machine."

"It can go invisible," Deirdre interjected. "Like the Fae."

Keegan snorted disdainfully. He paused at the door, his left hand on the back of Vonn's neck, his right holding his revolver. "Get the door for us, will you?"

Watson carefully unlatched it and pulled it open slowly. The door was heavy, made of four-inch thick planks of dark oak and bound by rivet-studded iron straps. Beyond lay only the gloom of the forecourt. "Would you like me to walk along with you?"

Keegan pushed Vonn through door. "I don't think that will be necessary, thank you."

A blinding blade of light stabbed through the murk, enclosing the doorway in a brilliant white disk. Keegan blurted in wordless surprise, squinting away. Shielding his eyes with one hand, Watson grabbed the man by the collar and sprang backward into the castle just as a rattling roar compressed their eardrums.

Bullets chopped dust-spurting gouges in the door-frame and lintel. Keegan uttered a sharp cry and went down, blood darkening the left leg of his trousers. He fired his revolver toward the source of the light. Vonn rushed away, shouting in panicked Swedish. The fusillade stopped, giving Watson the opportunity to drag Keegan away from the open door.

Holmes ran across the hall at an oblique angle to the open door. He squeezed the trigger of the machine pistol he held in both hands. The weapon stuttered and bucked in his grip, the rotating bores lipping flame. Spent brass cartridge cases arced and clattered against the stone floor. There was no return fire but the spotlight winked out.

Putting a shoulder against the heavy door, he shoved it shut. As he did so, he managed to peer around the edge toward the forecourt and beyond. On the other side of the low wall enclosing it, Holmes glimpsed gray figures. They fanned out and formed a long line, a chain of armed and armoured men. All of them appeared to be carrying the Rattler pistols.

A half-dozen of them had come out of the grounded aerocraft. Black hull glistening with rain-water, it rested on four thick tyres, each one about two feet in diameter. Two great wings were folded back in repose along the sides. He saw Vonn climbing up the right wing into an open hatch.

Holmes slammed the door and dropped the locking bar. He cast a glance at Keegan, who lay on the floor, back against the wall, clutching at his bullet-gashed leg. "Vonn got away."

Kneeling beside him, Watson examined the wound. "It looks to be a deep graze. Painful but not fatal...I'll get my medical kit and bandage you up."

Holmes checked the magazine of the Rattler. "Best hurry, Watson...I think we're in a for a siege."

Watson rose to his feet. He said sourly, "Well, that's just so bloody appropriate, isn't it?"

221B: On Her Majesty's Secret Service
The devil's agents may be of flesh and blood, may they not?
— Sherlock Holmes

CHAPTER 19

AS WATSON RAN across the hall toward the staircase, Loveday, Deirdre and Tesla appeared in the doorway of the receiving room. Loveday had taken her Bull-dog pistol from her reticule. "What is going on? Who is doing all the shooting?"

Watson's feet hit the first risers. "Holmes and Vonn's men—they'll be trying to break in to grab Nikola...the inspector has been wounded and I'm going to fetch my bag."

To Tesla and Deirdre, Loveday snapped, "Stay here!" and rushed across the stone floor to join Holmes at the door. He stood on the right side of the frame and indicated she should take up position on the left. He held up the repeater. "I'm not sure of the accuracy of this weapon or of the density of the door, so we should play it safe."

"Always my first impulse." She glanced over at Keegan. He kept his left hand clamped over the bullet-wound in his leg but liquid scarlet oozed between his fingers. He held his revolver in his right. His complexion was waxy but his expression remained alert. She asked, "How are you holding up, Inspector?"

"Well, I've been shot, Miss Brooke," he said wearily. "So I'm in a fair bit of pain."

"Dr Watson will return post-haste and fix you right up," Holmes assured him.

221B: *On Her Majesty's Secret Service*

He peered out the window, raising only his eyes above the sill. Four men jogged in broken-field style across the forecourt, toward the door. They wore gray coveralls of metallic mesh weave beneath a half-cuirass breastplate. Black bulbous helmets enclosed the tops and sides of their heads like the Deurne headgear of 4th-ceentury Rome. They carried Rattler pistols, and short-barrelled rifles were slung over their shoulders by straps. The helmets' nose-guards and the uncertain light made it difficult to see their faces.

Keegan said, "My men are out there with the wagon...I'm sure they've heard the gunfire and are on their way."

"They're armed, I hope?"

"Standard issue revolver and carbine apiece."

Holmes' lips tightened in a grim line. "I fear they are hopelessly out-gunned."

"Is there nothing we can do to warn them?"

"We could cover their approach by making our own noise," suggested Loveday. "Distract Vonn's men to draw their attention."

Holmes nodded. "Sound idea. Let's get these windows open."

His fingers explored the sash and found a double latch. He flicked it to the unlocked position. He grabbed it by the frame and pulled the window open and aside vertically. Glancing over at Loveday, he saw she already had the window open.

"Are you ready, Miss Brooke?" he asked, propping the barrel of the Rattler on the sill.

Loveday sighted down her revolver. "Let's make some noise, Mr Holmes."

Not really aiming, Holmes squeezed the trigger, firing a long fusillade. A constellation of sparks burst up from the forecourt's paving stones. The men veered away from their advance, running back to the cover of the wall. Loveday fired several shots, aiming at their heels.

As the uniformed men scrambled over and ducked down behind the wall, the spotlight on the bow of the aeroship blazed on, dazzling their eyes. Loveday and Holmes recoiled, whirling away as shafts of incandescence flooded through the windows and lit up the great hall.

As Holmes blinked away the dark floaters swimming across his vision, Vonn's hollow, amplified voice roared from the craft. "Sherlock Holmes! Loveday Brooke! Kevin McShinnock! Surrender Nikola Tesla or face complete destruction! Surrender must be unconditional and immediate!"

"Who the hell does he think he is?" came McShinnock's angry voice. "Ulysses bloody Grant?"

The man came clumping across the hall, one hand on his cane and the other holding a long-barrelled pistol with an engraved finish. Holmes assumed it was his U.S. Army sidearm, an 1860 Colt revolver. Éowyn and two other shotgun-wielding men marched beside him. Tesla and Deirdre trailed behind.

McShinnock shielded his eyes against the glare, moving between the two windows. He chose the left-hand one and crouched down. "I make out the distance to be twenty-five yards, Éowyn. What say you?"

Éowyn peered over the top of McShinnock's head. "More like twenty, Yer Highness."

"Close enough."

Taking a breath and holding it, McShinnock steadied his gun hand on the windowsill. He shifted position a fraction to the right, thumbed back the hammer and squeezed the Colt's trigger. The deep-throated *boom* of the big pistol echoed and re-echoed throughout the vaulted hall. The spotlight on the aerocraft exploded in a shattering of glass and a blaze of blue sparks. The hall became blessedly dim.

Vonn's voice rose in an enraged shout and a barrage of gunfire erupted. Bullets hammered against the door with a sound like a flock of infuriated woodpeckers. It shivered within the frame. After a few seconds, the firing ceased.

McShinnock snorted in disgust. "They'll waste a regiment's worth of ammunition trying to shoot through this door. It's original to the castle, made of oak that was ancient even then."

"Let's hope they don't unleash the ship's weapon," said Holmes. "It's a much higher calibre."

Nikola Tesla started to speak, coughed, and said, "Perhaps I should give myself up, let them take me and spare the rest of you."

McShinnock snorted again. "You're not getting off that easy, Professor. You've still a substantial bill to settle."

"I'm not really a professor," Tesla said apologetically. "Remember?"

"And I'm not really a king," McShinnock retorted. "But you still owe me."

"Even if you did the heroic thing," Loveday said, "after you complete the Ring's project you would end up like Julius Wendigee...or worse."

"Is the interior secure?" asked Holmes.

McShinnock nodded, but his expression was doubtful. "As best we can manage."

"How many hotel staff on the premises right now?"

"Three. I sent the cook and housekeeper home before we sat down to supper. I presume Swanton the stableman is in hiding. Can't say I blame him."

"How many ways are there to get into the castle?"

Éowyn said."Far too many, but you'd need to know where to find them."

Watson came down the stairs, two steps at a time, medical bag in hand. As he crossed the hall to Keegan, he said, "I looked out the window...armed men are creeping all around the grounds."

Kneeling down beside the inspector, he opened his case and removed the Webley. He handed it to Holmes. "I took the liberty of retrieving your pistol. I have my own service revolver but I don't know how much good any hand-gun will do if the flying machine gets airborne and attacks the castle from on high."

Tesla said, "It's possible, very likely in fact, that coming in contact with the geo-electrical discharge at Druid's Altar caused malfunctions aboard the *Terror*...perhaps a power surge affected some on-board systems. It may not able to fly properly until repairs are completed."

Watson ripped Keegan's pant leg open. A bullet had ploughed a thin, horizontal furrow along his thigh, a few inches above his knee. Working methodically, he swabbed away the blood with alcohol and applied a resorcisn paste. When Keegan winced, Watson said, "It's an antibacterial and a coagulant. But it stings."

Keegan asked, "How deep is the wound?"

"Not very...I can stitch it up if you wish, but these aren't the best circumstances, even for field surgery, and it will most definitely hurt like hell."

Keegan's lips twitched in a faint smile. "All things considered, just bandage it, please."

Watson instructed the inspector to squeeze the edges of the wound together while he bound the graze with several turnings of gauze.

Keegan gritted his teeth but made no outcry. Watson asked, "How is the pain level?"

"Tolerable, thank you."

"I can give you an injection of a morphine solution but you will be less than alert."

Keegan chuckled. "I think I'll need a clear head to deal with what is coming."

"Agreed."

Holmes turned toward Tesla and Deirdre, holding up the

221B: On Her Majesty's Secret Service

Webley. "Which one of you has ever fired a pistol before?"

After a silent second, Deirdre stepped forward and took the weapon from his hand. She popped open the cylinder, spun it while she checked the rounds and snapped it shut. Tesla stared at her in wide-eyed wonder.

"That answers my question, thank you," said Holmes.

Deirdre nodded. "Rebel county, remember?"

Peering through the window, Loveday said, "We've got a bit of fog blowing in from the bay. That could be to our advantage."

From outside, men shouted and guns began firing, a staccato popping sound, not the rattling roar of the repeaters.

Inspector Keegan twisted around, gazing up at the window. "Those are my men! Help me up, doctor!"

Watson hauled the man to his feet. Leaning against the windowsill, he stared out at the two uniformed constables running up the drive, both firing their bolt-action carbines in the direction of the armoured men behind the wall.

"Stop shooting, you fools!" shouted McShinnock. "Just run!"

"Open the door!" Keegan ordered. "Winston! O'Rourke! This way, lads!"

Holmes lifted the locking bar from the door while Éowyn pulled it inward. "Tell them to step it up!"

The undercarriage of the *Terror* snapped flame and noise. Bullets from the big Rattler stitched a line across the ground, spitting up gravel, tracking and intersecting with the two sprinting constables.

The men screamed, staggered and toppled, bodies jerking under the multiple blows. Keegan cried out in horror. Holmes felt a storm of bullets strike the door as if a work gang were pounding on it with heavy sledge-hammers. It shuddered violently amid a flurry of splinters. He staggered back, driven by the violent impacts transmitted through the wood. Éowyn snarled and put his back to the door as if against a cyclonic wind.

Tesla bounded forward and pushed. He and Éowyn shoved the door back into place and Holmes dropped the bar but it no longer fit tightly. The edge of the door sported a series of ragged holes. The volley ceased.

McShinnock shouted, "Fall back! Everyone fall back!"

Watson pulled Keegan away from the window. "Come away—there's nothing we can do about your men at the moment."

Keegan struggled. "No! I must see to them—"

Loveday grabbed him tightly by the arm. "The doctor is right...going outside now is suicide. There will be three murdered constables instead of two." She paused and added softly, "Live to fight another day, Inspector."

The man stared at her for a stretched-out tick of time, his face registering equal measures of grief and rage. Then he allowed her to lead him away. He limped but he was able to move at a rapid pace.

Inside the receiving room, Éowyn and the two McShinnock men overturned the long table, after first removing the dinnerware and the tureen of stew. They pushed it and three chairs toward the entrance to serve as a makeshift barricade.

Holmes gazed around at the cavities in the walls. "You don't intend to make a last stand here, I trust."

McShinnock chuckled, but his eyes were as hard as flint. "Not a bit of it. Clancahill Castle is seven centuries old...it was originally a Norman baronial estate before the Irish took possession."

He waved his pistol toward the niches. "Those lead to a network of tunnels and intersecting passageways inside the walls and into the hill. They were first dug by Baron Fitzgerald in the 12th century and further excavations were overseen by me in case I had to make speedy exit."

"From soldiers of the Queen, I suppose?" Keegan asked, an edge of sarcasm in his tone.

221B: *On Her Majesty's Secret Service*

"And there are still a few Johnny Rebs who think I did them wrong and might make their way here to settle some old scores. Most of the bolt-holes are warrens and lead virtually nowhere and some of them caved in over the centuries." He pointed to the cavity on the far wall. "But this part of the castle is built into the side of the hill itself...a remarkable feat of engineering. That tunnel is intact and will take you outside to the base of the hill — eventually."

"What's to keep enemies from simply following you through there?" Loveday asked.

Éowyn, from his place at the dining table barricade, said, "Remember when I mentioned the castle had its own gas-works?"

Loveday nodded. "I didn't make much of it at the time."

"Nor should you have." McShinnock's smile widened, but it did not reach his eyes. "Clancahill relies on coal gas for heat and light...from a supply and pumping system in the cellar, with adjacent fittings and fixtures worked into the passageways."

A line of consternation appeared on Watson's brow. "You wouldn't!"

"I haven't yet, but I would indeed, Doctor. I see you know that coal gas is composed of a highly flammable combination of hydrogen, methane and sulphur. And even if it is not ignited, the carbon monoxide is usually lethal in closed places...like tunnels."

"What are you proposing?" asked Holmes.

"It's simple... you and your companions, including the inspector, take the tunnel and get out while my men and I fight a holding action, if one is necessary. Once we think you've had enough time to make your escape, we'll make our own."

"And if you can't?" Loveday asked worriedly. "How will we know?"

"We'll fill the inner walls with gas. In addition to its many other qualities, coal gas stinks like the sump of hell. If you catch

221B: *On Her Majesty's Secret Service*

a whiff of it while in you're in the tunnels, do not strike a match or make the smallest spark. You can light your way as long as you don't smell sulphur."

Keegan leaned against the back of a chair to ease his wounded leg. "I prefer that plan to be a last resort —"

An eardrum-compressing crash reverberated across the entrance hall and into the receiving room. The massive door flew off its hinges, with a splintering of planks and screech of bolts being ripped from the wall. It toppled to the floor with a thunderclap that echoed and re-echoed. Tesla clapped his hands over his ears, his mouth forming an O of shock.

It took Holmes barely a second to realize the mechanics of the assault. The door had been propelled from its frame by the prow of the *Terror*. The craft rolled forward on its tyres, gathering speed and momentum until it struck the door squarely like a battering ram. He heard the thrum of an engine, so he concluded the ship had been piloted.

A quartet of gray-clad soldiers crouched between the doorframe and curving sides of the craft. They began firing their Rattlers in a left to right pattern. The bullets notched the walls and slammed into the surface of the dining table but did not penetrate the thick slab of wood.

Kneeling behind the table, Éowyn and his two companions triggered their shotguns in a triple volley, one after the other. A man using the *Terror* as cover slapped hands over his face and went down.

Holmes raised his weapon to fire a burst at the invaders but feared for the safety of the men at the barricade. Watson, Loveday and Deirdre squeezed off precise shots with their revolvers. the *Terror's* black hull rang with the impact of bullets. Return fire shattered glassware in the receiving room and pocked the walls. McShinnock manhandled Tesla toward the niche cut into the wall.

"Go!" he shouted. "These devils would rather shoot you to

221B: *On Her Majesty's Secret Service*

"That way," he said.

"Perhaps you should take the lead?" Watson suggested. "In case."

Holmes regarded him suspiciously. "In case of what?"

Watson lifted a shoulder in a shrug. "In case of bats, for instance."

"What about the gas?" Keegan asked pensively.

Holmes sniffed the air. "Clear so far. Let's go, bats notwithstanding."

The floor became cut into four steps that led downward. Rough rock walls appeared ahead of them, and vanished again into the pitch blackness behind them. The sound of shots tapered off to sporadic crackles and faded altogether.

Holmes only intermittently used the strike-lighter, wary of depleting its fuel or pinpointing their position to pursuers. The air smelled stale, but with no fumes of sulphur in it.

A passage opened to their left, angling downward. They started down the slanting tunnel, feet skidding slightly on the uneven floor. The tunnel levelled off then, and they stopped, Holmes holding the strike-lighter high. They saw signs of excavation, with rubble scattered across the floor. It could have lain there seven days, or seven hundred years.

Eyes narrowed, Holmes thrust his head forward, studying a series of vertical and horizontal grooves cut into the stone. With his free hand, he produced his magnifying glass from a jacket pocket and held the lens before the markings. "These look like Ogham inscriptions," he stated. "The so-called Celtic alphabet."

"So?" demanded Keegan impatiently.

"Some scholars date Ogham to the first century, which suggests this passageway predates the building of Clancahill Castle."

Sceptically, Loveday asked, "Who would have dug passageways this deep into the hill that long ago?"

pieces than have you escape them again!"

Tesla resisted, but did not struggle when Holmes dragged h[im] forward by his coat. "He's right! I don't know if Vonn has go[ne] mad or is obeying orders from the Ring to catch or kill, but the[re] is no point in negotiating at this juncture."

McShinnock took up a position at the dining table barrier. "A[ll] of you go! Get out and get help! We'll hold them here as long [as] we can."

He began fanning the hammer of the Colt as fast as he cou[ld] toward the uniformed men, the shots coming so rapidly the[y] sounded like the detonation of a string of firecrackers.

After pushing Tesla into the niche, Holmes helped Loveda[ce,] Deirdre and Keegan in ahead of him. Before he disappeared in[to] the darkness, he said to Watson who hesitantly hung back, "A b[it] more alacrity, if you please."

Watson's flesh tingled at the prospect of climbing into a pitch[-] dark passageway but it tingled even more at continuing t[o] exchange shots with enemies who outgunned the defenders of th[e] castle. Upon squeezing in, he saw the tunnel was only a split i[n] the rock walls, so narrow the six people moved in single file.

The darkness around them became complete, as if they were moving through a sea of black ink alleviated only a little by light from the receiving room behind them. The gunfire echoed hollowly. The passage debouched into a small, gloomy gallery with three fissures branching out from it. They came to halt.

"Which one should we take?" Deirdre murmured. "There's no way to know which is the right path."

"I guess we guess," said Holmes with a dour smile. "Just this once."

He took out his strike-lighter and after a couple of tries ignited the wick. He held it aloft, the tiny flame illuminating an area barely a hand's width in diameter. The flame guttered briefly when he held it before the centre opening.

Deirdre said softly, "Me mam told me about a farmer on his way home from a pub when it started to rain...he took shelter in a hillside cave and deep inside he found the royal court of the leprechauns who made him join their revels."

"I heard the same story," said Tesla. "Only it was kobolds, not leprechauns and they forced him into a bowling match. When he finally got out of the cave, twenty years had passed but he had not aged a day."

"Keep our minds on the problem at hand, shall we?" Keegan asked gruffly, voice tight with repressed pain.

Loveday chuckled nervously. "Leprechauns and kobolds need not apply."

Holmes extinguished the flame and they began groping through the blackness again. When the tunnel narrowed and branched, the strike lighter was called into service once more. The flame caught the gentle drift of air and flickered. They could smell wet vegetation, and the hint of the sea. Watson gusted out a relieved sigh, took a breath, then his shoulders stiffened. "Holmes —"

Instantly, Holmes blew out the flaming wick. The faint stench of sulphur wafted to them from deep in the tunnels. Keegan put a hand to his nose. "The old fox is gassing the passageways."

"Which may mean Ring troopers are in here," Loveday said grimly.

"Let's keep going," said Holmes, moving off.

They walked quickly, feeling their way in complete darkness. The walls of the tunnel drew in closer and the ceiling lowered until they had to stoop. A scattering of dried leaves crackled under their feet. They sidled around a projection of rock and paused to listen and sniff the air.

The sulphurous odour smelled stronger. From behind them they heard the clink of metal against stone and the murmur of men's voices. "They're back there, all right," Watson whispered.

"If we run, we'll make noise," breathed Deirdre tensely. "They may start shooting blindly."

Holmes said flatly, "That is a chance we must take, I fear...however, we can't be far from the exit so let's go as fast as we can.."

The six people rushed along the passageway, the scrape of their footfalls, rustle of their clothes and their little pants and gasps of exertion sounding obscenely loud. They had not gone far before they heard the stutter of a triggered Rattler and the whine of ricochets. Rock chips pelted them.

The darkness suddenly quivered, the tunnel floor feeling as if it had shifted beneath their feet. The air moved against their faces. Dust and grit sifted down from above like a snow flurry. Watson shouted, "The fools have ignited the gas!"

They began to run, stumbling on loose stones, banging knees and scraping elbows. Nevertheless, they kept running, lurching from wall to wall. A foul-smelling column of concussive force bellowed through the passageway, carrying with it the echoes of agonized screams. It slammed them up and off their feet.

They flew out into cold, clean air, rolling painfully over the wet ground and into a shallow declivity. A whorling ball of blue-white flame flung itself from the throat of the tunnel like a boulder launched from a catapult, roaring out over their heads. They all felt the wave of heat.

A series of consecutive blasts thundered and for an instant all that could be seen within the passage was a roiling whirlpool of flame. With a whoosh, it disappeared, as if sucked back into the heart of the hill. Loose stones and pieces of shale pattered down.

As they hiked themselves into a sitting position, a pillar of orange fire more than fifty feet high mushroomed up over the crest of the hill. Rolling balls of flame billowed up into the night sky. Burning debris inscribed glowing arcs.

"Oh, sweet Jesus" said Deirdre in a strangulated voice. She

crossed herself. "Poor King Kevin! His beautiful hotel—"

Tesla patted her shoulder reassuringly. "If the gas-works was indeed located in the cellar, the tunnels will act as vents for the thermal and kinetic shock of the explosion, so I imagine Clancahill Castle still stands, despite taking a considerable amount of damage."

"But what about him and his people?"

"He said he had a means of escape," Watson reminded him.

Grimacing, Keegan staggered to his feet. "And if King Kevin knows how to do one thing better than anyone else, it's how to survive."

Holmes got up, automatically brushing off his clothes. He extended a hand to Loveday, who allowed him to pull her to her feet. He said, "Perhaps a beneficial result is that the *Terror* will never fly again."

Watson, Tesla and Deirdre arose. All of them gazed upward as a winged shadow glided overhead before being swallowed up by a dense, scarlet-tinged cloud forming in the fog above the ridge line.

"Or," Watson darkly, "perhaps not."

"Blood in the sky," said Loveday in voice hushed by fear.

"An omen of devils?" Deirdre asked softly.

"Or a promise," Holmes said. He turned to face Tesla, his face a grim, uncompromising mask. "I expect you will tell us everything."

Tesla inhaled a deep breath, closing his eyes for a few seconds. His lips stirred as if in silent prayer. He exhaled, opening his eyes and saying simply, "I will."

221B: On Her Majesty's Secret Service
We can't command our love, but we can our actions.
—Sherlock Holmes

CHAPTER 20

4 March

DESPITE HIS INJURED leg, Inspector Keegan insisted they return to the hotel, arguing since the *Terror* had departed, most likely all active combatants had gone with it. Scaling the hillside in the fog in almost complete darkness seemed an impossibility, so the six people circled around the base to approach the castle from the front.

By the time they reached the mouth of the lane, a crowd of onlookers from the village had gathered in the forecourt to stare at the flames flickering through the shattered windows of Clancahill Castle. The six of them pushed past and entered the great hall. Swanton the stableman was attempting to extinguish small fires with a bucket of water dipped from a rain-barrel.

The tapestries and the McShinnock family crest showed only smouldering scorch-marks. The gas fumes had escaped through the broken-down door, so the flames when they ignited, had been of short duration.

Overall, the damage to the castle's interior was not as extensive as they had feared. Much as Tesla speculated, once the fumes ignited in the tunnel, the explosive blow-back was largely confined to the gas works in the cellar.

Still, the smoky air was poisonously redolent with the burnt rotten-egg odour of sulphur, so a full search of the castle was not undertaken. With handkerchiefs over their noses and mouths, Watson, Tesla and Holmes retrieved everyone's luggage from their upstairs rooms. The cases and valises were undamaged.

Neither McShinnock, Éowyn nor any other hotel staff were anywhere to be found. Swanton offered no intelligence as to their whereabouts. He had hidden in the hayloft of the stable during the short siege and only crept out upon the departure of the *Terror,* a scene he believed to be diabolical in nature.

If there were casualties among the crew of the aeroship, Vonn had collected them except for those caught in the tunnel inferno. The only bodies found were those of Winston and O'Rourke, the pair of hapless constables lying in pools of blood where they had been shot down.

Watson and Keegan walked down to the harbour to the police wagon, where, with Watson's help, they disconnected the dray horse's harness from a cast-iron carriage anchor. Keegan climbed into the driver's box and drove the wagon to the hotel. There, Holmes and Watson placed the corpses of the constables in the back, covering their bodies with one of the singed tapestries yanked from the wall. Deirdre studiously refused to look at their bullet-shattered faces. After leaving instructions with Swanton to wait for the fire brigade and more constables to arrive, Keegan drove the wagon out to the Cork Road, and thence to Skibbereen.

The ride to the town was slow, wet and miserable. The light shed by the wagon's lanterns barely penetrated the fog, so it felt as if they trekked through a mist-shrouded netherworld, making no progress. Other than the distant barking of a farm dog, the only sounds were the steady clop-clop of horse hooves on the hard-packed dirt road and the creak of axles. It was a cramped fit on the front and back benches, since no one cared to share the wagon's bed with the dead men. Holmes sat cross-legged on the roof. Everyone's clothes carried the stink of coal gas but since they all smelled the same, they had no choice but to bear it.

When he noticed her shivering, Tesla draped his coat over

Deirdre's shoulders and she leaned into him, her eyes haunted and tearful. She said, "To think just this morning, I said this would be fun." She brushed back tears and turned her face to Loveday. "You were right, Miss Brooke...I am a foolish creature."

Loveday patted her hand. "You're just young and perhaps too sure of yourself... but you've comported yourself bravely all through this. I misjudged you and for that, I apologize."

Watson rubbed his hands together and blew on them. "It's been a very long day, hasn't it?"

Holmes took his long-stemmed briar pipe from a jacket pocket. "Does anyone mind if I smoke?"

"Just exhale away from us, please," said Loveday.

After filling the bowl with tobacco, Holmes brought out his strike-lighter. After several attempts to kindle a flame, he said ruefully, "Out of petrol...good and bad , I suppose."

Watson said, "It worked when it counted. That's what's important."

Bedraggled, exhausted, and in Keegan's case, consumed with physical and emotional pain, the group of six reached the Skibbereen railyard at half-past one in the morning. Keegan remained in the wagon as the others climbed down to the station's deck.

"Do you think you can locate your train?" he asked, although he did not sound overly concerned one way or the other.

Holmes nodded. "The locomotive is rather hard to mistake. Will you get word to Mr Cronin that his horses can be found at Castle Clancahill?"

"I will. Do you wish me to wire London with a full report of your mission here?" Keegan suddenly grinned, a forced rictus that made his haggard face resemble a skull's. "Or should I just report it was successful and leave it at that?"

Watson stepped forward and said non-committally, "Just say

221B: On Her Majesty's Secret Service

we are returning with the person whom we sought."

Loveday stated, "We will be making a full report, Inspector, including details of the heroism of you and your men...a loss for which we are profoundly sorry."

Keegan nodded, hands tightening on the reins. "It might give some comfort to my men's families if they knew their killers would be brought to justice." He turned his head toward them. "But you three have no formal authority to do so."

Holmes reached up and squeezed the man's wrist. "We will bring our own retribution. Be certain of that."

Keegan snapped the reins and the wagon lurched forward. "I will hold you to it, Mr Holmes."

A blue-uniformed watchman came out of the building holding a lamp. He escorted the five of them to the siding on which the *Wraith* and its two cars waited. Surprisingly, they found Tennyson still awake in the Pullman passenger coach, although the train's engineer, fireman and mechanic had taken rooms at a nearby hostel that catered exclusively to the railroad trade.

Tennyson assured them the staff would report back before sunrise to ready the train for departure. He did not volunteer to go and rouse them, nor was it suggested. The earliest ferry back to Holyhead departed from the port of Dublin at five o'clock in the morning and there was little chance of reaching it, even if the *Wraith* left Skibbereen within the hour.

As it was, all five people were enervated and exhausted, wanting only to be dry, warm and safe — at least for a few hours. For Sherlock Holmes, sleep was out of the question. While his companions made themselves less damp and sulphurated, he took up a chair near a window and lit his pipe with a match. He smoked single-mindedly, his gaze both vacant and fierce, fixed on some distant point beyond the railyard.

Tennyson prepared a pot of tea and a platter of biscuits. When offered to Holmes, he declined them. He shifted his gaze to

221B: *On Her Majesty's Secret Service*

Tesla. Watson had seen that same steely glitter in his friend's eyes before and knew it did not bode well for the young scientist.

With the stem of his pipe, Holmes gestured toward a chair opposite him. "Nikola Tesla. Time to tell us everything. Please sit down."

Tesla's hand froze midway whilst bringing his tea cup to his lips. "Now, Mr Holmes? Really?"

"Now. Really."

Watson nudged the man toward the chair. "Unless you prefer to be left behind in Skibbereen. I know I'm tempted."

With a sigh of resignation, Tesla sat down. Loveday and Watson took seats on either side of him. Deirdre withdrew to lie down on a divan at the far end of the coach. Tesla asked, "What do you want to know that I haven't explained already?"

Holmes steepled his fingers and stretched out his legs, crossing them at the ankles. "How and when did you meet Robur?"

Tesla cast his eyes downward, hands around his cup. "Through Julius Wendigee. He and I met whilst working at the Société Electrique Edison in Paris. When I resigned, I returned to New York, hoping to find more lucrative prospects among investors for my inventions. Within a short time, I was reduced to the most menial of labours, just to pay my rent."

"Digging ditches for two dollars a day, you said," Loveday commented.

Tesla nodded. "A very lowly state. Then, much to my surprise, in late '86 I received a wire from Julius, urging me to make an appointment with Baron Maupertuis, who was a guest at the Windsor Hotel. The wire suggested the baron was very interested in new mechanicities and electrical applications. He wished to meet me."

"So you only knew him as Maupertuis?" asked Holmes.

Tesla nodded. "That was how he was introduced. We met in the hotel's dining room the evening of the very day I contacted him. He was an impressive man, in the company of a beautiful lady he introduced as Kathryn Koluchy. Since he was seated, I did not realize the shortness of his stature. He seemed somewhat familiar to me, as if I had glimpsed him somewhere before, but long in the past. Both he and Madame Koluchy gave the impression of superior intelligence, wealth and good breeding. Except..." He trailed off, his brows knitting at the bridge of his nose.

"Except what?" asked Watson.

"The baron was rather mercurial...twice during our meeting he began profane rants about fools who had tried to steal his inventions and twice the lady had to calm him down, speaking in French. The second time, she addressed him as 'Robur' and then I remembered. Robur the Conqueror! Some years before the portrait of this extraordinary man had been printed in all the European newspapers, when he drew the attention of the entire world to himself, and his wonderful airship, the *Albatross.*"

Holmes nodded. "All of that happened nearly twenty years before you dined with him in New York. Did he say where he had been and what he had been doing in the intervening years?"

"Not at that point — and even later, he only alluded to having designed a completely new flying machine which could conquer all the elements...he talked about a select body of devoted workmen constructing a prototype with a quadruple functionality. By that, I assumed he meant air, water, land and underwater. His major stumbling block was reliable motive power."

Loveday frowned. "Did you ever discuss your induction motor with Julius?"

"Of course...among many other things. He was a colleague...he was gifted but rather pedestrian in his thinking."

Watson asked, "Did Robur happen to mention the identities of the 'select body of devoted workmen'?"

"Not specifically...I was being sought out primarily for my

electrical expertise...Madame Koluchy explained the grand plans to make the upcoming Paris Exposition the wonder of the century, the doorway to the future. I was offered what seemed like a fortune to further develop my induction motor for a variety of different applications. The organization which they represented intended to invest in my work, and unlike my unhappy experience with Thomas Edison, I was offered a five-year employment contract which stipulated I could pursue all of my different lines of research, including how to harness the geo-electric grid of the Earth, to provide free energy...what I called the teleforce." Tesla smiled sadly. "It was a dream come true."

Holmes said, "I deduce that at some point, you realized that if the offer sounded too good to be true, it most certainly was."

Tesla tugged nervously at his long nose. "That realization took longer than it should have, I must confess. But once I signed the contract, I was caught in a whirlwind...not just wined and dined, but treated like royalty. Madame Koluchy entranced me with her brilliance and beauty. She was very attentive, very much a skilled flatterer. She introduced me to the so-called Echelon, technological masterminds in various fields... there was a Sikh prince named Dakkar who had developed a highly advanced submersible, Professor Mirzarbeau with his manipulations of a cosmic radiation he called the Violet Flame, a strange genetic scientist called Moreau, an elderly physicist who had created a substance to cancel gravity, and a doctor whose goal it was build a machine to travel through time. All very amazing."

Tesla shook his head. "Madame Koluchy, despite her reputation as a nutritionist, was particularly fascinated with what she referred to as 'artificial intelligence.' She and a man named Quevedo were devoted to completing electromechanical devices they referred to as integrated automata, including a telekino — a device to control machines remotely — and an Analytical Engine."

Loveday chuckled. "The names are rather whimsical."

Tesla regarded her broodily. "I assure you the brains behind them are anything but. These are very serious people."

He returned his gaze to Holmes. "I didn't realize how serious until I overheard a brief discussion between Madame Koluchy and Robur about a project called Thunderstrike... and how my telegeodynamics concept was necessary to bring it to fruition."

"Did you ask about the project's nature?" inquired Watson.

"They stopped talking as soon as they became aware of me, so I did not dare. The conversation took place in Paris at Madame Koluchy's home overlooking the Exposition grounds. She had earlier pointed out the Iron Lady tower to me, asking my opinion of its ongoing construction. Since we were preparing to embark to Cornwall, I didn't feel the time was right to question her. It was on the voyage over I met Basil Zaharoff who was introduced to me as an investor in technological futures." Tesla frowned. "I did not care for him."

Holmes exhaled a puff of smoke. "Not many do, I suspect. My brother, for one."

Tesla's lips quirked in a smile. "Once we arrived in Cornwall at Mr Zaharoff's foundry, I began to have serious misgivings about further involvement with this group. I saw very rough men in paramilitary uniforms marching about with vicious guard dogs. They carried large guns. When the baron's ship the *Friesland* arrived, I was very disconcerted by most of the cargo I saw being unloaded."

His eyes shifted to Loveday. "When the baron ordered Vonn to murder you in the coldest of blood, I decided my employment had come to an end, regardless of the contract."

Loveday smiled. "Thank you for reaching that decision when you did."

"Yes," said Holmes coldly, "that choice will no doubt save you from standing in the dock alongside the rest of the technological masterminds when they are brought to justice."

221B: *On Her Majesty's Secret Service*

"Mr Holmes!" Loveday glared at him. "That is hardly necessary —"

"And then you fled," Holmes broke in brusquely. "Where did you go after leaving Cornwall?"

Tesla coughed nervously, shifting in his seat. "I remained there at an isolated inn under an assumed name for several weeks. I had the money to buy anonymity. When I grew low on funds, I travelled to London...I feared I would be apprehended if I tried to board a ship to the Continent or elsewhere."

"Apprehended by whom?" Watson challenged.

"That was the conundrum, Doctor...I couldn't be sure. So, I changed my appearance as best I could and stayed only long enough to complete the sale of an earlier model of my induction motor to George Westinghouse in America. The transaction was done entirely through the telegraph and the post. After I received the cheque, I took the ferry to Ireland and decided to revive my telegeodynamics experiments, since I now had the money to build a transmitter. I visited many remote archaeological sites, sometimes staying a couple of months, other times only a couple of weeks."

Tesla dry-scrubbed his hair with one nervous hand. "Eventually, I came here to West Cork. I took a room at Clancahill Castle, and soon was living there on credit only because King Kevin took pity on me. You know the rest."

Holmes grunted disinterestedly and took another draw on his pipe.

Defensively, Tesla said, "I hope you don't hold me responsible for what Vonn did there tonight."

"Vonn made his own choices about the actions he took, but in my estimation, you set much of these events in motion when you fled from Penhallick instead of coming forward to tell what you knew. You would've been under the Crown's protection all this time, instead of living as a fugitive."

221B: *On Her Majesty's Secret Service*

Tesla's face registered defiance. "Why should I trust the British government with my life and my secrets?"

Watson spoke up angrily. "Because if you had, Robur most likely would not have been able to take the *Terror* from the prototype stage to fully developed war-machine with the capability of traversing the air, the oceans, and the ground while invisible. Two men who are now dead would not be. Not to mention whatever the Ring has planned for the Paris Exposition."

Tesla's defiance turned to defensiveness. "I was commissioned to install an electrical lighting system, so I have no details of what else they may have planned."

Holmes stood up and stared down at Tesla, pipe stem clenched tightly between his bared teeth. His hands knotted into fists. Tesla leaned back, as if fearing a blow.

With measured deliberation, Holmes unclenched fists, took the pipe from his mouth and inhaled a long, steadying breath. He intoned, "You're a fool, Nikola Tesla. You may very well be one of the most brilliant men who ever lived, but at the same time, you are possibly the most foolish man I've ever met and believe me, that is a high bar to reach, much less exceed."

He turned his back, staring out the window. "Kindly don't speak to me again unless I speak to you."

After a few seconds of contemplation, Tesla arose and crossed to the opposite end of the coach. He sat down, supporting his bowed head upon his right hand. Loveday said quietly, "You were rather hard on Nikola, don't you think?"

Watson uttered a scoffing laugh. "I know you feel you're indebted to him, but Nikola cut and ran rather than expose the Hephaestus Ring."

"John, he didn't know there was anything to expose. He did not understand what he was involved in. He only understood he was suddenly in grave danger and sought to remove himself from it as quickly as he could. This type of thing is not his milieu. Think of

221B: On Her Majesty's Secret Service

him as a child."

Watson began a rejoinder, but Holmes turned around, gesturing sharply with his pipe. "Enough, please. We've all come to the end of our collective ropes. Let's try to get some rest. If yesterday was long and arduous, there's no reason to assume today will be any different once we're underway."

He moved over to a bench and dropped onto it, assuming a half-prone potion. He relit his pipe, an action that was an unmistakable cue the discussion had come to an end. Loveday began to speak, but Watson touched her shoulder and shook his head. "He's in one of his mulish moods and there's no animal more intractable on the face of the earth than a mulish Sherlock Holmes." He raised his voice to ask, "Wouldn't you agree, Holmes?"

Holmes did not bother to glance his way. A veil of smoke obscured his features. Scowling, Watson stalked away, followed a moment later by Loveday, who muttered imprecations under her breath.

Resting the back of his head on the arm of the bench, Holmes finished smoking the tobacco in the pipe's bowl. His mind raced, providing images of the Eiffel Tower, moving them about to view from all angles. He could not visualize the vast space of the foundation, or what lay beneath or between the four massive support pillars.

After trying and failing to recall all that he had seen of the tower in Mycroft's office, he straightened up impatiently. Just as he did so, Deirdre sat down very close beside him, nearly crowding him against the coach wall.

Her blue eyes flashed bright with anger. "Yer a self-righteous sort, aren't ye? I heard what ye said to Nikola."

"I thought you were asleep."

She waved his words away. "I was acting. Why were ye so heartless to the poor lad? It's not like he's a skanger."

"I didn't claim he was," replied Holme irritably. "But he's certainly irresponsible to the verge of criminality."

"What do ye expect from him from here on, once he's back in London?"

"That would not be within my purview. I doubt Nikola will be officially charged with a crime, but he may be placed in custody for further questioning about the Hephaestus Ring." He paused and added, "You have no reason to worry about him, Miss Dalton. In a few hours you will be reunited with your mother in Cork City and you can put this all behind you."

Deirdre inhaled slowly through her nostrils. After few seconds, she said thoughtfully, "I'm not sure if I want to do that. I'm in rather deep in this affair now and I wish to see how it's all sorted."

Holmes lifted his eyebrows. "After what you experienced and witnessed tonight? That is a foolhardy wish."

Deirdre glared at him. "So ye think you can pay me off and drop me off, is that it?"

"To save your life, yes. You've had too many close calls in a single day. Think about your mother, even if you care little for your own safety. I should allow no daughter of mine to engage in such activities "

Deirdre stiffened. "Daughter?"

"Sister, then." Holmes realized instantly he had chosen the wrong word.

"Sister?" Deirdre echoed in outrage. "Is that how ye think of me? A little girl who needs protectin'? Who saved your pompous arse from the Fenians? It wasn't Loveday, I can tell ye that much!"

Holmes leaned his head back and sighed wearily. "I know you are intelligent enough to understand what I mean, regardless of how inelegantly I state it. Miss Brooke, Dr Watson and myself are professional agents of the British Secret Service. You may be a talented amateur but you are still a civilian. By retaining you to act as our guide less than twenty-four hours ago, we have put your life in jeopardy no less than three times, arguably four. That is more than enough."

Imitating his weary sigh, Deirdre leaned back beside him. After a moment's silent consideration, she said, "I suppose ye're right. I've earned me five shillings, haven't I?"

"More than. In fact, I think you've earned ten."

Deirdre closed her eyes and chuckled. "That should go well with the hundred pounds I earned from me starring role as Miss Millicent Monroe. It's been quite the successful tour."

Holmes chuckled too. They stayed like that, sitting side-by-side on the cushioned bench. After a minute, Deirdre's breathing became deep and regular. Holmes glanced at her, realizing she had fallen asleep.

This time she wasn't acting. He settled back and closed his own eyes.

221B: On Her Majesty's Secret Service

The highest morality may prove to be the highest wisdom.

— John H. Watson, MD

CHAPTER 21

AS TENNYSON SAID, the train crew arrived at the *Wraith* shortly before sunrise and began preparing the locomotive for travel. By then, everyone in the coach had fallen deeply asleep and were barely roused by the noise and the motion.

After replenishing the boiler with water, the engineer shoved the throttle forward, rolling the *Wraith* ponderously along the tracks leading out of the railyard. By then, the indigo of the night sky broke up into scraps of orange and yellow. Holmes slowly came awake, pulled from sleep by the aroma of freshly brewed coffee.

He saw that Deirdre still slept, her head resting against the shoulder of his Norfolk jacket. With her hair rumpled and her face in the repose of her slumber, she looked child-like and even cherubic. He gazed at her with an oddly sad but paternal feeling. He realized he would miss her, but he also knew he would have more peace of mind if she were out of harm's way.

Carefully, he dislodged her head and eased her down on the bench, placing a small cushion beneath her. He stood up and stretched, feeling twinges of pain in his elbows and knees from the multiple impacts against rock during their mad dash out of the tunnel in Glandore. From outside, he heard the switches being thrown for the main rail line. The train slowly rumbled over them, the wheels click-clacking rhythmically. The locomotive's whistle loosed a warning shriek along with a jet of steam. The train picked up speed.

Loveday, Watson and Tesla sat around a small table at the rear of the coach, sipping cups of coffee. Holmes joined them, walking up the aisle between the benches, arms spread to balance himself against the swaying of the coach. All three people looked tired and dishevelled. Holmes assumed he looked the same way. Tesla studiously avoided meeting his gaze, endlessly stirring his coffee.

"Good morning, Holmes," Watson said. "Did you sleep well?" He didn't sound as if he expected a positive response.

"I doubt it. Did you and Miss Brooke?"

"The same, I wager," said Watson. "Speaking for myself."

"Speaking for *my*self," Loveday said, "no, I did not."

Holmes filled a cup with coffee poured from a silver pot. "Miss Dalton is still asleep. I'll wake her on our approach to Cork City. I think we should pay her ten shillings instead of the agreed-upon five."

"I suggest fifteen," said Loveday. "Very few young ladies would have stood shoulder-to-shoulder with me and fired a revolver at armoured ruffians. She kept a cool head."

"Twenty then?" Watson enquired with a smile.

Holmes nodded. "Agreed."

The sun rose, a faint orange smudge due to the overcast. A gray mist hung in the air. The track curved through a huddle of old clapboard hovels. The trees there looked black against the few splashes of colour that spread up into the sky. In minutes the train was out of Skibbereen and rolling along at about thirty miles per hour. The train chugged around a gradual curve that descended into a shallow valley between a range of rocky hills. A few minutes later, they rumbled through Drimoleague Junction and then on to the South Coast Rail Line.

As Holmes drank his coffee, he noted how Tesla looked in

every direction but towards him. The man's eyes were red-netted, his shoulders slumped, his suit wrinkled. Holmes placed his cup on the table, put his hands into his pockets and after a self-conscious clearing of the throat, said, "Mr Tesla, I have had some time to think about your situation. It was brought to my attention that I dealt with you rather roughly. Although I feel you behaved irresponsibly in this matter, it is not my place to pass judgment on you. We offer the protection of the Crown, but we can't force it upon you. If you wish to remain a fugitive, that is your decision alone."

While Holmes spoke, Tesla slowly raised his gaze. "I've had some time to think myself, Mr Holmes. I realize now I was motivated by fear and humiliation...I was so besottted by Madame Koluchy and so taken with my new status, I refused to closely examine what should have been obvious. Although I was being paid, I was also being manipulated. When I came to that realization, I was so ashamed of my foolishness I could not bear to face up to it."

"Manipulated to what purpose?" asked Loveday.

Tesla's expression hardened. "To be completely in thrall to Kathryn and her ambitions. She tried to match me up with an attractive young lady she called Babiole. 'Trinket' in English. The name alone should have been a clue."

Watson smiled and shook his head. "Subtlety is apparently not her hallmark."

"Kathryn had done the same with Julius," Tesla continued, "who was totally seduced by a girl named Sara. I understood only in hindsight that both young women were far too beautiful and preoccupied with fashion and parties to feel any genuine attraction to either Julius or myself, much less affection. We were only their assignments, but I was so caught up in the mad whirl, I refused to heed my inner voice."

"If you had," said Holmes, "what do you think you would have learned from yourself?"

221B: On Her Majesty's Secret Service

Tesla exhaled a slow, shaky breath. "Madame Koluchy was more than intellectually fascinated by my telegeodynamics concept...I suspect the Thunderstrike undertaking I overheard her discussing with Baron Maupertuis is intimately connected to Eiffel's iron tower and —"

The steam whistle of the locomotive screamed an alarm. The brakes screeched and the great drive wheels locked, sending showers of sparks along the rails. The sudden deceleration caused everyone to stagger and grab at bench backs. The *Wraith* did not lurch to a complete halt, but its speed slowed considerably.

Deirdre, jolted awake, pulled herself to a sitting position and cried out petulantly, "Now what is happening?"

"Let's find out," Watson snapped, moving quickly toward the vestibule at the front of the car. He reached the midway point when the door swung open, pushed by Tennyson. Although the man appeared calm and composed, his voice trembled when he announced, "We have an emergency...Engineer Crampton requests the presence of someone in authority to join him forward."

Followed by Holmes, Watson went out on the coach platform, jumped over the coupler and carefully navigated a narrow footboard on the side of the fuel-tender. The train rolled forward at barely a crawl. On the right side stretched an overgrown thicket On the left a rock-littered embankment sloped upward. A man in a uniform of sorts consisting of a blue-striped cap and overalls stood amongst the heaps of coal in the tender. He extended a hand and pulled Watson and Holmes up.

A burly middle-aged man dressed in an identical cap and coveralls turned away from the controls when Watson climbed into the cab. Beneath a fresh film of soot, his round face was white with fear. "Who are you two?"

"John Watson and Sherlock Holmes," he said, pointing to himself and Holmes. "Representing Her Majesty's Secret Service. I presume you're Crampton. Why have we slowed?"

221B: *On Her Majesty's Secret Service*

Crampton pointed a gloved finger toward the window. "Take a look and maybe you can tell me."

Cautiously, Watson leaned out, looking down the tracks. For an instant, he wasn't quite certain what he saw. At a distance of about fifty yards, he saw a very large object straddling the rails. Then he recognized the outspread wings. He heard a sudden, sharp intake of breath from Holmes.

"It's the *Terror*," he said grimly. "Drawing a line in the sand."

"Daring us to cross it," replied Watson. "Or to give up Nikola."

"What is that infernal thing?" Crampton demanded.

"An aerocraft...a flying vehicle. The men aboard are interfering with our mission."

Holmes drew his head and shoulders back into the cab. "I doubt Vonn would want to risk a head-on collision with a locomotive of the Teutonic Class."

"I don't want to risk it either," Crampton said. He gestured to a wiry man perched on a stool on the opposite side of the compartment. He nervously wiped down a crescent wrench with an oily rag. "Neither does Hawley, my mechanic."

"No, I most certainly don't," Hawley said in a monotone.

Watson turned to look at him. "Surely the *Wraith* is superior in mass."

"Perhaps so, sir," replied Hawley, "but we're on a curve and a head-on crash with much of anything weighty could cause a derail if we hit it the right — or wrong— way."

Holmes thrust his head out of the window again and gave the configuration of the aerocraft a swift visual analysis. He said, "I recommend full throttle."

Watson nodded. "You heard him, Mr Crampton."

The engineer's jaw muscles bunched. "You two are in charge, I take it?"

"For the time being," Holmes said. "The responsibility is ours."

221B: *On Her Majesty's Secret Service*

"That makes me feel so much better," Crampton growled.

Slamming levers forward, the locomotive shuddered. The gauges and dials trembled as the steam pressure went up. The *Wraith* surged forward, black vapour erupting from the smokestack. Holmes reached for the whistle lanyard and yanked. As the alert shrieked forth, little spurts of flame came from the top of the embankment. A hailstorm of bullets pounded against the locomotive's side and bounced away. Others chocked into the coal heaped in the tender.

Watson crouched down. "Men up there with Rattlers."

Holmes said, "We should arm ourselves. They may have set up a gauntlet for us to run."

The train gained speed. More bullets spanged and sparked on the locomotive's iron hide. Crampton cried out, slapping at his upper left arm. A flower of blood bloomed on the fabric of his shirt. Holmes and Huxley pulled him away from the levers and settled him on the deck. Holmes took the throttle while Watson quickly examined the man's injury.

"Superficial," he said, improvising a bandage from a handkerchief that Crampton pulled from a pocket. "Probably a bullet fragment from a ricochet."

They heard more shots, much closer and spaced more evenly. Watson and Holmes looked behind the cab and over the fuel tender to see Loveday standing on the Pullman coach platform, holding her Bull-dog revolver in a two-handed grip and squeezing off precision shots at the embankment.

Deirdre stood behind her, holding the repeating pistol Holmes had appropriated at Clancahill. Crawling over to the tender coupling, Watson called the girl's name, drew her attention and motioned for her to toss the weapon into the car. She did so with a careful underarm throw. The fireman, crouching among the coal, caught the gun and passed it on to Watson.

He checked it over, fitting the grip into his hand and curling his index finger around the trigger. He noted that most of the weapon's weight was in the barrel. He aimed at the top of the embankment and squeezed the trigger. He managed the recoil with his other hand to keep the barrel from shimmying too far to the left or right. The big pistol hammered in a stuttering burst. Divots of dirt and rock fragments exploded along the crest. He glimpsed three helmeted heads ducking down behind the ridge-line.

"Fire at the *Terror*," Holmes called. "Perhaps they will give way."

Kneeling at the rear of the cab, leaning out and sighting down the barrel, Watson squeezed the Rattler's trigger again. Dust-spurting lines of impact scampered all round the bow of the *Terror* and struck flares from the rails.

The air-ship rose from the tracks, wobbling from side-to-side as the fan-turbines roared, blasting out grit and gravel in a blinding cloud. Wings quivering, the craft lifted vertically to an altitude of one hundred feet, then soared off to the east.

"You were right," Watson said, grinning in spite of the circumstances. Adrenalin pumped through him.

The train rocked steadily as it sped into more open country. Crampton climbed to his feet and took back the controls. He had stuffed his handkerchief under his shirt over his wound. Watson gave the injury a look and saw the bleeding had stopped. He said, "I'll fetch my medical kit and fix you up with a proper bandage."

"It just stings a little, so no rush." Crampton laughed and said, "In all my years as an engineer, the last three aboard this girl, I've had all sorts of truck and muck thrown at me, from chamber pots to rotten fruit. Never been shot, though."

"Medically speaking, you haven't now," Watson said. "You've been nicked. But I won't refute you if that's how you want to tell it."

Holmes peered out of the cab window at the sky, shading his eyes. He said, "The *Terror* will be back, most likely between here and Cork City, since it's so lightly populated compared to the Dublin route. Fewer witnesses."

Watson gazed upward. "Possibly Vonn decided the odds aren't in his favour... attacking us from the air would be like a hawk trying to seize an elephant." He handed the repeater to Holmes. "I'll get my bag and treat Crampton."

"Make sure the ladies and Tesla are prepared for whatever happens next."

"Right...whatever that may be."

Watson retraced his path around the fuel tender and to the passenger carriage. The train regained its speed of thirty miles an hour. Holmes stayed at the rear of the engine, watching the sky as best he could, although the roof of the cab blocked much of his view.

The locomotive laboured noisily against a steep upgrade. At the top, the track dipped between bulwarks of granite bordered by low cliffs. The puffing and chuffing of the locomotive's drivers echoed and rebounded from the throughway's walls, as it navigated the narrow channel with overhangs arching on either side.

Holmes caught a brief, almost subliminal glimpse of a shadow flitting overhead and of a black ovoid shape dropping down from the sky. A gout of flame, rock and smoke lifted into the air about twenty feet behind the passenger coach. He felt the concussive impact like a slap from an invisible hand. Stones rained down all around.

"Dropping bombs on us!" squalled Crampton, hunching over the throttle. "Filthy bastard's trying to bury us!"

"We need more speed," Holmes said, scanning the sky. "Get us out in the open before they start an avalanche and block the tracks."

With the double-roar of the fan-turbines at full output, the *Terror* skimmed overhead. Machine gun bullets kicked up dust and flurries of rock chips from the overhangs. Metal clanged and ricochets whined from the locomotive. Coal jumped and broke apart in the fuel tender. The fireman clutched at himself and fell over. Holmes fired the Rattler as the craft screamed by. When the firing pin clicked on an empty chamber, he tossed it aside in angry impatience.

Heart pounding, Holmes scrambled up and into the tender. The fireman's torso was stitched through with six bullet-holes, a seventh through his head. Closing his mind to the horror, he climbed over the coal, clawing and kicking the lumps aside. He hauled himself over the rear of the car and paused for a split second on the rim.

In the near distance, he saw the *Terror* banking and coming back, this time for a low-altitude broadside attack. He leapt the space between the tender and the platform of the passenger carriage. He landed clumsily, and for an instant, he tottered on the edge. Deirdre pulled the door open, reaching out a hand to steady him, just as the *Terror* shot by overhead. The left-side cliff erupted in a flash of yellow and red flames.

The concussion pushed them stumbling into the vestibule. Flying chunks of granite struck the windows, leaving spider-web patterns in the glass. Holmes and Deirdre fell to the floor. He sheltered her with his body as best he could.

A seething mass of rock slabs and dirt cascaded down from the cliff, breaking to pieces in the process. Dust and stone fragments gushed out of the mass. Metal clashed loudly and the locomotive's drive wheels locked as the *Wraith* braked. The entire train shook violently in a series of bone-jarring impacts. The *Wraith* plunged into a cloud of smoke and grit. Only when the pilot hit a tumbling boulder the size of a dog-cart did the locomotive crash to a full halt.

The Pullman coach remained coupled to the fuel tender so it didn't completely leave the rails but it tipped over to the right at a twenty-five degree angle. Loveday grabbed the back of a bench and managed to keep on her feet, but Tennyson, Watson and Tesla fell to all fours. Loose objects, chairs and tableware all went sliding toward the juncture of the floor and the walls.

The shuddering crash of rolling rock subsided, although the dust continued to surge in a gray pall. Everyone pushed themselves to their feet as best they could. They staggered and stumbled on the slanting floor. Loveday was the first to speak. "Is anyone injured?"

No one answered in the affirmative so she bent down, trying to see through the starred and cracked windows. "Should we expect more of the same?"

Holmes said, "Unlikely. The objective was to bring the train to a halt, which has been accomplished. We will have visitors, though."

Watson opened his medical bag and removed his service pistol. "Let's get ready to greet them." He tossed Holmes the Webley revolver.

Tennyson brushed off his sleeves and straightened his coat. "With our reinforced walls, the coach is defensible."

"It's also vulnerable since it's immobile," Watson said. "I think we stand a better chance outside. The airship will need to find a place to land so as to deploy men, and that will buy us time to come up with a strategy."

Holmes nodded. "I'll check the condition of the engine."

Pistol in hand, he went through the carriage's rear door, jumped down and ran toward the cab. He saw no sign of the *Terror* in the sky. Dust clouds boiled around the welter of broken stone. Rock clattered loudly under his boots but he could still hear the locomotive panting like an exhausted beast. Plumes of smoke and steam floated out from somewhere in the *Wraith*'s internal machinery, mixing with the dust.

Crampton's soot-streaked, fearful face peered down at him. He waved ahead toward the high heap of dirt, broken shale and boulders all but burying the tracks. Settling stone continued to grate and click. "We're not going anywhere for a long time."

Holmes motioned for him and Hawley to come down. "I suggest you two men either make yourselves scarce or throw in your lot with us. An armed squad will be here at any moment."

Crampton and Hawley exchanged worried glances. Hawley said, "I'd prefer to hide somewhere. After a lifetime on the railroad, I'm not much suited for running."

"Nor I," said Crampton. "Another train is due through here soon. We can flag it down."

"In that case," replied Holmes, turning away, "choose a place out of the line of fire and stay there."

He rejoined his friends at the rear of the passenger coach. Tennyson had elected to remain aboard as if the Pullman coach were a ship and he its captain. Without preamble, Watson said, "Nikola is who they're after, so we should divide our force. I suggest Loveday, Miss Dalton and Nikola go in one direction, while Holmes and I fight a rear guard action."

"What direction would that be?" Loveday demanded. She gestured around her. "There's nothing out here."

"All of us staying in one place will only make it easy for Vonn and his men," Holmes retorted. "I'm not inclined to do that. They've killed the fireman."

Loveday's eyes widened then narrowed. "The train provides some decent cover. We can hide Nikola and Miss Dalton in the vicinity and try to bluff our way out, convince Vonn they've escaped."

Tesla eyes shone with a mixture of guilt and fear. "I don't want to hide any longer. I should just give myself up. In the final analysis, all of this is my fault."

Deirdre said, "I don't think sacrificing yourself would save the rest of us, Nikola. Not wise."

"It may not be wisdom but it is the only moral thing to do."

"Let's not belabour the subject," Loveday snapped. "We don't have time for it." She pointed to the left. They saw three helmeted men jogging toward them through the settling dust cloud, all carrying Rattler pistols.

Watson said, "Best to take cover before they see us...hide in the dust."

"Dust won't keep out bullets," said Holmes. "Get behind the carriage."

As his friends did as he said, Holmes turned toward the Ring soldiers.

"What are you doing?" Loveday demanded.

"What they least expect...a direct confrontation."

Holmes moved quickly to a tumble of broken stone in front of the locomotive and kneeled behind it, cocking the pistol. When the soldiers drew closer, he fired a warning shot over their heads.

To his surprise, the men stopped running rather than breaking for cover. They halted at a distance of about twelve yards. The man in the centre carefully tugged off his helmet and raised both arms over his head. His left hand showed the white of a bandage. Vonn called, "Let's meet halfway and get this thrashed out before any more lives are lost, shall we?"

Holmes lifted his head above the pile of stones. "You're a murderer three times over, at the very least. Under the circumstances, why would I believe anything you have to say?"

"What other choice do you have, Holmes?"

Slowly, Holmes stood up, thumbing back the revolver's hammer. He stepped forward. From behind him he heard Watson's incredulous whisper: "Holmes, what the hell —?"

Holmes did not reply. He walked toward Vonn and the soldiers. He could hear the panting of the halted locomotive. The smell of oil and hot metal tickled his nostrils. He saw no one in the cab.

When he was within ten feet of the three men, he stopped. "I prefer to talk to Robur."

Vonn smiled contemptuously. "Even if you were in a position to bargain, that is not possible."

"Because he's not really with you aboard the *Terror*?"

Vonn hesitated before replying, "I did not say that. Besides we don't need him to settle this. Where are your friends?"

"They're not here at the moment, so if any thrashing out needs to be done, it will be between you and I."

Vonn chuckled. "I'm not interested in them at this juncture. Bring forth Nikola Tesla."

"He's not here, as I said. "

"You're a very unconvincing liar, Holmes. After all you've gone through in the last day or so, you wouldn't just let him run off. So bring him out, transfer his custody to me and we will leave. No more blood needs to be shed."

Holmes casually lifted his Webley. "Only yours, it could be argued."

Vonn's smile vanished. "You will die, too."

His anger making him reckless, Holmes pointed the revolver directly at Vonn's face. "That's rather the point, isn't it? We kill each other and in the aftermath, Nikola and my friends get away."

Vonn swallowed hard. "We could always wait — or bomb — you out. You are sitting ducks, as the Americans say."

Holmes laughed scornfully. "You don't have time to stage a protracted stand-off. This is a public railroad, remember? I've been reliably informed a train could be along at any minute. I don't think you have orders to destroy another one, especially if it's full of passengers. Even the Hephaestus Ring won't be able to suppress the news of that kind of slaughter."

Uncertainty flickered in Vonn's good eye, then it glinted hard in building rage. "You have no idea of the extent of what we're able to do —"

221B: On Her Majesty's Secret Service

A sudden commotion and a babble of angry, frightened voices commanded their attention. Holmes and Vonn swivelled their heads toward the train just as Nikola clambered over the coupling connecting the fuel tender to the locomotive. "Stop!" he shouted. "The madness must end!"

Loveday and Deirdre held his arms, trying to pull him back. He struggled furiously, shrugging free of his coat. He slipped out of it, leaving them holding the empty sleeves. He stumbled over the rocks, raising both arms over his head. "I give myself up! Take me and spare these people!"

The soldiers snapped up their repeating pistols. Vonn slapped down their barrels. *"Nej! Döda engelsmannen!"*

Holmes understood the order to kill the Englishman. Instantly he squeezed the trigger of the Webley, the heavy round striking the nearest soldier in the right leg. Although the metallic mesh turned the bullet, the shock of impact caused him to go down with a scream, plucking at his dislocated knee. Vonn rushed for Tesla, who allowed himself to be violently wrestled forward and placed before Holmes' pistol.

The second soldier swung his weapon around toward Holmes. Watson fired his service revolver from his position between the tender and the front of the passenger coach. The bullet slammed into the man's cuirass but did not penetrate the alloy. The kinetic force knocked him backwards, his finger convulsively tightening around the trigger.

The multiple muzzles spat flame, first at the rock-littered soil, then in a wild, spraying arc, rounds hammering against the side of the locomotive with semi-musical clangs. Bullet-driven stone splinters jumped from the ground. Something hard and hot smashed across Holmes' forehead and sent him flailing back. He felt himself falling, blinded by a fiery wetness. Eyes stinging, he tried to clear his vision with desperate swipes of his free hand. fright.

A rush of bodies knocked him sprawling and he heard the

221B: On Her Majesty's Secret Service

characteristic *dut-dut-dut* of another Rattler pistol. The stutter of the weapon ceased, but the sharp cracks of Watson's service revolver continued for a few seconds, followed by silence. He heard the rapid scutter and crunch of feet running across rock, and then Watson leaned over him.

"Holmes, don't you dare be dead!"

Holmes lurched into a sitting position, swiping at the scarlet liquid streaming down his face. "I'm not. Where's Vonn?"

"Getting away — with Nikola."

Holmes came to his feet in an enraged rush, pistol questing for a target. He nearly fell as a wave of dizziness swept over him. His head began to throb in agonizing cadence with his pulse. "Have to go after them —"

Watson caught him and probed at the wound on high on Holmes' forehead with his fingers. "Nikola went with them willingly...we've no choice but to let them go. Looks like you were struck by a rock, not a bullet."

Holmes impatiently pushed Watson away and sluiced the flow of blood from his eyes with his left hand. He snarled, "What do you mean 'no choice'?"

He froze, blinking through a veil of scarlet. He saw the distant figures of Vonn dragging Tesla across the rockscape, the soldiers following, one helping the other to hobble along. He turned his head and saw Deirdre, her back against one of the locomotive's massive drive wheels. She slowly slid toward the ground. Loveday eased her down. She looked toward Holmes and Watson with helpless, heart-stricken eyes.

Deirdre's right hand pressed against her chest, just below her left breast. Crimson glistened between her splayed fingers. She kept her hand there as though she were trying to catch the pain.

Watson and Holmes rushed forward. Watson placed a hand behind the girl's head and pulled her away from Loveday. "Lay her flat."

Holmes sat down and lowered Deirdre's head into his lap. "Miss Brooke, go fetch Watson's medical bag."

Loveday arose as Watson lifted Deirdre's limp hand from her chest and grimly examined the flesh around the wound. Her breathing came harsh and shallow. Her eyes didn't open.

"Will she be all right?" Holmes asked, oblivious to the blood streaming down his face.

Watson's lips compressed into a tight white line. He tugged on the hem of Loveday's dress. Softly, he said, "Sit. Let's all just sit here with her for a little while."

Loveday sat down and took Deirdre's right hand in hers, clasping it tightly.

"Will she be all right?" Holmes demanded, louder.

Watson kneeled beside him. He whispered, "A gunshot wound to the chest, Holmes. Thoracic penetration. Cardiac trauma at best, irreparable heart and lung tissue damage at worst."

Holmes stared at him, not comprehending, his hands on either side of Deirdre's head, smoothing her hair. "No, go get your bag. Do something."

"The bullet can't be removed here and even if it could, she's haemorrhaging internally."

Loveday bit her lip and tears sprang to her eyes.

Deirdre's eyelids fluttered and flicked open. Her eyes were glassy but when she looked up into Holmes' face, her expression registered concern. She attempted to rise. "Yer hurt, Mr Holmes!"

He gave her a faltering smile. His throat constricted but he huske out, "A little scratch and bit of a scrape, nothing to it. Just lie there and let the doctor take care of you. And you might as well call me Sherlock."

She glanced over at Watson, saw the expression on his face and smiled with rueful humour. "I think the doctor has done all he can." Her smile turned into a grimace of pain and then became a smile again when she looked at Loveday. "This is what is called 'winging it' on the stage, Miss Brooke...I think I'm doing fairly well, wouldn't ye say?"

Loveday tried to smile. "You're brilliant...rave reviews all around."

Deirdre's eyes shifted to Holmes, looking up at him again. She asked playfully. "Do ye remember what I said when ye quoted some Andrew Marvell at me, Sherlock?"

He nodded and said hoarsely, " 'The grave's a fine and private place, but none I think there do embrace.' "

Deirdre's hand reached up for him. "Do ye think we can prove the smarmy bastard wrong?"

Holmes carefully took her in his arms. She pulled his head down to hers and their lips touched. After a moment, she sighed and made no sound afterward. Lifting his head, he saw the faint smile on her lips but no life in her blue eyes. Watson reached forward and closed them with gentle fingers.

Holmes gazed into the face of Deirdre, then at Loveday and Watson and Deirdre again. He did not move. He could not. He sensed something ease out of him, from his mind and muscles, his nerves and his bones. He suddenly felt more tired and alone than he had in his entire life.

He closed his eyes

221B: On Her Majesty's Secret Service
PART FOUR

***T**HE SPRING WHICH immediately preceded my marriage was made memorable by three cases of interest, in which I had the privilege of being associated with Sherlock Holmes and of studying his methods. The first of these, however, deals with interests of such importance and implicates so many, that for many years it will be impossible to make it public. No case, however, in which Holmes was engaged has ever illustrated the value of his analytical methods so clearly or has impressed those who were associated with him so deeply.*

I still retain an almost verbatim report of the interview in which he demonstrated the true facts of the case to Monsieur Dubugue of the Paris police, and Fritz von Waldbaum, the well-known specialist of Dantzig, both of whom had wasted their energies upon what proved to be side issues. The new century will have come; however, before the story can be safely told.

— John H. Watson, MD

221B: On Her Majesty's Secret Service

No free energy device will be allowed to reach the market.

— Nikola Tesla

CHAPTER 22

5 March, Location Unknown

BLINDED BY DARKNESS, Tesla stopped struggling and squeezed his eyes shut —at least he thought he squeezed them shut. He guessed he had been sitting in the tiny, lightless cell for nearly an hour. He was weary of fighting his fear.

The air smelled foul, tainted with the chemical effluvium of formaldehyde and carbolic. Other odours were less familiar. Tesla kept alert for any sound, but all he heard was his own respiration, as his breath dragged into and out of his lungs past the wet gag crammed between his jaws.

The stone floor felt damp beneath him but he couldn't shift position to find a dry spot — not with his hands bound tightly behind him and his ankles tethered to an iron ring deep-sunk into the flag stone. Drawing up his knees, Tesla rested his forehead against them. He hadn't expected to be drugged once he had surrendered to Vonn and dragged aboard the *Terror*. He did not remember the sequence of events after he gave himself up very clearly, only a chaotic set of impressions.

The recollection of being immobilized by powerful arms and a small black tube held before his face was very vivid, as was the white liquid flushing out of it. He was aware of the burn of the fluid on his skin, in his eyes and his nostrils, and then only blackness.

He shook his head and waves of pain swallowed his thoughts. He focused on the rasp of air in his throat until the throbbing in his skull abated somewhat.

Images swam through Tesla's consciousness, primarily the stricken faces of Loveday Brooke and Deirdre as they struggled to prevent him from surrendering to Vonn. He remembered the sound of gunfire and shouts, and then running madly over rocky ground, alternately pushed and dragged by gray-clad men.

Tesla swore around the gag, the profanity swallowed up by the thick fabric. He would have cursed Robur's name had he been able, although he hadn't encountered the man aboard the *Terror*. He slept through its flight for which he felt both cheated and disappointed. Satisfying his scientific curiosity about the aerocraft was not an acceptable trade-off for surrender, but it would have helped reduce some of the humiliating sting out of his decision.

Upon awakening in a small metal-walled chamber in the airship, Tesla found his wrists bound by what felt like rawhide thongs. Just as he came to wakefulness, a burlap sack was tugged over his head and the drawstring pulled so tight around his throat, he feared imminent death by suffocation. After being pulled to his feet, he was marched along a short passageway, then guided down a ladder. He smelled and heard a horse and the jingle of a harness.

He managed to ask in a hoarse whisper, "Where am I?"

A voice he recognized as Vonn's growled in his ear, "I'm putting you aboard a carriage. Don't resist and you won't be harmed."

Assuming Vonn would have no qualms about harming him severely if he tried to put up a struggle, Tesla decided to lay quietly on the floor of the carriage. Since he was still groggy and off-balance due to the effects of the fluid sprayed into his face, the decision was not a difficult one to make. He guessed the *Terror* had landed in some remote spot and he was being conveyed to what most likely would be his final destination.

After a rough journey with the carriage rocking and jouncing on its springs, it rolled to a slow stop. By the time it did, Tesla had recovered most of his faculties. He heard the door open. Hands pulled him up and out, setting him on his feet. He allowed himself to be manhandled down a flight of slippery stone steps. At their foot, the sack was yanked from his head and a strip of cloth jammed between his jaws. The ends were knotted tightly at the nape of his neck.

A door opened and a hand propelled him through it into an unlighted cell. There a burly man in traditional butler's livery waited. Although his black coat and trousers were impeccable, his flattened nose and cauliflower ears identified him as an ex-pugilist. The deeply ugly scar on the left side of his face marked him as something far more sinister than a boxer. He wore untraditional work-boots on his feet. His shaggy red sideburns looked familiar, but Tesla's fogged memory could not immediately place where he had seen them before.

Swiftly and expertly, the man knelt and bound Tesla's ankles with a length of rope to an iron ring in the floor. When he was done, he left the room, closing the door behind him. Plunged into complete darkness, Tesla stood motionless for a few minutes before easing himself down into a sitting position. He had been sitting ever since.

At first, abject fear kept him from stirring overmuch. Curiosity and anger gradually forced him to squirm around, exploring his surroundings with what little feeling remained in his fingertips. He expended little time speculating about his location.

Bent over with his forehead on his knees, aware of his aching lungs as they laboured to pull in the clammy air past the gag, he felt his thirst increase to agonizing levels. Bruises inflicted by Vonn throbbed. He wondered if the Hephaestus Ring intended to kill him. If so, he hoped they would do so before his discomfort grew intolerable.

The door to the cell boomed open. He feared his head would come loose from the echoes.

The light from outside, as feeble as it was, all but dazzled him. "You all right, boyo?"

The words were overlaid by a Scots brogue. Assuming the question was rhetorical, Tesla declined to even grunt in response. A fist clutching a knife entered his field of blurred vision. The blade sawed briefly at the ropes around his ankles and they parted easily.

A pair of big hands fitted themselves beneath his armpits and hoisted him to his feet. The man said quietly, "Sorry about this, laddie," and pulled the sack over his head again. Tesla did not feel despair, only outrage. When the hands pulled him backward toward the door, he resisted. The man uttered a coarse laugh. "All the same to me if you stay in here — but the lady waitin' for me to bring you to her wouldn't be very understandin'."

The man pulled at him again and Tesla twisted away. The man shook him by the collar of his frock coat and snarled, "You come on your own, or I'll drag you out by yer scruff and yer privates. Yer choice."

Tesla tamped down the urge to kick backward. He allowed himself to be directed out of the cell. Heavy-soled boots clomped on the floor behind him. He heard a clink of metal against metal, a squeal of hinges, and after a few more steps, he was jerked to a halt. A moment later, the footfalls receded. He jumped at the bang of a door slamming shut behind him.

Waiting silently, not moving, Tesla tried to catch even the faintest of sounds. He felt a quick pressure against his wrists and his bonds fell away. Footsteps, much less heavy, moved away from him. He detected the whiff of tobacco smoke. A woman's soft voice, touched with amusement and an elegant Parisian accent, said, "You may remove your bag and gag, Nikola."

221B: *On Her Majesty's Secret Service*

The voice triggered a surge of co-mingled dread and hope within him. Fingers prickly with returning circulation, Tesla snatched away the hood and worked to loosen the knot of the gag. Tearing it away with loathing, he squinted around, looking first to the left and then to the right. He waited until his eyes had adjusted to the light before so much as shifting his feet.

Tesla stood within a long chamber, with stained wood-panelled walls, silver-filagreed wallpaper above, and brass lamps with pale purple shades. The room was dim but somehow not gloomy. Knuckling his eyes, he glanced behind him at the red-headed man with the untidy sideburns. He remembered the brief glimpse of him at Penhallick Wharf on that wild night nearly two years before.

He kept his expression composed, not reacting when he saw the familiar faces seated around a table shaped like a narrow ellipse. The men he knew as Mirzarbeau and Prince Dakkar regarded him unsympathetically. Kathryn Koluchy lounged in a chair at the squared-off head of the table.

She gazed at Tesla with hooded eyes as she smoked a black cheroot. She was dressed far less formally than when he had last seen her — tan jodhpurs, black riding boots and a loose blouse of bleached muslin with the sleeves unbuttoned and rolled casually to her forearms.

After smoothing his hair, he bowed to her. "Madame." He turned to the men at the table. "Gentlemen."

"It's been rather a long holiday for you, Nikola," she said. "Too long, perhaps?"

"Perhaps," Tesla said. "But I would not call the last twenty-four hours a holiday."

"Mr Vonn can be rough, but he had his orders."

"So he said. I only surrendered to him to spare my friends."

Kathryn arched an eyebrow. "Surrendered? Nikola, I'm still waiting for Mr Vonn's report, but no matter. You have been returned to where you belong."

As they spoke, Kathryn's right hand dipped out of sight beneath the table. It came back up holding a calvary sabre with a gently curved blade and steel basket hand-guard. She pointed it toward a vacant chair beside Dakkar. "This is not a formal meeting of the Echelon...in fact, we have yet to vote on who should replace poor Julius...Silvanus Cavor is proving to be unreliable so Westmoreland Moreau is the prime candidate to replace him. You may sit."

Tesla did not move "Where is Baron Maupertuis?"

"He is indisposed at the moment," the woman replied smoothly. With the tip of the sabre, she tapped the tabletop. "Sit, please."

Slowly, numbly, Tesla pulled out the chair and dropped into it. He reached for a pitcher of water at the table's centre and poured a tumbler. He drank it down in one swallow, refilled it and drank again. After alleviating the worst of his thirst, he asked, "Where are we?"

"At the Foods on the Rise research annex beneath my home in Paris. You were brought here through the rear courtyard."

"I've never been to the annex before."

"There was no need before. Since I was meeting with potential vendors of my Herakleophorbia VI hormone, I thought it best to keep you sequestered and quiet until Professor Redwood and Mr Bensington took their leave. I was also demonstrating an automation exhibit simply for their amusement."

Tesla poured another tumbler of water. "Why am I here?"

"You now have less than three weeks to complete preparations on the Iron Lady. Tomorrow I will begin sending out invitations for my reception on the 30th of March and the inauguration tower tour scheduled for the following day, the 31st. We are woefully behind schedule."

Tesla tried to hide his sudden surge of fear. "Behind schedule

221B: *On Her Majesty's Secret Service*

for what? I do not understand. You never explained your plans."

"That is because you panicked and ran away like a startled fawn that night at Penhallick. If you had not betrayed Robur and abided by your contract, you would even now be sitting at this table as a full member of the Echelon." She paused to blow a stream of smoke. "Poor Babiole was inconsolable, by the way."

Tesla ignored the comment. "I did not proffer my interest in being a member of your Echelon, let alone my consent, Madame."

Kathryn Koluchy grinned at him around her cheroot. "Your interest or lack thereof is no longer germane. On the matter of consent, I beg to differ. For the term of your contract, the Ring does not require your consent to exploit any of your intellectual or technological creations, if we see a use for either... in the instance of Eiffel's tower, your application of telegeodynamics is integral to Thunderstrike."

Tesla stared at her, stunned into silence for a handful of seconds. All he could think of to say was, "Are you mad?"

The woman's grin faltered but then returned. "That's a rather metaphysical question... but the simplest answer is no."

Tesla said, "Madame Koluchy, you possess a remarkable intellect, but certainly you — all of you — must know that harnessing any kind of electromagnetic wave energy is only one factor in the process. Transmitting it safely is quite another."

She tapped off an inch of ash from her cheroot in an ashtray, uttering a thoughtful "hm" sound. "Pray, how is the Iron Lady markedly different from your telluric current transmitters, other than its size?"

Turning her question over in his mind, Tesla said with slow deliberation, "Theoretically it isn't different ...if all the necessary cabling and transformer circuits were properly configured. Even so, do you expect me to master a new form of high-energy physics in less than three weeks?"

Mirzarbeau tittered. "You've already accomplished that, *mon coquin*...during your absence we reviewed your diagrams for fabricating all the hardware and concluded your engineering is sound...what you lacked was a reliable wave propagation medium. Gustave Eiffel has unknowingly provided that."

"I've never experimented with telegeodynamics on this scale," Tesla said desperately. "I have no idea what would happen."

Prince Dakkar smiled thinly. "We do. Thanks in part to Julius Wendigee."

Tesla swallowed hard and reached for more water. "I was told he suffered an accident."

"Yes," replied Kathryn, tapping an ash from her cheroot onto the floor. "Poor Julius. A fatal accident in judgment."

She rose swiftly, with the grace of a gymnast. She stubbed out the cheroot in the ashtray. "Come with me, Nikola."

Tesla hesitated. "Madame, please understand —"

Kathryn Koluchy whirled, teeth bared, whipping the point of the sabre toward Tesla's face. "You understand! Just because you were not given twenty lashes upon your arrival here, don't delude yourself into thinking you have any choice whatsoever from this day forward." She gestured with the blade. "Get up."

Tesla obeyed, feeling the pressure of Dakkar's and Mirzarbeau's eyes upon him. The sudden aura of lethal violence was strong enough to taste. The three pairs of eyes pierced him, and none was more dagger-like than those of the Madame.

Meekly, he followed Kathryn Koluchy across the room, through a set of double doors and into a long corridor. Electric lights inset into ceiling sockets cast a cold and sterile illumination on the white floor and walls. Trying to match the woman's long-legged stride, he asked, "Once I fulfil the terms of my contract, I will be given my freedom, *ja?*"

Sabre swinging from her hand, Kathryn voiced a scornful laugh. "Unchecked human freedom leads only to unchecked lunacy, you know."

Tesla blinked at her. "But the principles of democracy —"

The woman slashed the air with the sabre. "Look at the world around you, Nikola. Freedom and democracy lead only to self-indulgence, to conflict and waste, and perpetuate the stagnancy of the human mind."

They strode past open rooms full of scientific instruments, such as centrifuges and microscopes. Other tables were loaded down with complicated networks of glass tubes, beakers and retorts. The left wall was composed of panes of glass, beaded with condensation. Peering through them, Tesla saw rows of slim, bright green trees towering many feet high. He realized they were stalks of corn with ears of fabulous size, half again the length and thickness of his forearm.

His pace slowed and he came to a stop, his eyes widening as he stared through the glass at the garden on the other side. "You are growing corn down here?"

Kathryn smiled pridefully. "Among other crops, such as tomatoes and beans. Those plants which look like hazel bushes are the tops of carrots. It is the science of hydroponics, producing crops without soil."

"How are they growing so large?"

"They are rooted in beds of water enriched with the Herakleophorbia growth hormone. The sperm of the earth, I like to call it."

Tesla pressed closer to the glass, peering upward at the array of overhead lights. "Are those arc lamps?"

"Yes, they shed a light on the bluish spectrum which emits a high amount of ultraviolet light to simulate solar radiation and stimulate growth. Professor Mirzarbeau blended his Violet Flame research and built on the work of Edison...and yourself."

"You could feed thousands."

"Millions. That is the key to the Hephaestus Ring's overall plan

221B: On Her Majesty's Secret Service

to transform humanity for the twentieth century...we will not accomplish this through invading armies but through the simple expedient of feeding them and keeping them strong and healthy."

"Through nutrition?"

"Partly." They began walking again. Kathryn asked, "Do you know what pharmacology is, Nikola?"

Tesla shrugged. "A new name for patent medicines."

"Hardly." Kathryn Koluchy did not appear to be offended. "Pharmacology is a biomedical science still in its infancy. Pharmacologists such as myself largely deal with finding the correlation between the chemical structure of substances and their effectiveness as drugs. With the Herakleophorbia as the foundation, a person's physical resistance to injury, the body's ability to fight off infections is increased tremendously. We can develop cures for scores of bacterial diseases, such as typhoid and tuberculosis."

Tesla angled an eyebrow at the woman. "Cures available for everyone or only for a select few?"

Kathryn made a negligent gesture with the sabre. "Like most other things in life, that depends on the circumstances."

The corridor opened into a wide square chamber like the interior of a cube. The floor space was dominated by a black-topped trestle table and a tall man wearing a bright red, gold-braided jacket, and a plumed shako — the uniform of a Napoleonic-era Hussar. He held the naked blade of a cavalry sabre crossed over his chest. Startled, Tesla stepped back but then realized the figure was but a life-sized likeness with wide-open eyes and carefully sculpted features, including a dashing, painted-on pencil moustache. His booted feet rested upon a slightly raised metal disk. Tesla saw small rollers on the underside.

Noting his reaction, Kathryn chuckled in genuine amusement. "Meet Brigadier Etienne Gerard...or his automata doppelgänger.

221B: *On Her Majesty's Secret Service*

He was built by an artificial limb manufacturer named Gumpel for the Galerie des Machines at the Exposition. He plans to display him along with his chess-playing android, Mephisto. Working with Leonardo Quevedo, we blended his advances in remote control with the theories of Ada Lovelace and Charles Babbage to create something totally unique... an artificial human possessing a rudimentary form of artificial intelligence."

Tesla nodded. "I recall your mention of that, ja."

Kathryn walked to the rear of the automaton and lifted the hem of his jacket. Her fingers busied themselves beneath it. Upon hearing a series of clicks, Tesla received the impression she was pressing buttons or keys. "The physical form of the Brigadier was constructed around a computing machine."

"Ah. Your Analytical Engine."

"Not that advanced. Basic fencing moves were input onto a series of punched cards which consisted of the formulae...variable data known as algorithms. Powered by Quevedo's telekino technology, the Brigadier can engage in a limited form of swordplay."

The eyes of the automaton suddenly flashed yellow, lit up from within. A faint drone filled the room and it raised the sabre in a salute, and then extended it straight out. Kathryn Koluchy assumed a fencer's stance, and sidled forward, leading with her sabre. The tips of the two blades kissed, then engaged with the furious clash of steel against steel.

For a few seconds the woman and the man-shaped machine exchanged sword-strokes. Then with a flick of a wrist, Kathryn Koluchy beat aside the Brigadier's blade. Instantly, she lunged forward, touching the centre of the automaton's braided chest with her sabre's tip. The glow in its eye sockets went out with the suddenness of a pair of candles being blown out. The machine's sword-arm returned to its first position, with the blade resting across its torso.

Tesla clapped his hands. "Amazing."

221B: *On Her Majesty's Secret Service*

She nodded in gracious acknowledgement. "Thank you, but this bit of entertainment is not what I brought you here to see."

She walked across the room to the long trestle table. It was covered from corner to corner by a miniature scale model of the Exposition Universelle grounds. Eiffel's tower rose nearly two feet from the middle. All of the buildings and even the waterways had been cunningly constructed.

"This is based on the architect's model," Kathryn continued. "It's actually more accurate, since it was put together within the last year."

"It's very detailed," Tesla said lamely.

She frowned at him. "The tower model is constructed of the same puddled iron alloy as the original. You said you had no idea what would happen if the Iron Lady were turned into a telegeodynamic energy transmitter. The teleforce, as you termed it."

Anxiety knotted in his chest. "I did."

Kathryn reached under the far end of the table. Tesla heard a switch being thrown. "Julius was able reproduce steps in your process and craft this simulation."

Tesla heard a faint, familiar bee-hive hum, and felt the skin-crawling sensation of static electricity. Loose hairs on his head rose. The miniature tower suddenly shimmered with a dull blue halo. Sparks flashed along its length. Little threads of energy gathered in a pulsing knot at the top, then formed into random twisting patterns. They fountained up and out at the very top of the spire with a sharp *pop!*, enclosing the tower within a translucent sheath of light. Many of the tiny buildings around it burst into flame and blew away as if exposed to a high wind.

Reaching under the table again, Kathryn threw a switch. The hum and the energy discharge faded. From a shelf, she picked up a damp length of cloth, shook it out and threw it over the display, extinguishing the dozen little fires. "Now you see why we call our project Thunderstrike. Obviously we require a primer to touch off the reaction, but that has already been developed."

221B: *On Her Majesty's Secret Service*

Tesla's thoughts felt frozen, overwhelmed by horror. He knew his mouth hung open but he was unable to close it. After two attempts, he rasped, "The safeguards against lightning will be of no use against geo-generated electricity...hundreds could die!"

Kathryn shook her head. "That is not the plan. Yes, all the people who are on the tower tour will most probably die from electrocution and perhaps some of the Exposition buildings will be destroyed. For the sake of the demonstration, all are acceptable losses."

"Demonstration?"

"The world is out of control, global wars are pending. Calls for freedom and democracy will lead to revolution and chaos in the coming century. Only technocracy can make over humanity into something worthy of the future."

"My teleforce was designed to transmit free energy all over the world, to bring light and warmth to darkness."

"My dear sweet, sad Nikola." Kathryn bestowed upon him a sympathetic smile. She reached for his right hand, taking it hers. She squeezed. "Darling, the Ring wants that, too."

"But without capacitive couplings to act as receivers for the energy, you will turn my telegeodynamic system and Eiffel's tower into a weapon of terrible destruction."

"Sometimes visionaries must burn down in order to build something better."

"But—"

Kathryn Koluchy's face lost its warm placidity. Her lips compressed. Her eyes glittered. She closed her fingers around Tesla's hand and squeezed with such force and ferocity that he cried out in surprised pain. He dropped to his knees, trying to prise her fingers open. Raising her left leg, the woman drove the sole of her boot into the middle of his face.

It felt as if he had been hit by an iron sledge-hammer. The impact slammed him backward onto the floor. She released his hand just as the rear of Tesla's skull struck the concrete with cruel force. Tiny white stars of pain danced behind his eyes. Kathryn Koluchy stepped away from him and handed him a white linen handkerchief. "Get up."

Tasting blood, cradling his throbbing hand, Nikola Tesla tottered to his feet. He stared at her in dazed, fearful confusion. He suddenly comprehended that although the woman possessed an extraordinary intellect, she was also floridly insane and superhumanly strong. He dabbed at his split lower lip with the handkerchief and frowned at the spots of blood. "With all of the boons the Ring can bestow upon humankind, endless food and energy, why engage in this monstrous plan?"

"Because," Madame Koluchy replied with a half-smile, "in any negotiation, first you have to get their attention. I hope I've finally gotten yours, Nikola."

221B: On Her Majesty's Secret Service
Any truth is better than indefinite doubt.

—Sherlock Holmes

CHAPTER 23

25 March, London, Baker Street West

"A LOGISTICAL NIGHTMARE," said Mycroft Holmes. "A diplomatic nightmare, and taking into account the damage inflicted upon the Crown's property, a financial nightmare."

"A mother's nightmare," Loveday replied coldly. "The death of a child trumps all the other nightmares."

Mycroft glared at her, then nodded contritely. He murmured, "Quite so, quite so. Forgive my insensitivity...comes from working alone for too many years."

Loveday turned her face away, gazing out the black coach's window at Baker Street rushing by. She saw carriages dashing through puddles and wagons bouncing over wet paving stones. Working men clad in raincoats scurried along the sidewalk, heads bowed against the rain and the raw, chill wind. Although the hour was before noon, the sky continued to darken with leaden clouds, mirroring those filling her thoughts.

Mycroft asked, "When was the last time you saw Sherlock and John?"

Loveday continued to stare out the window, at the drops of water dancing on the glass. "Not since the debriefing session at the Home Office, the day after we returned to London."

Mycroft blew out a long, weary sigh. "A truly ghastly day, that.

Sherlock did himself or his reputation no good by assuming all responsibility, not just for Nikola Tesla's abduction but also for the poor girl's death."

"Deirdre," Loveday intoned. "That was the poor girl's name." She glanced towards Mycroft with a small smile. "Deirdre D'Alton. She preferred the more elegant French pronunciation of the pedestrian Dalton. She considered herself an actress...and she was a talented one."

The carriage jounced over a fault in the road. Mycroft's top hat fell from his head, very nearly onto Loveday's lap. "Confound it."

Loveday caught and returned it. "Cobb is rather reckless with the reins today."

"That isn't Cobb in the box...he tendered his resignation two weeks ago."

Loveday raised an eyebrow. "Oh? And Commissionaire Tangey?"

Mycroft frowned. "I learned he decided to take early retirement around the same time. Are the two events related?"

"I couldn't say."

"Couldn't or wouldn't?"

Loveday shrugged as if disinterested. "Your choice."

Mycroft didn't try to resettle the hat on his head. Instead, he pretended to flick away dust from the flat crown. Softly, he said, "I'm not quite as heartless as I sound, Miss Brooke. What befell Miss Dalton is a tragedy. But we must put it behind us and return to the work of safeguarding the nation."

Loveday didn't roll her eyes but nor did she repress the contempt in her voice. "The work of safeguarding the nation is a very cold comfort to Deirdre's mother and family. I'm fairly certain it's of little solace to your brother, who feels the blame for her death is his alone."

"I was under the impression all three of you agreed to retain her."

221B: *On Her Majesty's Secret Service*

"We did. I had my reservations about her character based on a brief interaction, and it turned out that for once I was very wrong. Regardless, Sherlock assumed the role of the girl's protector...therefore, he steadfastly refuses to share the responsibility of her death with anyone else, including the Hephaestus Ring."

Mycroft grunted. "He always favoured the hair shirt. I remember how he convinced himself he was at fault for the death of our mother —" He broke off, covering his sudden embarrassment with a cough.

Loveday straightened up on the cushioned seat, eyeing him keenly. "When did this happen?"

Mycroft waved away her question. "Old family matters, Miss Brooke. Best not spoken of."

Loveday nodded. "Regardless, your denial of permission to allow us to attend Deirdre's funeral only contributed to Sherlock's self-anger."

"Not *my* denial," Mycroft corrected her. "Whitehall's denial. Or more specifically, the Defence Intelligence Branch. This has become a matter of national security and a serious operational failure on our part. Not to mention the *raison d'etre* for the mission to Ireland in the first place surrendered himself to the opposition."

"Nikola sought to save us."

"Or just himself," Mycroft retorted. "It doesn't matter either way at this point. The priority is to salvage what can be salvaged."

"Salvage?" Loveday echoed. "Just why did you come and fetch me, Mycroft? I thought you hated leaving the Diogenes."

"I do, but I have news which needs to be shared, and I prefer to do it only once, and since neither Sherlock nor Dr Watson responded to my summons —" He shrugged. "In this instance, the mountain must come to Mohammed."

221B: *On Her Majesty's Secret Service*

The coach slowed, rocking to a halt at the kerb before 221B. Loveday climbed out, pulling up the hood of her cloak. Fortunately, the rainfall had slackened to a misting drizzle. She waited for Mycroft to ponderously disembark with a creak and squeak of relieved springs. At the stoop, Loveday rang the bell and felt only a little surprise when the door was opened by Mrs Hudson herself. Although primly dressed, the older woman's blue eyes were dulled by worry and fatigue. They brightened with relief at the sight of the two people.

Grasping Loveday by the hands, she pulled her into the foyer. "Miss Brooke, thank heaven! And you too, Mr Holmes. I've been at my wits' end for days now because of your brother!"

"What has he been up to now, Mrs Hudson?" Mycroft asked, closing the door behind him.

The gray-haired woman opened her mouth to speak when the sharp crack of a gunshot rolled down down the stairwell. Mycroft's eyes widened. "Indoor target practice again? I hoped Sherlock had outgrown that."

As Loveday and Mycroft mounted the stairs, Mrs Hudson said, "He's not been eating or sleeping or seeing anyone. He even sent away that friend of his from Scotland Yard, Mr Lestrade. I hear him playing his violin at all hours. Dr Watson and he have been having terrible rows about it."

"We'll see if we can't get him sorted," Mycroft assured her. "You'll be compensated for any damage done to the flat."

"I'm less concerned about that than I am your brother's health, Mr Holmes."

At the landing, Loveday paused before the door. On other side of it, she heard voices raised in anger and what sounded like furniture being roughly tossed about. Rapping sharply on the panel, she called, "John! Mr Holmes! It's Loveday and Mycroft — we're coming in."

Mycroft added, "So don't shoot us."

221B: *On Her Majesty's Secret Service*

Watson's voice responded, "No promises. Just watch your step."

"Do you mean literally or figuratively?" Loveday asked.

When no reply was forthcoming, Loveday cautiously turned the knob and opened the door. She hesitated a few seconds before entering. She had visited the lodgings of Sherlock Holmes and John Watson only twice, so she knew their attention to housekeeping was casual. She had not expected to step into the aftermath of a natural disaster.

Two chairs had been overturned and a lamp knocked from a table. Newspapers were scattered all over the carpet. Cups of cold tea and plates of half-eaten food could be seen on tabletops, the mantelpiece and even the floor, along with articles of clothing.

The wallpaper beside the bow window was covered by a complex tree diagram rendered in different coloured crayons. The name "Moriarty" was scrawled several times along the branches. A bright red hand-drawn question mark comprised the root of the dendrogram which was punctuated by a bullet-hole. The acrid scent of gunpowder hung in the air, along with other, less identifiable odours.

John Watson stood before the cold hearth, his unshaven face flushed with anger. His collar was askew and his clothing rumpled. He breathed heavily, holding a long-barrelled pistol in his right hand. He glared at Sherlock Holmes who sat cross-legged on a rug wrapped in his dressing gown, like a volcanic island rising from a sea of newsprint and file folders. His Stradivarius lay beside him.

Dark rings surrounded his red-netted eyes, his face haggard and sallow of complexion. He had not shaven in days or even bothered to comb his hair. His unlit black clay pipe was clenched between his teeth. A fading bruise and small scabbed over abrasion was visible on his forehead at his hairline.

Mycroft peered in over Loveday's shoulder and uttered a noise of dismay. "Good God," he said hoarsely. "What have you boys been up to?"

"Beginning from only a minute ago," Watson snapped. "Using a pistol as a writing implement."

"I used a bullet for emphasis," Holmes said dismissively. "No harm done."

"Except to Mrs Hudson's wall and my nerves," Watson half-shouted. "Not to mention what is left of our friendship." He displayed the pistol. "After he fired it, I asked him to hand it over and he refused...he forced me to take it from him."

"*Tried* to take it from me," Holmes corrected, lifting a finger. "After a bit of a tussle, I willingly gave it over."

"You —" Baring his teeth, Watson took a threatening step toward Holmes, raising the gun as if to use it as a hammer.

"John!" Loveday said sharply, crossing over the threshold. "We need to talk." When Holmes began to rise, Loveday added, *"All* of us, Mr Holmes."

Holmes sat back down, groping in his pockets for a match. "No one needs to talk, Miss Brooke."

Watson uttered a scoffing sound of derision. "Unless it's about Professor Bloody Moriarty, and then he doesn't know when to shut up. He's completely turned his attention away from the Hephaestus Ring and Robur to Moriarty."

Holmes found a lucifer and struck it into flame. "He's represents an ever-growing menace."

"Yes, well, so do you, Holmes...at least to those foolish enough to share lodgings with you. That bullet you fired came very near to taking my ear off."

Holmes applied the flame to the bowl of his pipe. "Oh, stop being so melodramatic. You were just startled because your back was to me."

"Oh?" enquired Watson, a dangerous edge in his voice, his eyes narrowed. "Do you want me to demonstrate just how melodramatic I can be?"

"Enough," announced Mycroft loudly. He up-righted a fallen chair. "That is quite enough from both of you two cockwombles."

Loveday picked up a plate of what was once sliced roast beef and peas from the floor. "You two should be ashamed. You're not at university."

Mycroft extended a slab of a hand toward Watson. "The gun, please."

Watson smiled humourlessly. "It's a one-shot target pistol. It's already been fired." He slipped it into a pocket. "It belonged to my brother, so I'm keeping hold of it so your brother doesn't get any more ideas about emphatic punctuation."

Inhaling and exhaling a weary breath, Watson began trying to restore a semblance of order to the sitting room. Loveday and Mycroft offered what aid they could. Holmes sat and smoked in silence, watching them.

Loveday, hoping to lighten both the mood and the gloom, drew aside the curtains to allow weak daylight to enter the room. She asked, "How is Mary, John?"

Scooping up several days worth of newspapers from the floor, he chuckled. "She is well...when I suggested I might take a hotel room, she urged me to stay here in Baker Street in case I'm needed."

He nodded towards Holmes on the rug. "But as Holmes has made plain over the last few days, he doesn't need anyone or anything...except for maybe his crayons."

Mycroft glanced over the diagram on the wall, pursed his lips as if he tasted something sour, and dropped into the armchair. "Get up, Sherlock."

"I can hear just fine from here."

"Good." Loveday whirled on him, eyes blazing. "You're not the only one who is grieving, Mr Holmes. John and I both are, and it pains me to think of Deirdre's family in Ireland and the way they are struggling to come to terms with how and why she died."

"The how is obvious," Holmes retorted, removing the pipe stem from his mouth. "The why is because she trusted me to keep her safe. I doubt anyone at Whitehall," he cut his eyes toward Mycroft, "or the Diogenes has made them aware of that."

"Of course they haven't," snapped Loveday. "Because is isn't the truth. It's just your habit to play the knight-errant, the protector. The hero. Force of habit. You said so to me, remember?"

Holmes did not respond.

"We gave Deirdre the chance to walk away," Loveday continued. "She chose to stay, partly due to her infatuation with you."

Holmes winced as if in pain and lifted his eyes to meet hers. "Is that intended to make me feel better?"

"No, it's intended for you to accept the reality of the situation. When Nikola bolted at the train, I went after him and Deirdre went after me." She paused to take a quavery breath. "I could have pulled her back, but I didn't...I was caught up in the moment. Nikola took precedence, not me and not Deirdre. I should have chosen her."

"Tesla was the mission," Holmes intoned.

"Exactly," said Mycroft. "Even if Miss Brooke had successfully restrained the girl, it would not have made any difference...Nikola Tesla would have still surrendered himself."

"Except Deirdre might still be alive," replied Loveday.

Mycroft shook his head. "Speculation. She might have lived, or all of you may have died. I suppose we could perform an analysis of probabilities, but that will not change your doubt of the outcome."

Holmes regarded his brother with narrowed eyes. "Is that what we need to talk about...probabilities?"

221B: *On Her Majesty's Secret Service*

Watson looked toward Holmes, his expression and voice weary. "No, it isn't. I've had enough, Holmes. No more indulging your Moriarty obsession or arguing you out of your misplaced guilt. Sit where you are. But you can sit there forever and it still won't bring Deirdre back. You can squat on your little hearth rug until the end of bloody time and that still won't make up for what happened. The only thing you can do — the only thing we can all do — is to make it right, to balance the scales."

He pointed to the doorway. "I'm going out there and by God try to do that very thing. If I live through it, I'll come back to let you know. I'm sure you'll be still be sitting there on your tuffet, playing with your pipe, your fiddle and your crayons."

Watson stalked toward the door. He paused when Holmes said, "Wait."

He glanced over his shoulder, hand on the knob. Holmes slowly arose, drawing his dressing gown about him. He swept his gaze over Mycroft and Loveday and rubbed his lower back."My tuffet is getting awfully sore. Perhaps indefinite doubt does have its limits. Give me a few minutes to dress and have Mrs Hudson bring up some tea and toast."

Watson said wryly. "I probably should just go down to the kitchen and fetch it myself, under the circumstances. Mrs Hudson has been through enough without exposing her to the state of our rooms."

Holmes returned his smile with an uncertain one of his own. "I won't debate you."

While Watson went downstairs to confer with Mrs Hudson, Holmes retired to his bedroom to make himself more presentable. Loveday and Mycroft did what they could to make the sitting room the same with a bit of judicious tidying and rubbish collection. The table was cleared and the window opened to allow the chill breeze to air the place out.

Within a few minutes, Holmes re-emerged wearing a sedate black frock coat and unpressed trousers. He had washed his face

221B: *On Her Majesty's Secret Service*

and combed his hair. He also smelled strongly of cologne, a stop-gap measure to forestall a full bath. Watson carefully made his way up the stairway, balancing a tray loaded with teapot, cups, saucers and wedges of toasted bread. Holmes reclaimed his armchair from Mycroft and after settling in and pouring the tea all around, he said quietly, "Thank you, John."

Watson nodded brusquely and sat down on the sofa beside Loveday. "No worries, Holmes."

Holmes sipped at his tea, his hand trembling slightly. He cleared his throat and asked, "Is there any news from Inspector Keegan about King Kevin?"

"Regrettably, no," Mycroft answered. "However, at last report only the two cooked bodies of Robur's men were extracted from the castle's tunnels. The inspector's suspicion is that McShinnock and his people survived but they are laying low, probably among Fenian friends."

"If so," replied Holmes, "he will resurface. Is there any news about Robur?"

"Not a whisper, even though in your report you mentioned glimpsing him."

"More of a sense, an impression. What about Nikola Tesla's whereabouts?"

Mycroft bit off the corner of a toast triangle. Chewing it slowly, he said, "He might as well have fallen off the face of the Earth. Through my contact at the Deuxieme Bureau, I had Monsieur Dubugue of the Paris police make discreet enquiries of Madame Koluchy. She claimed ignorance of anything relating to Tesla...through her solicitors, of course."

"Of course," Loveday repeated bitterly.

"Because of her social station, her response was accepted at face-value, but Dubugue is not satisfied. Curiously, early this morning a communique from Madame Koluchy was forwarded to me by the Foreign Office."

221B: On Her Majesty's Secret Service

From an inner coat pocket, Mycroft produced a large rectangle of stiff, buff-coloured paper. He handed it to his brother who ran his fingers over the embossed symbol on one side of it and brought it to his nose. "Double-sided. Expensive coated stock. It's perfumed as well."

He passed the card under Loveday's nose who sniffed at it delicately. She said, "Guerlain."

Mycroft grimaced impatiently. "Just read it, Sherlock."

Holmes flipped it over and scanned the text, printed in a delicate cursive typeface in both English and French. He uttered a grunt of surprise. Watson leaned forward. "What is it?"

Holmes handed it to him. "It's an invitation to a reception on the evening of the 30th of March at Madame Koluchy's home on Avenue de la Bourdonnais in Paris."

"The invitation has been sent to at least 200 people throughout Europe, perhaps even America," said Mycroft. "To diplomats, investors, patrons of the Exposition, all drawn from the upper echelons of European officialdom — including France's newly elected Prime Minister, Pierre Tirard. They've all been invited to an inauguration tour of Eiffel's 'Iron Lady' on the morning of the 31st."

Loveday read the text and said, "The Exposition itself doesn't open until May."

"A pre-opening day publicity event." Mycroft shrugged. "The tower isn't fully operational, either. Most of the lifts aren't working so the tour will be by foot." He feigned a shudder. "That will require considerable exertion."

Loveday, still reading the invitation, said, "According to this, a private tour of some of the fair's exhibitions may be arranged by contacting Madame a week in advance."

"Which exhibitions?" Watson asked.

Loveday handed the card back to Holmes. "Suspiciously non-specific."

221B: *On Her Majesty's Secret Service*

Holmes took it and held it up to the light. "Why and how did the invitation come into your hands, Mycroft?"

He stirred in his chair. "Mathis at the Deuxieme Bureau. According to him, labour on the tower's electrical system continues day and night, even though the official word from the Exposition's representatives is that there is no chance the work will be completed by the 31st of March. There is a select crew of engineers who are engaged in the installation of both cables and devices that are described as small one-legged stools made of ceramic and metal. Reportedly, they are being placed at all four corners of every level of the tower."

"Let me guess," said Loveday. "And the man overseeing the work fits the description of Nikola Tesla?"

Mycroft frowned. "No. The overseeing authority is a woman and if she fits any description, it is of Kathryn Koluchy. But her face is always veiled, according to the report conveyed to me."

"So," ventured Watson, "there is no actionable proof Tesla or the Ring is involved."

Holmes chuckled and held out the invitation. "None of you looked at the embossing closely, I take it."

"No," said Mycroft. "The invitation was delivered to my desk and upon reading it, I contacted Miss Brooke and we came here straight away."

Loveday took the card and angled it toward the light. Rising in relief on the paper's surface she made out a small circle enclosing a short-handled of a hammer hovering vertically above an anvil."The Hephaestus Ring," she said, passing it to Watson. "They're not even trying to hide any longer."

"No reason why they should," replied Holmes. "The more that evil can stroll about in broad daylight, the less evil it appears to be. It becomes a matter of perception, of familiarity."

Watson said dryly, " 'For if it prospers, none dare call it treason.' "

221B: *On Her Majesty's Secret Service*

"Just so," said Holmes with a grimly approving smile. He turned toward Mycroft. "I presume you have access to more of those invitations?"

For the first time since arriving at Baker Street, Mycroft chuckled. "You anticipate me, brother." From his coat pocket he removed four more cards and fanned them out on the table-top like a man playing a hand of bridge. "I do indeed. And I also have a plan of what use we can put them to."

221B: On Her Majesty's Secret Service
The great ordeal was in front of us.

— John H. Watson, MD

—

CHAPTER 24

30 March, The English Channel

A LOW MIST floated over the water's horizon and diffused the milky light of dawn. A few lights showed through the fog, bright dots against an irregularly shaped black background.

"Calais," said Loveday, thumping the deck with the tip of her umbrella. "Huzzah."

She stood between Holmes and Watson at the bow rail of the steam packet *Brittany,* gazing forward across the surprisingly calm sea. The three people had stood at the bow for the past hour since the ship departed the port at Dover. Loveday was dressed in a deep burgundy travel suit with a short jacket, two-layered skirt and round-brimmed sailor hat. Watson and Holmes wore neatly pressed dark suits. Both men were clean, clear-eyed and well-groomed.

Watson said, "This was a shorter voyage than the ferry to Dublin."

"If you factor in the train trip from London," replied Holmes, "the travel time is not markedly dissimilar...we might be saving thirty minutes more in the Channel crossing than we did the Irish Sea."

"At least John and I aren't seasick this time," Loveday said. She glanced over at Watson. "Are we?"

221B: *On Her Majesty's Secret Service*

He shook his head. "Not to speak of, but I do feel just a bit more apprehensive about the prospect of arriving in France than I did about arriving in Ireland."

"Just a bit?" Loveday enquired.

Watson lifted his right shoulder in a shrug. "A lot."

"As do I," admitted Loveday.

Holmes leaned forward, placing his elbows on the rail. "I hope Ebenezer is not seriously discommoded by you being conscripted by the Secret Service twice in one month."

"I asked for a fortnight's leave from the Lynch Court agency," replied Loveday.

"I see. Good."

"It wasn't granted."

Watson scowled. "Why not?"

"I suspect Mr Dyer is hoping to make me choose between Lynch Court and 221B. I believe he's a bit jealous of the time I spend with, as he calls you, the Baker Street Boys."

"Not very fair-minded of him. Have you made a decision?"

"I'm here, aren't I?" she retorted. "Although I'm not sure I'm making the proper decision, under the current circumstances."

Watson raised his eyebrows. "What circumstances?"

"I have my doubts about the clarity of my thinking." She cast a glance at Holmes and then back to Watson. "I'm not if sure any of us are clear-headed. We're still dealing with Deirdre's death."

"It's called grief," said Holmes stiffly. "Or so I've been told."

Loveday shook her head. "It's more than that or guilt. I remember my father talking about battle fatigue."

Watson nodded. "Combat stress reaction, yes. We army doctors were told how to treat it amongst soldiers in Afghanistan. I suffered a touch of it myself after Maiwand."

"So did my father, involved as he was in the bombardment and occupation of Alexandria. Like you, he was wounded and retired from the service shortly thereafter. He wasn't seriously injured but he was still in enough pain physically and emotionally to seek relief in laudanum, morphine and even cocaine."

Holmes pushed himself up, continuing to stare impassively straight ahead.

"He became addicted," Loveday continued. "In fact, I think his physical reliance on narcotics contributed to his early death."

Holmes turned his face toward her. "Are you making a point, Miss Brooke?"

"An observation. You showed the oh-so-familiar signs of being under the influence of a narcotic when Mycroft and I visited you the other day. I have a feeling that was one reason John was so angry with you."

Watson forced an unconvincing grin. "No, it was all pretty much due to poor housekeeping, poor company and indoor target shooting."

Holmes held up a hand. "No need to dissemble on my part, old fellow. I've put you in an uncomfortable, if not untenable situation." To Loveday he said flatly, "I had been the under the influence of a seven percent solution of cocaine earlier that day... around three o'clock in the morning, in fact. Watson awoke early and removed my..."

He paused, groping for a term. "Accoutrements. I resented him for it and had been in a sulk for quite a few hours before you and Mycroft arrived. I obviously had not slept or eaten since the previous day."

He took a deep breath and exhaled it. "Withal, I am not an addict in the textbook sense. Intermittently, I desire the artificial stimulus it provides, but it is not a physical craving; therefore, I am not reliant upon it."

Loveday turned to regard Watson with challenging eyes. "You've been aware of this?"

"For some years...but never did I enable the practice. I hoped I

221B: On Her Majesty's Secret Service

had weaned him from the solution's usage, but after the death of Deirdre, Holmes once again invited the fiend into his veins."

Holmes shook his head in weary exasperation. "Reserve the melodramatic metaphors for your literary efforts, please."

Facing Loveday, he said earnestly, "Miss Brooke, I am being candid with you because we find ourselves in a partnership, and we need to depend upon one another. Therefore, what Watson knows, you should know. I admit, I have been wracked with guilt and rage for the last three weeks, and consumed with an intense need for vengeance. I unfortunately dealt with those emotions by returning to a destructive pastime, for which I have been rightly chastised by Watson and my own conscience. However, please set your mind at rest...I have not invited the fiend back into my veins or any other part of my anatomy since that morning in Baker Street."

Loveday gazed at him steadily for a long stretch of time. Holmes stared into her eyes unblinkingly. Her lips curved in a wan smile and she glanced back to the lights of Calais. "I believe you."

A shrill boatswain's whistle pierced the morning sea mist and a man's voice loudly announced the *Brittany* would be docking at Calais within half an hour. The ferry was not crowded, so there was no rush to the disembarkation gate.

At the Calais port, the *Brittany* made an easy entrance into a waiting slip. After collecting their luggage, which consisted of one valise apiece, they crossed the deck and walked down a ramp to a granite pier. The air smelled of kelp and hot engine oil. They passed through the customs booth where their passports were examined by a sleepy uniformed gendarme.

They saw a plain carriage drawn by a brace of bay horses on the other side of the checkpoint. A man with a cap pulled low sat in the box, apparently napping. As they approached, a middle-aged man climbed out. He was short and curiously egg-shaped, with a thick moustache and heavy jowls. He wore a crushed velvet trilby hat and a long tweed coat. He waved. "Monsieur Vernet?"

Holmes stepped forward, extending a hand. *"Oui.* Inspecteur Dubugue?"

The man shook his hand twice in the traditional pumping manner of the French. "Yes. I have been assigned as liaison with the Sûreté. We should converse in English. If there are any eavesdroppers about, they most likely only understand *Francais.* Spies are everywhere in France, like maggots in cheese. "

Holmes introduced Watson and Loveday. Dubugue waved them into the carriage ahead of him and took the seat opposite. The interior smelled of damp leather, strong tobacco and garlic. The driver snapped the reins and the carriage rolled forward smoothly.

"An honour to meet you, Monsieur Holmes," Dubugue said. "Your monograph about the tracing of footprints has become required reading for new recruits in the Sûreté."

"Ah." Holmes smiled. "And as I recall, you and I corresponded briefly about the poisoning of Monsieur Leturier in Montpellier some years ago."

Dubugue frowned. "A miscarriage of justice that one." He folded his arms over his chest. "May I ask why you chose Vernet as a recognition word?"

"My family is of French descent through a grandmother who was the sister of the artist Vernet."

"Ah!" Dubugue's face registered impressed surprise. "I would not have thought it after meeting your brother."

"Mycroft is in Paris already?"

"He arrived at the Hôtel d'Alsace yesterday, where he is ensconced as Monsieur LeCoq."

Watson laughed. "That's a little obvious even for Mycroft."

Dubugue grinned. "I said as much to him but he defended his choice of aliases on the grounds that if any one of you is being watched for, he and that name would draw the most attention."

"We're not hiding from anyone," Holmes stated confidently.

"Quite the opposite," agreed Loveday. "If we are expected in Paris, there's no reason to disappoint anyone waiting for us."

The carriage wheeled along the coast road as the gray of the post-dawn sky slowly faded, melting to mauve. They saw copses of tall, straight-boled trees on the left and the open sea on the right. The road curved around and abruptly terminated at a railyard. The carriage halted on the cindered roadbed beside a locomotive. Waiting beneath a white canopy of steam, it appeared older and much smaller than the *Wraith* and drew only a coal car and passenger coach.

Dubugue opened the carriage door, allowing Loveday to climb out first. He said, "This is a commuter train...we are its only passengers. The police have commissioned it for the day even though it is only a short trip into Paris."

"Then why take it over for the whole day?" asked Loveday.

"Spies," he replied curtly. "Perhaps assassins. Secretly boarding a train would be difficult even for the most accomplished espion."

They boarded the coach and took two bench style seats facing each other. Unlike those in the *Wraith*, they were not well-padded. The train got underway with a shrill trumpeting of vented steam and within minutes it rumbled and ratcheted along the track. Dubugue tried to make conversation but due to the incessant clatter, it was not worth the effort. After half-an-hour, the inspector fell into a doze. Not long after, so did Watson, Loveday and Holmes.

Three hours after departing the Calais station, a change in the train's motion caused Loveday to raise her head from the cushion she had propped up against the coach wall. She looked out the window.

The clouds seemed to open up revealing a bright blue expanse.

221B: *On Her Majesty's Secret Service*

Like a theatrical spotlight, a shaft of brilliant mid-morning sunshine fell upon a skyline that appeared to be gilded in gold-leaf.

Paris rose like a fairyland city but Loveday knew from prior visits it was a distance-based illusion. Still, she felt her pulse quicken at the sight of the Notre Dame spires and the gilt-edged Dome des Invalides. She glimpsed the skeletal silhouette of Eiffel's tower reaching up from the horizon and she experienced a moment's awe. Paris held a special place in her heart, although she had only visited the city twice.

As the train chugged into the Gare du Nord station, Loveday saw the platforms were thronged with people. They looked prosperous, with men in dark suits and top hats and women in long skirts moving briskly to and fro. Boarding whistles seemed to shriek from everywhere. She remarked, "Very busy morning."

Dubugue leaned forward to look out the window. "Typical, actually. The Nord is a travel hub to all parts of the Continent. It is constantly being expanded and rebuilt, and it can be rather confusing in the main terminal, so please follow me. A cab should be waiting for us out front. Watch for Les Apaches."

"The fabled street gang, I presume," said Holmes. "Not the American Southwest Indian tribe?"

"Some of them are more savage than their American counterparts," replied Dubugue grimly.

The train came to a shuddering halt beside a platform and the four people disembarked. The inspector led them from the boarding platforms into the crowded main promenade of the cavernous, high-ceilinged terminal. Watson overheard at least a dozen different accents and dialects as soon as they entered. The station was truly an international flux.

His eyes swept about, scanning all of the different faces, noting bearded and turbaned Sikhs, Orientals and a few colourfully clad men from an African nation. His gaze passed over, then returned and rested on a quartet of young men. They wore red cummerbunds and headgear that looked like flat-caps crossed with berets.

They swaggered about the promenade, elbowing aside people and talking in loud, aggressive voices. As they approached their party, an outside member of the pack swung directly in their path. Dubugue stopped and fixed a slit-eyed stare on the young man's face. His right hand made a casual show of stealing inside his jacket. The man's eyes caught the inspector's gaze. He blinked, and at the last second, veered to one side, avoiding him completely.

Dubugue smiled at his companions without humour. "Welcome to gay Paris."

They began walking through the promenade again. By bulling his way forward, parting clots of people like the prow of a ship, the inspector led them out of the terminal. It felt surprisingly cool outside. Holmes glanced around at the crowds streaming in and out of the many glass and steel doors. He said, "When the Exposition opens, I imagine the daily in-and-out traffic will increase dramatically."

Dubugue nodded. "The conservative estimate is by a factor of four, especially during the height of summer. The Gare du Nord will become the mecca for pick-pockets throughout Europe."

A grey coach pulled by two horses of a matching shade rolled up to the parking apron. Dubugue spoke to the man in the driver's box and gestured for everyone to climb aboard. The carriage navigated the traffic-heavy street running alongside the facade of the train station and then entered the great wheel of Place de l'Etoil that circled the massive and lofty Arc de Triomphe.

The architecture of the neighbourhoods branching off from the wheel was surprisingly plain, even dull in their mass-produced similitude. Saint-Germain-des-Pres was no exception, due to the extensive renovation of the old buildings and houses, some of which dated to the Middle Ages.

Hôtel d'Alsace on Rue de Beaux Arts did not have a reputation of being among the quality Parisian hotels. The hostelry was old, rather run-down and not very well-known, except to members of various intelligence services of various European nations. Due to its location, lay-out and age, it was considered a safe haven, a neutral ground. The hotel had corollaries in every European capital.

The cab deposited Loveday, Holmes, Watson and Dubugue before the dingy front steps at a few minutes after 11 o' clock. No valet appeared to help them with their luggage nor was there a bell-hop in the small, shabby lobby.

The décor was muted, the over-stuffed maple furniture implying comfort with great age. Sprays of fresh flowers bloomed from vases set on walnut pedestal tables at intervals along the walls. Their scent helped repress the odour of must and mildew.

Holmes crossed the once-lush purple carpet to the front desk where an elderly concierge in a threadbare blue coat greeted him politely. When Holmes gave his name, the old man nodded toward a doorway to the left. "Monsieur LeCoq asked me to direct you to the restaurant where he is having an early lunch."

"And our luggage?"

The man gestured with a white-gloved hand. "You may leave it here after you sign the register."

Holmes, Watson and Loveday signed the book with a thick, old-fashioned fountain pen. With the inspector in tow, they entered the hotel's small restaurant. They saw Mycroft seated at a table covered in a red-and-white chequered tablecloth. Across from him sat a smooth-faced man with long dark hair parted in the middle framing a blandly aristocratic face. He wore an odd coat of serge with a fur collar and cuffs. Upon seeing the approach of Holmes and his party, he quickly arose from the table and walked toward the rear door, glancing self-consciously over his shoulder.

Mycroft gestured the four people to chairs. "Welcome...I've

been waiting for you to arrive for the last hour and I finally put in my lunch order."

"Which is?" Holmes asked.

"The classic quiche Lorraine. I can recommend it."

"Who was that man you were talking to?" Loveday asked. "He looked familiar."

"You might have seen his likeness in *Vanity Fair* and elsewhere...that was Oscar Wilde, the Irish writer and editor...he took a room here at the hotel to research a play he is writing. We met a few years ago at a function in London. Interesting fellow."

"I've read one of his essays," said Watson diffidently. "I don't remember much about it."

A male server in a starched apron brought them tea and coffee in fine china and a tray piled high with pastries and croissants. Without speaking Holmes took one and began eating it without so much as adding a half-pat of butter. Mycroft smiled. "I see your usually healthy appetite has returned, Sherlock."

Loveday poured coffee for Dubugue, Watson and Holmes. She preferred the tea. "You appear to be enjoying yourself here, Mycroft."

He shrugged. "I had forgotten Paris has its charms and travel its benefits. This is the closest to a holiday I've had in ten years. Which reminds me –"

Reaching into a coat pocket, he produced a brown envelope and extracted invitations and several pieces of paper bearing stamps, crests and logos. "Sherlock, Miss Brooke... here are your invitations to Madame Koluchy's *soiree* issued from and bearing the stamp of the Foreign Office. You can personalize them by signing beneath the stamp. Your wardrobe for the night waits for you in your rooms. Dr Watson, here is your press pass issued by the *Globe* identifying you as one of their correspondents."

Watson eyed the small half-tone photograph glued to one corner of the card. " 'Hubert Willis'" he read aloud. "He looks only a little like me."

"The resemblance is close enough," said Mycroft. "A white male with fair hair. He is a couple of years older than you."

"He has a moustache," Watson pointed out.

"Men shave them off occasionally, you know...or you can wear false whiskers. I brought a selection in case you choose to go in that direction."

"Where is the real Hubert?"

"On paid leave in Wales, so don't fear running into him here."

Holmes asked, "Will you be attending the reception as Monsieur LeCoq?"

Mycroft shook his head. "I will not be there, nor will Dr Watson. He and I will be on standby and embarking on the tower tour tomorrow morning."

Watson's eyebrows rose. Incredulously he asked, *"You* will?"

"I've been exercising."

"Doing what?"

"Javelin throwing. Twice a day for the past week."

Loveday eyed him sceptically. "I find that hard to believe."

"Mycroft's javelins are under six inches long with pointy metal tips," said Holmes. "The rest of the world calls them darts."

There were chuckles all around until Dubugue said, "As amusing as I find all of you, I am still waiting for an explanation about what you hope to accomplish through all of this subterfuge. I was told to cooperate unless I determined you were violating the laws of our Republic. At this juncture, I am starting to grow wary of deeper engagement."

Mycroft said, "Understandable, but I was informed you were briefed about an illicit cartel that has involved itself with the Paris Exposition."

"The Hephaestus Ring." Dubugue nodded impatiently. "We are aware that the Ring is an organization overseen by a dangerous woman, Madame Kathryn Koluchy of the Brotherhood of Seven Kings."

"She's not merely a dangerous woman," Mycroft said, "but the most dangerous woman alive. She is a brilliant brain by any measure and is a member of the higher councils of several European criminal societies, like the Camorra of Italy. The police and secret services of half a dozen nations would dearly love to be able to pin something on Madame Koluchy, but she has been too cunning for that, hiding behind a curtain of respectability as a producer of health foods. She has earned a degree of legitimate fame in that field. Although she may be the power behind the Ring's throne, she has been never been out in the open, preferring to work from the shadows."

With a big blunt finger, he tapped the embossed image on the surface of the invitation."Now for some reason, she feels sufficiently safe to come into the light."

Holmes said, "Her Majesty's Secret Service has reason to suspect that Madame Koluchy and the Hephaestus Ring are on the verge of staging a major crime during tomorrow's tour of Eiffel's tower."

"That was explained to me, but not the nature of the crime."

Mycroft shifted in his chair uncomfortably. "Unfortunately, all we really know is a possible code-name – Thunderstrike. Regardless, inasmuch as the tour group will consist of representatives of international concerns, including foreign governments, it has become a diplomatic matter."

Dubugue cocked his head at a quizzical angle. "Then should not diplomats be dealing with it?"

"They are," replied Mycroft gravely. "That is why we are here."

"As far as I know, only the British Secret Service has been accorded this accommodation."

"That is the operative term, Inspector. As far as you know. Last night I encountered an agent of Bismarck, Fritz von Waldbaum, in this very lobby. We had been introduced some years ago at a diplomatic function in Geneva. We spoke briefly...he informed me he would be at the reception tonight and present on the tour tomorrow, acting as a specialist for the German government."

"What kind of specialist?" asked Dubugue.

Mycroft shrugged. "He did not elucidate, and I did not ask."

Dubugue nodded but he still seemed uncertain. Loveday said, "So, it's just Mr Holmes and I breaching enemy territory this evening?"

The inspector helped himself to a pastry. "Not entirely, Mademoiselle. There will be policemen present, and I presume agents of the Deuxieme Bureau, although I do not know for sure."

"Nor I," Mycroft said darkly. "I fear the Bureau may have been compromised. My last two enquiries to Mathis went unanswered."

"As I warned you earlier," Dubugue said to Loveday. "Spies are everywhere in France."

Loveday smiled. "Like maggots in cheese?"

Dubugue returned her smile. "Precisely like that, Mademoiselle Brooke."

Holmes said.,"And that is precisely why I am not inclined to adopt an alias or a disguise, pretending to be someone I'm not. It would be a waste of time and effort, since I intend to question Kathryn Koluchy directly."

"Under the circumstances," Loveday commented, "cage-rattling may be the best strategy."

Mycroft said reluctantly, "That is an exceedingly dangerous tactic, Miss Brooke."

"Actually, it's about standard," said Holmes. "For us."

221B: On Her Majesty's Secret Service
I don't think I have ever had a more difficult game to play.
— Loveday Brooke

CHAPTER 25

THE CARRIAGE RUMBLED along the Avenue de la Bourdonnais, drawn by two horses with glossy black coats. Ornately sculpted lamps atop metal columns illuminated both sides of the thoroughfare, casting a steady yellow glow bright enough to read a newspaper by, even within the interior of the coach. Loveday said, "They have electrical street lighting in this neighbourhood."

"Carbon arc lamps," replied Holmes. "Also called Yablochkov candles, named after Pavel Yablochkov, a Russian electrical engineer. Similar ones were installed along the Victoria Embankment but they're much more common here in Paris than in London. I think it will be a while longer before our city's tried-and-true gas lamps are replaced by electric ones."

Loveday's breath condensed on the glass of the carriage window. Outside, the air was cold. The people she saw on the sidewalks walked hurriedly, clutching their coats tight about them. Fortunately for her hairstyle, it was not raining. Except for one tress hanging over her left shoulder, her hair was artfully braided at the nape of her neck, and caught by a golden brooch with four small emeralds — a gift from her father, many years before. Too many years, she thought bleakly.

She, Holmes and Watson had spent the day catching up on their rest and preparing for the reception at the home office of

221B: *On Her Majesty's Secret Service*

Madame Koluchy. Mycroft had arranged for a hairdresser and personal maid to attend to Loveday's preparations. Holmes took care of himself, except for allowing a barber to trim his hair and give him a perfunctory shave.

Loveday wore a satin evening gown of white and pink, lent to her for the evening. The sleeves were short and the bodice trimmed with a frilly lace and small silk roses. She had chosen it from the clothing made available by the Defence Intelligence Branch. Nothing like it could be found at the Diogenes Club, of course. A fur-trimmed purple velvet collar stole draped her shoulders.

She said thoughtfully, "Electric street lights, flying machines and free energy...I don't know if England is ready for the future. I don't know if I am."

Holmes replied, "It doesn't matter whether anyone is ready for it...all we can do is try to shape the future in a fashion that doesn't repeat the mistakes of the past."

Loveday smiled playfully, "Then perhaps we should not stand in such opposition to the Hephaestus Ring and their technocratic ideals...humanity in general could use a few more, you know."

"Their ideals can be distilled down into one word: tyranny...with humanity united like a team of dray animals, yoked together and obeying one whip." His tone held an edge of barely repressed loathing.

She laid her hand on his. "I was just teasing." To her surprise, he did not pull away.

"Miss Brooke, your hand is very cold...don't you have gloves?"

"Of course...but they're tight and elbow length and I don't like wearing them."

"Perhaps you should...they are part of your chosen ensemble, I believe."

Irritably, she said, "I don't require fashion advice from you, Mr Holmes."

"I submit that is a good thing," he retorted. "Regardless, if your hands are cold, you should put on your gloves."

"I will if you will."

Holmes obligingly slipped on a pair of white gloves and held up his right hand, waggling his fingers. "All digits properly shod and warm."

She admitted to herself that Holmes cut a dashing figure in his tailored black tailcoat, matching vest, boutonnière and white tie. His patent leather shoes and smooth black hair both gleamed with highlights in the lamp-glow. A red-lined black cloak hung from his shoulders.

On impulse, she said, "You look very handsome."

His face registered surprise. "It's a costume. Camouflage."

"Nevertheless."

After a few seconds, he said haltingly, "You look very..." He trailed off.

"Very what?"

"Exquisite?"

"That's acceptable, thank you." Loveday tugged on her gloves. "Are you armed?"

He adjusted his shirt cuffs. "A couple of items up my sleeves. You?"

She patted her beaded reticule. "Just my loyal Bull-dog. I doubt ladies will be searched."

The carriage rolled under a brick archway and into a walled courtyard. It faced a short flight of marble steps leading up to the main door of a three-story town-house. The baroque façade looked as if it dated back at least a century, probably to the reign of King Louis XVI. Somehow, it had withstood the efforts of Napoleon III to modernize and standardize Paris architecture and retained its flying buttresses and windows with Gothic arched frames.

Holmes consulted his pocket watch. "Just now eight o' clock.

We're still fashionably late."

Loveday realized her nerves were wire-taut. Her stomach had a chill, empty feeling. She glanced over at Holmes. "Aren't you nervous?"

Restoring his watch to his vest pocket, he shook his head. "Not so much nervous as recalling my antipathy for entering a trap."

"You think this reception was staged as a trap for us?" Loveday asked doubtfully.

"Not specifically for us, but anyone curious enough to stick their heads into it."

"Like I said to you a few weeks ago, it's not really a trap if you know it's a trap."

"Let's not be under any illusion as to how dangerous this place can be. It is our lion's den."

Loveday eyed the courtyard uneasily, gauging the height of the walls. "John and Mycroft are waiting for word from us at the hotel. Inspector Dubugue and a contingent of gendarmes are watching the house."

"The exterior of the house...unfortunately, that is not where a trap will be sprung."

The carriage joined a queue at the foot of the steps to allow coach passengers to disembark. Unsurprisingly, the people they saw with invitations in their hands all looked very affluent. When their coach pulled up, a red-coated servant opened the door and helped Loveday to step out.

As they climbed the steps, a grave-faced man in a white jacket opened the oak door. Yellow light spilled out as well as the music of an orchestra. He held up a green-gloved hand. "Invitation, *s'il vous plait.*"

Holmes placed his and Loveday's invitations into it. He unfolded them, looked at the stamps and the signatures, and tapped the side of his nose with an index finger. "Very good, Monsieur Holmes, Mademoiselle Brooke."

He nodded to Holmes and waved them into a foyer where Holmes handed his cloak to a young woman in a black-and-white maid's uniform. Loveday opted to keep her wrap. Once inside, Holmes offered Loveday his arm. She took it, murmuring, "I have sometimes wondered if you and your brother were ever taught etiquette."

"We were...by our mother. We occasionally forget the lessons and revert to what we learned from our wild lupine friends."

A mosaic floor echoed with their footsteps. The walls on either side were pillared at intervals of one yard. Between each fluted column stood a pedestal, each one occupied by a white marble bust. Holmes noted them as they passed by. "Hippocrates, Euclid, Pliny, Asclepiades Pharmacion, Jacques de Vaucanson...rather an eclectic group of physicians, mathematicians and engineers to deify in marble."

The two people walked through a wide doorway into the great vaulted ballroom. Stone columns topped by intricately sculpted Corinthian capitals rose here and there around the hall. Since they did not reach the ceiling, they were there for effect. They admired the richly brocaded furnishings and the vividly painted ceiling, an imitation of Francois Boucher's *Boreas Abducting Oreithyia*. A magnificent birdcage chandelier hung from the apex, bright electric light glittering from the multi-faceted pieces of rock crystal.

Glass bulbs glowed in brass fixtures on the walls, and a champagne fountain bubbled within a recess that might once have been a hearth, huge enough to have easily accommodated the carriage they had arrived in. Miniature replicas of Eiffel's tower served as centrepieces on every table.

Loveday's eyes flitted over the crowd. She noted the guests were of a curious assortment, even for cosmopolitan Paris. Her mind catalogued and evaluated. A number of the guests fell into an expected pattern — bureaucrats, middle-aged industrialists accompanied by their young mistresses, and even a high-ranking

French military officer in full-dress uniform. But she also saw a few people who were atypical of such affairs.

One was an elderly bowed man with the look of an aged rodent, with a bristle moustache and thin white hair swept back over a receding hairline. His trembling, gnarled hands rested atop the silver knob of a polished black cane. His tiny round eyes shone like wet agate on either side of a long, pointed nose.

She shifted her attention to a very tall man with dark lensed half-glasses. A medal-heavy red sash crossed from the epaulette on the left shoulder to the right hip of his ivory-coloured coat. The cuffs and brass button eyelets were trimmed with gold thread. He leaned against one of the columns, a glass in his left hand.

He had a great seamed face with a sweeping tawny moustache that almost hid his mouth. His shaggy lion's-mane of hair was nearly white, which made his deeply bronzed skin seem even darker. Their glances met. His eyes were pale, faded to the colour of old pewter, void of any depth. Loveday quickly averted her gaze.

Holmes said, "I see a few academics, a handful of the aristocracy, half-a-dozen foreign agents and even two police officers in mufti, but I do not see Madame Koluchy."

"That's not surprising, since we don't know what she looks like."

Holmes nodded distractedly, his gaze continuing to jump from face-to-face. "I'm certain we will recognize her when we see her."

"How many people do you think are here?"

"In this room alone, I counted one hundred and eighty-seven. I presume there are others I cannot see, so that number is variable."

The babble of voices suddenly rose in volume. They heard an outbreak of spontaneous applause. Turning, they watched a stout but very well-dressed, bearded man making his way into the hall. He beamed and nodded at the people clapping their hands around him. An elegant young woman hung on on his right arm, regal and slender in an ice-blue gown with a wealth of dark blonde hair piled atop her head. A number of men and women followed in his wake.

"Gustave Eiffel and his entourage," commented Loveday. "And his wife?"

"He's a widower...the young lady is perhaps his daughter. Or more likely a companion hired for the evening. He is basking in his time of triumph."

"I don't suppose he can be blamed."

The orchestra arrayed against the far wall struck up with a new burst of music, playing to Loveday's ears, a composition by Johann Strauss. Couples began whirling over the vast expanse of the dance floor. Although Loveday had little knowledge of music theory, she found the melody thrilling. For a moment, she wondered what it would be like to be out there, dancing and spinning like a tiny toy figures on a music box. But she hadn't danced since she was a child, and would only make a spectacle of herself – which was the exact opposite of the night's mission.

Holmes touched her elbow and with an arched eyebrow and half-bow indicated the dance floor. She blinked at him, nonplussed. "You wish to dance?"

"Why should we not? We would be less conspicuous."

"You do know how?"

"Dancing lessons came with the ones in etiquette at no extra charge."

"Very well." She managed a curtsy and Holmes took her extended hand.

As they joined the dancers on the floor, Holmes placed one hand lightly on her waist and held her right hand. He said, "Johann Strauss, *The Emperor's Waltz*... have you ever danced a

Viennese waltz?"

"No, but at least I recognized the composer."

"That is a good start, Miss Brooke. Three beat increments. While dancing a waltz, our feet should not leave the floor. Ideally, we will glide."

"I think I should probably follow your lead."

Holmes smiled in genuine amusement. "For all things there is a first time." He slightly flexed his knees. "One, two, three. Here we go."

Within a second, they were among the dancers, turning with the best of them, sliding around the floor counter-clockwise in time with the music. The tension in her body and her mind eased as Holmes turned and twirled her with a surprising grace and confidence of movement.

The music ended on a stirring fanfare. After a smattering of applause, the dancers bowed, curtsyed and drifted away. Arm-in-arm, Loveday and Holmes walked across the marble floor, toward the champagne fountain. Loveday said, "Thank you, Mr Holmes. You never fail to surprise me."

"Nor I myself. For instance, I found Kathryn Koluchy by *not* looking for her." He inclined his head slightly to the right. "I spotted her during the last allemande."

Loveday squinted in the direction he indicated and said, "Apparently so did many other men."

She saw a tall, copper-haired woman sipping from a fluted champagne glass while engaged in spirited conversation with a man wearing a tuxedo. With his back turned to them, they could not see his face. Several other men stood attentively around her.

Her long hair, glinting with radiant highlights, was done in a regal coronet. A scandalously tight black gown encased her taut-muscled body. The neckline plunged almost to her sternum. Her tight evening gloves gave the visual suggestion she had dipped her arms up to the biceps in India ink. The contrast with her white skin was startling.

Loveday sensed an aura about her, a glow not cast by the diamond necklace around her throat but exuded from some power source deep within her. The words *the Black Queen* popped unbidden into her mind.

She hesitated, slowing Holmes's advance across the floor. For an instant, he strained against her arm, like a hound against a leash. Impatiently, he demanded, "What is it?"

Loveday spoke in an urgent whisper. "Are we just going to walk right up to her?"

"Wasn't that our plan?"

"That's not a plan, that's an intention."

He sighed. "I have already located five, possibly six points of escape from this hall. I've looked for armed guards and not found a single one."

"That doesn't mean they aren't here."

"I've taken all of that into consideration, but I understand your apprehension. Perhaps it would be strategically best if we separated at this point."

Her grip tightened on his arm. Forcing a smile and speaking sibilantly between clenched teeth, she said, "The last time we did that, I had to pull you out of a bog. If you can keep your anger in check, I'll continue to follow your lead — for the time being, at least."

"I'm not angry," he replied but some of the tension went out of his body.

They started off again, wending their way through the crowd. They heard various languages, from Russian to Spanish. A man's accented voice spoke quietly behind them: "Herr Holmes, Fräulein Brooke?"

They turned to see a small man with gray side-whiskers framing a narrow, bald skull standing there. His sallow face was dominated by a beak of a nose and a single bright blue eye. The right one was covered by a black patch. Dressed in conservative evening garb, he held himself ramrod straight.

"You have the advantage of us, sir," said Holmes politely

He clicked his heels and bowed his head. "I am Fritz von Waldbaum. I encountered your brother, Mycroft, at the Hôtel d'Alsace yesterday. I glimpsed you and Fräulein Brooke in the lobby this morning."

Holmes smiled, but it was little more than a distracted lip twitch. "Herr von Waldbaum, the specialist from Germany."

"Dantzig to be specific. I shall get to the point. I am wondering if your invitation to the reception includes the private tour of the Exposition grounds later this evening?"

"I'm not sure. How would I know?"

The man held up his left hand, displaying a ring with a hammer and anvil setting. "You would have received one of these at the same time as your invitation."

"We did not."

"Apparently the tour group list is short and exclusive, restricted to representatives of certain business interests."

"Is the tour the only reason you are here?"

Von Waldbaum nodded. *"Ja,* I was not dispatched from Berlin solely to attend this superficial social function."

Loveday leaned closer to him in order to hear over the babble of the crowd. "According to Mycroft, you identified yourself as a specialist. What is your field?"

"Primarily forecast economics. I've been informed the private tour Madame Koluchy has arranged is not so much a preview of the fair but a preview of the future...she presents it as a rare investment opportunity."

Holmes narrowed his eyes. "Do you mean the point of the tour is actually to —as the Kent Street jewellery sellers say— 'make a pitch'?"

"Ja, that is accurate, Herr Holmes."

"What is Madame Koluchy hoping to sell, exactly?"

Von Waldbaum pursed his lips, pondering the question. In a measured tone, he replied, "Shares in the twentieth century would be the least fanciful description."

"Why is she so sure the twentieth century is worth buying?"

"Due to something I've heard talked about for several years — the Analytical Engine." He grinned, displaying several gold teeth. "I have not seen any such thing, of course. Perhaps that will change tonight. If you wish to learn more, it is probably not too late to arrange your place on the tour. Possibly I shall see you there."

"Possibly."

Von Waldbaum bowed and sidled around Holmes and Loveday, swiftly crossing the floor space in the opposite direction. They stared after him. Loveday commented, "An odd little fellow."

"But helpful. He's provided us with an entree to speak directly to Madame Koluchy."

"You want us to hear her pitch?"

"I do indeed."

"That's a different tactic than demanding information about Nikola and Robur."

He shrugged. "Anticipate and adapt, Miss Brooke."

"Oh, spare me," she shot back. "Just for tonight."

Voices raised in an angry exchange commanded their attention. They saw the red-haired woman pivoting sharply away from the man with whom she had been speaking. She put her back to him as if offended by something he had said.

The man turned around slowly, wearily lifting a wine glass to his lips. His dark eyes locked onto Sherlock Holmes and Loveday Brooke. They widened in shock and he froze in mid-motion.

221B: On Her Majesty's Secret Service

On Basil Zaharoff's right hand gleamed a ring made of a coppery metal with the setting in the form of a smith's hammer and anvil.

221B: On Her Majesty's Secret Service
I play the game for the game's own sake.

— Sherlock Holmes

CHAPTER 26

"BELIEVE ME, SIR," said Zaharoff desperately. "I have less wish to be here than you could possibly wish me not to be here."

"That's a peculiar way of putting it," snapped Holmes. "Where I wish you to be at this moment is six feet down. At minimum."

He, Zaharoff and Loveday stood outside the ballroom on a terrace, away from the crowds and the ambient drone of conversation, but in the cold. Loveday hugged herself and declared, "Mr Zaharoff, you made it clear a few weeks ago that you were avoiding further contact with the Ring."

"I also said I had one final contractual obligation to fulfill," he responded desperately. He craned his neck to see past Holmes. "Your brother Mycroft isn't here, is he?"

"He had a prior engagement. Miss Brooke and I were sent in his stead."

"He was invited?"

Holmes said carefully, "Our invitations were conveyed through the Home Office. What about yours?"

"A week after our meeting in Soho, I received an invitation to tonight's function. It was delivered by hand to my villa in Spain, so obviously Madame Koluchy knew where to find me. I interpreted it as a summons. Mandatory attendance."

Holmes uttered a short, taunting laugh. "I did not realize Basil

221B: *On Her Majesty's Secret Service*

Zaharoff was so easily intimidated."

The man's dark eyes glinted like pieces of hard obsidian. "The possibility of forfeiting a hundred thousand pounds would intimidate anyone, even Basil Zaharoff. That is the amount I am owed by the Ring"

"For what?" asked Loveday. "More weapons?"

"If you must know, the delivery of a prototype tripod mounted, gas-operated heavy machine gun."

"I presume it's a superior design to the Rattler." Holmes commented.

Zaharoff's face showed surprise. "Very much so. It will change the face of modern warfare. The next military conflict will be fought with such weapons."

"And as a top-flight merchant of death, you'll sell them to both warring parties, won't you?"

Zaharoff shrugged. "All part of the *Bolshaya Igra* — the Great Game — isn't it? That is why I am here tonight, to negotiate an exclusive license with the Hephaestus Ring and to settle a debt."

"Judging by Madame Koluchy's reaction," Loveday said, "the negotiations are not going well."

"In truth, they are not. I primarily want the money owed to me as part of the development fee and to simply go on my way...I fear she may withhold payment unless I agree to her terms."

"And the tour tonight?" enquired Holmes. "Does she expect you to be part of it?"

Zaharoff nodded grimly, displaying the hammer-and-anvil ring on his hand. "She made that abundantly clear. By the way, Mr Holmes ...I have not reneged on or forgotten my agreement to compile a dossier on James Moriarty. It has proven to be a more difficult task than I originally thought, but my top London operative is working on it, even as we speak."

"At the moment, I am less concerned with Moriarty than I am about the whereabouts of Nikola Tesla and Robur."

221B: *On Her Majesty's Secret Service*

"Tesla?" Zaharoff echoed, eyebrows knitting at the bridge of his nose. "Why—?"

The double-doors leading from the hall to the terrace opened, pushed by a man in dark evening clothes with short-cropped red hair. Rust-coloured sideburns framed his scarred face. He held his blackthorn shillelagh in his right hand. He said, "Mr Zaharoff, Madame is asking for you."

"Thank you, Cuthbert," Zaharoff said.

Holmes gazed at Cuthbert Rubadue, their eyes locking. He said, "Hello again, Cuthbert. I had been led to understand you were in service to Kathryn Koluchy now."

"Holmes," the man said in a menacing drawl. "To whom I'm in service is none of your bloody affair, ye jumped-up jack."

"Still using the same tiresome material," Holmes retorted. He glanced toward Zaharoff. "Whose coat does he wear now?"

"Mine," said Zaharoff, moving toward the doors. "I paid more for it. Considerably so. We reached a new accord when he came to deliver Madame Koluchy's summons — I mean invitation."

"Perhaps you'll consider facilitating a formal introduction with Madame."

"No need." Rubadue said gruffly, pointing at Holmes and Loveday with the end of his walking stick. "She is asking to see you both, as well."

Loveday exchanged a surprised look with Holmes. "Does she know who we are?"

Rubadue held the doors open. "She knows your names, that's all I can tell ye."

Holmes and Loveday allowed Zaharoff to precede them as they walked across the floor toward the starkly dressed figure of Kathryn Koluchy. She smiled at their approach and lifted a slim black-gloved hand in greeting.

"We still have business to conclude, Basil," she said in a quiet, modulated voice. "But I can neglect the formalities no longer, Mr

351

Holmes. I'm so glad to finally make your acquaintance. Miss Brooke, I remember our very brief meeting in Cornwall, of course."

Loveday smiled wryly. Madame Koluchy's deep blue eyes contained a self-confidence that was rarely shaken but they also held the watchful look of the wolf and the hawk.

Loveday said, "As do I...particularly how you stood by while Robur ordered his man, Vonn, to murder me. If not for the intervention of Mr Zaharoff here, it might well have happened."

The copper-haired woman laughed, waving a dismissive hand through the air. "How very gallant of you, Basil. Yes, Robur was so irrepressible in those days."

"And now?" challenged Holmes.

Her eyes met his. "He has mellowed some...he is more deliberate and measured. Perhaps you two should meet again and work out your issues."

"I would very much enjoy that," Holmes said impassively. "Especially if his hired man, Vonn, participated in the exercise."

"Oh, that goes without saying, Mr Holmes. Nikola Tesla might be inclined to take part, as well."

"You know of his whereabout?"

"Of course...he is very busy at the moment, but perhaps he can be persuaded to desist in his labours for a few minutes to have a chat with you and Miss Brooke."

"We would very much appreciate that opportunity," said Loveday.

Kathryn Koluchy's lips drew back over her teeth in a smile that was more of a snarl. "You will come on my tour to the Exposition grounds, will you not? Most of your curiosity will be satisfied then, I'm certain."

Holmes raised his hand, displaying both sides. "We don't have the club rings, I fear."

"I'll make a special dispensation in your cases. Consider it a professional courtesy."

"Thank you. I must admit I am interested to learn why your organization has chosen this point in time to crawl out of the baseboards and play your game in the light of day."

"The rules of the game have changed." The woman's smile disappeared. "All the more reason for you and Miss Brooke to accompany us." By her tone of voice, there was no choice in the matter. "Be in the courtyard in five minutes, please. Two coaches are waiting."

Holmes nodded curtly. "I shall retrieve my cloak and we shall go there forthwith."

He pivoted and strode across the ballroom, with Loveday hurrying to catch up. She called to him and he slowed down, casting her a peevish glance. She demanded, "Are we really going?"

"We really are."

"Have you forgotten you called this our lions' den?"

"I have not. Like Daniel, we should have faith in our deliverance."

"In that case, shouldn't we get word to Mycroft or Dubugue if we can?"

"That is exactly what I have in mind."

They retraced their steps to the foyer, where Holmes asked the maid for his cloak. As she went to fetch it from a closet, Loveday saw Holmes and the man in the white jacket exchange quick, almost perfunctory nods, after which the man closed and opened his right eye.

After retrieving his cloak, Holmes and Loveday went through the door and down the steps into the courtyard, where they saw two coaches waiting near the arch. A handful of people milled about nearby. The breeze was cold and sharp but it had scoured the sky of clouds until the stars and moon shone brightly.

221B: *On Her Majesty's Secret Service*

Loveday asked softly, "How will we apprise Mycroft?"

"I already have," Holmes replied. "The man taking the invitations is a police officer."

She stared at him, then back at the door, and demanded, "How do you know?"

Holmes brushed the tip of his nose with his index finger. "Because he did this after taking our invitations and recognizing our names. It's a universal recognition signal between police officers working undercover. By nodding to him, I let him know to alert his superiors to keep watch on us. He responded with an affirmative wink."

"Oh," said Loveday, mollified. She rubbed her arms briskly under her stole and shivered.

Holmes draped his cloak over her shoulders. She said, "Thank you."

"I have no need of it."

"Thank you, anyway."

A footman opened the doors to both coaches and gestured for four men to climb aboard the first. Two of them were dressed identically in tuxedos and wore burgundy fezzes over their oiled hair. Another was a compactly built man with black hair combed back from a widow's peak. A neatly trimmed pencil moustache adorned his upper lip. Other than Loveday, there were no women.

Holmes murmured, "Quite the distinguished guest list...the rat-faced old gentleman is Jacques Delbray, who has the dope trade in Marseilles in his purse; and I recognize Señor Rinconete of the Garduna society which controls every penny's worth of major vice in Barcelona. Not quite certain of the other two but their remarkable resemblance to one another and choice of headgear suggests they are the Alabora twins, representing their family's smuggling syndicate that operates on both sides of the Bosporus Strait."

Loveday allowed the footman to help her inside the second

coach. Holmes sat down beside her on the cushioned seat. A third man climbed aboard. He was the tall fellow wearing the military-style coat and half-spectacles she had seen leaning against a Corinthian column. In a disdainful tone, as if he begrudged speaking even two words, he said, "Good evening."

Loveday gave him a practiced smile. "Good evening, sir."

Holmes said nothing. He gazed intently at the man for a long moment, then glanced away, looking out the window. Another man pulled himself inside. Fritz von Waldbaum nodded to Holmes and Loveday and sat down beside the tall man.

The footman closed the door. Holmes said, "I presume Madame has her own mode of transportation and will meet us at our destination."

The tall man folded his arms over his deep chest. "That's a safe assumption, Mr Holmes."

"Not to mention an obvious one, Colonel Moran."

His eyes widened slightly behind the lenses of his glasses. "You recognize me, do you?"

"I had a little investigative involvement with the Nonpariel Club card scandal."

Moran grunted. "None of my affair."

Holmes lifted one shoulder in a shrug. "Except you were a member of the club, served in India with Colonel Underwood and then denied you knew anything of his atrocious behaviour. Speaking of which —"

Holmes nodded toward Loveday. "Miss Loveday Brooke, this is Colonel Sebastian Moran, late of the First Bangalore Pioneers. Celebrated author, too."

Moran responded with a gruff, "Miss."

"Have you met Fritz von Waldbaum? He's a specialist in economic forecasts, much like professional card-players."

Von Waldbaum frowned but said only, "Colonel."

221B: *On Her Majesty's Secret Service*

Despite the sudden electric tension in the air, Loveday said, "That is an interesting uniform, Colonel...I don't believe I've seen its like before."

"It is of my own design," replied Moran coldly. "But not the medals I wear."

Holmes chuckled dryly. "I'm a bit surprised to see you showing off all of those gongs at a civilian affair in France, since you are long retired from the British service."

"I'm here on business, so I wear what I like. Why are you here, Mr Holmes?"

"The same as you. Business."

"What kind of business?"

"I might ask you the same question."

"If you did, I might answer 'none of yours'."

"That would suffice as my answer, as well."

With a snap of reins and a jingle of harness, the coach started off, wheels rumbling against the cobblestones of the courtyard. No one spoke once the coach made its way out onto the street. Everyone sat unspeaking, jostled occasionally against one another in silence.

After a few minutes of travel, the two conveyances crossed over a bridge spanning the Seine and approached a stone wall. Peering out the window, Loveday said, "According to the signage, I believe we've arrived."

The smooth walls surrounding the grounds of Exposition Universelle rose ten feet above the surface of the street. The uniformity of the stone was interrupted by a wrought iron gate. The coaches were reined to halts outside it and the passengers disembarked. Fritz von Waldbaum and Moran exited first. Loveday commented, "Those gentlemen are not much on observing the forms, are they?"

"I can't speak for Herr Waldbaum, but Colonel Moran is definitely not a gentleman."

221B: On Her Majesty's Secret Service

"You'll have to tell me more about him one day."

"One day."

An arc-lamp lit their way to the gate. A blue uniformed man on the other side of the black bars caused it to slide sideways by turning a crank handle. The group of people filed through without speaking, and he guided them forward by swinging a lantern. "This way, please."

Loveday looked up and caught her breath. Less than an eighth of a mile northward rose Eiffel's iron citadel, a tower dominating the surrounding structures, a giant sceptre set amongst scatterings of children's building blocks.

Even at such a distance, they could see the immense base and how it was constructed in looping, soaring traceries of black metal. The tower stretched arrogantly upward, the interconnecting complexity of iron-work tapering in sharply close at the top. On its highest point glinted a reflective object, like a beacon or a captive star.

"Do you see that, Mr Holmes?" she asked in an awed whisper, her head canted back.

"The tower? Very clearly."

"It's an astounding achievement."

Holmes smiled slightly. "I will not dispute that."

A series of street-lamps cast a reflective glow on a line of white paving stones that led to a little tree-shaded depot, a square, low-roofed building made of red brick. A black and brass shunter locomotive engine rested on a narrow railway outside of it. Only one carriage was coupled to it, an open coach with cushioned seats and a gold tasselled Surrey roof made of dark green canvas.

The man with the lantern announced, "Welcome to the Decauville railway. We will take you to the Palais des Machines, the Hall of Machines, where Madame Koluchy awaits you. Please climb aboard and make yourselves comfortable."

221B: On Her Majesty's Secret Service

Everyone took seats on the cushioned wooden benches. Holmes and Loveday chose places at the very rear of the carriage, so as not to have their backs to Moran and the others. The uniformed man climbed into the cab and pulled the whistle cord. It hooted happily. With an increasing number of huffs, the train began rolling along the rail-line into the Exposition grounds proper.

Illuminated by streetlamps and strings of coloured light bulbs, the place looked like an enchanted kingdom put together by architects influenced by the dreams and fantasies of children. The sprawling compound was a city within a city. Although Eiffel's tower clearly was the focal point which continually drew the eye, they chugged past scores of ancillary pavilions and buildings. Spacious gardens and gazebos with gilded roofs were interspersed between them.

The train followed a curving side-track and braked to a halt under a broad porte-cochere. Above it loomed the Hall of Machines, a vast building which combined the features of a Gothic cathedral of high arches with modern iron, steel and glass. A manicured lawn of at least an acre spread out around it.

Kathryn Koluchy and Basil Zaharoff stood outside the double doors. A dark red cloak draped her from neckline to ankle. Zaharoff appeared pensive as the passengers disembarked. He did not meet the glances of Loveday or Holmes. At a word from Madame Koluchy, he stepped further beneath the overhang and rapped sharply on the door.

Light blazed through the windows, shining up through the glass panes composing the roof. Faintly came the sound of switches being thrown. The doors opened, pulled from within. Madame Koluchy announced, "Follow me, please."

The old rat-faced man Holmes had identified as Jacques Delbray stepped forward and hesitated. "Follow you to where and what, Kathryn?"

"To Things To Come." She stepped over the threshold.

221B: *On Her Majesty's Secret Service*

Obsequiously, Zaharoff held the doors open while Madame Koluchy and the others filed in. As Loveday passed him, she sarcastically murmured, *"Bolshaya Igra."*

They entered a great echoing space and walked down a wide marble-floored aisle. A constellation of light fixtures shone down from the ceiling high above their heads. The people looked around in wonder and puzzlement. On either side, great gear wheels slowly turned, huge ratchets caught and released and massive pistons thrust and returned in a complex dance of motion and steel. Rather than a clanging cacophony, the air vibrated with a soft, almost musical tick-tock rhythm.

"It's like being inside a giant Swiss clock," Loveday murmured.

"That's definitely the effect they're striving to achieve," replied Holmes, looking around at the plenum of machinery surrounding them. "These are props... all for show."

"It's a well-crafted decor, regardless."

Zaharoff walked quickly around the people in the aisle and joined Kathryn Koluchy. She began speaking, the acoustics of the hall carrying her words perfectly. "Most of you know me, either through doing business with my late husband, Count Carlos Koluchy, or directly with the Brotherhood of Seven Kings. You know I am not given to hyperbole, so listen very closely to what I have to say."

She paused, took a breath and declared matter-of-factly, "The world suffers from famine and plagues, it stews and percolates in waste and bulges at the seams with useless people. Governments could end these fundamental evils but they see no immediate reason to do so. Maintaining power in the present and discarding concerns about the future is their credo. Due to this arrogance, civilization on a global scale will fall into complete chaos within our lifetimes."

"No one can argue with that, Madame," said Von Waldbaum. "How do you propose to check the fall?"

221B: *On Her Majesty's Secret Service*

"With an immediate change of focus. And that focus is building a technocratic European government. But to make such a change, cooperation is essential, even if that cooperation is coerced."

She swept into a pavilion on the right side of the aisle. A yellow banner stretched across the entrance bearing the words: *Etonnant Automates*. "One way to coerce cooperation is through distraction and delightful diversions such as the Amazing Automata."

Two figures stood within the pavilion — one was a tall, sword-bearing man in a Hussar's uniform standing on a raised metal disk and the other a red-garbed, Satanically smiling man seated at an oversized chess-board. Madame Koluchy waved toward them. "Meet two diversions — Brigadier Gerard, swordsman *par excellence* and Mephisto, the champion chess-playing android."

"An oversize toy soldier," grunted Moran contemptuously. "And a chess-playing devil-doll. Playthings."

The copper-haired woman favoured him with a slit-eyed stare. "They are far beyond mere playthings in implication, if you have the imagination to see past the here-and-now. Shall I demonstrate?"

Not waiting for a response from anyone, Kathryn strode purposefully over to Brigadier Gerard and touched small buttons beneath his uniform jacket. Lights flashed in the automaton's eye-sockets. It saluted with the naked sabre, then rolled forward aggressively toward Moran, blade outstretched. Its legs did not move but the disk on which it stood was equipped with a series of directional wheels.

Moran took a reflexive backward step, lifting his hands. His eyes widened flickering with fear. "What is this?"

The Brigadier came to a halt, the tip of the sword mere inches from the end of Moran's nose.

From a corner of the room, Madame Koluchy picked up a

221B: On Her Majesty's Secret Service

scabbarded sabre and offered it to Moran. "I understand you consider yourself an accomplished swordsman...do you think your abilities are superior to those of a toy?"

Colonel Moran's face reddened with barely suppressed anger. With a forefinger he pushed the blade away. "I am a professional soldier. I will not perform for your entertainment, Madam."

She smiled. "I assure you, Colonel... it would not be solely for mine."

Several of the people nearby laughed, including Loveday. She asked, "How does the Brigadier move by its own accord?"

"By combining the principles of a galvanometer which measures electrical current and what is known as thermocouples which are sensitive to infrared wavelengths." Kathryn gestured to the automaton's eyes. "The sensors are there, but he does not have the same vision as humans. Brigadier Gerard responds to movement and body heat but is incapable of bipedal locomotion at present. From a purely mechanical point of view, walking is a very complex process. Fortunately, Mephisto has no need of it."

Kathryn strode over to Mephisto, lifted its feathered cap and touched the back of the automaton's head. Like Brigadier Gerard, the figure's eyes flashed but with a blood-red light. She called out, "Mr Holmes!"

He stepped forward. "Madame?"

"Would you be interested in matching your chess skills against Mephisto? Perhaps just an opening gambit?"

"I would be very interested."

He walked to the edge of the chessboard, briefly studied it and picked up a pair of pawns. Putting his hands behind his back, he closed his fingers over the pieces then held them out. With a faint mechanical whine, Mephisto's right arm reached across to touch Holmes' left hand. Opening it, he placed the black pawn on the board, followed by the white.

Kathryn said, "Mephisto grants you the first move and a slight advantage."

"Uncharacteristically thoughtful of his Infernal Majesty." Holmes moved the pawn across the board, saying, "Classic Queen's Gambit opening...I see no need to get fancy."

The glow of Mephisto's red eyes brightened. The automaton's hand pushed the black pawn into position. Although its moulded lips did not move, a hollow male voice, sounding as if it spoke from the bottom of a bucket, intoned, "2c6."

Holmes said, "Standard Slav defence." He glanced toward Madame Koluchy. "And the voice?"

She touched Mephisto's red-velvet covered chest. "A speaker horn within, responding to his move."

"How?"

The woman laughed, a coquettish dismissal of the question. "Perhaps I'll explain later. I've other, even greater wonders to let all of you see first."

She returned to the aisle and the men fell into step behind her. Holmes and Loveday lingered for a moment, staring at the figures of Mephisto and Brigadier Gerard. She whispered, "Impressive display...frighteningly so, if you see past their novelty value"

He nodded grimly. "Exactly. My suspicion about the state of existence of Robur is now a full-fledged theory."

His words chilled her but she refrained from asking for clarification. They followed the tour party into the next pavilion. A banner spread across the top read, in bright yellow letters, *Maître du Monde*.

Loveday commented dryly, "Master of the World.... wasn't it Diogenes who said modesty is the colour of virtue?"

"Not if you're colour-blind," replied Holmes.

A long display table occupied most of the floor space. Atop the right side, in a little cradle, rested a Rattler repeating pistol complete with magazine drum. A paper target imprinted with the outline of a man covered the centre of the far wall.

Appearing to hover above the opposite end of he table floated a two-foot long, scale model of the *Terror*, wings stretched out to maximum. It quivered as it floated, as if straining against the thin, threadlike cord stretching from its undercarriage to a heavy iron weight anchoring it to the table. Loveday wondered what would happen if the cord were severed.

One of the fez wearing men cleared his throat. "What is this, Madame? More toys?"

"A preview of some tools to command the future," she answered. "Colonel Moran, as a military man, would you care to inspect the weapon?"

With a barely repressed smirk, Moran swaggered to the table and picked up the big pistol, hefting it in both hands, sighting down its length and turning it over and over. He said, "Similar to a Maxim, but on a much smaller scale...almost a composite of the Gatling and a pepper-box system. How many rounds in the magazine?"

She cut her eyes toward Zaharoff. "Basil?"

He shook his head, made uncomfortable by the question. "This is a revised version of the original model...thirty rounds, perhaps?"

Holmes said casually, "I was told 50 rounds of 45-70 calibre ammunition."

The woman threw a smile at him. "Thank you. So, there you are, Colonel." She pointed to the target on the far wall. "Would you care to test its accuracy?"

Moran grunted his assent. He raised the weapon in a two-fisted grip at the end of his extended arms, braced his feet and squeezed the trigger. Spear-points of flame flickered from the barrel. The bullets tore across the room and ripped savagely into the outline of the man affixed to the wall.

The pavilion filled with staccato thunder and the sharp sweet smell of cordite. Spent shell casings arced up and clattered down. Sections of the target dissolved in flying scraps of paper. Fritz Von Waldbaum and Señor Rinconete clapped their hands over their ears. The Alabora twins retreated into the aisle. Loveday fanned the smoke away from her face.

Easily managing the recoil, Moran played the bullet stream over the square of paper as if he were washing it down with a hose-pipe, stitching the target across from left to right. It fell apart. Releasing the trigger, he turned toward Madame Koluchy, eyes bright and feverish. He grinned broadly. "I will take as many of these as you have."

"Not for sale," Madame Koluchy snapped. "None of these tools are for sale at any price."

Moran stared at her in angry incredulity. "Then why —?"

"You cannot own the future," she broke in. "You may only invest in aspects of it."

"We've only seen the aspects with toys and guns," challenged Von Waldbaum.

She walked over to the model of the *Terror*. "I'm sure some of you are aware of the newspaper reports about flying machine in the skies of the United States?"

Jacques Delbray made a spitting sound of contempt. "Some of us are old enough remember the hoax about the *Albatross* and the man known as Robur the Conqueror."

"No hoax, Jacques." She gestured to him. "Come closer, please."

Reluctantly, he hobbled to her side, eyeing the small bat-winged ship. She asked, "What do you think keeps this model in the air?"

"Some charlatan's trick."

"A scientist named Cavor discovered a substance that, for all intents and purposes, cancels out of the force of gravity. He named it after himself, calling it 'Cavorite.' A tiny container of it, perhaps the size of your thumbnail, rests inside this model. If you were to cut this cord, this small ship would rise straight up, and if it could, pass through the ceiling and continue into the ether."

The Alabora twins moved closer, expressions of interest on their faces. One of them asked, "Can the material be reproduced? Manufactured or synthesized?"

"Perhaps," replied Kathryn. "If we find there is a need. Jacques, touch the hull. Tap it."

Very cautiously, as if he feared receiving a shock, the old man followed her instructions. A faint violet glow spread over the surface of the model then faded, leaving only the faintest of smudges in the air where it hovered.

He stumbled back, mouth opening in astonishment. "Invisible! How can this be?"

"With the Violet Flame, a discovery of the astronomer, Professor Mirzarbeau. He harnessed a form of cosmic radiation, a high frequency of light that exerts changes upon matter."

Moran stared at her in baffled rage. "Why was this not mentioned to me weeks ago?"

"Because, Colonel, you are not a full member of the Ring and definitely not one of the Echelon. Nor is your employer, despite our invitation."

She faced Rinconete and Von Waldbaum. "Imagine a ship over thirty feet long capable of operating as a boat, a submersible, an automobile or flying machine. It can travel at the speed of 150 miles per hour on land and more than 200 miles per hour in the air. Imagine it can render itself invisible and is armed with larger models of the rapid-firing gun you see here. Now imagine a fleet of them, soaring over the continent."

Von Waldbaum said in a voice high and quavery with fear, "No nation's armed forces could stand against you."

"No," stated Madame Koluchy confidently. "They could not, if military action were the objective of the Hephaestus Ring. But

221B: *On Her Majesty's Secret Service*

our mission is to restore order to the world, and war is very disorderly. That's why we prefer to avoid it."

Holmes declared, "You've shown us playthings and weapons of war...the open hand and the closed fist. What is next?"

The woman smiled, showing the edges of her teeth. "I'm so glad you asked." She turned toward the aisle and called loudly, *"Nous sommes prêts!"*

Footsteps and the rumble of wheels sounded on the marble floor. Holmes and Loveday swung around just as Cuthbert Rubadue appeared, pushing an upright cabinet of ominously dark walnut. The process was awkward since he carried his walking stick in one hand and the cabinet appeared to be very heavy, despite rolling smoothly on ball-and-claw casters.

Another man came in behind him, not walking but standing upon a rolling disk of metal. Dressed all in grey, he was very tall, his physique built on a heroic scale. He looked to be over six feet in height, with massive breadth of shoulder and chest. A neat black beard followed the line of his chiselled jaw.

Holmes looked into the man's dark hollow eyes and felt as if he had been struck a deep, painful blow in his belly. He realized he had glimpsed the man three-plus weeks ago aboard the *Terror* as it hovered over the Druid's Altar. If he had any doubts, Loveday's quick, shuddering gasp of recognition confirmed it.

The man's eye sockets suddenly blazed yellow. Robur's raspy, distorted voice boomed, "Sherlock Holmes. Loveday Brooke. We have all travelled far to finally meet in this place, have we not?"

221B: On Her Majesty's Secret Service

Don't you think that ghost-seeing is quite as catching as scarlet fever or measles?

— Loveday Brooke

CHAPTER 27

"THIS IS MADNESS," breathed Loveday, her eyes darting back and forth like those of a panicked animal. "It can't be him."

"Just another automaton, built to represent an idealized version of Robur." Holmes' hand sought hers and gave it a quick, reassuring squeeze. He whispered, "Steady. We'll soon see through this trick."

"If trick it is," she responded.

The men gave way before the rolling figure of Robur. None of them spoke but they stared in wide-eyed puzzlement as Rubadue halted the walnut cabinet just inside the Maître du Monde pavilion. The manikin of Robur came to a stop with a faint double-click.

"What are the purpose of these things, Kathryn?" demanded Delbray.

"I cannot explain the one without explaining the other, Jacques."

"Then get on with it," said Colonel Moran. At the flash of anger in her eyes, he hastily added, "Please."

At a gesture from Madame Koluchy, Rubadue flung wide the doors of the cabinet. A low droning hum filled the aisle, a tone that vibrated gently against the eardrums. They saw a maddeningly intricate pattern of circuitry criss-crossing within. Tiny lights blinked synchronously with a medley of barely

221B: *On Her Majesty's Secret Service*

audible clockwork ticks.

There were uneasy murmurs from several throats. Fritz von Waldbaum leaned forward for a closer look. He enquired, "A computing device?"

"The Analytical Engine, the beginnings of machine intelligence...artificial intelligence, if you will. It is based on the blueprints of Charles Babbage and the notebooks of Ada Lovelace, two of the most brilliant minds of the century. The Analytical Engine has the potential to be the greatest invention ever conceived. There are only two in existence and the Hephaestus Ring has both. They will render the 19th century obsolete."

She cast a mocking smile toward Holmes and Loveday. "Including the manner in which you two ply your trade."

Señor Rinconete uttered a scoffing laugh. "Forgive me, Señora, but it is still just a machine...gears and wires, nuts and bolts."

Kathryn's smile became a scowl. "Don't be so foolishly short-sighted, Ramon. The Analytical Engine has extrapolated from what is happening in the world right now to what will happen in the coming century. In the next fifty years, a series of small and large wars will rend Europe and Asia asunder...fifty years after that, overpopulation and pollution will result in the air being fouled, the waters poisoned and the sea life left to die. Forests and farmlands will wither and the climate will be drastically altered. In a hundred years, most of mankind will be dying of starvation as natural resources are depleted. Politicians will refuse to undertake hard measures in the interim...instead, they will use the chaos and crises for their own advancement."

Holmes asked blandly, "And will the Hephaestus Ring use its own resources to stop this apocalypse, or to hurry it along?"

"Neither...we will manage it. At this juncture, the world is in a state of flux and most of the turbulence is due to disparate opinions from different cultures about the definition of freedom.

Most seem to feel it's an all-or-nothing proposition. All of us in this room know that true freedom is an illusion but we also know such illusions are dangerous and destructive.

"Therefore, it falls to the Ring to achieve a balance between the illusion and the reality of freedom...however, we must first make an indelible impression of what we can do for the benefit — or detriment — of humankind. After that, the future will follow the course we set. The impression is scheduled to occur tomorrow at Eiffel's iron tower."

Fritz Von Waldbaum stiffened. "I plan to be on the tour of the tower tomorrow."

"I would change my plans, if I were you."

Basil Zaharoff said thoughtfully, "So the Hephaestus Ring will hold the monopoly on advanced technology and will dole it out to the nations that do your bidding, and withhold it from those who don't."

Kathryn Koluchy shrugged. "More or less."

"The old carrot and the stick principle," said Moran sarcastically. "Not a very advanced approach."

"That is a bit more crude than I would phrase it," she replied. "I prefer 'what is good for one is good for all,' but in order to reach that point, yes, we will have to employ the carrot and the stick. Hopefully only short-term."

Holmes chuckled dryly. "More like 'they supply the war, you supply them with the means to wage or lose it.' "

"Does any of that really matter?" asked Kathryn in a silky-soft voice of challenge.

"It's a protection racket," Holmes said. "The Ring is no different from the Elephant and Castle Gang but operating on an international scale."

Zaharoff caught his eye and shook his head in warning negation.

Holmes ignored him. "But I suppose having been a criminal

gang-leader for so many years, the practice is hard to give up, despite your long and unsuccessful masquerade as a nutritionist."

Madame Koluchy swung her head toward him, sudden rage swirling in her eyes. Holmes smiled. "Oh, I'm sorry...did I think that aloud?"

The woman stepped forward and back-handed him across the face. It was not a chastising slap. Holmes was rocked back on his heels, and would have staggered to the opposite side of the pavilion if Loveday had not caught him. Face feeling as if it had been scalded, senses reeling, Holmes regained his balance, astonished by the force of the blow. Moran did a poor job of repressing a chuckle but the Alabora twins did not even try.

"I will not tolerate disrespect, Mr Holmes," Madame Koluchy said, voice sibilant with barely repressed fury. "I told you I would extend a professional courtesy and I require the same in return."

Holmes nodded. "So noted."

She turned away from him as if he were beneath her notice.

Señor Rinconete eyed Robur suspiciously. "What use would any nation have for these mechanical men of yours? They cannot even walk, so they would not make serviceable infantry."

"Not yet," she said. "But that will change. In the example of Robur, his gifts reside within him."

"He is still an automaton."

"So was Talos," retorted Kathryn. "The bronze giant forged by Hephaestus as a gift for King Minos. According to legend, Talos was a mechanical entity that combined basic truth with simple logical equations — intelligence produced by mechanical means."

Holmes stepped closer to Robur, scrutinizing his perfectly sculpted face. "You claim you have developed artificial intelligence for these artificial humans?"

"Not entirely. The Brigadier and Mephisto operate on a simplified binary system...not true thought, and certainly not

221B: On Her Majesty's Secret Service

sentience, either."

The woman opened her cloak, revealing a leather harness worn over her torso and cinched at the waist by a belt. Metal devices resembling the parts of telegraph units were attached to the frontis-piece and the harness straps. "With the telekino, encoded commands are transmitted using a telegraph module and sent as electromagnetic waves to internal receivers within the automatons. The receivers convert them into movement impulses. Quevedo calls it remote control. Mephisto and Brigadier Gerard work perfectly within a limited radius. But Robur is quite different."

She reached out to affectionately pat the automaton's grey clad arm. "The effigy standing before you does not possess a skeletal structure as we understand it, although his arms and hands are fully jointed and articulated. His thermoplastic and layered aluminium body was built around a duplicate of my Analytical Engine. The automatonic Robur serves as a repository for everything that was salvageable from the organic Robur — from his force of personality and his vast technical knowledge."

Holmes snapped his head toward her, his gaze intense. "Explain."

"The mighty Robur the Conqueror was dying, Mr Holmes. We fished him out of the sea, Cuthbert and I, as we sailed away from Penhallick Wharf. He was half-drowned, his right arm torn from the socket, his legs and back broken, all due to your interference. He had only his brain between life and death. We returned with him to Paris. where I kept him alive and conscious with my treatments. Even so, he was in agony for over a year but he refused sedation or anaesthesia. When we both agreed his body was beyond restoration, we determined to save what was most important about him — his mind."

Loveday's face twisted with revulsion. "You put a man's brain inside a celluloid skull?"

Madame Koluchy directed a scornful glare her way. "Don't be

ridiculous, Miss Brooke. I said his mind, not his brain. They are not the same thing. The brain is simply a container."

Loveday enquired darkly, "And is not the brain the organic repository of a person's knowledge and personality?"

"After Robur's biological functions ceased over a year ago, we swapped out containers. Instead of a container made of viscera and fluid, we placed his mind within one composed of metal relays, pegs, and a system of tiny, delicate gear wheels designed by Leonardo Quevedo, based on the work of Babbage and Lovelace. Over a long tedious period, we transferred the essence of Robur's consciousness."

Moran uttered a wordless exclamation of disbelief. "Such a thing cannot be possible!"

The copper-haired woman fluttered an angrily dismissive hand. "You know nothing of what is possible and what is not, Colonel. As you said, you're a soldier, most certainly not a scientist. You cannot even begin to comprehend the endless weeks and months of transcriptions, of impressing Robur's voice onto wax cylinders, of milling and tooling and retooling the hardware, of trial and error. By the time his noble heart gave up the fight, we had finished duplicating his vital essence."

Loveday barely caught herself from rolling her eyes as Kathryn continued, "Following his last wish, this body was built in the image in which he saw himself in life...tall, powerful and god-like. Depending on the signal transmitted by the telekino, Robur's actions are determined by formulae that mirror his personality. Watch."

Her fingers manipulated two keys on the harness. The yellow of Robur's eyes blazed brighter. The disk on which the figure stood rotated suddenly, facing Holmes and Loveday. Under that unblinking hot stare, Loveday barely kept herself from shrinking back. She forced herself to meet the gaze. The wide mouth framed by the beard did not move, but after a few seconds during which they heard faint whirs and clicks, a hollow voice intoned,

"Sherlock Holmes. Loveday Brooke. I last saw you in Ireland, did I not?."

"Yes," said Holmes. "There you tried to kill us again. You failed. Again."

The response, when it came, was a voice in which the cadence and even the volume changed from word to word. "Yes. But you are here now and thrice is always the charm, n'est-ce pas ?"

Holmes cast a questioning glance toward Kathryn Koluchy. She said, "His formulae searches through his voice recordings to put together the proper words and match them with the best response."

Loveday said, "So the real Robur is not communicating with us, just a collection of wax phonograph cylinders?"

The woman's eyes clouded with anger for a few seconds. "Robur's interfaced consciousness controls what is said to you. For all intents and purposes, this is Robur."

"This is Robur's ghost," Loveday shot back. "Not even that, actually. A copy of a copy...a machine that physically resembles the original enclosing a copy of the Analytical Engine which holds within it a copy of his mind. This Robur is at best a composite."

Holmes asked, "Is the composite capable of independent thought and movement or does it need you to key them in?"

Robur's arm suddenly lifted and shot forward. A gloved hand closed around Holmes' throat and swung him completely clear of the floor. He clutched desperately at the automaton's wrist in order to keep his vertebrae from being dislocated.

"Is this independent enough for you?" Robur's voice rasped.

Loveday lunged forward, prising at Robur's fingers. Cuthbert Rubadue slid the walking stick around her upper body and pulled her back. She struggled as the man placed the length of studded blackthorn against the base of her throat and exerted pressure. He growled, "Stay."

Zaharoff blurted, "Kathryn, stop this! You can't make us a party to murder!"

The other men murmured in anxious agreement and backed away. Madame Koluchy cast them a disgusted glance and said, "Robur, dearest...you must release him. This is not the time nor place for retribution. You're upsetting the delicate sensibilities of our guests."

"I decide. A long time coming, this...the reckoning. A long time."

Robur's fingers continued to squeeze Holmes' throat. Blood thundered in his ears. He dangled like a kitten in the hand of a sadist, toes barely touching the floor. He kicked at Robur, struggling as his body began to convulse due to lack of oxygen.

Kathryn's hands went to the harness. "Darling, don't force me to—"

Whatever else she intended to say was drowned out by the sound of a handclap, magnified many times. Robur's right temple acquired a deep gash, revealing the gleam of metal beneath. Kathryn cried out in anger at the same time Loveday twisted around just far enough to plant the bore of the Bull-dog pistol against Rubadue's midsection. She demanded, "Well?"

Immediately, he whipped the shillelagh away from her and stepped back. Loveday pointed the pistol in the direction of Madame Koluchy. "Turn that automatic abomination off."

The woman tapped a key on the harness. The yellow glow in the eye sockets faded. Its hand opened and Holmes sagged to the floor. He knelt there, trying to cough, trying to breathe, to move. Loveday turned toward the men in the aisle and gestured with the pistol, thumbing back the hammer. "Go!"

The five men hesitated, looking toward Madame Koluchy for permission or instruction. She said, "You now have a grounding in what the future holds. We will meet and talk again after tomorrow. For now, *bonne soirée.*"

They hurried toward the door as Loveday waved Rubadue over to stand beside Zaharoff and Kathryn. "Raise your hands."

Zaharoff made a tentative move toward the aisle and ventured, "Perhaps this is the most opportune moment for me to make my own exit?"

"No," Loveday said, reaching down to secure a hold on Holmes' arm with her free hand. "You are not excused."

Holmes allowed himself to be dragged to his feet, pulling mouthfuls of air into his straining lungs. When he regained enough oxygen to speak, he said, "You were right when you opined ladies wouldn't be searched. Thank you, Miss Brooke."

"Saving your neck is becoming a habit."

"Let's try not to break it."

"The habit or the neck?"

"That's a conundrum we will address later." Massaging his throat, Holmes faced Kathryn and said hoarsely, "So Robur is capable of independent movement as long as you keep the power on. I presume he's aware of that."

Madame Koluchy nodded. "He is. But his hatred for you is so deep and fierce, it survived the grave. You shouldn't have provoked him, either tonight or two years ago in Cornwall."

"Robur was doing his damnedest to kill me on that night and I did my damnedest to keep him from being successful." He cut his gaze toward Zaharoff. "All part of the *Bolshaya Igra,* correct?"

Zaharoff did not reply. Holmes stepped forward and cautiously examined Robur's bullet-scored temple. "It's not damaged too badly, I trust?"

Madame Koluchy smiled. "No, rest easy on that score. Purely cosmetic."

Training her pistol on Madame Koluchy, Loveday demanded, "What is Thunderstrike?"

Kathryn frowned, casting a questioning glance toward Zaharoff. "Where did you hear that word?"

Zaharoff gave Loveday a pleading up-from-under look. Pretending not to notice, she said, "From Nikola Tesla. He was fearful of asking for details. Obviously, Thunderstrike is the event you have planned for tomorrow."

"Perhaps you should wait until then to satiate your curiosity."

"And perhaps you will be more forthcoming when questioned by the Sûreté." She waggled the barrel of the revolver in the direction of the exit. "Let's find out."

Madame Koluchy uttered a sneering laugh. "Don't be absurd. I am a sponsor of the Exposition and a French citizen. I have every right to be here. You and Mr Holmes possess neither of those qualifications. If you bring the police into this, at best you'll be detained until you can be shipped back to England in disgrace, at worst you'll be arrested and thrown in La Santé Prison."

"Perhaps we can all share a cell and settle the issue." Holmes walked over to the long table and picked up the Rattler. He detached the magazine, checked it, and popped it back into place. "Eight rounds left out of fifty. Colonel Moran is quite the spendthrift."

Gun in hand, he joined Loveday and herded Zaharoff, Rubadue and Madame Koluchy along the aisle. As they passed the adjacent pavilion with its *Etonnant Automates* banner, Holmes heard a faint tap-tap. A sudden blur of movement caught his attention. He shouted "Loveday!" as he pivoted on his heel.

Whirling, he brought his right hand up and under his left arm. Even before he had completed his turn, he depressed the trigger and the six bores of the Rattler blazed, stitching a line of holes across the front of Brigadier Gerard's red jacket. Eyes glowing, the automaton continued to rush forward, swinging its sword over the top of its shako. The multiple impacts of the bullets knocked the machine off-course but did not slow its momentum. The Rattler's firing pin clicked on an empty chamber.

221B: *On Her Majesty's Secret Service*

Loveday aimed her pistol and squeezed off two shots at Brigadier Gerard, tearing away the fringe of an epaulette. Cuthbert Rubadue struck out at her with the heavy knob of his walking stick, striking a clump of nerve ganglia on her wrist. She cried out in pain as the revolver fell from suddenly numb fingers. Madame Koluchy plunged forward, shouldering Zaharoff aside as she clawed out for the gun.

Loveday kicked the firearm and sent it skittering across the aisle. Kathryn screeched and dived after it. Loveday leapt atop her and the pair went down on the floor in a furious tangle of arms, legs, and French profanity.

Rubadue lashed overhand at Holmes with the shillelagh, intending to split his skull. Holmes blocked the blow with the frame of the Rattler and drove the man back with a heel kick. He spun around as Brigadier Gerard's sabre hacked downward for his face. He managed to deflect the blade with the long barrel of the repeater but the force of the sword-strike tore it from his grasp.

As the weapon clattered to the floor, Holmes threw himself against Rubadue, slamming hard into him with his left shoulder, pushing him bodily backwards, off-balance and flailing. Reaching inside his left sleeve, he withdrew a flat black-bladed knife from its forearm sheath and then grabbed a handful of the Scotsman's coat. The two men grappled until Holmes smashed the back of his head against the bridge of Rubadue's nose. Cuthbert cried out, dropping his stick to clap both hands over his face. Half-bent over, he staggered backward.

Holmes lowered himself to one knee, swiftly measured the distance and flipped his knife across the aisle. The razor keen point entered the left eye of Brigadier Gerard with a crunch of glass. The automaton veered sharply to the right, slashing blindly with the sabre. Holmes rolled away just as the blade chopped into the left side of Cuthbert Rubadue's head. The man screamed and stumbled away, scarlet streaming down his face.

221B: *On Her Majesty's Secret Service*

Holmes snatched up the shillelagh and delivered a running kick to the circular base upon which the Brigadier stood. The automaton wheeled around in an 180 degree turn, sabre rising and falling like a butcher's cleaver.

Holmes deflected several strokes with the tough varnished blackthorn, although the blade chopped notches along its length. His free hand groped beneath the hem of Brigadier Gerard's jacket, fingers finding a row of small inset buttons. He pushed them at random. The automaton abruptly froze in place in mid-stroke, the glow fading from its single eye.

Breathing hard, Holmes turned toward the two struggling women on the opposite side of the aisle. All at once came the *crack* of a shot followed by a cry of pain. Loveday stood up shakily, with the pistol in her hand. With her other hand she brushed away the tangle of auburn hair from her face. At her feet Kathryn Koluchy writhed, hugging herself. In an aspirated half-shriek, she said, "You shot me! You bitch! *You shot me!*"

Holmes started forward, mind momentarily blank with surprise. Panting from exertion, Loveday said, "I shot that bloody control harness of yours so you can't activate your mechanical pals through remote control. The bullet didn't penetrate all that metal and leather. I hope it hurt, though."

Holmes blew out a half-laugh, half-sigh. "I wish you'd done that about twenty seconds ago."

He glanced toward Zaharoff. "Thanks for your help."

Zaharoff lifted his hands palm-upward and shrugged. "Violence is not my forte'."

"It's not too late to be given a lesson," Holmes stated, working the throwing knife from Brigadier Gerard's eye socket.

Rubadue lay on his side, one hand covering the laceration across his scalp. He made wordless, whispering squeals, like a distressed piglet. Holmes pried his blood-wet fingers away from his head and gave the laceration a quick inspection. It was long and unsightly but not critical. The blade's edge had not penetrated his cranial bone but it had nicked the top of his ear.

In Rubadue's coat pocket he found a discoloured handkerchief. Wadding it into a ball, he pressed it against the wound. After a moment, he placed the Scotsman's hand there. "You'll be all right, Cuthbert...Mr Zaharoff will see you're stitched up and you'll have another scar to add to your collection. Keep pressure on it."

"Damn you, Holmes," he wheezed in a nasal snuffle. "You broke my nose."

"If so, it's most likely the fifth or sixth time it's been in such a state. Perhaps you should have it properly set this time."

Holmes rose, roughly pulling Rubadue with him. "Get up. Places want us to go to them."

Loveday nudged Madame Koluchy with a foot. "You heard him. Up."

Groaning, Kathryn staggered erect. Pieces of bullet-shattered metal tinkled down from her harness, chiming against the floor. Probing her rib-cage with her right hand, she swept Loveday and Holmes with eyes seething with rage. "I now understand why Robur hated you two so much."

She moved past them slowly, favouring her rib-cage, teeth clenched as if in great pain. Loveday said, "I've been in the company of a good actress long enough to recognize a bad one."

The copper-haired woman straightened up and imperiously stalked away, red cloak belling out behind her. Eyes and gun barrel trained on her retreating back, Loveday side-mouthed to Holmes, "She nearly tore the gun away from me. I squeezed the trigger in desperation. She's terrifyingly strong."

Holmes gingerly touched the side of his face where he had been slapped. "I can attest."

With Rubadue and Zaharoff a few paces ahead, they strode past the oversize gear wheels and pistons display. Kathryn

Koluchy reached the door, paused and turned to face them. She made a "come along" gesture with both hands, a smile creasing her face.

Holmes and Loveday glimpsed the glint of many gun barrels from between the giant machine props on either side of the aisle. They halted, starting to turn, but hands pushed them forward. They felt the painful prodding of gun muzzles in their backs.

Half-a-dozen men wearing gray metallic mesh uniforms and berets circled them. Above the Rattlers in their hands, their faces were hard and expressionless. A tall figure marched around and put a massive hand on Loveday's pistol, almost covering it. She resisted for only an instant and allowed Vonn to take the Bulldog. In a mocking croon, he said, "Ah, Fröken Brooke, again finding yourself in circumstances you shouldn't."

He took the throwing knife from Holmes' right hand but ignored the shillelagh in the other. Holmes said pleasantly, "I've been waiting to meet you again. When did you get here?"

"I've been here along...who do you think opened the door when Zaharoff knocked?"

"Ah. That explains the smell."

Vonn did not respond. With hands planted against their backs, he pushed Holmes and Loveday along the aisle to where Madame Koluchy, Rubadue and Basil Zaharoff waited. The woman laughed as they approached. "You did well, Basil, by staying out of this."

Not making eye contact, he muttered, "I only want what is owed to me and then our business is concluded."

"That will be the Echelon's decision," she replied smoothly. She surveyed the faces of Holmes and Loveday. "I hadn't given much thought about what to do with the pair of you if you came calling, although Nikola was certain you would show up eventually. I suppose I was too preoccupied with Thunderstrike business to devote much thought to it. Fortunately, my confidante

221B: On Her Majesty's Secret Service

in the Deuxieme Bureau apprised me of your arrival yesterday."

Holmes commented sympathetically, "I understand proper time management is one of the drawbacks of choosing criminal mastermind as a career."

Kathryn nodded. "Agreed. I will focus on the matter of your dispositions."

She struck Loveday with her right fist. The impact of flesh against flesh sounded like a gunshot. The blow rocked her head to one side. Loveday fell, tripped by a clever boot inserted by Vonn. She lay on the floor, dazed, eyes unfocused.

"Esperance d'enfoiré, tu m'as tire dessus!" hissed Madame Koluchy, drawing back a foot. Holmes tried to tamp down his rising fury as he saw only cruelty and arrogance on the woman's face, as if a paper-thin human mask had slipped and exposed the monster beneath.

He knew he had no chance to reach the second knife in its sleeve sheath. Surrounded by Rattlers, it would mean certain death if he tried to use it anyway. He still held Rubadue's walking stick so he lunged forward, leading with its knob. He drove it toward Kathryn but a heavy gun barrel crashed against his skull and he fell to his knees. He tried to rise again. Through a haze shifting over his vision, he saw Vonn's maimed half-face grinning down at him.

Another blow landed on the back of his head with a blinding flash of pain. He felt the marble floor come up—and slap him down into a black pit of oblivion.

To run here and there and lie on my face with a lens to my eye – it is not my métier.

— Mycroft Holmes

CHAPTER 28

31 March

AT HALF-PAST midnight, Mycroft and Watson left the Hôtel d'Alsace by the rear entrance and navigated a narrow alley. The air was cold and a mist hung over the street, softening the sharp angles of the buildings and blurring the rubbish. The two men paused just inside the alley mouth and watched the street. They saw nothing of importance on the avenue. Watson tugged down the broad brim of his hat and raised his coat collar.

He and Mycroft had passed the bulk of the evening in the hotel's restaurant, waiting for the return of Holmes and Loveday or word from Dubugue. They spent the time considerately ignoring one another, with Mycroft hiding behind the pages of *Le Figaro* and Watson pretending to be immersed in the latest issue of *The Lancet*.

Watson read the journal, sipped at brandy and smoked cigarettes. He was accustomed to waiting. Due to his time in the military, he knew that the ordeal of waiting to take action was only alleviated by concentrating on patience. He thought of Mary, he thought of his brother and he tried not to think of Loveday and Holmes. When the concierge came to the table with a note and handed it to Mycroft, he felt great relief when the big man bestirred himself and announced, "We have been summoned by an agent of Dubugue to the Chez Vous cafe. We must go now. We were cautioned to make sure we are not followed."

The two men exited the restaurant through the kitchen and through the back door to the alley, where they waited together in silence and watched the street beyond.

"I understand you intend to marry soon," Mycroft said suddenly.

Watson cast him a puzzled glance and replied cautiously, "Yes."

Mycroft smiled at Watson's reticence. "Married life and this sort of work rarely mix well."

"I am quite aware of that, thank you."

"You don't think you will miss it?"

Watson forced a chuckle. "I'm standing in the cold rain in a dirty alley in Paris at nearly one o'clock in the morning waiting to talk to a police spy — what do you think?"

"Field work holds little appeal for me, either."

"So you've said, more than once."

Both fell silent again. Then Mycroft asked bluntly, "You don't care much for me, do you, Dr Watson?"

Watson was surprised into voicing an uncomfortable chuckle. "What makes you ask that now?"

"We've known each other for several years. You've never invited me to address you by your Christian name."

"Even Sherlock doesn't do that very often."

"Why do you think that is?"

Watson shrugged. "My guess is it's his way of maintaining an emotional distance from people he might actually care about."

"I note that you feel free to address me by my first name."

"Only because if I address you as 'Holmes' in the presence of your brother, we'll be engaging in a music hall comedy routine."

"That is what I assumed."

"As to your question," Watson continued, "I don't dislike you, but I don't overly trust you, either. I'm still ashamed I didn't see your hand in the first service you manoeuvred your brother and I into performing for the Crown....the Tide-Waiter case, remember?"

"Of course. Unfortunate bit of business."

"I'd say 'unfortunate' was a dire understatement," replied Watson coldly. "Both Holmes and I nearly lost our lives because you withheld vital information. A man did die."

Mycroft grunted. "Need to know, doctor. Official secrets. This is a silent war, where even random straws in the wind are of utmost importance."

"Straws?"

"Small episodes of no apparent weight but are actually straws which could tip the world balance toward war or peace, chaos or order. We discussed this a long time ago."

Watson nodded curtly, feeling the heat of an old resentment kindle within him. "We did. And just because you keep repeating that position doesn't make the consequences miraculously disappear."

"Yet here you are, years later, standing in the cold rain in a dirty alley in Paris at nearly one o'clock in the morning, waiting to talk to a police spy."

Mycroft's unemotional delivery doused the flame of anger and for a long moment Watson struggled with the impulse to curse or to laugh. Finally he decided to heave an exasperated sigh. "Fairplay to you, Mycroft. And you can call me John if it means that much to you."

"It doesn't...I was just remarking on the contradiction." Mycroft eased out of the alley, looking both ways. Watson felt a twinge of surprise at how cat-footed the big man seemed. He said softly, "It is safe. We may go."

"You don't see anyone on the street?"

"No, but that means very little in Paris at midnight."

"You've been to this cafe, before?"

"Once, as a much younger and thinner man. It's a message-drop used by police informers and intelligence operatives."

They walked around the block to the Rue de Beaux Arts and along cobblestone streets surrounded by old, tall buildings. The windows of most were dark and they reminded Watson of headstones marking past centuries. They went down a stone stairway to the riverbank. Near a lamp they saw a man wearing a black beret leaning over the balustrade, staring at the flowing waters of the Seine, single-mindedly smoking a cigarette. As they passed him, Watson noticed how he straightened up, flicked away the cigarette and after a moment, fell in step behind them. Under his coat, he wore a red cummerbund.

Watson tensed, fingering the derringer in his pocket. Inasmuch as Mycroft appeared oblivious to the man's presence, he figured he meant them no harm. He was either Dubugue's agent disguised as an Apache or he worked for the Deuxieme Bureau with orders to shadow their every move.

The cafe was a short distance from the river, squeezed between store-fronts. A dirty red-and-white awning overhung three tables outside. Men and women were visible through the window, standing at the bar in yellow gaslight. They spoke in loud, argumentative voices and gestured with glasses of wine. Strains of accordion music filtered out the shuttered door.

A man wearing a flat-cap and turtle-neck sweater of loose

green wool sat at one of the tables, three empty cups and a pot of coffee before him. His face was thin, with bright, alert eyes on either side of a sharp nose. He reminded Watson of someone but he was unable to put a name to the face.

He glanced up as Mycroft loomed over him and enquired politely but with a sly smile, "Monsieur LeCoq?"

"The same."

"Sit, *s'il vous plaît.*"

Watson and Mycroft did as he requested, pulling out wooden chairs damp with mist. Watson said, "My name is Willis. You are?"

"Gabriel Lestrade. I work with Dubugue. No need for an alias, Dr Watson. Both you and Mr Holmes have been compromised." He spoke English fluently.

Watson eyed the man's face closely, noting the set of his brown eyes and the shape of his chin. "Do you happen to have a male relative in London, a detective with the Metropolitan Police?"

The man smiled blandly. "My father's cousin, a member of an old, extended family. Cousin Gervais mentioned you and Sherlock Holmes several times in letters to me."

"In a complimentary fashion, I hope," replied Watson.

Lestrade's smile faded and he turned toward Mycroft, looking past him. "I see you picked up a tail despite my warning. He's from the Deuxieme Bureau."

Watson looked in the direction of Lestrade's gaze and glimpsed the man in the beret and cummerbund loitering at the corner. "Yes," Mycroft said. "We noticed him. I presume he's a freelance confidential informant, looking to make a few francs."

Lestrade poured coffee from the pot into Mycroft's cup and then his own. "The Bureau watches the Sûreté and the Sûreté watches the Bureau. That is how we know your cover identities have been penetrated. Not that 'Monsieur Lecoq' would fool anyone for long, if I may be so bold."

Mycroft dropped several sugar cubes into the cup. "The choice of names was more a statement than a disguise."

Watson declined the offer of coffee and said, "We understand you have officers watching Madame Koluchy's home and the Exposition grounds...Mr Holmes and Miss Brooke have yet to return, and we've been waiting for word from them. A little while ago, we received a message at the hotel to meet an agent of Dubugue at this cafe for news."

"The message was from me. Less than an hour ago I learned Dubugue had been suspended from duty. I'm sure I'm next to be ordered to stand down."

Watson stared at him in surprise. "Suspended by whom?"

"Our superiors," Lestrade answered. "They are only following orders from *their* superiors."

Mycroft, holding the cup by thumb and forefinger, took a sip of coffee and said dolefully, "I suspected as much... the French police and intelligence services have been contaminated by the Hephaestus Ring."

"Don't underestimate the Bureau or the Sûreté," replied Lestrade defensively. "There are still a few patriots in office and some of them have had their eyes on the Ring for a long time."

Watson shifted in his chair impatiently. "Is that the only reason you summoned us here?"

"No." Lestrade sighed. "At a little after nine o'clock this evening, I personally observed Monsieur Holmes and Mademoiselle Brooke leave Madame Koluchy's home in a coach. I followed them to the grounds of the Exposition Universelle, where they disembarked with other guests. At approximately half-past ten, the guests returned. Monsieur Holmes and Madamoseille Brooke were not amongst them. At last word from an officer who worked undercover on the premises, they have yet to return. The reception appears to be over, as well."

Watson and Mycroft exchanged glances. Watson asked, "Do you have any idea where they went within the grounds?"

"The Hall of Machines was illuminated for quite some time. Apparently it still is, but we have no authority to breach the grounds, much less search any of the exhibitions."

"No authority'?" echoed Watson incredulously, leaning forward over the table. "You're the bloody police!"

Lestrade's eyes flashed. "We're the bloody police without a warrant at one o'clock in the morning. Even if I could find a sympathetic judge, there is no guarantee such a warrant will be granted. Your reasons for it would be dismissed as specious — your friends, an adult man and woman, haven't returned from a party at the time you think they should have."

Mycroft said with a hint of menace, "There is a British embassy in Paris, is there not? My name has been known to open a few judicial and bureaucratic doors in Europe."

"That may be so, but I would not expect much in the way of local cooperation or support," Lestrade replied. "I presume in your line of work it is best to keep things detached from the authorities. You do not want to provoke an international situation so close to the Exposition's opening day. There are plenty of people in government who would be only too happy to accuse you of clandestine sabotage against the Exposition. Interference in national affairs. Cultural jealousy. That kind of thing. Madame Koluchy is a well-known and respected figure. She would make full use of any such excuse, given the ghost of a chance, to fire up anti-British sentiment on the eve of the fair's opening."

"We're dealing with a large and well-financed conspiracy," Watson said, trying to keep his temper from rising further.

"So Dubugue told me...or least, told me that is what you

believe."

"Do you want your country's strings pulled by a conspiracy?"

Anger suddenly glinted in Lestrade's eyes "My country has faced monarchists and anarchists over the last twenty years. The prospect of dealing with a group of technologists isn't very intimidating, particularly when they have connections with the government."

Mycroft said flatly, "The Hephaestus Ring is a criminal organization with deep roots in underworld secret societies. Even here in Paris they employ criminal tactics. They kidnap, steal, murder and terrorize with impunity. The men in the government with whom they are connected are either naïve, coerced into non-action or simply corrupt."

"Whether that is true or not, m'sieu, I have been told this is now a matter of internal security and the primary concern is that an anarchist group will attempt to disrupt tomorrow's ceremonies. I strongly suggest you and your friend stand down and not meddle in French affairs like a pair of amateur detectives found in cheap fiction."

Mycroft's eyebrows dipped down on either side of the bridge of his nose. "Meddle?" he echoed. "Did I hear you correctly, Lestrade? Meddle?"

Lestrade gestured casually. "Perhaps I misspoke. Would 'interfere' be more accurate?"

"No, it would not." Mycroft carefully placed the cup back on the saucer. In a quiet, almost contemplative tone, he said, "Since Her Majesty's Secret Service and the Deuxieme Bureau have long maintained cordial relations and cooperate like true allies, there should be no objection to me or my friend conducting our own personal investigation...as long as the French authorities are made aware of it. Therefore —"

From a breast pocket, Mycroft took a small notebook and

fountain pen. He quickly scribbled a few lines on the paper, blew on them to dry the ink, folded it twice to make a square and gestured to the man in the black beret lounging at the corner. He called, *"M'sieu, s'avancer."*

The man stared at him curiously, glanced over his shoulder and back to Mycroft, pointing to himself with eyebrows at a questioning angle. Mycroft nodded impatiently. *"Oui, vous."*

The man sauntered over, making a show of being nonchalant by putting his hands in his pockets. Mycroft held up the square of paper. *"Apportez cette note à Monsieur Mathis. Immédiatement."*

The man stared without responding. With his other hand, Mycroft folded a blue 50 franc bank-note around it. *"Dis-lui que Mycroft t'a envoyé."*

The man took it, a smile spreading over his face. Mycroft snapped his fingers imperiously. *"Immédiatement!"*

Tipping his beret, the man turned and began a shambling trot down the street, sliding both notes into a coat pocket.

Watson asked, "What was that all about? I understood a little of it but—"

Mycroft said, "I despatched our shadow with a note to Mathis of the Deuxieme Bureau, who for all intents and purposed, is my opposite number. Although I would not necessarily call him a friend, he is a trusted colleague and we have collaborated on several successful missions when we were both younger...and of course, thinner. He has become strangely non-responsive over the last few days, so I wrote a communique making him aware of our intent and itinerary...I let him know that tomorrow you and I will be among those taking the tour of the Eiffel Tower. I invited him and as many agents as he can trust to join us there."

Mycroft swivelled his gaze toward Lestrade. "After all, I would not wish us to be confused with amateur detectives who meddle and interfere."

"And if Mathis does not respond to your note?" Lestrade challenged.

Mycroft smiled and shrugged self-consciously. "It has fallen to me in the past to initiate diplomacy through direct coercion instead of appeals for cooperation. If it falls upon me again, so be it."

Lestrade stared him, eyes seething with anger. "You are very arrogant, regardless of your motives, Monsieur Holmes. We in France are proud of our Republic. We don't need to be coerced to stand in defence of it."

"Some men do, Lestrade. Consider — when a democratic government conceals its agenda from its own citizens, it has divorced everyone in the democracy from any understanding of the circumstances affecting their own lives. If that's your standard, all you have is a conspiracy disguised as a democracy."

Lestrade stood up so suddenly his chair nearly tipped over. "The French Republic has a commitment to freedom, equality and fraternity. We enshrined those values in our Constitution."

"If you cannot or will not help us safeguard those values, then do not hinder us."

Lestrade's face twitched in reaction to Mycroft's words as if he were in pain. He said in a low voice, "If you persist in your actions, I very well may be given orders to arrest you and Dr Watson as enemies of the Republic."

Mycroft said with studied indifference, "You'll know where to find us tomorrow."

Lestrade turned sharply on his heel and stalked from the cafe and into the mist-occluded night.

Watching him go, Watson said dryly, "I think you struck a nerve, Mycroft."

Mycroft nodded. "That was the idea, John."

221B: On Her Majesty's Secret Service

As a rule, the more bizarre a thing is the less mysterious it proves to be.

— Sherlock Holmes

CHAPTER 29

THE CRASHING CAME from inside his skull, a ladder of sound Holmes had to scale to reach consciousness. He saw himself in staggering, zigzag images, climbing hand-over-hand, rung after rung with the sound of pounding as an accompanying rhythm. After what seemed like a chain of interlocked eternities, he identified the sound of a hammer beating repeatedly against metal.

The clangour was not within his head but close enough so he could feel the air vibrate with every crash. He lay still, noting how his body ached all over and how his limbs felt arthritically stiff. He kept his eyes closed, not reacting to the mildly sweet and pungent odour of ozone. The air had an underground feel, cool and faintly redolent of earth. The clammy smell of water filled his nostrils. He sensed a pressure overhead as if he lay under a giant hand.

Between the hammer-blows he heard a man's voice saying, "Disgraceful! Absolutely disgraceful!"

Another man asked, "What are you complaining about? At least now you have some company."

"There was no need to beat him half to death!"

The man said, "Shut up, you fool! Shut up and work! The clock is ticking!"

Holmes recognized the husky rumble of Vonn's voice. "Do you understand me, Nikola?"

"Only too well, *du Schläger!*"

"What did you say?"

"I called you a thug!"

"Don't make me angry, Nikola!"

"Or what — will you kill me right before your beloved Kathryn glories in the final triumph of the Hephaestus Ring and Thunderstrike?"

"The next time you see me will be the last, Nikola."

"That time cannot come soon enough."

Holmes heard a profanity-seasoned growl and then the heavy stamp of Vonn's boots as he marched away, then the whisper of doors closing. Slowly, by degrees, he opened his eyes and looked into the bright glare of arc-lamps. Blinded, he turned his face away, squeezing his eyes shut.

"You can get up now, Mr Holmes," said Nikola Tesla. "Vonn has left the premises for the time being"

Slowly, Holmes opened his eyes again, looking in the direction of the man's voice. Pushing himself to a sitting position, Holmes gingerly touched the back of his throbbing head and felt half-dried blood in his hair. His fingertips explored a swelling lump, painfully tender to the touch. He was surprised he could move his arms and legs. He had expected to find himself bound hand and foot. An acidic taste coated his tongue and made him want to spit. His thirst was intense.

He began to rise and the floor heaved sideways beneath him. He clenched his teeth against a surge of nausea and vertigo. His vision swam with semi-transparent specks, and he cleared them away with a swipe of his hands.

"Don't over-exert yourself, Mr Holmes...most likely you've been dosed with a drug to keep you tractable." A thin man in a rumpled lab coat scuttled into view. He was a strange, untidy figure, carrying a clipboard in one hand and a sledge-hammer in the other. He walked with a springy, nervous step. With his dark hair an uncombed mess and his face bristling with several days worth of whiskers, it took Holmes a moment to recognize Tesla.

"Madame Koluchy is quite the believer in sedatives," he said. "As I can attest."

"I had hoped to find you," Holmes croaked, by way of a greeting. "I hadn't anticipated reuniting this way."

Tesla grinned bleakly. "Nor I, Mr Holmes."

Holmes cleared a dirt-dry throat. "Where are we?"

"In a grounding chamber beneath Gustave Eiffel's tower on the Exposition grounds...the iron frame is bonded as protection for static build-up and lightning, but grounding minimizes the risk during the discharge of electrical energy from within."

"I presume I was brought here from the Hall of Machines via the Decauville railway. How long have you been down here?"

"I was put here late in the day on the 5th of March. I have not left since. I sleep and take my meals here. Occasionally I am allowed to bathe." He feigned sniffing an armpit. "But not recently."

"That was more than three weeks ago," Holmes replied. "What have you been doing all this time?"

"I work, as per my employment contract." Tesla walked over to a braided metal cable coiled on the floor. He took one end, laid it on the floor and struck it hard with the hammer, flattening the braids at the tip. "I'm on a deadline, so forgive the noise."

Holmes winced at the resumption of the metal-on-metal crash. Repressing a groan, he tottered to his feet, silently checking himself. Nothing seemed broken but his entire body ached. Without much surprise, he noted that the second throwing knife was no longer scabbarded to his arm. Brushing off his coat and straightening his vest, he surveyed his surroundings. He stood inside a round, hollow room, with cement walls that rose upward twenty-five feet to a white ceiling. The diameter of the floor space looked to be approximately the same size.

On a low balcony that encircled the room at the midway point, he saw a line of arc lamps, and a bank of humming, keg-shaped turbines. They were attended by three men in gray uniforms. They gazed at glass-fronted needle meters attached to the cast-iron casings. They wore goggles and heavy canvas gloves.

Below the balcony stood several control board consoles bolted to the concrete. All the switches, dials and light-indicators on the board were powered down, although cables snaked from the turbines to the machines. Other items and apparatus were ranged at various points around the floor of the chamber.

The centrepiece was a pair of angled chromium steel pipes mounted in concrete sockets protruding from equidistant points on opposite sides of the chamber. The two cylinders shot upward, forming an upside down V.

At the point where the ends came together, they connected to a round steel ball at least six feet in diameter. The top quarter of it rested within a metal collar in the ceiling. A black cylindrical object resembling an oversize camera lens protruded from the lower surface of the orb.

On a raised concrete ledge behind Tesla, he saw a narrow camp cot, a broom, dust-pan and a small table with a tin water cooler resting atop it. A cup dangled from the container by a thin chain. Holmes walked over and held the cup beneath the spigot. He filled it and drank. Three cupfuls later, most of the vile taste in his mouth had been washed away.

Holmes visually swept the room a second time before fastening his gaze on Tesla. "Have you seen Loveday?"

Hammer poised in mid-air, Tesla's eyes widened in surprise. "She was with you?"

"Of course. We came together to Madame Koluchy's reception."

Tesla swallowed hard. "I am sorry, Mr Holmes...Vonn carried you in here alone and dumped you on the floor only a minute before you regained consciousness. He did not mention Miss Brooke. I was afraid to ask about her. I am sure she is very cross with me."

"She was, but she — all of us — were far more distressed by what happened to Miss Dalton."

Tremulously, Tesla asked, "What was that?"

Knowing he was being dreadfully cruel, Holmes said bluntly, "She was shot when she tried to prevent you from surrendering to Vonn. She died shortly thereafter. Within minutes, in fact."

Nikola Tesla stared at him silently for a long moment, his lips working as if he were groping for something to say. His eyes filled with tears and he dropped the hammer as if it had increased in weight ten-fold. It thudded heavily to the floor. Shoulders sagging, he said hoarsely, "Like you said, I am a foolish man, Mr Holmes. A profoundly stupid man. I hoped by returning of my own free will to Paris, I could possibly convince the Hephaestus Ring to choose a different plan for my teleforce. Instead, I am a prisoner...slave labour. For weeks now, I hoped you and Dr Watson and Miss Brooke would rescue me, you see, so I cooperated. If I had known about poor Deirdre, I would have refused."

"That's why you weren't told," Holmes said. "You're still needed."

"Not much after today, I imagine. What do you think will be done with us?"

"With you, I do not know. But my fate and that of Loveday is definite. We will be killed."

Dolefully, Tesla said, "If she hasn't been already."

Knotting his fists in anger-fuelled anxiety, Holmes asked, "Is there no way out of here?"

Tesla nodded toward the opposite side of the chamber. "There is a lift. But a key is needed to open the doors."

"I thought none of the tower lifts were operational."

"One is, for construction purposes but only to the third level."

A gray-uniformed man on the balcony barked, "Nikola! Get back to work!" He pointed to a meter. "Turbine three needs the static pressure adjusted."

Tesla kneeled beside a floor socket and began feeding the copper cable into it. "The friction turbines are of my design," he explained. "They are bladeless, so few engineers understand the operating principle."

Glancing up, Holmes studied the steel ball hanging at the apex of the pair of pipes. "This is an a much larger version of the telegeodynamics resonator you had in Ireland?"

"Yes. By connecting it to Eiffel's tower, it also serves as an energy transmitter."

"I gathered as much. But why this structure in particular? Due to the nature of puddled iron?"

"The location is just as important," replied Tesla.

"Is this part of Paris significant?"

Tesla nodded. "What was around the Druid's Altar in Ireland?"

"Other than brambles, bogs and standing stones?"

"Yes."

Holmes frowned down at him, then his brow smoothed. "Water. The Atlantic currents. And of course the Seine flows through and beneath the Exposition grounds."

"Of course." Tesla flashed him a jittery grin as he continued to work the cable down into the socket. "Moving water is the perfect propagation medium for the transmission of wireless energy."

Holmes eyed the steel ball and the machinery again. "But the Hephaestus Ring is not interested in free energy...it is your teleforce they wish to harness."

Tesla nodded, swallowing hard. "They think it can used as a death-ray, to destroy from afar."

Comprehension sprang full-blown into Holmes' mind. "They intend to employ Eiffel's tower as a projector of the teleforce. That is very bizarre."

"It is science."

"Is such a thing possible?"

"Very. A few years ago, I experimented on a small scale and very nearly brought down my apartment building in New York City. The effect radius of the energy field is unpredictable and unstable. The tower itself could be destroyed, along with a sizeable portion of the Exposition grounds, perhaps even this part of Paris."

"Thunderstrike indeed." Holmes patted the pockets of his vest, pulled out his watch and thumbed open the cover. He noted the time at close to eight o'clock in the morning. "Obviously, I was drugged. In a short time, the tour of the Iron Lady commences. We need to find a way to stop the Ring and their scheme."

"I have a concept of a plan."

"We need more than that." Holmes turned toward a double set of steel doors recessed into the concrete wall. He strode toward them, noting how the men on the balcony paid him no attention, focused as they were on the turbines. He reached the halfway point when the door panels hissed aside, revealing a box-shaped lift cage. He rocked to a halt.

Loveday stepped from within, pushing a four-wheeled tea-cart before her. Her gaze flew about the room, evaluating it, and then she saw Holmes. She rushed forward, the big phonograph atop the cart rattling. "You're alive." Loveday's voice conveyed her relief.

"Most likely," Holmes replied, keeping his voice steady but giving her a reassuring smile.

"Most likely it's a temporary condition for the two of you," said Madame Koluchy, following closely behind Loveday. She carelessly pointed Loveday's appropriated Bull-dog pistol at the back of her head.

Loveday's hair hung in untidy strands over face. Her gown was torn in places and she was missing her stole. A bruise darkened the line of her jaw, but she seemed otherwise sound. Madame Koluchy had exchanged her black evening dress ensemble for the grey Hephaestus Ring uniform with the hammer and anvil symbol emblazoned upon the breast.

With the barrel of the revolver, she waved Loveday forward. "Over there, Miss Brooke."

"Are you all right?" Holmes asked quietly.

"She is fine," Kathryn said. "Her face will be sore for a day or two, but that is unimportant under the circumstances. I won't apologize for your own rough treatment, Mr Holmes." She uttered a disdainful scoff. "Your schoolboy heroics earned you a battering. I had to send Cuthbert away with Basil to prevent him from using his blackthorn cudgel on you."

"And just where is Basil?"

"He decided he had enough excitement and retired for the evening."

Holmes rubbed the back of his head. "I can sympathize."

"No doubt, but you did catch a bit of a rest, after a fashion. To keep you and Miss Brooke manageable, you were sedated with a soporific of my own manufacture. There are no ill after-effects, except an extreme thirst and an unpleasant taste in one's mouth."

"Those are more than sufficient, thank you," said Loveday, stepping around the kneeling Austrian to stand beside Holmes. She glanced down at Tesla who presented the image of a man totally engrossed in his work. She said, "Hello, Nikola. I'm happy to see you."

"Don't distract him," snapped Kathryn. "He cannot afford to have his attention divided at this juncture."

Holmes arched an ironic eyebrow. Putting his hands in his pockets, he made an exaggerated show of looking around. "So this is Thunderstrike. Not quite as impressive as I imagined."

The copper-haired woman laughed with genuine amusement. "What could you have possibly imagined? Thunderstrike is not a material thing, Mr Holmes...it's a strategy, an agenda."

"Which entails what exactly, other than trying to turn Monsieur Eiffel's tower into a weapon and hoping you don't destroy it in the process?"

Loveday swivelled her head toward him. "I beg your pardon?"

"In case our hostess was not forthcoming," Holmes replied, "we're beneath the Iron Lady in a chamber sandwiched between the Seine and the tower's foundation." He nodded toward the steel ball in the ceiling. "I calculate that orb is directly connected by means of conductive cables to the tip of spire, over a thousand feet above our heads."

Madame Koluchy nodded approvingly. "Very astute, Mr Holmes."

"I assume there are myriad technical details for the plan of

221B: On Her Majesty's Secret Service

which I'm unaware?"

"There most definitely are but rather than divert Nikola's attention further, I'll provide a brief overview. The Iron Lady is fundamentally an enormous version of his small prototype you saw in Ireland. What we have here is an electromagnetic energy vacuum, drawing the power up from the Earth much like a pump, and then transmitting the accumulated charge into the atmosphere, through a valvular conduit. Which, unsurprisingly enough, is at the very tip of the spire atop the tower."

Holmes gestured to the balcony. "This specific generator is run by turbines and not telluric currents, correct?"

"To a point. The turbines accelerate the current within the charge to produce both a field and a beam of high-powered energy of several million volts." She pointed to the steel sphere in the ceiling. "They are transmitted to the accelerator which then spits them out through the conduit at the tip of the spire. A high-energy electromagnetic pulse opens the conduit much like priming a pump connected to a well. Then the charge inside the sphere is released."

Loveday stated, "The only way to reach the tip of the spire to deliver the pulse is by air. The *Terror* should make that very easy."

"I don't know if 'easy' is the proper word, but the airship will certainly facilitate the procedure."

"And electrify the entire tower, as well?"

Madame Koluchy smiled. "You cannot have one without the other. It will be a remarkable, once-in-a-lifetime display of pyrotechnics, talked about for decades."

Holmes said sarcastically, "I'm sure the people on the tower will appreciate this once-in-a-lifetime display, although they won't have the opportunity to talk about it."

"Eggs and omelettes, Mr Holmes."

Loveday asked, "After you break all of the eggs, what kind of omelette does the Hephaestus Ring intend to make?"

Kathryn's smile widened. "I've always hated contrived stories where the villain reveals all the information the heroes need to thwart his plan. But in this situation, there are no heroes, no villains...only a world that needs saving from itself."

She raised the ornate sound horn of the phonograph and turned the big key on the side of the box. A black wax cylinder attached to a gear-and-roller mechanism began to slowly turn. "This is an improved model of Thomas Edison's phonograph...I understand he will unveil it during the Exposition."

A man's deep voice, pitched at an unemotional level floated out from the flare-mouthed horn. "Inasmuch as you will play this communication for the British and Americans, I will speak in English and save you the time and trouble of interpreting."

"That is Robur," said Holmes.

Madame Koluchy nodded. "Recorded mere days before his passing. His epitaph, as it were."

"My name is Baron Robespierre Robur de Maupertuis. Some may know me as Robur the Conqueror. I now represent the Hephaestus Ring but that is not important. What is important is to accept we control a force that can destroy armies from afar. You witnessed a demonstration only a short time ago. That force cannot be wrested from us without incurring the most terrifying consequences. I should not have to add that what we accomplished once, we can accomplish again and again from any point on the continent.

"However, we have no intention of doing so...at least, not yet. That is entirely up to you. We have had enough of wasted time and opportunities, of self-indulgence and corruption and decadence. The great nations of Europe must reclaim their superiority on the global stage. We cannot do that while weak and pallid democracies persist in allowing so-called freedom to destroy us."

Sherlock Holmes snorted.

"The misconception of freedom prevents us from sharing a united purpose," continued Robur's voice. "Calls for democracy will lead to revolution and chaos in the coming century. Only a technocracy can make over humanity into something worthy of the future. We must be disciplined and driven. Europe cries out for such discipline, for a safe and sane world. We can save ourselves. Such a goal can be accomplished in a short time, without bloodshed, without incident by the institution of a technocracy."

Holmes glanced briefly at Madame Koluchy, noting how her lips stirred as she silently recited Robur's words as they issued from the horn. She seemed to be visualizing Robur as he spoke. Without turning his head, Holmes watched Tesla continue to work, attaching the free end of the cable to the base of a console near one of the angled chromium cylinders. After a few turns with a half-moon spanner, a yellow light glowed on the surface of the apparatus.

"Some of you have had past dealings with the Hephaestus Ring," went on Robur, "and understand our technocratic ideals. Perhaps you even agree with them. Regardless, for the technocracy to succeed, we will require a covert cooperation between the leading European nations and the Ring. In return, marvels of mechanical, industrial and medical science will be shared in order pave the way for the new century. We will also control crime on an international scale. Yes, sacrifices will need to be made in regards to judicial systems, but the end result is more than worth it...a Europe that is technologically twenty or more years ahead of the United Kingdom and the United States.

"The Hephaestus Ring will ask for certain legislation to be

passed, certain laws to be created or repealed, certain trade agreements to be made. We realize the wheels of bureaucracies turn slowly, and we can afford to be patient.

"However, you cannot afford to ignore us. Within a fortnight, a motion to amend the French Constitution will be presented to the National Assembly. The motion will be carried as a show of good faith. If it is not, then we will be forced to take extreme measures. If the motion is carried, then we will communicate with you again. If it is not, further communication is unnecessary. You know our position. Let us know yours."

Robur's voice faded, replaced by a faint series of rustles. Madame Koluchy lifted the arm of the phonograph. She said, "Copies of this recording will be in the hands of every minister of every European government no later than tomorrow. The Ring has worked diligently towards this day for more than three years — three years of meticulous planning, strategy, meetings, and all the work of smuggling in the components of our teleforce projector."

Loveday asked, "How many French officials have you entangled in all of this?"

Kathryn Koluchy showed her teeth in a grin. "Not as many as you might suspect. Only a few key ones susceptible to bribes, disguised as appeals to their patriotism."

Holmes demanded, "And the number of European criminal societies that are involved? More than we suspect?"

The woman laughed. "If you suspected all of them, you would be close."

"So," said Loveday, "all you are really doing is consolidating a gang of international crooks."

"What is a government *but* a gang, Miss Brooke? Like-minded men and women uniting around a principle, whether it's business, scientific or sociological. Technocracy blends all three. Certain approaches were made by the Ring to certain officials, inviting their participation in a joint venture. Most of them accepted because technocracy possesses the organizational structure by means of which they could retain their positions of leadership, yet still impose their personal ideals onto a blueprint for the future."

"A quiet and civilized *coup d'etat,*" remarked Holmes. "The criminal networks are also attracted, because such a scheme is good for business."

"They are investing in an orderly world. The different syndicates and networks have no formal organization. At best, they have isolated cells, pockets of agents and members, all of them busy scheming and suspicious of one another. Barely contained chaos. The Ring offers them a different way of doing business."

"And a more orderly world is a more profitable world," said Loveday.

"Of course."

Holmes forced a chuckle. "I have a difficult time accepting that the Ring and its associates are idealists."

"That is wise, because we are decidedly not. In the long run, we are the ultimate pragmatists. The threat of the teleforce is only a tool to be used to build a better, cleaner world. The Ring will transform France into the prototypical nation of the future, a standard by which other countries will measure themselves."

"By blackmailing your way into the 20th century," said Loveday. "Coercion by threat can accomplish only so much."

"The teleforce is a fulcrum to move the governments to the proper position to agree to our terms. After all, the agreement is covert, and every European nation will benefit. In the final analysis, many decision-makers in the German, Russian and British governments believe in the tenets of technocracy as put forth by the Hephaestus Ring. They are willing to bargain for the Ring's technological advances. They will pay vast sums if they are properly impressed."

"And the reasoning behind the fiction that Robur the Conqueror is the mastermind?"

"Come now, Miss Brooke. You must know what it is like for a woman to work within a primarily male field of endeavour. Besides the name Robur carries with it an impressive cachet, at least in government bodies."

"What happens if a government body requests a face-to-face meeting with Robur?" Holmes asked.

She brushed aside the question with the wave of a hand. "We evade, we dissemble, we delay. They will have weightier matters to attend to, like concocting a reasonable cover story for today's accident at the Iron Lady, which most likely will cost the lives of numerous influential people."

"You have yet to name the specific target of the teleforce projector."

The woman laughed with genuine delight. "There isn't one...there is no need. The teleforce is a wave, not a focused beam. Whatever matter interacts with the wave will either be destroyed or severely damaged, depending on whether it is organic or inorganic."

"Therefore the destruction you envision," said Holmes, "is random."

Kathryn's smile widened. "Why not?"

"There's a word for such an action," stated Loveday. "It was coined here in France. Terrorism."

"In this instance, there is an objective to the terrorism. A future to be won."

Loveday and Holmes exchanged surreptitious glances, silently questioning one another. Madame Koluchy caught the brief eye exchange and chuckled contemptuously. "You're stalling for time, hoping you can do something disruptive with the information I just imparted. Let me disabuse you of that conceit right now — you cannot. Vonn will be on his way to rendezvous with Robur and the *Terror* in a few minutes."

"I need help!" announced Tesla, so loudly and suddenly that both Loveday and Holmes jumped a bit.

All eyes turned to him. The man had returned to the task of feeding the cable into the floor socket. "I'm not able to move the conduit any further—it seems to be caught on something. If Mr Holmes and Miss Brooke could twist it while I push, I can wiggle it through to the turbine level."

Loveday squinted at him in disbelief. "Are you joking, Nikola?"

Kathryn paused for a thoughtful second, then gestured with the revolver. "Help him. Do as he says."

Holmes pursed his lips as if thinking it over, and then bent down, grasping the coil of cable. "I'm assuming we have little choice in the matter."

"You assume correctly," said Kathryn. "If nothing else, you'll earn a few more minutes of life."

The heavy cable consisted of many stiff intertwined strands of oiled copper wire and therefore, a tight grip was difficult to secure. Tesla instructed Holmes and Loveday on how to hold the cable while walking backwards, all the while twisting it back and forth. Loveday said under her breath, "This is bloody ridiculous, but my manicure is already ruined."

After a few moments of back-walking, they found themselves stepping up onto the elevated lip of the wall. "We can go no further," Holmes called.

Tesla looked over his shoulder, muttered in wordless

exasperation and arose, walking over to the edge of the lip. He said tersely, "Let it go."

They did so, dropping the cable onto the floor. Tesla reached for the table as if he meant to use it pull himself up. He tipped over the water cooler. The cannister toppled to the floor with a clang. The lid popped off and the liquid within splashed out, spreading quickly across the concrete. It drained down into the floor socket and flowed around Madame Koluchy's boots. She scowled. "Nikola, you clumsy —"

Whatever else she intended to say was drowned out by a chorus of agonized yells from the men monitoring the turbines on the balcony. They performed mad dervish dance steps, wrenching themselves away from anything metal.

Kathryn Koluchy screamed, her body convulsing. She hurled away the revolver as electrical current raced up her legs, through her arm and into the pistol. She made a leap for the ledge where Tesla, Loveday and Holmes stood. Loveday grabbed her tightly by a flailing hand, yanked her up and slammed the crown of her skull into Kathryn's forehead. She let her drop unceremoniously and unconscious onto the camp cot.

Holmes gave her a wry grin. "I suppose Madame had it coming."

Loveday nodded grimly. "And then some." She rubbed a spot at her hairline. "Luckily, she didn't know about my exceptionally hard head."

"Unlike your colleagues."

Speaking loudly to be heard over the cries of the men on the balcony, Tesla said, "I improvised an induction coil which used the cable and the water as a voltage circuit. The current isn't lethal, but it delivers a robust shock."

Holmes stared at him at him in silent surmise for a handful of seconds and then intoned, "Your concept of a plan?"

Tesla nodded. "Thank you for your participation."

221B: On Her Majesty's Secret Service

The French enjoyment of the Sunday seems to me infinitely more rational than our custom.

— John H. Watson, MD

CHAPTER 30

THE DAY DAWNED grey and ghostly. The little train chugged through the morning mist amongst and around the pavilions toward the massive arches between the support pylons of the Iron Lady.

Watson shifted position on the hard wooden bench, pushed to one corner of it by Mycroft's bulk. The two men sat in the rear of the third open carriage, drawn by a compact shunter engine. In front of them they saw only hats and backs — top hats, bowlers, homburgs and a few festooned with flowers. Watson guessed female journalists, wives or secretaries of officials wore those.

He felt very tired. After returning to the Hôtel d'Alsace after the meeting with Gabriel Lestrade, he had slept fitfully, his thoughts constantly returning to Loveday and Holmes. He knew they were extremely competent but by the same token, neither of them had strolled into enemy territory with such blithe bravery before, either.

Or blithe foolhardiness, he thought glumly.

Mycroft had roused him at seven o'clock. After two cups of black coffee and the application of a neat blonde moustache by the stinging application of spirit gum, the two men took a cab to the entrance of the grounds of the Exposition Universelle.

They joined a crowd of well-dressed men and women, a few of whom were members of the British diplomatic service. Despite the fog and the chill, they seemed to be in cheerful frames of mind. After having their invitations and photographic identification examined by uniformed men at a turnstile, the visitors were conducted to a small and picturesque railway depot. Mycroft preferred to occupy the last bench of the last carriage, claiming he never felt comfortable with strangers sitting at his back. Watson didn't blame him.

The locomotive clanked and clattered its way further into the fairgrounds, seeming to travel with infuriating slowness. Due to the fog, sightseeing was limited but Watson glimpsed several of the pavilion and exhibition halls still under construction, with scaffolds and ladders arranged around their facades. No labourers were in sight, but since it was Sunday, their absence was not a surprise.

Watson squirmed around on the bench, trying to find a more comfortable position. He ran a thumb over the moustache glued to his upper lip, making certain the adhesive had a firm hold.

"Suits you," said Mycroft without preamble.

"I beg your pardon?"

Mycroft touched his face between his nose and mouth. "The soup filter. Gives your face more gravitas."

"You're not the first to say so. I only stuck it there to avoid issues when I presented Mr Willis' credentials or if I ran into one of his colleagues from another newspaper."

"Sound tactic."

"And what about your own?"

Mycroft eyes slid toward him in a puzzled glance. "Explain."

"For when we reach our destination."

"Any tactic will be formulated upon what — and whom — we encounter at the so-called Iron Lady."

The train punched through the fog and in successive waves, the people aboard the carriages uttered exclamations and murmurs of awe and wonder. Watson leaned to one side, staring out and up and beyond the fringed tassels of the carriage's canvas roof.

He craned his neck as he studied the gigantic tower looming overhead. Although he had glimpsed the structure rising from the Parisian skyline the day before and seen illustrations, he felt overwhelmed by its size and magnitude. Approaching the base of it, he could see the structure in its true proportions. It was colossal, intimidatingly so.

He estimated each of massive pylons stood nearly two hundred feet tall and extended well over thirteen hundred square feet from corner to corner. The first level constructed atop an elevated superstructure looked to be a minimum of 150 feet above a flat stone promenade. He studied the metal stairways that went up in geometrical patterns to the first level platform. Tilting his head back, Watson tried to see the pinnacle but experienced a momentary surge of dizziness and gave up.

Somehow, Eiffel's Iron Lady looked less like a majestic achievement in architecture than a sinister structure radiating an aura of menace, like an evil wizard's castle from a book of fairy tales. He felt a stirring of dread within him, despite the festive air contributed by the many colourful pennants and gaily coloured tents serving refreshments.

The train clanked to a halt at the edge of the esplanade. A cluster of formally dressed people stood there, greeting the passengers as they disembarked from the carriage. Watson recognized only Gustave Eiffel, who tipped his top hat and shook the hands of all those who came forward to greet him

Watson continuously scanned faces, looking for Holmes and

Loveday. His gaze fell upon a thin man with weather-beaten features wearing a shabby old gray raincoat with a velvet collar, and a derby hat that looked too small for his head. The man stared intently at him and Mycroft for an uncomfortable length of time, then moved toward them with a deliberate stride. He carried a furled umbrella and swung it like a cane.

Upon reaching Mycroft, he said simply, "I received your message." He spoke in English.

Mycroft nodded. "Thank you, Rene. I hoped you would be here."

"It wasn't just your message alone that drew me...a short time after it was delivered, a handwritten note from Fritz von Waldbaum, identifying himself as a specialist from Danzig was passed on to me. The note suggested in the strongest possible terms this morning's tour of the tower should be cancelled."

"I know Herr Waldbaum," Mycroft said. "Did his note provide reasons the tour should be cancelled?"

"No, but a direct communique from a confidential informant specifically mentioned a threat to the government by a plot code-named Thunderstrike."

Mycroft's eyebrows lifted. "Indeed? Are you aware of the informant's identity?"

"I can surmise. The report was signed 'Z'...earlier in the evening, one of my agents at Madame Koluchy's reception reported the presence of Basil Zaharoff."

Watson exhaled a disgusted sigh. "So much for his wish to be done with the Hephaestus Ring."

Mycroft chuckled. "Perhaps acting as a spy is his way of achieving that. Rene, you did not come alone?"

The man gestured negligently behind him with the umbrella. "I asked for volunteers and got them, especially when I mentioned a threat to Prime Minister Tirard. The men who issued the stand-down order to the Bureau and the Sûreté were themselves ordered to do the same — by me. Once they realized the extent to which their authority was being questioned, they had no belly for a direct challenge."

Watson surveyed the crowd and glimpsed Dubugue and Lestrade walking amongst the people. Mycroft said, "Apparently the Ring's influence is not as pervasive as we were led to believe."

"I suppose that is something we will conclusively learn today." He glanced toward Watson. "Dr Watson, I presume?"

Watson automatically smoothed his moustache. "More or less. Monsieur Mathis?"

"The same." The two men shook hands. "As I understand it, two of your operatives have gone missing here on the fairgrounds."

"One of them is my younger brother," Mycroft said.

Mathis smiled coldly. "Let's go find them."

Following Eiffel and his party, the tour group walked across the flat expanse of white stone that occupied the grounds directly beneath the tower. The overall tenor was convivial and excited.

"What are we looking for?" Mathis asked, his eyes scanning the grounds and the milling people.

Mycroft's lips quirked in a humourless smile. "I suspect it will be one of those we'll-know-it when-we-see-it type of things."

The group followed Eiffel to the gigantic pillar beneath the west-facing arch. A seven-man military honour guard in full uniform stood at its far corner, rifles at the ready. On the opposite side, a pair of men in grey uniforms, high black boots and berets posed in parade rest positions — backs stiff, legs wide-braced, hands clasped behind their backs.

Watson pointed them out to Mycroft who murmured "Perhaps they are an added security detail provided by the Ring?"

Watson stared at them, noting how Rattler repeater pistols hung from their shoulders by lanyards. "You may be half right."

Gustave Eiffel climbed a few of the metal risers of the stairway, cunningly concealed within the wrought-iron latticework of the pylon. A husky, middle-aged man with a square-cut gray beard joined him, carrying an open case which held a folded Le Tricolour — the national flag of France.

"Have you apprised Monsieur Tirard of the threat?" asked Mycroft.

"Yes, without getting into specifics. He did not seem overly concerned."

Eiffel gestured for silence and announced in French, "I thank all of you for attending this historic event on this rather drab Sunday morning. I assure you it will be worth it...at least in the years to come. My tower is not just a structure or even a sculpture, but a work of art which showcases and symbolizes French innovation and engineering."

He paused for a smattering of polite hand-claps and continued, "If you would be so good as to form a queue, then you will follow my good friend Prime Minister Tirard and myself up 1,710 steps to the top of the tower, where we will hoist the Tricolour—making our beloved flag the highest-flying one in the world and worthy of a 21 gun salute."

A wave of appreciative laughter and applause rippled through the crowd as the people surged forward. Mycroft and Mathis stepped back. "We should bring up the rear," Mycroft said.

They watched as the gray-uniformed men took up positions on either side of the staircase, ushering the people up the steps. They appeared very efficient and official, so no one questioned them. Even the few gendarmes in the vicinity gave them little heed.

221B: On Her Majesty's Secret Service

By degrees, Watson became aware of a tingling vibration passing through the ground under his feet. It felt so faint at first, he barely noticed but the closer they drew to the stairway, the stronger it became. In sudden alarm, he asked, "Do you feel that, Mycroft?"

The big man frowned. "Feel what?"

"Like a tickling underfoot...I last felt something like it at the Druid's Altar when Tesla was performing his telegeodynamics experiment." He gestured toward the pair of Ring soldiers herding the tour group up the stairway. "Those men are trying to get as many people onto the metal steps as quickly as they can. Why?"

Mathis glanced their way and frowned. "I will find out who sent them here."

As he began pushing his way through the crowd, a flutter of pink, white and wispy gray smoke caught Watson's eye from the other side of the pylon. He caught the scent of hot metal. For a split second his mind could not identify the nature of the image his eyes registered. When it did, all he managed to husk out was a hoarse cry of, *"Loveday!"*

221B: On Her Majesty's Secret Service

Violence recoils on the violent.

— Sherlock Holmes

CHAPTER 31

HOLDING ONTO TESLA'S belt, Holmes anchored himself by hooking a leg around the frame of the camp cot. Having it weighed down by the senseless Kathryn Koluchy helped keep it in place. The Austrian leaned out over the wet floor as far as he dared, using the blunt end of the broomstick to tap the control surface of the console. Voice tight with strain, he said, "I conceived of the plan earlier in the week, but it required more than one person to pull it off."

"Lucky for you we just happened to drop by," replied Holmes, holding Tesla at arm's length.

After three attempts, Tesla managed to tap the switch beneath the glowing power light to the off position. Instantly, Loveday jumped from the lip and raced to retrieve her pistol from the floor. The pained howls of the men on the balcony ceased and were replaced by sputtering streams of profanity. One of them made a move as if to come down, but Loveday trained the revolver on him.

"Get back up there," she snapped. "All of you raise your hands." She cast a backward glance toward Tesla and Holmes. "Now what?"

"I did not plan much further than this," Tesla admitted.

221B: On Her Majesty's Secret Service

Kathryn Koluchy groaned and stirred. Pushing herself to a sitting position, she gingerly rubbed the spreading red spot on her forehead. "Ow. A Glasgow Kiss is very unsportsmanlike, Miss Brooke."

"So is a sucker punch," Loveday retorted. "Consider it quid pro quo."

As the woman attempted to rise, Holmes held up a hand. "You're fine where you are, Madame. The lift key, please."

Kathryn Koluchy grimaced. "Nothing you do will make a difference to Thunderstrike. The charge has already built to maximum within the accelerator. Can't you smell the ozone?"

Before Holmes could answer, the glass cylinder protruding from the bottom of the metal sphere on the ceiling exuded a blue-white glow. A thready pulse of vibration suddenly tickled his skin, synchronized with a low hum, like the after-vibrations of a gong which had been struck. The hum gradually became a whine, seeming to shiver in the air all around them.

Tesla said dolefully, "I'm afraid she's right, Mr Holmes. The current within the accelerator will automatically be directed into the coils, and then through the resonant transformer circuits installed at key points in the tower. The level of voltage is variable, controlled by the turbines, but it is most likely high enough to be fatal."

"We can't stop it?"

"No...we can only exert a degree of control over it." Tesla pointed to the metal rods, the turbines and the steel orb. "Picture this room as a spillway for a dam or reservoir...an uncontrolled discharge of surplus water past the dam would be catastrophic, so governors are in place to hold it check, although the water is still overtopping it. A steady but exponential increase in the discharge is the ideal but unfortunately, when the peak discharge rate is reached, there is no reducing it."

"In other words," Kathryn Koluchy said, "unless there is a release of the teleforce energy, the Eiffel Tower could quite literally melt in on itself."

Loveday spared the woman a contemptuous, over the shoulder glance. "And you would quite literally be guilty of mass murder."

Madame Koluchy shook her head in mock pity. "You're really new to this, aren't you? Technically, the Hephaestus Ring would be guilty, but we will not be blamed. We've already provided a very plausible culprit."

"I'm not quite as green as you might think," retorted Loveday. "A renegade Austrian-Serbian electrical engineer with mad ideas and alleged to hold even madder anarchist beliefs would be the perfect scapegoat."

"Especially," interjected Holmes, "if that scapegoat happens to perish while executing his terrorist plot. It is an elegantly simple solution, since anyone in government who suspects otherwise would be compelled to cooperate with the cover story for the sake of restoring order."

Tesla said glumly, "I suspected I was being set up to take the responsibility, so I factored in a few tricks to delay the final phase of the operation."

"How much of a delay?" Holmes asked.

"Fifteen minutes...enough to skew the baron's part of the schedule, hopefully."

"Perhaps we can extend that." Holmes squinted at the lens on the steel ball. The electric glow pulsated steadily within its thick glass walls. He asked, "What purpose does the cylinder on the accelerator serve?"

Tesla frowned, then his face brightened. "It's a voltage stabilizer...designed to deliver constant voltage, regulating the energy input before it's fed to the load. It's possible to adjust the settings and siphon off some of the voltage before it reaches the peak discharge rate." He paused and added, "Disabling it will be dangerous and leave us exposed to the naked current."

"Don't a be a fool, Nikola!" exclaimed Madame Koluchy, eyes wide with apprehension.

The man ignored her. Facing the balcony, he shouted, "Turn off the turbines! Turn them all off!"

The copper-haired woman struggled to stand up from the camp cot. "Don't listen to him!"

The attendants stared at her, then at Nikola Tesla but they did not move. Holmes said, "Miss Brooke, perhaps you should explain it to them."

She squeezed the trigger of the Bull-dog revolver. The report sounded like the breaking of a tree branch. The bullet struck the wall above the middle turbine and keened away, leaving a dust-spurting pockmark to commemorate its impact.

The grey-uniformed men instantly busied themselves throwing switches on the keg-shaped exteriors of the machines. One by one the turbines fell silent but an underlying throb continued to climb in scale and pitch, becoming painful to the ear. The air around the accelerator sphere wavered with a shimmer, like heat waves rising from a sun-baked road. Holmes felt the feathery touch of energy as if he were washed by waves of static electricity.

Tesla eyed the lens, saying grimly. "We may be too late. By the time we deactivate the stabilizer, the peak discharge level will have been reached."

"What can we do?" asked Loveday.

Tesla's face registered confusion and fear. "Shoot it?"

Holmes demanded, "Will a bullet penetrate the stabilizer case?"

"The glass is very thick, so perhaps not. But all we need is a crack to effect a fluctuation."

Holmes and Loveday locked glances. He said, "You've got the gun."

"And only one bullet."

"Best put it to good use, then."

Lips compressed, Loveday lifted the pistol in a two-handed grip, sighting down the barrel. She held her breath and squeezed the trigger. The gunshot and the crash of shattering glass were almost simultaneous. The lens burst apart in a nova of showering sparks.

Madame Koluchy voiced a wordless shriek of rage. She lunged forward, elbowing both Tesla and Holmes out of her way. She rushed toward Loveday, face a bare-toothed grimace of homicidal fury. Loveday backed away, encumbered by her gown. She reversed her grip on the revolver, intending to use the butt as a bludgeon if necessary.

A crooked finger of energy crackled down from the sphere, impaling Kathryn Koluchy's upper body. Little jets of fire, gold, orange and pale blue, danced over her limbs, creating a nimbus around her. Her screech of anger turned into a full-throated scream of agony. She fell heavily, thrashing and convulsing.

Holmes snatched the blanket from the cot and threw it over her, swiftly smothering the flames. The sickening odour of scorched human hair and flesh crept into his nostrils. He pulled away the blanket. Kathryn Koluchy lay sprawled face-down. Smoke curled from her clothes and moans of pain bubbled past her blistered lips.

Kneeling down, Loveday helped Holmes turn Madame Koluchy onto her back. Much of the woman's hair was crisped a dark brown, her face covered by red, raw patches and leaking blisters. Holmes quickly began patting down her clothes. "The material of the uniform is fire-resistant, so if there are pockets — ah!"

He brandished a wafer of metal, double-pronged at one end. "The lift key."

A jagged arc of electricity struck the floor very close to them, inscribing a black starburst on the concrete. Holmes tossed the key to Loveday. "Unlock the doors...Nikola and I will bring Madame."

As Loveday rose, Holmes carefully lifted Kathryn to a sitting position. She felt surprisingly heavy, all hard muscle and sinew beneath the gray uniform. She moaned, head lolling, eyelids fluttering. "I can't move..."

"Where is the *Terror*?" he snapped.

"I need Herakleophorbia."

"First we have to get out of here." He glanced toward Nikola Tesla who remained on the lip, casting his eyes about uncertainly. He still held the broom, his fingers tightening around the handle. The steel sphere continued to spit sparks and corkscrews of current. The men on the balcony crouched down, using the turbines as cover. A console took a direct strike and burst apart in a shower of sparks and acrid smoke.

"We can't stay here, Nikola!" Holmes shouted impatiently. "Come help me."

Reluctantly, Tesla stepped from the ledge and crossed the floor, dropping the broom as he did so. He took Madame Koluchy's legs and lifted. At that instant, a man leapt down from the balcony, barring Loveday's path to the lift doors. Reaching out for her, he shouted, "Give over the key, bitch!"

Without hesitation, Loveday raked the frame of her pistol across the man's forehead, the blade sight tearing the flesh. Crying out in pain, he staggered backward, almost immediately blinded by a sudden flow of blood. She stiff-armed him aside and reached the doors, inserted the key into the slot and turned it sharply to the right. The panels slid open. She glimpsed a shadowy shape rushing toward her from the interior of the cage, arms outspread.

Loveday threw herself backward, barely avoiding the massive fist thrown at her face. She retreated into the room, ducking another blow from Vonn. His maimed face twisted in a rictus of disbelief as his gaze fixed on Holmes, Madame Koluchy and Tesla. For a handful of seconds, the big man stopped in his tracks as he tried to make sense of what he saw.

"What are you doing?" he bellowed. "What is happening?"

Holmes laid Madame Koluchy down and stood up, bringing the broom with him. "Thunderstrike is done, Vonn. And if we don't get her medical attention, so is Kathryn. Best not to interfere."

Emboldened by Vonn's sudden arrival, the two turbine mechanics jumped down from the balcony. One of them paused long enough to examine his comrade's pistol-inflicted injury. A crooked lance of energy launched from the sphere struck him on the shoulder. The voltage sent both men careening way from each other like a pair of drunken dancers.

At the sound of their screams, Vonn whirled around toward them. Holmes shouted, "Go, Miss Brooke! Send the lift back down when you can!"

She paused only an instant before running to the cage. The third technician raced forward, intent on reaching it first. He was a shade slow. Loveday fell into the cage and slammed the door shut in his face. Upon the sealing of the latch, the lift began to rise.

The man snarled in frustration and put his arm between the bars, securing a grip on the bodice of Loveday's dress with his right hand. She sank her teeth into his wrist. Howling, he thrashed in pain, trying to escape. Releasing him, she fetched his knuckles a sharp rap with the butt of the Bull-dog for good measure. Cradling his arm, he stumble-footed backward until his legs tangled and he fell down. With a squeak of pulleys and cables, the cage rose up the square shaft, a column of smoke following it.

She called down, "Be back soon! Don't wander off!"

Vonn bulled toward Holmes, his head lowered, a savage grin on his his wide mouth. Holmes brought up the broom handle and caught him on the jaw. Grunting, the big man staggered back, his eyes widening with surprise.

Reaching behind him with his right hand, Vonn whipped out a flat knife. As the scar-faced man thrust for his throat, Holmes recognized the black blade. He leaned away from its point, cautiously stepping between Madame Koluchy and Tesla. He said, "I wondered what happened to my other knife...thank you for finding it."

Vonn swung the knife at Holme's midsection with an exaggerated sidearm slashing motion. He snarled, "I'll leave it for you in your bollocks, Holmes!"

Holmes stepped aside as the man made a half-cut, half-thrust at his groin, seeking to sever the femoral artery. The lens of an arc-lamp on the balcony exploded in an eye-dazzling flare. Everyone shielded themselves from flying fragments of glass. Thick smoke filled the room, abrading throats and stinging eyes.

Holmes assumed a combat stance, holding the broomstick horizontally in front of him, grasping it mid-length so the right palm faced his torso and his left away from it. Bartitsu borrowed shamelessly from many martial art sources, from savate to bojutsu.

Rushing to the attack, Vonn wove a web of steel with the knife-blade held before him. Standing his ground, Holmes balanced on the balls of his feet, pivoting from the waist, knocking the knife aside. For a long moment, the two men exchanged a flurry of knife-strokes and broom-stick parries.

Baring his teeth in frustration, Vonn set himself, and as Holmes half-expected, he feinted to the right with the knife, then launched a roundhouse kick at his belly. With the broom, Holmes swept the man's leg to the left, causing him to stumble while he tried to maintain his balance on one foot.

Before Vonn could recover his equilibrium, Holmes brought the blunt end of the broom handle down on Vonn's right forearm. He cried out as the knife clattered to the floor. Without pause, he thrust the blunt end of the stick into the man's sternum, slamming half-a-lungful of air out of his lungs in a protracted wheeze. Vonn bent double but managed to catch and secure a tight grip on the length of wood. He pulled it toward him and hammered at the side of Holmes' head with his left fist.

Holmes managed to partially deflect the blow with a forearm but he staggered as the punch jarred him. Savagely, Vonn twisted the broom handle from Holmes' grip, broke it over a knee and tossed the two pieces aside.

"Games," he snarled. "Bloody childish games, playing tricks with sticks. Fight like a man, if you know how."

With a rise of cold anger, Holmes realized he had underestimated Vonn as a mere back alley brawler, not as a trained professional soldier and therefore, an extremely formidable opponent. He saw no point in prolonging the contest. He nodded. "As you like it."

Vonn lunged for him. Leaning forward, Holmes delivered a *La Baffe* open-palm strike to the man's nose. Blood spurted from both nostrils like opened spigots and the man howled. When Vonn clapped both hands to his face Holmes kicked him in the crotch and he sank to his knees, clutching his groin.

"Does that meet with your manly approval?" Holmes asked.

Vonn groaned between gritted teeth, *"Din jävel..."*

Matter-of-factly, Holmes said, "The longer we stay here, the greater the chance we'll be electrocuted. Nikola and I plan to carry Madame Koluchy to safety. You can choose for yourself what action to take."

Voice thick with pain, Vonn said, " The baron waits for me."

"Good. You can take me to him once we're out of here."

Vonn nodded almost imperceptibly. Then he flung himself forward, hand closing around the knife on the floor. He coughed out a hoarse laugh of triumph. He half rose from the floor on one knee, cocking back his arm for a throw. A tendril of energy brushed the blade held between his fingers. A door-slamming report shook the chamber.

For a moment Vonn writhed within a cocoon of flame. Limbs spasming, he toppled onto his left side. The knife was gone. Little blobs of molten metal clung to his blackened right hand and scorched sleeve. Tesla and Holmes stared, stunned into momentary immobility. Tesla murmured faintly, *"Lass die Strafe dem Verbrechen angemessen sein."*

"Yes," Holmes said."You might also say that violence does in truth, recoil upon the violent." He glanced over at the semi-conscious Kathryn Koluchy. "And the schemer falls into the pit which she digs for another. Speaking of which, let's get her out of here before we end up in a similar condition."

Tesla's dark eyes unblinkingly fixed on Vonn's smouldering body. "Deirdre is avenged, at least."

Holmes bent down to pick up the woman. "Not yet," he replied. "Not quite yet."

221B: On Her Majesty's Secret Service

The present is theirs... the future, for which I really worked, is mine.

— Nikola Tesla

CHAPTER 32

BY THE TIME the lift doors opened, the shaft had filled with astringent black smoke. It billowed out after her. Loveday's eyes brimmed with tears so she could barely see her surroundings. Fanning the smoke away from her face, struggling with a coughing fit, she pushed open the cage door and groped around on the wall for the key-slot.

She found it, closed the cage, inserted the key and turned it to the right. The door panels slid closed and she heard the creak and clank of machinery. Clearing her vision with a torn scrap of her dress, she saw the same narrow passageway within the support pillar she had been forced to enter less than an hour before.

Upon awakening from a deep, drugged slumber inside the Hall of Machines, Loveday had been ordered by Madame Koluchy to get up and out to the little train, where a pair of armed gray-uniformed men waited. She was surprised to see the sun was up, although its early-morning light was filtered through a pall of mist.

Too woozy to do anything but cooperate with the woman's commands, she trundled the phonograph on its wheeled cart aboard the carriage and sat quietly until it conveyed them to the esplanade beneath Eiffel's tower. Although people were already assembling, they were ignored. The armed men escorted them and presented a very official image to the casual glance.

It wasn't until Loveday and Madame Koluchy had entered the small passageway within the pylon that clarity returned but she refrained from showing it, not asking after Holmes. The two-man escort did not accompany them. They encountered Vonn, who engaged Kathryn in a hurried, whispered conversation. Loveday kept her eyes down but listened intently. Although they spoke in English she understood very little, other than that Vonn would check back in with her before going to the farmyard to meet with the baron.

The babble of the crowd brought her back to the present. Loveday moved toward the weak daylight and the promise of untainted air at the end of the passageway. Upon reaching it, she had paused to take several cleansing breaths, when she heard a male voice shout, *"Loveday!"*

Turning in the direction whence the voice came, she saw a moustached blonde man hustling toward her from the edge of a crowd. Although his voice was familiar, she could not place his face for a second. Then she did and despite the situation, couldn't help but laugh in relief. "I didn't recognize you at first, John. The moustache suits you."

He nodded impatiently, taking her by the arm. "So I hear. Are you all right?"

She smiled wanly, coughed into her hand, and said, "For the most part, yes."

"Where've you been? Where is Holmes?"

With the pistol in her hand, she gestured back toward the passage. "To answer both of your questions — Sherlock and I have been held prisoner down below with Nikola...Madame Koluchy and Vonn are there, too. I sent the lift back down for

Nikola and Sherlock."

Watson stepped around her, peering into the smokey passage. "Is there any other way down there?"

"I don't know." Loveday saw the people climbing the stairway and pulled away from his grasp. "We have to stop the tour from going further up into the tower — it's been rigged to electrocute them!"

Watson's face registered incredulity, also a sudden fearful realization. Loveday laid a hand on his shoulder, her face stark and white. "We've got to get everyone away — an electrical charge is building! Can't you feel it in the ground?"

Watson whirled away from her. "I'll deal with it — you see to Holmes and Nikola!"

He ran back toward the crowd queuing at the foot of the stairwell. "Mycroft! Mathis! Keep people from climbing into the tower! It's electrified!"

Mycroft turned toward him, eyes widening. "Electrified? How?"

"Never mind how," Watson retorted, reaching around him to grab Mathis by the sleeve. "Alert your agents to keep everyone away from the tower! Tell all the people to come back down immediately!"

Mathis blinked at him but did not otherwise move. Then he turned his attention to the uniformed men standing at the foot of the stairs. He shook his umbrella and shouted, *"Espece de salaud! S'enfuir au nom de la loi!* Get away from there, in the name of the law!"

They paid him no heed and continued directing people up the stairs, even pushing some of them so hard they tripped on the risers. From under his shirt Mathis took out a tin whistle, placed it between his lips, and blew out a piercing *toot-toot-toot* rhythm.

The sound was apparently a familiar alarm signal to many within earshot. Much of the crowd came to a dead stop, milling about uncertainly. The people climbing the stairs halted. Watson saw half-a-dozen men in long tan overcoats rush toward Mathis' position. The two men wearing the Hephaestus Ring grey glanced around with startled eyes, and reached for their weapons.

Watson drew his Adams revolver from a coat pocket. He aimed it at the Ring men. "Back away!"

He spoke in English but he doubted the men would follow his order even if they understood. They unlimbered the Rattlers and crouched down behind the latticed stanchions on either side of the stairway. Watson did not hesitate. Dropping to one knee, he squeezed the trigger of his pistol twice. At the sound of gunshots, the murmur of the crowd ceased and was instantly replaced by cries of fear.

A Ring soldier spun around on his toes as the revolver's bullets pounded into his right shoulder. He fell flat on his back. His companion returned fire with the Rattler, but in trying to control the recoil of the fusillade, the barrel dropped too low. The rounds stitched a path across the esplanade toward Watson. He flung himself to one side as a shower of stone chips swept against him. As he rolled, he heard more screams, more shouted commands in French.

He saw people running in all directions and more men wearing long coats. They brandished handguns and shouted contradictory orders. The people on the stairs bent low but did not move, their faces stamped with expressions of fear and confusion. Mathis continued to blow the three note alarm signal on his whistle.

Watson came to his feet and pushed his way closer to the stairwell through a knot of frightened people and armed men in overcoats. He hoped the latter worked for the Deuxieme Bureau or the Sûreté. He feared the Ring had their own disguised men disseminated throughout the crowd to aggravate the growing pandemonium.

As soon as the thought registered, the tarpaulin enclosure of a refreshment tent slid away. A dozen men dressed as labourers in overalls and red neckerchieves charged forward, all armed with pistols and carbines. Black cloth hoods completely concealed their heads, except for narrow openings for their mouths and eyes. They chanted, *"Pas de dieux, pas de maitres!"* as they fired enthusiastically into the air with their guns.

After a few seconds, Watson realized the labourers shouted, "No gods, no masters," an old anarchist slogan. He wondered if they had chosen the inauguration day of the tower to stage a workers' revolt.

When rounds spanged off the wrought-iron of the support pylon behind him, Watson did not give the possibility of an insurrection much more thought. He aimed his revolver at the hooded men and picked his targets carefully, dropping three of them with crippling shots to their legs. He closed his mind to the cruelty of his actions. He imagined he felt recriminating sympathy pains from the Jezail bullet wound in his leg.

Over the clamour, he heard Mathis bellowing, *"Depechez-vous, imbeciles!"* He and Mycroft stood at the foot of the stairway, literally dragging people down the steps while gesturing to Gustave Eiffel and Prime Minister Tirard, who still stood on the risers, their eyes blank with stupefied surprise at the appearance of the masked men.

Watson circled around to flank the man in in the Ring uniform but was hampered by a back-and-forth exchange of gunfire between the men in overcoats and the men in hoods. The shooting became brisker, and he heard cries of pain. The fire from both factions wasn't accurate, but men toppled like bowling pins, clutching at themselves. He saw Inspector Dubugue slap a hand to his left hip while he fired a revolver with his right hand.

The military honour guard jogged across the esplanade, their rifles at the ready. At a barked order from Mathis, three of the soldiers halted, put their rifles to their shoulders, aimed and fired together at the labourers. A burly, bellowing masked man wielding a double-barrelled shotgun was struck by the bullets.

Bawling in angry agony, he crashed over on his back, his finger tightening reflexively on the trigger. Flame and a spray of steel pellets smashed into a pair of his confederates. They all went down in an arm-flailing tangle.

The closer to the foot of the stairwell Watson came, the more pronounced was the tingling static charge, both in the air and at his feet. The last few people on the steps rushed down in a pell-mell wave to escape the electrical current passing through the risers. Eiffel and Tirard stumbled past Mycroft and Mathis, shouting questions in angry, pain-wracked tones.

Watson gestured to them. "We need to get as far away from the tower as possible!"

Mathis, his eyes bright with rage and fear, snarled, "Anarchist scum! This is a monstrous act! A plot to overthrow our Republic! All who are responsible for this will lose their heads!"

Mycroft pulled the man away by his coat collar. "Let's worry about keeping our own, shall we?"

As they trotted away, Watson caught a blur of movement from the stairwell. He turned, raising his revolver, although he realized he had fired the cylinder dry. He also knew the range was too great for the derringer, even if he could have drawn it from his vest pocket in time. He saw the Hephaestus Ring soldier prop the barrel of the Rattler on the hand-rail, training it on Tirard and Eiffel. Little sparks danced beneath the weapon's brass fittings.

A skein of blue-white energy suddenly sheathed the metal railing and stairs. Ragged tongues of flame spurted from the weapon in the man's grasp. All the rounds in the magazine detonated with a bone-jarring concussion. The weapon flew apart. Up to the man's wrists, his hands flew apart with it. He fell heavily and made no movement after.

As if the sight of the pyrotechnics was a signal, the hooded men began throwing down their weapons and running. The few who didn't run stopped chanting *"Pas de dieux, pas de maitres!"* and instead shouted *"Nous nous rendons!"* They raised their arms in surrender. It was the wise thing to do, since they were outnumbered by over-coated agents and the uniformed honour guard.

"Anarchist scum," growled Mathis. "We should execute them now."

"I wouldn't rush to judgment if I were you," warned Mycroft. "This chaos has all the hallmarks of a staged diversion."

A small man with sandy sideburns and wearing a tailored dark gray suit strode past, glanced their way, did a double take and paused, staring at Watson intently. "Willis? Is that you? I heard you were on leave."

Watson saw the man's notebook and guessed he was a journalist from London. Rather than continue the pointless imposture, he peeled the moustache away from his upper lip and said, "No, I'm someone else entirely."

The journalist stared at him in total confusion. Before he could reply, a deep humming pressed against their eardrums, as of a gigantic beehive. All eyes turned to the tower as crackling streams of silver-blue energy played all along its length, reaching to the uppermost levels and the spire. The intricate latticework designs glowed with a luminous mist. The milling crowd stared fixedly at the display, eyes and mouths wide in wonder.

"What is this?" Mathis demanded gruffly, as if he took personal affront. "What is happening?"

"Whatever is happening" replied Watson, "it's does not bode well."

"Watson!"

He turned to see Holmes, Loveday and Nikola Tesla hurrying toward them. Mycroft blew out a relieved sigh. "Slow but sure. Where have you been, Sherlock?"

"Saving your skins, for one thing," Holmes retorted. His and Loveday's once elegant evening clothes were torn, dirty and dusty. Both of their faces showed bruises. However, Tesla looked in much worse condition than either of them.

Holmes quickly updated everyone on the circumstances. When informed of the appearance of masked anarchists, he did not react with surprise. Waving toward the corner of the pillar, Holmes said, "Madame Koluchy is back there in an access passageway. She's badly injured, but we now know the extent of the Thunderstrike plot. Hopefully, we've managed to derail it."

"And Robur?" asked Watson. "Is he involved?"

Loveday said, "That's not a yes or no question, but something answering to his name is here on the Exposition grounds. I overheard Vonn and Madame Koluchy mention a rendezvous with the baron at the farmyard...wherever that is."

Holmes regarded her reproachfully. *"Now* you share that bit of data?"

"We've all been preoccupied saving Paris — and ourselves — for the past hour, you might recall."

"Where is Vonn?" Watson asked, hand tightening on the grip of his revolver.

"Down below and no longer our concern." Holmes turned toward Tesla. "What will happen if Robur deploys the *Terror* to trigger the teleforce reaction in the central conduit, since the accelerator is destabilized and the turbines are depowered?"

"What?" Mycroft asked, mystified.

Tesla spread his hands in a gesture of helpless frustration. "I have no idea, Mr Holmes. Madame Koluchy's plan to use the tower as a telegeodynamic transmitter was totally theoretical. If Robur succeeds with his part of the operation, nothing at all could happen or anything at all could happen."

"What?" repeated Mycroft, his tone now edged with angry impatience.

Holmes angrily stabbed a finger at the threads of energy streaking along the girders and beams of the tower. He half-shouted, "Something is happening right now, Nikola!"

"The current could bleed off harmlessly over a period of time with no power source to renew it." Tesla spoke hastily, his words tumbling over one another. "An electromagnetic pulse discharged into the conduit could conceivably jump-start the process and might — again, over a period of time — degrade the integrity of the structure by overheating it....causing the tower to melt in on itself, as Kathryn said."

Holmes spun around, surveying the surroundings, trying to fix their position in relation to Eiffel's tower. "Is there a farmyard on the grounds?"

Before anyone answered, he stiffened, staring across the esplanade at the shunter engine with three passenger carriages waiting at the railway. Little puffs of white vapour floated from the smoke-stack, indicating the boiler possessed a full head of steam. He kicked himself into a sprint. "There!"

Watson and Loveday exchanged a quick glance then chased after him. Loveday paused only an instant to snatch the umbrella from the hand of Mathis. "I'll return it," she called over her shoulder, gathering her skirt in one hand. She didn't add, *Hopefully in the same condition.*

221B: On Her Majesty's Secret Service

I am not the law, but I represent justice so far as my feeble powers go.

— Sherlock Holmes

CHAPTER 33

HOLMES, WATSON AND LOVEDAY dashed across the promenade, dodging groups of people. Mycroft shouted their names, but he did not run after them. When Holmes reached the train, he saw the carriages were almost full of passengers, seeking to leave the vicinity as rapidly as possible.

Jumping into the open cab of the little locomotive, Holmes roughly pushed the astounded engineer out of the other side. Rather than lodge a protest or argue, the man simply stood and watched as Holmes studied the gauges and controls.

When Watson and Loveday reached the train, Holmes snapped, "Watson, uncouple the carriage. We'll need as much speed as we can build."

Breathing hard, Watson positioned himself on the back of the engine and wrestled with the locking pin, straining to pull it up and out of the coupler. Loveday slid the curved handle of the umbrella through the eye of the pin and between the two of them, worked it free. The people seated in the first row of benches on the carriage shouted at them, demanding they desist.

"All aboard!" Holmes called, releasing the brake and pushing the throttle forward. The locomotive started down the tracks.

Watson and Loveday scrambled atop the little platform at the rear of the engine, ignoring the angry questions of the passengers left behind in the carriages.

The locomotive rattled and lurched as Holmes opened the throttle wider until the needle of the speedometer trembled at twenty-five. Loveday's hair flowed back in the wind. She asked, "Do you know where we're going, Mr Holmes?"

"To a point," Holmes replied, speaking loudly in order to be heard over the deep panting of the engine and the clacking of the wheels. "When Mycroft showed us the artist's map of the Exposition grounds at the Diogenes, I committed to memory the route of the Decauville rail line. I distinctly remember it ran directly alongside open areas labelled the Ministry of Agriculture and the Pont d'Iena."

Watson nodded. "Open fields would be a good place to hide the *Terror*. If seen, most people would think it's just another exhibit, probably a new piece of farming equipment."

"A field would provide a launch site for the *Terror* as well," put in Loveday.

Holmes opened the throttle all the way. As the train sped on past the Exposition's pavilions, they heard only the steady chuff of the little engine and the clatter of the iron wheels. The track curved gently toward the dark waters of the Seine. To their right, they saw a large open pasture, bordered on one side by a dozen rectangular wooden panels. Eight feet long and tilted upward at forty-five degree angles, the railway ran alongside them.

Watson asked, "What are those structures supposed to be?"

"Hen-houses," replied Holmes. "For a model poultry farm, according to a brochure. It is still under construction."

Over the sound of the engine, they heard a throbbing undertone which increased to a muffled roar. Holmes pulled back on the throttle, reducing the train's speed. He half stood up, eyes

221B: On Her Majesty's Secret Service

searching the field. At the edge closest to the riverside, a flat-roofed clapboard structure shifted as if the entire foundation had shivered. A few seconds later, the walls fell outward in a spill of lumber.

A black contoured spindle rolled forward, bouncing slightly on four tyres. The *Terror's* wings had been retracted and lay folded against the fuselage, just below the square outline of the portside hatch. Barely visible behind the glass enclosure above the long prow, they saw the silhouette of a man.

Holmes slammed the throttle to full open, and for a long moment the locomotive and the aeroship raced side-by-side. He said loudly, "I suppose it's too much to expect that any of us are armed?"

"I have a pistol," said Loveday. "But no cartridges. That's why I nicked the umbrella."

"I have a derringer," Watson declared. "With two cartridges."

"Even if a derringer could bring down the *Terror*," Holmes said, "we're not in range. I fear it's time for yet more of my signature schoolboy heroics." He held out his right hand.

"We won't even ask what you intend to do," retorted Watson sourly, digging into his vest. He produced the derringer and slid it into Holmes' palm.

"That is wise because I don't know myself."

Leaning forward, Loveday placed the curved handle of the umbrella over Holmes' forearm. "In case it rains."

He cast his friends a quick, over-the-shoulder-grin. "You do know I'm best suited for what comes next, don't you?"

Watson returned the grin. "Other than the fact that you don't have a game leg—"

"—Or are wearing a ball gown," Loveday interposed.

"—Yes," said Watson. "We do."

221B: On Her Majesty's Secret Service

Placing the derringer in his coat pocket and holding the umbrella in his right hand, Holmes balanced himself on the edge of the cab. Watson took his place at the controls. He saw the track ahead angled sharply away from the field and declared, "We're running out of rail."

Holmes nodded. "I'll return as soon as I can. We'll have lunch, something nutritious at the hotel."

"I'll make reservations for noon," Loveday said. "So don't be late."

"If I am, make sure you save my place."

Holmes left the locomotive as if launched from a catapult. He hit the ground running in a long-legged, distance-eating stride, head back and arms pumping. The pilot of the *Terror* kicked the rudder. The machine veered to the left and the nose lifted, rising skyward.

He ran up a hen-house roof, his feet gaining uncertain purchase on the upslanting plank surface. He sprinted up it as if it were a ramp. Using the topmost edge as a springboard, he bounded into the air, arms extended.

Slamming hard against the *Terror's* hull, he hooked an empennage strut with the umbrella handle and pulled himself up far enough to seize a cable connected to the wing housing. The aerocraft lurched and the fan-turbines roared.

The lift-off came smoothly and suddenly, with breath-taking swiftness. He felt little sense of motion, only a sinking sensation in the pit of his stomach. He wondered if the quick ascent could be attributed to the Cavorite mentioned by Kathryn Koluchy. To Holmes it seemed as if the earth simply vanished, replaced by patches of mist and fog.

The *Terror* inscribed a great circle. The ribbed wings slowly sprouted from the fuselage, unfolding until they popped open at full extension. The aerocraft shuddered briefly, and continued to climb.

Hugging the strut, Holmes worked his way along the fuselage and reached the hatch, set flush with the hull. After a couple of muscle-straining attempts and the aid of the umbrella, he managed to release an exterior latch and slide the door aside with little resistance. Ducking his head, he stepped inside.

Streamlined to the point of minimalism, the interior of the *Terror* was not at all like the crowded space full of pipes, gauges and other clockwork mechanisms he had imagined. In the small bridge above the prow, Holmes saw the ridiculously broad-shouldered figure of Robur standing immobile before a control console. His hands held the up-curving horns of a steering yoke. The manikin did not turn away from the glass viewport or appear to be aware of his presence.

Closing the hatch, Holmes eased forward, treading lightly on the vibrating deck plates. He saw no one else aboard, which he found both comforting and alarming.

He took another sidling step closer, and Robur's distorted voice droned, "We have been in this situation before, Holmes. Remember?"

Managing to keep the uncertainty he felt from being detected in his voice, Holmes replied, "Very clearly. I'm a little surprised that you do, however."

"Kathryn explained it all to you. I am Robur so obviously I have Robur's memories. All of them." His voice held no particular inflection, the lack of which made the effigy at the controls seem even more inhuman.

Holmes moved closer and saw the scar inflicted by Loveday's bullet still gleaming on its temple. "You have echoes of the real Robur's memories...only his monumental ego was transferred intact into this mechanical body."

The yellow glow of eyes brightened. "Silence."

221B: On Her Majesty's Secret Service

The aerocraft banked, soaring over the swiftly running Seine. Robur manipulated the control yoke and the *Terror* banked again, settling into a long, steady climb. Holmes glimpsed the loom of Eiffel's tower to the left but the fog hid it before he could ascertain if it glowed with electric current.

"Shouldn't you have waited for your man, Vonn?" Holmes asked.

"I trained Vonn. This is my machine. His presence is not necessary to complete the mission."

"It might interest you to know that the first phase of your mission has been foiled. There will be no mass electrocution on the Iron Lady today. The Hephaestus Ring has been exposed as a gang of criminals and insurrectionists. Vonn is dead, Madame Koluchy is so seriously injured she may die before the day is out. There is no reason to continue on this course of madness."

Without pause, Robur's voice said, "It is my mission. I will complete it."

"Like a spring-driven, wind-up toy soldier that can only perform a single task? Is that all you are now?"

"I am Robur the Conqueror."

"Prove it. Turn this craft about and live to conquer another day."

Robur's left hand reached out and closed over a knob-tipped lever rising from a console. He pushed it up. Directly behind where Holmes stood, a pair of deck-plates fell open with a metallic clang. A strong suction began, with a sound like a hundred tea-kettles on full boil. His hair and clothes fluttered, drawn in toward the opening.

"Look down."

Taking cautious steps, Holmes leaned forward, peering over the edge of the rectangular, three-by-four opening. He saw a small mushroom-shaped object about two feet long connected to the aerocraft's undercarriage by a web of thin wires. It appeared to be composed of a gleaming metal dome with a narrow ceramic stalk centered beneath.

"What is that thing?" he asked, speaking loudly to be heard over the rush of the wind.

"It is a pulsed voltage coil, drawn from the mind of our mutual friend, Nikola Tesla. He designed it to discharge electromagnetic energy in short bursts, creating high-voltage arcs. Once connected to the valvular conduit at the tip of the tower's spire, the pulse will engage with the accelerator. The teleforce wave will then be transmitted. The mission will be complete."

Robur's hand pulled the lever and the deck plate panels resealed, with barely a seam visible between them. "I will manoeuvre the *Terror* to link up to the conduit. Only I possess the precision and pilot's skill to perform such a task."

"There is no damned point to the task," Holmes said angrily. "Thanks to our 'mutual friend,' the teleforce generation system will not function. It has been sabotaged beyond any hope of repair."

Robur did not immediately respond. Holmes thought he heard a faint mechanical whir, followed by a series of clicks, as if the thousands of tiny relays which constituted Robur's mind struggled to process the information.

After several seconds, Robur intoned, "Care not."

Holmes stood and stared, digesting Robur's two words. Looking past him through the viewport, he saw the mist thinning. The spire of Eiffel's tower swelled in size, blue energy flashing along its joists, beams and lattices. A blast of hot rage and adrenalin threw him forward, his hands reaching for the steering yoke.

The upper half of Robur's body rotated in a complete one

hundred and eighty degree pivot. His open right hand caught Holmes on the side of the head and slapped him across the cockpit. The motions were swift and effortless.

Holmes slammed against the bulkhead, pain radiating out from his back and the rear of his skull. The daylight coming through the viewport dimmed. The unexpected force of the blow jarred him all the way down to his toes. He struggled to retain a grip on consciousness.

He felt the trickle of blood from an abrasion on his right cheek — the same one Robur had fractured two years before. Blinking away the translucent amoebas floating across his vision, he glared at Robur, hating him. He felt suddenly convinced the man's evil and egomania had indeed transcended the limitations of flesh and were preserved in an automatonic body for all eternity.

Pushing himself away from the bulkhead, Holmes feinted to the right and caught Robur's left arm at the elbow and wrist. He tried to twist it up behind automaton's back, but the effort felt like trying to bend an oak log. Robur again spun at the waist, easily pulling away from Holmes' grasp, his right arm coming around hard and fast. Holmes ducked the backhand aimed at his face, but Robur's arms locked around him, squeezing the air from his lungs. He felt himself lifted bodily from the floor, the toes of his shoes scrabbling on the deck.

The tower outside the aerocraft wavered in Holmes' eyes. He could not breathe. He brought up his arms to break Robur's grip, to wrench apart the excruciatingly painful hug. Robur's metal reinforced limbs pressed him to its chest and crushed the derringer in Holmes' breast pocket against the cartilage of his rib cage.

Although Robur's lips could not move, Holmes imagined them lifting in a cruel smile as he stated flatly, "You realize if I increase the pressure, your ribs will puncture your lungs and you will choke to death on your own blood."

Holmes did not — could not — reply. He could barely breathe. He felt panic touch him, realizing too late he had underestimated the manikin's physical abilities. He heard a roaring in his ears, and he tried again to break Robur's double-armed hold, straining with all his strength against it.

Recalling his bartitsu training, he stopped resisting, exhaled and let everything go limp. His entire body sagged. The tactic was too sudden and unexpected for an automaton to react quickly. Before Robur could tighten its hold, Holmes slipped down and out, under its arms.

Biting at air, he rolled to one side, cramming himself into a corner. Robur spun around on its wheeled disk, eyes blazing as they fixed Holmes' position on the bridge. Holmes reached for the derringer, drawing it from his pocket with a ripping of fabric.

Robur rotated, coming toward him. Its raspy voice crooned, *"Meurs, bâtard."*

Holmes remembered the same words Robur had screamed at him that long-ago night in Cornwall: "Die, you bastard!"

Levelling the little pistol, Holmes sighted down its short length and squeezed the trigger. With a sound like a distant finger-snap, the bullet struck the knob atop the control lever and ricocheted away, piercing the glass of the foreport. The deck-plate panels fell open.

A pattern of white cracks spread through the glass. A corner section of the port blew inward with a scream of air. Sharp-edged fragments shattered against the bulkheads. The sudden influx of wind pushed Robur forward. The disk on which it stood tipped over the lip of the of the opening. Overbalanced by the ponderous weight, Robur's body teetered for an instant, then toppled, much like a tree sawn through at the base of the trunk.

The prominent bearded chin struck the edge of the opening, the combined force of impact and mass tearing its great head and neck free from its shoulders. The grey-uniformed body continued falling, ripping through the support wires beneath, and carrying the pulse coil with it.

Robur's head remained on the deck, rolling slightly from side-to-side, staring at Holmes with fury-filled yellow eyes. Then by swift degrees, the glow faded and the eyes became blank pieces of moulded glass again.

In sudden revulsion, Holmes kicked the conqueror's faux skull through the opening. "Tit," he whispered hoarsely, "for tat."

The ship suddenly bumped and swayed around him, his eardrums compressing with the howl of the wind as more pieces of the foreport broke away. Holmes staggered to his feet, dragging himself to the control board and the steering yoke. The spire completely filled the frame of the port, the black iron latticework interwoven with blue threads of electric energy. Moving on instinct, he clutched the yoke and turned it sharply to the right.

The deck underfoot tilted as the *Terror* heeled over on the starboard wing, just as the tip struck the spire a glancing blow. A violent concussion slammed through the hull at the same instant a flash of blue lightning dazzled him. A ball of light exploded on the wing. For a shaved sliver of a second, Holmes glimpsed a tangle of electrical current streaking along the prow.

Smoke and the odour of metal turning molten filled the cramped cockpit. Holmes kept his hands on the controls as the aeroship dropped, wobbling violently. The *Terror* went into a long corkscrew spin. The centrifugal force hurled him tight against a bulkhead. Gusts of air shrieked up through the opening on the deck.

He heard the muted roar of the engine and then the protracted groan of ruptured metal. That sound was followed by a high-pitched squeal as the strain on the extended wings bent them backward.

Through the broken glass in the port he glimpsed a spread of dark waters whirling below. Straining to move, he drew in a deep breath as The *Terror* struck the surface of the Seine at a ninety-degree angle. The jolt of impact felt as if the ship had received a head-on blow from a medieval battering ram. He braced both feet against the control console as the prow cleaved through the river and beneath the surface. The vast, bubbling crash of cold water flooding through the viewport swept Holmes up and around the bridge like a cork caught in a maelstrom.

The light grew very dim as the ship began to sink, but the violent buffeting of the water eased. Holmes righted himself, resisting the impulse to struggle through either the opening in the floor or the foreport until the water pressure equalized. He waited until the pounding of blood in his temples and the fire in his chest became intolerable. In semi-darkness, he found the deck opening and wriggled his way through it. He kicked upward, pulling himself along the *Terror's* fuselage. When his hands encountered the umbrella still hanging on a strut, he grabbed it.

His head broke the surface in the shadow of the tail section of the *Terror*. He forced himself not to cough and gasp as he cleared his vision. Pieces of the starboard wing floated around him. Treading water in a circle, he saw the Pont des Invalides bridge only a score of yards away. A short distance past it, Eiffel's tower loomed gigantic against the cloud-streaked tapestry of the sky.

The Iron Lady no longer glowed with a blue-white radiance. Although he abhorred guesswork, he felt sure the electrified tower had acted like a gigantic closed circuit and when the *Terror* struck the spire, the wing broke the flow of the current.

Pedestrians on the bridge gaped in wide-eyed amazement at

the aerocraft and the lone man floating in the river holding a furled umbrella. Ignoring their calls, he swam away from the bridge, noting that the water temperature wasn't cold enough to be dangerous but it did not feel comfortable, either.

By swimming steadily for five minutes, he reached the splintery pilings of an ancient stone quay. He feared he would be too fatigued to climb one of them, especially burdened by the drag of his wet clothes and the umbrella. Then he heard Loveday Brooke call out, "Thank you for remembering to return Monsieur Mathis' umbrella, Mr Holmes."

Looking up, he saw Loveday and Watson kneeling at the end of the quay, reaching their hands out for him. Holmes stretched up the umbrella so Watson could secure a grip on the handle. "Despite the lack of rain, it turned out to be more useful than I thought, Miss Brooke."

"Brollies always are," she replied. "Are you all right?"

He was aware of various aches and flares of pain all over his body but decided not to mention them until he had been fished out of the Seine. "It seems so."

Between Loveday and Watson, Holmes was heaved up and out of the river. He was so exhausted, all he could do was sit and stare at the black cylinder of the *Terror* projecting up from the surface of the Seine. It had not sunk any further. He assumed its apparent buoyancy was due to the Cavorite aboard.

Watson and Loveday sat down on either side of him. Eyeing the abraded, bruised skin on Holmes' face, Watson said, "It appears you dropped your guard again."

"This time," Holmes replied, "I wasn't cheated out of a tit-for-tat. How did you two get here so quickly?"

"Fortunately the rail line followed the riverside," said Watson. "It brought us to within a quarter mile of the bridge just as the *Terror* went down. Your doing, I take it."

"We ran cross-country the rest of the way," Loveday said, ruefully eyeing the torn and soiled hem of her gown. "I hope Mycroft isn't in charge of expense accounts."

"All the police and intelligence officers in Paris will descend on us in a few minutes," said Watson. "Even with Mycroft's influence I imagine we'll be occupied for the rest of the day."

Holmes nodded. "So...lunch while we can?"

Loveday smiled. "That depends on our appetites. Mine would improve if we knew what happened to Robur."

"He lost his head," Holmes said bluntly. "Quite, quite literally. Details later. I suppose both it and his body can be found at the bottom of the Seine if anyone cares to trawl for them."

"Decapitated." Watson smiled grimly. "An appropriate demise, him being of the French aristocracy and all."

Holmes chuckled. "A distinct touch, that."

"Justice has been done, then...for Deirdre."

Holmes did not reply.

"Nikola will be happy to learn the future is safe," Loveday said.

Holmes lifted a shoulder in a shrug. "That task is more up to him than to us."

Shading her eyes with a hand, Loveday gazed out at the broken pieces of the *Terror* and the fuselage rising above the water like a tombstone. She recited softly, " 'The grave's a fine and private place, but none I think there do embrace.'"

Holmes smiled sadly. "Miss Dalton would appreciate the irony." After a thoughtful moment, he added, " 'Had we but world enough and time.' "

He closed his eyes.

221B: On Her Majesty's Secret Service

A man is only as good as those he loves.

— Mary Morstan-Watson

CHAPTER 34

1st May, Camberwell, South London, St. Mark's Church

THE WEDDING PARTY arrived at the chapel a bit before ten o' clock in the morning. Wednesday weddings weren't common, but neither were the bride and groom. Fortunately, the weather was mild and the sky sunny.

Holmes, Watson and Mrs Hudson arrived together in one carriage and Mary in another, accompanied by her matron and maid of honour—Mrs Cecil Forrester and Miss Loveday Brooke. Guests had already been summoned by the pastor to take the pews. There were not many on the groom's side — Mycroft, Gervais Lestrade and Michael Stamford, a friend from Watson's days at St Bartholomew's. Mary's guests were limited to less than a dozen people, mainly the Forrester family and their domestic staff. A handful of other people had been invited, but sent their regrets.

Mrs Hudson had earlier volunteered to take the place of the organist, since the regular one was not available at such an inconvenient day and hour. She played the proper mood music, despite her unfamiliarity with the keyboard. Her rendition of Handel's "Viscount Envoy" held a few flat and missed notes. Holmes, sitting beside Loveday in the front pew, winced but voiced no criticism.

The Anglican vicar, a white-haired elderly gentleman named Paget was soft-spoken but efficient. He made sure all the proper papers and licenses were in order before indicating the wedding service could commence. Watson and Holmes took their places, both very neat and trim. Watson wore his crimson-jacketed military uniform and Holmes an elegant black morning suit with the lavender vest and tie Mrs Hudson had suggested.

When Mrs Hudson played the fanfare of Wagner's "Bridal Chorus," Mary swept down the aisle with Mycroft on her arm. Since Mary had no living male relatives and Mrs Forrester was a widow, Mycroft had been inveighed upon to give her away. Mrs Forrester and Loveday flanked them, with two of the teen-aged daughters holding the train of Mary's white satin dress.

With the sunlight shafting in through the high, arched stained-glass windows, Loveday and Holmes joined Watson and Mary before the altar table. Vicar Paget recited the vows service from the Book of Common Worship, which fortunately were straightforward and blessedly short. Holmes experienced only a few seconds of consternation when he had difficulty producing the ring from his vest pocket, but no one commented — or laughed.

The vows and rings exchanged, Watson lifted Mary's lace veil and kissed her. After the registry was signed and legally witnessed, Vicar Paget introduced the assemblage to Doctor and Mr. John Watson. As Mrs Hudson fingered the proper organ keys for the exit processional, the younger Forrester children threw confetti, despite having been expressly forbidden to do so by their mother the day before.

The guests congregated in the churchyard, facing Cogburn Road. Mrs Forrester passed around champagne, and toasts were given. Even the vicar imbibed. Mary and Watson mingled, talking about ordinary, everyday things. Mary's large blue eyes sparkled as she laughed and chatted.

"John and I chose St. Mark's for the ceremony, since it is small and intimate," she said to Inspector Lestrade. "We have no living family members and our social circle is small, so there was no reason for a larger church. Neither of us wish to draw attention to ourselves."

Mrs Hudson asked, "Have you still not decided on a honeymoon destination, child?"

Mary chuckled. "I mentioned to John that the Paris World's Fair might be fun, but he seems very unenthusiastic."

"I can't imagine why," Loveday said with an enigmatic smile.

Watson frowned at her but said nothing. He excused himself to say his goodbyes to Stamford and to speak privately to Lestrade who waited for him at the gate. After a word of congratulations, the small, wiry man said, "Gabriel wrote me how much he enjoyed meeting you."

"That's not how I remember it," Watson replied. "But send him my regards, nevertheless."

Lestrade chuckled and moved on. "We'll miss you at the Yard, Doctor."

Mycroft stepped over, eyeing Watson's face closely. He ran a forefinger over his own upper lip, he said, "Trying for a real one again?"

Watson sighed wearily. "I had a real one for years. I shaved it as men often do. Now I'm regrowing it — again, as men often do."

"Hopefully you won't be mistaken for Hubert Willis a second time. By the way, I received a wire from Rene Mathis yesterday...he mentioned there is talk of awarding 221B the Legion of Honour for your efforts to save the Republic."

" 'Efforts'?" Watson echoed. "I suggest that we all succeeded — you and Monsieur Mathis included."

Holmes joined them. "Succeeded at what?"

"Saving the Republic of France," replied Watson. "We might receive commendations for our 'efforts.' "

"Ah," said Holmes. "A medal would look quite toney on the mantelpiece in Baker Street."

"Certainly more picturesque than a jack-knife or bullet-pocks in the wall," said Watson dourly.

"Depends on the commendation, I suppose. Have you and Mary decided where you're going on your honeymoon?"

"She's pushing for the Paris Exposition."

"You told her you'd just been there, didn't you?"

"I did. On business for the Crown."

Mycroft regarded him disapprovingly. "I hope you didn't provide details."

"None of any note. At this juncture, matters of marriage will take precedence, not matters of state secrets."

"Like your honeymoon," Holmes stated.

Watson swallowed the champagne left in his glass. "Among others, but that subject is currently at the top of the list."

With a clatter of hooves and rumble of steel-rimmed wheels, an open carriage drawn by two white horses clad in polished, patent-leather harness rolled up before the gate. Looping garlands made of intertwined ribbons and flowers festooned the sides and rear. The driver in the box wore a bright red jacket and gold-trimmed top hat.

Consulting his watch, Holmes said, "Your honeymoon chariot has arrived, surprisingly on time."

Watson stared at it for a handful of seconds then fixed Holmes with an incredulous stare. "I didn't arrange for this."

Holmes shrugged. "Part of the best man's duties, isn't it?"

"No, not really. Who did the decorating? Mrs Hudson?"

"Actually, Miss Brooke is the designer and craftswoman. Mrs Hudson enjoyed some input, I imagine."

Loveday, Mary, Mrs Forrester and Mrs Hudson came to the gate. Mary stared at the carriage and laughed. "Oh, John, it's beautiful...it will be like travelling in a wheeled florist's shop."

"Holmes's doing," said Watson. "So much for not drawing attention to ourselves."

"Thank you, Sherlock." Mary embraced him and after a second of hesitation, he put tentative arms around her.

He whispered into her ear, "Take care of him. He is the best and bravest man I have ever known."

She whispered back, "A man is only as good as those he loves."

As he disengaged, he said, "The chariot will take you and Wat — John — to wherever you want to go in this world. Paris or Pekin. My gift to you both."

Farewell hugs and kisses were shared all around. Watson shook the hand of Mycroft and kissed Loveday's cheek. He helped Mary aboard the carriage and swiftly turned to Holmes, extending his right hand. "Mr Holmes."

Holmes took his hand and shook it hard. "Doctor Watson."

Their eyes met. They both smiled and nodded at the same time. Watson climbed aboard the carriage, careful not dislodge the roses. He gave an instruction to the driver, and the coach started off. After the farewells, the guests began drifting away. Mrs Forrester offered to drop Mrs Hudson back at Baker Street.

When only Holmes, Mycroft and Loveday remained in the churchyard, Holmes turned toward his brother. "It's been a month," he said without preamble. "I assume there has been no recent news about the whereabouts of Madame Koluchy or any other member of the Hephaestus Ring."

With an edge of impatient asperity in his voice, Mycroft said, "Obviously that is the case or I would have told you. The French government has expended much time, effort and money on either explaining away or outright suppressing the news of what happened on the 31st of March. The Exposition opens in less than a week, and they're on tenterhooks, fearing another disruption on opening day...this one much more public and destructive. My office receives several cables a day from Whitehall and the Deuxieme Bureau, querying and fretting. "

Loveday said, "Their anxiety is understandable but most likely all agents of the Ring are too busy finding bolt-holes to risk drawing attention to themselves. What allies they might have had in officialdom are of little use to them now."

Mycroft grunted thoughtfully. "I've expressed as much to Mathis but their fear level remains high, particularly since no piece of the Robur automaton has yet to be recovered from the Seine. Madame Koluchy seems to have vanished."

"And her Analytical Engine?" Loveday asked.

"No sign. It was missing from the Hall of Machinery."

"The French authorities have custody of the *Terror*," pointed out Holmes. "And presumably whatever marvels they laid claim to when they raided Madame Koluchy's home and offices. That should keep them quite busy."

Mycroft's lips twitched a wry half-smile. "I understand Monsieur Eiffel was so enchanted by the effect of electrical current on his Iron Lady, he now wants to drape the entire tower, top to bottom, in lights. He's consulted Nikola Tesla about the feasibility."

"I thought Nikola had returned to America," Loveday said, "to continue his experiments in telegeodynamics."

"Regardless." Mycroft cast a challenging glance toward Holmes. "We should remain vigilant."

Holmes arched a sardonic eyebrow in response. "By that do you mean 221B should be on alert?"

"I do."

"Both Miss Brooke and I have our own agencies, you know. And with Watson no longer involved in a meaningful way, 221B is spread a bit too thin to be an on-call service."

"Mycroft, I appreciate you intervening with Ebenezer on my behalf," Loveday said, "but surely you have other agents whom you can trust."

"None with your experience and expertise dealing with the bizarre," Mycroft replied with a smile.

"What about that Sexton Blake fellow?" asked Holmes.

"I mainly rely upon clerks with guns."

"In that case, you should consider updating Her Majesty's Secret Service recruitment standards...preparing for the future as recommended by the Hephaestus Ring." Holmes cast his gaze down the street. His eyes narrowed and his shoulders stiffened. "I may be too busy with my own mission to focus on the business of the Crown."

Loveday and Mycroft followed his gaze and saw a lean man striding purposefully down the sidewalk toward them. The brim of his slouch hat cast much of his face into shadow, but they could make out the ginger tint of his side whiskers. He carried a square package under his left arm and a blackthorn walking stick in the other.

Loveday slid her hand into her reticule as the man approached. When he was within a few yards, Holmes stepped forward, raising a hand in greeting. "Hullo, Cuthbert. You're looking well."

Cuthbert Rubadue's scarred face twisted into a grimace that was either a forced smile or a scowl. "I'm improvin'."

He tapped the brim of his hat with his cane. The white edge of bandage peeked out from beneath it. "Like you said, Holmes, the cut wasn't deep but 'twill leave a nasty scar."

"A plus in your line of work," Holmes said. He nodded toward the brown-paper wrapped package. "What have you got there?"

"What Mr Zaharoff promised you," he replied. "I'm to tell you that it squares the business 'twixt you and he."

"I'll be the final judge of that," said Holmes, reaching out his hand.

Rubadue placed the package onto his palm. Holmes hefted it, as he were gauging the weight of a cut of meat. "Seems a bit light."

The Scotsman shrugged. "I don't know what it is nor do I want to. Mr Zaharoff keeps his word."

Mycroft snorted disdainfully. "So do I. Tell him to stay out of the way of the Secret Service from herein out or I'll see him hanged."

"Tell him yourself, sir." Rubadue nodded toward Loveday and touched his hat with a forefinger. "Miss."

He turned and marched away, resolutely not looking back.

Tearing away a bit of the wrapping paper from a corner of the bundle, Holmes thumbed through bound ream of foolscap. Most of the pages bore type-written lines of text. Loveday peered over his shoulder and saw one word repeated several times.

"Moriarty," she said. "Professor Moriarty is your mission?"

"Perhaps more than one," Holmes answered cryptically, tucking the package under an arm.

Mycroft rolled his eyes but said only, "I need to return to the Diogenes. I still have many daily reports to digest." He beckoned to a carriage parked a bit down the lane. The driver snapped the reins and the pair of horses trotted forward.. "Shall I drop you two somewhere?"

Holmes shook his head. "No, thank you. It's such a pleasant day, I think I'll walk a bit."

Loveday smiled. "Same here. I could use a break from Lynch Court business. Dreadfully dull at the moment." She glanced at Holmes. "Perhaps we can take a stroll through Peckham Rye Common."

The eyes of Holmes were both vacant and thoughtful. He said, "As you wish, Miss Brooke."

Mycroft tipped his hat to Loveday and climbed aboard the coach. It started off with creak of springs and a jingle of harness. Holmes didn't move until Loveday presented him with her arm. "Shall we, Mr Holmes?"

Holmes slipped her arm through his. As they walked along the path, under the spreading pink and white boughs of cherry blossom trees, Loveday said, "You seem strangely somber on such a celebratory day."

"Somber? Perhaps a little. I was thinking about absent friends. One in particular."

"Deirdre?"

"She would have enjoyed playing a bridesmaid."

Loveday nodded. "Or a bride."

"I suppose, if the part called for it."

After a moment's silence, Loveday asked, "Will you miss him? John, I mean."

"I have grown accustomed to his presence in my life. After a time, I'm sure I will grow accustomed to his absence."

Loveday shook her head in good-natured exasperation. "You're such a sentimentalist, Mr Holmes."

"Pot meet kettle." Holmes smiled ruefully. "Both you and I find the emotional qualities antagonistic to clear reasoning, Miss Brooke. As much as we — or others — might wish otherwise. Would you not agree?"

Loveday presented the image of seriously pondering the query. After a moment, she said, "I agree that you and I do a creditable job of playing the part."

"Be the part, Miss Brooke."

Loveday tightened her hold on his arm. "I prefer to anticipate, Mr Holmes."

Holmes' smile widened. "And adapt, if the part calls for it."

EPILOGUE

CUTHBERT RUBADUE TURNED right two blocks beyond the churchyard. He waited at the corner of Cogburn Road for a count of sixty. When he was fairly certain he hadn't been followed, he continued down the narrow side-lane to the black brougham waiting at the mouth of an alley. Nodding to the driver seated in the box, he squeezed between the alley wall and the big horse. He rapped sharply on the coach door.

A slim, green-gloved hand thrust aside the dark red curtain over the window. "You made the delivery?" The woman's voice was a low, strained half-whisper.

Rubadue took off his hat. Bandages swathed the top of his head. "Yes, m'lady. Mr Holmes is none the wiser, but seems like he expected more than what he got."

"That doesn't matter." The woman withdrew her hand and a few seconds later, it reappeared holding a small cloth pouch closed by a drawstring. "Here are ten sovereigns, Cuthbert. You've done well. Return to Basil. I will be in touch."

Rubadue took the pouch from her hand. He did not open it to count the coins. The faint clink of gold against gold was sufficient. He carefully settled his hat back onto his head and crab-walked out of the alley.

Kathryn Koluchy drew the curtain closed and leaned back against the cushioned seat, a motion made awkward by the tilt of her Duchess-of-Devonshire hat. A dark veil fell from the brim, concealing her face. She was able to see well enough through the lace to observe the man sitting opposite her. A large book lay open on his lap. He ran his right hand over a page before turning to the next, as if he were reading the typed text by absorbing the words through his palm.

"Fascinating reading, Professor?" she asked in a hoarsely

"Very."

"Because it is all about you?"

"No, and that is the problem." He lifted his gaze. "Zaharoff was frightfully thorough. I can only hope the false report your man Rubadue gave to Holmes will pass muster — at least temporarily."

"Basil entrusted Cuthbert to deliver the report to Holmes," she replied. "I doubt Holmes will question its authenticity much less suspect a switch for quite some time."

"For the sake of your sanctuary," Moriarty said, still running his hand over the pages, "you should pray that is the case. It is unlikely the heat of the search for you and the rest of the Ring's Echelon will cool in the foreseeable future...probably not until closing day of the Exposition in October."

Madame Koluchy repressed the urge to utter a dismissive comment. When she looked into James Moriarty's eyes, she saw the glint of implacable cruelty in their pale depths, glimmering like the fires of a furnace that had only been banked, not extinguished.

Although of medium height, Moriarty was so excessively thin he appeared taller. His hair was cropped so short it resembled a grey skullcap of bristles. His raw-boned, leathery face was deeply seamed, as if it had been lashed by desert wind and cooked by the sun until only bone, sinew and a layer of tight, parchment-thin flesh were left.

Reaching up, he knocked sharply on the ceiling of the coach and said loudly, "Home. Past St. Mark's."

The brougham lurched forward. Speaking loudly to be heard over the clopping of iron-shod hooves on cobblestones, Moriarty said, "I believe it is nearly time for your scheduled Herakleophorbia treatment, is it not?"

"Noon."

"Hopefully you are nearing the end of the regimen and your burns are healing properly. The odour of the stuff is objectionable. If I had known my London headquarters would be turned into a field hospital, I might have reconsidered taking you in. But Sebastian insisted."

"The Colonel is perceptive. He can smell a rare opportunity when it is presented to him."

"Just as I can smell the Herakleophorbia," Moriarty said scornfully. "The worth of your Analytical Engine has yet to be proven." He closed the book on his lap with a forceful clap. "In any event, having this file in my hands will buy the House of Moriarty a bit of time."

The coach swayed as it took a corner. Madame Koluchy asked, "Buy time for a specific purpose?"

"Of course."

"Would you care to share what that might be?"

Moriarty did not answer. Instead, a half-smile creased his lips. He leaned forward, pulling aside the curtain just enough to permit a glimpse of the street. Madame Koluchy peered out as the brougham rumbled past Loveday Brooke and Sherlock Holmes, strolling arm-in-arm on the sidewalk.

"What a charming picture." James Moriarty shook his head in feigned sadness and murmured, "Dear me, Mr Holmes." He let the curtain fall closed. He sighed, staring directly at the woman sitting opposite him. "Let us hope those two young people will enjoy the spring weather while they can. We wish them well, do we not?"

Kathryn Koluchy whispered, "Dear me, Miss Brooke." She bit out the words. "Dear me."

221B: On Her Majesty's Secret Service

Author's Afterword

In my nearly forty years as a professional writer, I've learned a lot...one enduring lesson is that a good core idea always remains a good core idea. One of those core ideas started with the old "What if?" approach. In this instance it was "What if Sherlock Holmes and Dr Watson had actually operated as agents of Her Majesty's Secret Service?"

That is not a startlingly original "What if?" since in several canonical stories by Sir Arthur Conan Doyle, Holmes and Watson work directly and indirectly in the service of the Crown. In "His Last Bow," the final story in the official chronology, Holmes, Watson and Mrs Hudson are all engaged in a mission to expose and apprehend a German spy on the eve of World War I.

Not only is the mystery element negligible, but the story is one of the two Sir Arthur wrote in third person instead of the usual first person narration provided by Watson.

Sir Arthur Conan Doyle by way of Ian Fleming seemed like an interesting idea to explore — one day. Like most professional writers, I had far more ideas than the time or the energy to develop them. Despite my lifelong love for the work of Sir Arthur and his immortal creations, I back-burnered the concept, as I had so many others.

Fast forward through creating/writing scores of comics stories and more than fifty novels onward to January of 2017... my wife Melissa Martin-Ellis and I retired to Ireland, and so I could at last pick and choose writing projects without worrying how I was going to keep the lights on.

My brain — that old thing — kept returning to the Holmes and Watson as secret agents concept I'd crafted many years before. I concluded it was still a workable idea. Because I'm a very visual writer, I at first planned it as a graphic novel, but soon realized that such a format would be too unwieldy for the story I had in mind.

I wondered if I could apply a tonal quality similar to my popular and long-running *Outlanders* novel series — a sense of enhanced realism, nudging science-fiction but not crossing the line into fantasy. In order to emulate that quality, I determined to introduce new characters into the Holmes and Watson dynamic and employ a third person omniscient narrative form, rather than Watson's first person point of view.

Some years before I had discovered the stories featuring Miss Loveday Brooke, Lady Detective created by Catherine Louisa Pirkis. Like Sherlock Holmes, Loveday was a private investigator, but unlike Holmes, she was employed full-time by an established London detective agency. Loveday therefore was the first female *professional* investigator in English literature, not a talented amateur, which was the standard for women protagonists in Victorian Age crime fiction.

Loveday was an engaging heroine, quick-witted and a little acerbic, definitely far ahead of her time, and I've always been surprised so little has been done with her since her initial peak of popularity. I decided to make her the third member of the 221B team and rather to my surprise, the interplay worked very well.

As for the plot, I chose the Paris World Fair of 1889, The Exposition Universelle, as the centrepiece. The Exposition was notable for many reasons, primarily because of the unveiling of the Eiffel Tower, the tallest man-made structure in the world — until 1930, and the opening of the Chrysler Building.

The Exposition also served as a public acknowledgement that the world was changing, particularly in the sudden surge in science and technology, with the message the old ways could no longer be relied upon. With the dawn of the 20th century barely a decade away, many so-called technologists feared European cultures would not be up to the challenges facing them. Inventors like Edison and Tesla were but two of the many visionaries who rose to the forefront during that time.

Of course, there are always those who wish to exploit the creations of others, and so I crafted a mix of adversaries from various and sundry sources. I put them together under the umbrella designation of the Hephaestus Ring and gave them free rein for their deviltry.

I chose to loosely follow the chronology of the Canon as put down by William Baring-Gould in his classic *Sherlock Holmes of Baker Street,* the first "biography" of Holmes. The book remains my favourite piece of Sherlockiana, and the timeline contained therein worked within the context of the story I wanted to tell.

The dating was important partly due to my wish to present Holmes and Watson as young(ish) energetic men, in their thirties. Too often in pastiches and certainly cinematic ideations, the tendency is to present the pair as locked in perpetual middle or late middle-age. In reality, they were at their most active while in their late twenties and through their thirties. Old duffers in their tweed jackets harrumphing and fumbling with their pipes would not have fit the action-oriented story I envisioned.

As it is, *221B: On Her Majesty's Secret Service* is a novel I wish I had written years ago. I'm not quite sure why I feel that way, but when in doubt, I refer back to what I call the Rex Stout Dictum: "If I'm not having any fun writing a book, no one will have any fun reading it."

I can't think of a better explanation than that.

Mark Ellis
County Cork, Ireland
May 2025

221B: On Her Majesty's Secret Service
Who and What They Are.

Loveday Brooke was created by Catherine Louisa Pirkis. *The Experiences of Loveday Brooke, Lady Detective* first appeared in serialized form in Ludgate Monthly in 1893.

Her adventures were very well-received by the reading public, although as compelling mysteries they do not amount to much. The cases assigned to Loveday are the standard of the day — upper class robberies, murder, and an heiress involved in a rather silly marriage fraud. In fact, chapters seven and nine of *221B: On Her Majesty's Secret Service* are a slightly rewritten and repurposed version of the latter story, originally published as "Drawn Daggers."

Madame Koluchy made her debut in *The Brotherhood of the Seven Kings,* a ten-part serial by L.T. Meade and Robert Eustace, published in *The Strand* from January through October of 1898. "L. T. Meade" was the pseudonym of Elizabeth Thomasina Meade Smith (1844-1914) and "Robert Eustace" was the alias of Eustace Robert Barton (1854-1943).

The Brotherhood of the Seven Kings is a secret society led by the beautiful and charming Madame Katherine Koluchy. She is described as "a scientist of no mean attainments." Of course, she is thoroughly evil and the mastermind behind a variety of unnamed wicked crimes.

As a worker of miracle cures she insinuates herself into London's high society and becomes the talk of the town, the rage of the season, the great specialist, the great consultant."

Over the course of the ten-part tale, Katherine Koluchy

perpetrates various crimes in order to carry out her goals, which includes luring enemies into her secret lair in order to murder them with an overdose of x-rays. When the police finally to try to arrest her, Madame Koluchy apparently kills herself in a furnace.

The Brotherhood of the Seven Kings is interesting in a historical context, presenting the first female criminal mastermind in English crime fiction.

Robur the Conqueror/Baron Maupertuis are two characters combined into one. In Sir Arthur Conan Doyle's "The Reigate Squires," Watson alludes to the terrible toll Holmes suffered while defeating the baron and his "colossal schemes" which involved the Netherlands-Sumatra Company. Watson offers no further details.

In "The Adventure of the Norwood Builder," he refers to the "shocking affair of the Dutch Steamship *Friesland*, which so nearly cost us both our lives" and again, Watson declines to provide details. Pairing the untold tales of the Netherlands-Sumatra company with that of the *Friesland* seemed a natural combination.

I decided the baron is actually Robur the Conqueror, the central character of two novels written by Jules Verne—the eponymous *Robur the Conqueror* and the much later sequel, *Master of the World*. The first appeared as a serial in a French language journal in 1886, and the second was published in book form in 1904.

In his inaugural appearance, Robur resembles Verne's earlier anti-hero Captain Nemo from *Twenty Thousand Leagues Under The Seas* — a before-his-time technological genius. Although something of an embittered egomaniac he is presented as basically sympathetic.

By the time of *Master of the World,* Robur is a full-fledged super-villain. The reasons for the change in his character between the novels are never addressed. His airship in *Robur the Conqueror* is named the *Albatross* and is essentially an advanced model of a Zeppelin.

Conversely, the *Terror* in *Master of the World* comes across as a dark multi-purpose prototype of the 1960s "Supermarionation" TV series, *Supercar*. As the theme song went, "It can journey anywhere." In the case of the *Terror*, that wasn't a good thing.

Professor Mirzarbeau appeared in *The Violet Flame,* a 1899 novel by Fred T. Jane. In it, Professor Mirzarbeau, a disreputable astronomer, discovers a cosmic radiation he names the "violet flame".

Mirzarbeau is not only disreputable, he is also despicable, much like the title character in the Despicable Me films...both in attitude and appearance. He builds devices that can manipulate the destructive energy of violet radiation and his first act is to vaporize Waterloo Station in London. Before the novel is over, he seizes control of England and creates a comet made of the Violet Flame and threatens to destroy the world with it.

The Violet Flame is notable for being one of the first novels to feature a power-mad scientist who threatens to destroy the planet if his demands are not met. As such, Professor Mirzarbeau is the precursor to tyrannical scientist characters that became a staple of pulp fiction.

Colonel Sebastian Moran was introduced by Sir Arthur Conan Doyle in "The Adventure of the Empty House," although it was revealed he and Holmes had met before. A former Army officer, albeit one retired under a cloud, Moran found lucrative employment as Professor Moriarty's chief of staff. Holmes referred to him as "the second most dangerous man in London."

221B: On Her Majesty's Secret Service

Prince Dakkar is of course Captain Nemo, the anti-hero of Verne's *Twenty Thousand Leagues Under The Seas* and *The Mysterious Island*. Dakkar, using the alias of Nemo (which means "nobody" in Latin) is a genius and wreaks havoc about the world in his highly advanced submarine, the *Nautilus*.

Silvanus Cavor is the pivotal character of HG Wells' *First Men in the Moon* (1900), a reclusive self-proclaimed physicist. He develops a material he has named "cavorite" which can cancel the force of gravity. Lacking a first name in the original work, I took it upon myself to christen him "Silvanus."

Julius Wendigee is mentioned briefly in the last chapter of *First Men in the Moon* as a Dutch electrician, who has been "experimenting with certain apparatus akin to the apparatus used by Mr Tesla".

Herakleophorbia IV is a food growth hormone introduced in HG Wells' 1904 novel, *Food of the Gods*. Also known as "Boom-food," the substance can speed up the healing process and increase cellular growth in plants, animals and eventually humans.

Mephisto, the Chess-playing Android was real and enjoyed a brief vogue in Europe. It/he even had his own fan club in England. It was created by Charles Godfrey Gumpel, a manufacturer of artificial limbs. "Android" was the favoured term applied to human-like automata such as Mephisto. "Robot" wouldn't come into common usage until years later in *R.U.R.* (Rossom's Universal Robots), a 1920 play by Karl Capek.

To this day, it is not known how Mephisto operated, although it seems clear it was controlled remotely through a wireless radio system. Strangely enough, after Mephisto was on display at the Paris Exposition, it was dismantled and never seen again.

The Analytical Engine was a digital general purpose computer designed by mathematician and computer pioneer Charles Babbage (with the help of Ada Lovelace's algorithms). The technology did not exist at the time to build the machine, although he assembled a small part of it before his death in 1871. In the years following his demise, many scientists attempted to complete the engine — including his son Henry — but most were again stymied by its complexity and the lack of engineering technology.

The Telekino was a pioneering device invented by Leonardo Torres Quevedo.With it, Quevedo established the operating principles of the modern remote control using using Hertzian radio waves.

Phantom Airships was a phenomenon that thousands of people in the late 19th and early 20th witnessed; sightings of mystery aircraft similar to, but markedly different, from dirigibles. The typical reports were night-time observations of unidentified lights in the sky, flying in such a way as to suggest they were attached to an airborne craft. Contemporary consensus of opinion was that the phantom airships were the inventions of private geniuses who were test-flying or withholding their aeronautic creations from public.

Skibbereen was known as the epicentre of revolutionary sentiment and activity in West County Cork, often referred to as the "Cradle of Fenianism." In "His Last Bow", Holmes assumes the persona of an Irish-American rebel by the name of 'Altamont' in order to penetrate a German spy ring just before the outbreak of World War One. In this role, Holmes states he gave "serious trouble" to Skibbereen's constabulary.

Drombeg Stone Circle (known as the Druid's Altar until 1957) is a megalithic ritual centre two kilometres west of Glandore village and is the best known archaeological site in West Cork, Ireland. Dating roughly to the 11th century BCE, Drombeg served as both a ceremonial and social gathering place for the ancient Celts.

Nikola Tesla and **Basil Zaharoff** although real people, provided the templates for iconic figures in fiction such as heroic inventors like Reed Richards and the scheming, sinister criminal businessman like Lex Luthor or Ernst Stavro Blofeld.

ACKNOWLEDGEMENTS

My sincere thanks to **Jess Nevins** for his always entertaining and insightful *Encyclopedia of Fantastic Victoriana*; **Caroline Tobin** for providing me with *Leap and Glandore: Fact and Folklore* by Eugene Daly, as well as *And Time Stood Still: A Pictorial History of Skibbereen and District*. Thanks also to **Catherine Pirkis, Jules Verne, HG Wells** and **L.T. Meade**, as well as to fellow helpful Holmesians **Will Murray** and **Paul Bishop**.

Most of all, a huge thank you goes to **Melissa's** great contributions, from proofing and editing to design in the final version of this work, and of course, to **Sir Arthur Conan Doyle**, without whom, none of it would have been possible.

MARK D. ELLIS

A novelist, journalist, and comics creator, Mark was introduced to Sherlock Holmes when he was gifted a Golden Pictures Classics edition of the stories on his sixth birthday.

In his 40-year career as a professional writer, he has amassed hundreds of published credits. A busy comics creator in the 1980s and 90s, Mark created the popular *Death Hawk* character and also created/developed *Star Rangers, The Justice Machine* and *Ninja Elite,* as well as writing such popular properties as *Doc Savage, The Man From U.N.C.L.E., H.P. Lovecraft's Cthulhu, The Wild Wild West, The Saint* and more.

In 1995 Mark took over the *Deathlands* novel series published by the Gold Eagle imprint of Harlequin Enterprises. Under the pseudonym of James Axler, he created the best-selling *Outlanders* series, which was consecutively published for over

18 years. He has also contributed to the *Remo Williams:The Destroyer* and *Mack Bolan:The Executione*r franchises.

He has been featured in *Starlog, Comics Scene* and *Fangoria* magazines and was interviewed by Robert Siegel for NPR's *All Things Considered.*

His most recent books are *Death Hawk The Complete Saga, Nosferatu: Sovereign of Terror, Knightwatch: Invictus X* and *Lakota: Serpents of Aztlan.*

Mark lives with his wife, best-selling author and photographer, Melissa Martin Ellis in rural Ireland.

www.ingramcontent.com/pod-product-compliance
Lightning Source LLC
LaVergne TN
LVHW021616010825
817526LV00007B/193